Tempest and Treason

L.L. Gray

Heroic Rose Publishing

Your FREE book is waiting

A killer pair of shoes, a party of a lifetime, and a demon.
What could possibly go wrong?

Cameron Blaze owes a demon a favor and what better way to pay off a debt than to have a girl's night out? The plan was simple. Find a killer pair of heels, go to a great bar, and party into the early hours of the morning. Cameron thinks that she has everything planned. The shoes on are, the drinks are poured, and the party is in full swing. She just forgot to account for one small thing. Magic going haywire. Suddenly, gods are out of control, myths are throwing punches, and Cameron is running for her life. Will she be able to stop the magical mayhem in time or has the clock run out for Cameron and her friends? Sign up here to get your free book!

https://www.subscribepage.com/llgray

To Becky

Thank you for being my dragon-spotting, fairy-chasing, adventuring partner for over thirty years.

Chapter 1

An innate sixth sense dragged me out of my nightmares. Something was out there. In the dark. *Watching* me.

Magic sprang to life inside me before consciousness. The insubstantial form of my shadow blade slapped into my palm before I opened my eyes. Instinctively, I ran the shadowy form along the whetstone of my will. The blade sharpened from a wavering dream into a dark blade with a razor-sharp edge almost instantly. My subconscious mind had selected the familiar form of the yatagan I'd left back on Earth. When the hilt formed and solidified in my hand, it felt like I was grasping a weapon molded to my grip rather than a newly formed blade of pure magic. All of that happened in less time than it took to tell it as I rose to a crouch and scanned the darkness, careful to keep my eyes averted from the dying embers of the campfire so as not to affect my night vision, searching for the sound that had awakened me.

Nothing.

I looked at my companions to see if the noise had disturbed them. Both were still asleep on the hard-packed earth. I was wary of waking them, especially if it turned out there was nothing prowling through the night. Ever since we had crashed through the portal to Fae, everyone's nerves were stretched tight. Mine felt like discordant piano strings, jangling at every unfamiliar sound. I looked back at the slumbering forms. Sloane and Andrei needed their sleep. Unless something was coming to murder us in the night, I was determined not to wake them.

A low whistle caught my ear, and a whisper of movement snagged at the corner of my eye. A tall, lean man with dark hair and enough stubble to form the start of an impressive beard stepped briefly out of the sparse tree line, marking the end of the forest.

Magnus.

The werewolf raised a finger to his lips and made a circling gesture with the other hand before fading back into the foliage.

It hadn't been my imagination then. If Magnus was on high alert too, something was out there. I ghosted across the campsite and placed a hand on Andrei's shoulder and then Sloane's, waking them silently. It was a credit to the trials of the past week that they woke swiftly, reaching for weapons as soon as I touched them. I made the same circling gesture Magnus had. In unison, the three of us left our rumpled blankets on the ground around the campfire and faded into the tree line, waiting with bated breath.

We had been tracking Kroxius for the past week across the unfamiliar, and often murderous, land of Fae. Kroxius was a lich, a nigh-unkillable undead sorcerer with unbelievable powers over the dead. Until my friend had given his life to destroy the lich's soul jar, making the undead sorcerer mortal again.

Ben.

My heart squeezed painfully as I crouched behind a small bush covered in a smattering of dying leaves. I scanned the darkness but could see no movement. My mind drifted back to the events that had led me to this spot. Memories tore at my fragile heart. Ben had sacrificed himself to protect the unsuspecting people of New Orleans. In doing so, he'd given us this infinitesimal chance to kill Kroxius before the lich made himself another soul jar. It was a noble, selfless act of bravery. The old man was a hero. He'd also been one of my closest friends. A surrogate father to this fatherless girl.

I ruthlessly squashed down the wellspring of grief that sprang to life inside me until it was merely a trickle. A trickle I could ignore. I'd mourn Ben properly once I had killed the lich, burned his corpse, and danced a jig on the bastard's grave.

Soft rustling in the long grass off to the northwest caught my ear. I squinted through the darkness, tapping into my extraordinary night vision. There were benefits to being a Supe other than being able to make weapons out of shadows, although that was one of my cooler tricks. I squinted at the grass, which came nearly to chest height, making it difficult to spot anything approaching our campsite. The moon wasn't helping things either, not being bright enough tonight to illuminate an approaching enemy clearly. If only there had been a better place to camp! But we needed rest, and this had been the safest place to camp for miles. I'd been warned that everything here in Fae was a potential enemy, even down to the smallest things like the flowers. Nothing in my time here had dissuaded me from that warning. Another crunch and snap of dried grass sounded. It was closer this time.

I flexed my fingers against the hilt of my shadow sword, waiting to glimpse whatever undead creature Kroxius had raised. The lich had escaped when we all unexpectedly tumbled through a portal into Fae. He knew we were tracking him across Fae, and he was cunning. Kroxius had been using his powers to raise any creature he stumbled across and turn it into a zombie to distract, deter, or deadify our small party. He just needed to buy enough time to either give us the slip or make another soul jar.

We needed to keep him on the run. If he didn't have the time or magical energy to create a new soul jar, we stood a chance at killing him and ending the death curse he'd placed on the fae contingent from New Orleans. If he remade the soul jar, then our job would become infinitely harder. However, to kill him, we also had to catch him and so far, we were at a stalemate. Something had to tip the balance one way or the other, and soon.

Another rustle whispered through the darkness. I saw a twitching ripple slither through the tall grass. My eyes widened. It was closer than I'd expected. That small shiver was all the warning I had. Three blurred shapes flung themselves out of the tall grass on the opposite side of the recently vacated campsite. As one, the monstrosities viciously attacked the empty blankets strewn on the ground. In the glowing embers, spindly legs coated in bristling orange and black fur scuttled over the blankets. The legs supported a furry round body, about the size of a basketball, and a knobby head with too many eyes.

Spider-tigers? Huh. That's a new one, I thought.

Fae was filled with many things that storytellers left out of fairy tales. Things that would've sent all the good boys and girls screaming for their mommies. Danger in Fae didn't just come from the strange and horrible creatures like the spider-tigers murdering our blankets, either.

Leaves were so sharp they could slice you into smithereens. Trees could move and liked to indulge in murder. Babbling brooks really talked and tried to lure you close enough for sylphs to drag you under the water. Faeries were not the only things that lived in Fae. Both creatures of myth and fae nightmares populated the realm. From what I'd seen, if you could imagine it, it lived in Fae. Hybrid monsters lived alongside their Earthly counterparts as if the laws of interspecies mating didn't hold true in this bizarre realm. We'd seen badger-deer, wasp-monkeys, and scorpion-otters. The latter were devilishly cute with a deadly sting to their tail.

I started inching through the sparse foliage to get into a better position to attack. Magnus was closer. He leaped out of the darkness in his massive silver wolf form. He was both beautiful and deadly. I was thankful he was on my side.

The werewolf snapped his powerful jaws around the base of the nearest spider-tiger's neck. Magnus threw his head back and forth, shaking the monster violently until the thing's neck cracked, and the head popped off, revealing a host of maggots feasting on the internal organs of the undead creature.

This wasn't a chance attack. Kroxius had reanimated the fae spider-tigers and sent them to murder us in our sleep. The sooner we dealt with the lich, the better.

With a snort, Magnus tossed the body into the embers of the campfire. The bristly dead fur lit up like a Christmas tree in February. The fire popped and snapped as it greedily crawled up the zombie's dead-undead body. Magnus finished the job by shoving the thing's head into the fire with his nose.

Andrei followed Magnus's lead and charged into the fray. The younger werewolf snapped another spider-tiger's head off and tossed the body into the fire. The two wolves converged on the final spider, dispatching it in short order. Seeing that they had the situation under control, I stayed hidden just in case there were unseen threats still lurking in the night.

Andrei yipped at Magnus, who let out an answering rumble. They melted silently back into the darkness, working together as easily as if they'd been Pack for years instead of weeks. Magnus wasn't even officially part of the New Orleans Pack yet, and Andrei was still a battle-green kid. However, I had to hand it to the teenager. Andrei had been so green that he was more of a detriment than an asset a week ago. However, between the frequent skirmishes with Kroxius's minions and the evening training sessions with Magnus or me, he was shaping up to be a quick student and a clever opponent. Even Sloane tried to help. She wasn't much of a fighter, but helped where she could in demonstrations or sparring. Hopefully, the kid would survive his adventure in Fae. If he didn't, I had a feeling his dad, the Alpha of the Pack of New Orleans, would make sure I didn't survive it either.

As the third and final spider's head collapsed in on itself with a shower of angry orange sparks, Sloane crept into the camp from her hiding place in the darkness. I followed her, silently, scanning the darkness for any more movement. The charred smell of rotting flesh hit my nostrils and made me gag. I started breathing through my mouth to avoid the worst of it. Fire was an excellent way to deal with zombies, but I hated the resulting stench.

"Well, that was easy," the petite leprechaun commented as she gathered the blankets, pulling them away from the sparking fire before any embers could burn holes in the thin fabric.

"Almost too easy," I muttered. "Any idea what that was?"

Sloane shook her head. "I've never seen anything like it before. But that's Fae for you. It's always coming up with new and bizarre ways to kill you."

I chuckled in wry agreement, but kept my eyes on the gently swaying grass, just in case there were any more undead creatures out there. I waved my free hand at where the two wolves had disappeared.

"Once they finish scouting, let's move camp. No sense in staying put if Kroxius has already found us once," I said.

"Agreed," Sloane replied, shoving a blanket into one pack at random.

I let my shadow blade dissolve as I bent to help Sloane. I'd been practicing with my shadow magic whenever I found a spare moment since arriving in Fae. However, I still couldn't keep the blade corporeal if it wasn't directly in contact with me. It was annoying, but I was working to see if I could find a solution. I had to do it on my own because I hadn't been able to get in touch with Barqan, my mysterious magic tutor, since arriving. I didn't know if crossing over into Fae had disrupted the magic of my enchanted necklace or if he'd worn himself out by summoning me to meet him in the ether. He had warned me of the possibility of magical exhaustion after the astral projection thing. Regardless, he wasn't answering my summons.

Not that I had a great deal of time for practice or magic lessons. I'd spent nearly every waking minute of the last week fighting, tracking, or trying to survive whatever Kroxius and the Fae realm threw at us.

Now wasn't the time to bemoan my lack of magical tutoring. We needed to get out of here as quickly as possible, in case Kroxius had more surprises heading our way. Working efficiently, Sloane and I packed up the camp. I kept half of my attention on the grass swaying in the night breeze as I worked, just in case something slipped past the wolves.

Sloane spoke up again as we worked. "I still think that he's getting weaker. Those zombie spiders didn't stand a chance."

"Only because we weren't asleep. If they'd caught us off guard, we all would've been dead before we knew what happened," I said as I shoved things at random into packs.

"Look who's cranky this morning!"

"It's not morning, and that's the problem," I grumbled.

"Well, I still think that this relatively lame attack is a sign that we are wearing him down." Sloane sounded irritatingly chipper for someone who hadn't gotten a full night's sleep in about a week.

"Maybe. Or maybe those things," I pointed at the charred remains in the fire, "were the only corpses he could find today to reanimate. Or maybe he's lulling us into a false sense of security."

Sloane snorted. "He's been on the run for almost a week now, with no provisions and very little rest."

"You could say the same about us," I pointed out.

"Yeah, but at least we have the stuff Letitia shared with us. He's got, what? Anything he can scavenge? No matter how powerful the lich is, he has to be running on fumes soon. You need energy to do magic, and he is flinging around some massive spells by turning dead Fae creatures into zombies two or three times a day. His energy and his magic have to run out sometime."

"I could say the same for us and our energy," I pointed out dryly. "How long can we keep up this pace without making a mistake? As you said, Kroxius isn't letting up the pressure. We never know when the next attack is coming."

Sloane fastened the last of the straps on the last bag. "Fae has done weird things to you, Cam. Not sure that I like all of them."

"Well, Fae is a weird place," I retorted.

"You don't have to tell me that. I spent a lot of time here when I was younger. There's a reason I got out as soon as I could," Sloane said with a little shudder, the smile fading slowly from her face.

"You haven't ever talked about your time in Fae before. Not really," I said.

"That's because it sucked. Big time. And after the kind of discrimination that my people faced?" She shuddered. "Would you want to relive the most traumatic events of your life repeatedly?"

I reached out and grabbed her hand, squeezing it reassuringly. "No. And you don't have to. Not with me, at least. Just know that I'm here if you need me, however you need me."

Sloane squeezed back and nodded tightly. "It's just hard, you know? Being back. I never thought I'd be back here and now that I am?" She bit her lip and cast her eyes around furtively. "It's bringing back a lot of old memories. Few of them are good."

"Yeah, based on the past few days, I'm getting an inkling of why you wanted to leave. The truth behind the fairy tales isn't all princesses and glitter, is it?"

"Not even close," Sloane said seriously. Memories chased the good humor from her eyes and her face clouded over with anxiety that she'd never fully divulged before. She blinked and shook her head before offering me a bright smile. "But you should hear the stories the fae tell about humans. Those manling tales are crazy! I bet you'd laugh until your sides hurt if you heard some of them."

"Sounds like you're volunteering to be our entertainment tomorrow night," I said, trying to lighten her mood.

"Well, I don't know about that. It would be much better if we could find a bard or something. One of the traveling musicians would do a better job than I ever could!"

"Great. I'll just tell Kroxius that he needs to make a pit stop in a fae town so we can grab a pint at the pub and listen to the local gossip," I said sarcastically.

"Wow! Attitude much? Want me to remake your bed for you so you can wake up again and get out on the right side this time?" Sloane's smirk belied her words as she hefted a bag onto her back. Her teasing made me feel better.

"Yeah, that'd be great, thanks. While you're at it, can you also make some breakfast and a nice cup of tea?" I joked.

"Sorry, the kitchen is closed," Sloane grunted as she shifted the bag to a more comfortable position.

I ignored the bags for now. They could wait until the werewolves got back from their scouting. Instead, I focused on searching the darkness for any signs of ambush. I pulled a shadow blade into existence. It was harder when I was fully awake, which I found strange. Whenever I tried to use my magic instinctively to form a shadow blade in Fae, it worked easily. Like slicing a butter knife through thin air. However, when I concentrated on *making* the magic happen, it felt more like forcing a butter knife through hard-packed snow. It worked. Eventually. It just took a hell of a lot more effort.

The hilt of my new shadow sword thudded comfortingly into the palm of my hand. I smiled. It had formed a little faster than last time. Before I congratulated myself on my slight magical accomplishment, a thin, striped leg tipped with five glistening claws flashed out of the long grass on the edge of the campsite.

I yelped in surprise and jumped back. The claws swept through the space where my knees had been just a moment before. If I hadn't reacted so swiftly, I'd be about twelve inches shorter now.

"Cam!" The desperation in Sloane's voice was clear. I took a quick look. She scrabbled at the straps of the bag, trying to get it off her back so it wouldn't encumber her fighting. The straps didn't move. She shot me a wild look of fear as she redoubled her efforts.

"Get behind me, but stay near the fire. Use it as a shield if anything comes at you," I hissed.

Sloane nodded. She hurried to follow my directions, still struggling with the bag.

I braced myself in front of her with my sword uplifted. Another bandy leg whipped through the grass at me. This one was much larger than the spindly things attached to the smoldering spider-tigers in the fire. I threw myself over the leg in a diving forward roll. I lost control of the blade in the frantic move to escape. The sword melted back into shadows as soon as my focus wavered. Which is when the body attached to the clawed legs lumbered into view.

A rasping yowl curdled my blood as the beast rose out of the long grasses. It was a dark smear against the night, making it difficult to see details. However, I could tell that it was big. Much bigger than I imagined. Compared to the little spiderlings who'd attacked us first, this thing was huge. They were kittens compared to a saber-tooth-tiger. Mixed with a spider. I was going to have nightmares for days if I survived this fight.

The creature interrupted my thoughts as it swiped at me again, coming closer to the fire, and I finally got a good look at it. The sloping dome of the narrow body wasn't very high, but it was wide. Eight thin legs attached to clawed paws sprouted from the creature's thorax. Bristling orange and black fur covered the entire beast, and it smelled like it had never had a bath in its life. But that wasn't the worst part. The giant spider monster's face was covered in eyes of all shapes and sizes. It locked every single one directly on me.

And I no longer had a weapon.

Chapter 2

I pulled on more shadows to cloak my movements as I rolled out of the way of the wickedly curved claws. In the wavering light from the fire, I hoped my magic was enough to hide me from the monster until I could make another sword. I imagined a longer version of my yatagan, dragging the shadowy form through the fiery forge of my focused will. Unfortunately, none of my weapons had made it through the portal to Fae, so I had to rely on my shadow magic if I wanted to mount an attack.

The creature swiveled its head, trying to locate me in the deceptive dancing of the light from the dying fire. My shadow trick must've worked because all of its eyes slid right over me and the beast turned its attention towards Sloane, who was still fighting with her pack. I made the most of my moment and *focused.* The insubstantial blade sucked up the shadow magic thrumming through me and snapped into existence with a silent pop I felt more than heard. Just in time, too.

The giant spider swiped a claw-tipped leg over the fire towards my best friend's head. Sloane let out a little yelp and dove to the ground. The lethal leg whizzed over her head, barely missing her. She started army-crawling towards the edge of the clearing, the pack on her back making her look like a drunk turtle. I would've teased her if not for the murderous zombie right in front of me.

I needed to pull the monster's attention away from Sloane so she could get away. With my new sword firmly in hand, I dropped my shadowy cloak and leaped to my feet. A few of the spider's many eyes swiveled towards me the second I popped back into its line of sight. Another striped leg whizzed towards me, but this time, I was ready. I met the attack with the razor-sharp edge of my sword. That wasn't fair.

The magical blade was sharper than any mundane sword I'd ever used. It passed through the creature's thin leg with almost no resistance. The claw-tipped paw went spinning off into the night. It locked all of its dead eyes on me.

"Sloane! Get out of here!" I shouted in warning as I dodged another swipe from the beast. She might be hell on wheels with a gun, but technology didn't work as expected in Fae. Rather than wait for her sidearms to explode and take her arm clean off, Sloane had opted to leave the guns with Letitia rather than bring them with us on the hunt across Fae for a murderous lich. A decision I'd fully supported at the time. Without her guns, though, it meant either putting her questionable skills with a blade to the test or keeping the monster's attention firmly focused on me.

The spider-tiger barreled towards me at unbelievable speed, scuttling awkwardly with its injured leg flapping uselessly in the cool breeze. Blood so dark that it looked black splattered across the smashed grass as it attacked.

I waited until the last minute and dove to the side, trying to see a weakness besides the missing leg. The spider-tiger's enormous head swiveled to keep me in focus. This close, I could see the glistening fangs that descended from its upper jaw. A droplet of venom fell from the exposed incisors and splashed on the ground with a smoking hiss. The grass shriveled and died on contact. The smell of chemical burning assaulted my nostrils.

Great. Acid-spiked venom. Fan-fucking-tastic.

I smiled grimly, pulling at the shadows to form another blade. A shadowy knife sprang into my hand, solidifying as soon as it touched the power thrumming through my veins. It mildly surprised me that the knife formed so easily. Fae sucked. Spider-tigers sucked more. But the positive of all this fighting was the continual magical practice. Although, I could've done without the life-threatening scenarios. Maybe a nice dojo somewhere? With a soft mat and a gruff teacher with a tiny mustache who grunted when I did something, right? I shook my head. Things had to be bad when I was daydreaming about my perfect sensi and a training montage. If I couldn't have a thirty-second movie-esque acquisition of skills, I'd settle for just being able to make a shadow blade easier.

Focus Cam!

I ducked under a swipe from one of the creature's clawed front paws and continued the trajectory of my momentum to roll under its belly. I rose to my feet in a low crouch, searching for a soft spot on its unprotected underside to attack. From my vantage point, I could see that something had gouged a ragged tear in the spider-tiger's abdomen. Maggots crawled and writhed in the dead flesh. I gagged. I *hated* maggots.

The spider hissed and arched its body upwards, out of my reach. I grunted in disappointment. The monster tucked its head and sprayed venom at me, and I dodged. No way was I letting that venom hit me! I used the magical powers of my enchanted boots to increase the power of my jump. The acidic venom spattered on the ground, dissolving the steaming grass into a noxious puddle of goo. Silently, I sent up a prayer of thanks for the brownie who had made these boots for me. I'd hired her to make me a pair that muffled any noise I made. She came back with silent, fireproof boots that boosted my jumps and looked sexy as hell. At least, they would if they weren't covered in a week's worth of muck.

The spider swiftly overcame its surprise at my unexpected elevation. It raised itself higher, trying to aim another volley of venom my way. With a curse, I dove to the side and abandoned the idea of slashing into its belly. I'd find another way to kill it that wouldn't result in being showered with maggots. Knowing my luck, if I killed it from underneath, the beast would land on me and crush me to death.

Instead, I slashed out with my sword as I ran out of the danger zone. My sword sliced through the bottom joint of the articulated leg. The spider tried to turn to keep me in its line of sight. Without its support leg, it crashed awkwardly on its side. I skidded to a stop and reversed direction, trying to take advantage of its momentary lack of coordination. However, the beast was faster than it looked. It scrambled to its feet before I could capitalize. I was grudgingly impressed that Kroxius still had enough power to animate something so large without his soul jar. The soul jar that Ben had destroyed.

Ben...

Tears clogged my throat. I shook myself and dodged another swipe. I couldn't afford to lose focus. Emotions were a luxury. One I would indulge in *after* I'd killed this zombie spider. And Kroxius. And burned his corpse. Then Ben…no. I shoved my feelings over Ben's death to the side until I had the time to properly self-flagellate.

A grimace twisted my lips as I sprang towards the creature in front of me. Venom spun off its curved fangs to spatter over the grass. Small craters erupted with smoke anywhere the sizzling venom struck. The puddles of steaming goo forced me to approach carefully, which limited the speed of my attacks. On the plus side, the creature wasn't fast enough to keep me in sight with its missing appendages.

This stalemate had to end. I needed to tip the fight in my favor. Something was moving in the grass behind the spider; I glimpsed a flash of silver through the dried stalks. A crazy idea coalesced in my mind, and I let out a long, low whistle. Then I stopped moving. I tried to slow my breathing and calm my heart rate as I readied for the next move. The abrupt halt confused the giant spider, and it tottered unsteadily on its uneven legs. Its head wavered back and forth uneasily, unsure as to the change in tactics.

A rumbling growl vibrated through the darkness. The spider wasn't the only dangerous creature hiding in the night. The spider-tiger whipped its head around in search of the imminent threat and lost focus on me. In the confusion, I drove forward with as much speed as I could muster. I raised my weapons and slashed any part of the monster I could reach. It took a moment for the spider to recover and retaliate, but that was all I needed.

I dove over the first clawed leg, sliced the second off at the lowest joint, and kept moving, searching for my opening. I heard Magnus let loose a bone-chilling howl behind me and the spider's head twisted towards the sound. Something about the eerie howl spoke of apex predators and frosty nights. A lifetime of instinctive survival reactions was hard to overcome even when you were dead. For the moment, I was forgotten once again.

An uninjured leg appeared before me as the spider tried to compensate for the expected flanking attack from an angry werewolf. Amid the flashing of furred spider legs, I saw my opening. Two quick steps brought me within striking distance. The stench of rotting flesh was overpowering, but this was my best chance. I held my breath as I propelled myself upwards, aided by my boots. The power in my jump was incredible. It felt like I was flying for a moment—until my foot landed solidly on a spindly leg. Without hesitating, I pushed off the thin limb. I felt it crack as I soared skyward once again.

This time, I landed on the tough bristles of the spider's back. I dug my knife and sword into its furred exoskeleton to keep myself from sliding off. The spider didn't like that one bit. It bucked like a fake bull in a Western-themed bar. I bared my teeth and held on. It would take a hell of a lot more to toss this cowgirl off target than a zombie spider-tiger hybrid.

I saw a blur of silver as Magnus finally dodged in from the darkness. I didn't know what had kept him away for so long, but I was grateful he was here now. Magnus sprang into the clearing and started doing what wolves do best: harrying the prey to distract it from the Pack member about to make the lethal blow. Namely, me. If I could land it.

Magnus nipped at the spider's legs, then danced away as the spider spat venom at him. In a flash, he was right back within striking distance. The werewolf sank his teeth into a spindly leg. With a sharp, short wrench of his head, he tore it free. The werewolf trotted off into the long grass with his prize. The spider let loose a rasping yowl as it tottered around in search of its equilibrium amid the muddy blood-and-ven-om-drenched ground.

I smiled grimly, glad for the werewolf's distraction. After a week of fighting together, we'd became a decent team. A well-oiled machine of death lubricated by the blood of the creatures Kroxius threw into our path. It was as though Magnus could read my intentions, even as they formed in my head.

I made the most of the reprieve he had bought me. I pulled my blades out and scrambled across the spider's back towards its head. The bristly fur poked at my exposed skin. It felt rough and itchy under my palms. A bead of sweat dribbled down my cheek. I wiped it away with the back of my hand. The itchy sensation on my palms transferred to my face. I made the mistake of rubbing at it. Soon all of my cheek was itching. I couldn't help myself. I sneezed violently.

The spider jerked to a halt, finally remembering that it had an un-wanted Cameron-sized flea on its back. Another yowl tore through the night as it redoubled its efforts to dislodge me. I had to do a quick little jig to avoid being tossed off its back, but lost my grip on my knife. The blade immediately dissolved back into shadows.

Shit. That wasn't good.

I tightened my grip on my sword. I couldn't afford to lose my only weapon now.

The spider rose into the air and started to slam its body down. Anticipating the move, I stabbed my sword deep into the spider's back to brace myself. The creature halted its downward movement and screamed an unearthly shriek that tore at my eardrums. I used the embedded sword as an anchor as the bucking resumed. However, the monster was injured, bleeding, and missing multiple limbs. Surely, it couldn't maintain this kind of furious thrashing much longer. I just had to hang on long enough for it to tire itself out.

I closed my eyes and focused on maintaining my position. Eventually, I felt the spider slowing down. Using my upper body strength, I swung myself forward around the anchor of my sword. I worked the blade loose, releasing it with a sickening sucking noise. The spider roared its outrage at being used as a pincushion. It tried to resume the furious bucking, but it seemed sluggish. Maybe blood loss was catching up with it. Did blood loss matter to the undead? Perhaps that was a philosophical question for armchair adventurers. I didn't have the time to contemplate it now in the face of acid venom and too many eyes.

I crept as quickly as I dared toward its head. The orange and black fur grew denser underfoot as I reached the thing's neck. I raised the blade to chop its head off. Decapitation followed by burning the corpse was the ultimate way to make sure that a zombie wouldn't ever come in search of your brains again.

My blade descended. My aim was true. At the last second, the spider dodged by twisting its head to the left. I almost severed one of its furry ears. The flap of skin dangled over half of the spider's eyes like a pirate's eyepatch.

I gritted my teeth. Displeased at the messy strike, I raised my weapon high and swung it hard. The shadow blade bit deeply into the spider-tiger's neck. It didn't cut as cleanly as it had the spider's thin leg. I repeated the motion, hacking with grim determination at the thick skin protecting the base of its skull. The spider's thrashing grew weaker and weaker. Finally, the heavy head tumbled free of the body. It hung in midair for a split second as multiple eyes blinked up at me in surprise. Then the eyes glazed over, and the spider's head landed with a hiss of venom on the dry ground. I rode the slowly collapsing body to the ground, bending my knees, and leaping free of any potential venom spatter as the spider-tiger's corpse crashed sideways.

Despite decapitating the monster, I kept a firm grip on my blade. If there was anything I'd learned from fighting the undead sorcerer's minions over the last few days, it was to never think that the dead were really dead. That's how *you* got killed. And without a lich on our side, there was no coming back for a second chance. Not that I'd really wanted a lich, however friendly, to raise me from the dead. Something about being an animated rotting corpse didn't work with my aesthetic.

I waited for three slow breaths. When the creature didn't twitch, I rose from my crouch and let out a quick series of low whistles in a repeating rhythm. Magnus, in his massive silver werewolf form, padded out of the grass and came over to me. He glanced at the spider, then sat back on his haunches, his long tongue lolling out of his mouth in a canine smile.

I dug my fingers into the soft ruff behind his neck. "Are you ok?" I asked, keeping my eyes fixed on the darkness. He snuffled an affirmative, nosing at my free hand.

"What do you think?" I asked him. "Are we getting closer to Kroxius?" I felt Magnus's heavy shoulders move under my hand in the wolf's semblance of a shrug.

"Yeah, I don't know either, but it begs the question: Is he getting weaker, or are we getting stronger?" I asked.

"Why not both?" A cheery voice rang out behind me. I glanced over my shoulder to see a small bobbing flame approaching. Sloane carried a makeshift torch in one hand and kept the fingers of her other hand firmly woven through the fur of the dark wolf at her side. She dipped the torch in the embers of the campfire until the end of the leaf-studded stick caught.

"Let's burn this thing fast. I don't want it coming back to life or un-life or whatever. That venom looked nasty," the leprechaun said.

She let go of Andrei as she neared the bristly corpse. The teenage werewolf started snuffling around the muddy battleground. I snapped my fingers at him. "Stay out of there. There's too much venom. We don't know what it does, and we don't need it getting up your nose. We don't have time to waste as it eats you from the inside out."

Andrei gave a happy little yip and trotted over to my side, tail thumping hard against my legs. If I didn't know any better, I would've thought that Andrei was thrilled to be here. Like he viewed this entire trip through Fae, where everything wanted to kill us, as nothing more than an outstanding field trip. And the best part? No homework.

I rolled my eyes. However, the young werewolf's joy was infectious. My hand dropped to his shoulder, and the shadow blade dissolved the moment I let go of it. I patted the teenage werewolf affectionately.

"I hear you," I whispered to the young werewolf. "We'll work on training you up a little more, and then maybe you can come along with Magnus and me on a scouting mission soon."

Andrei gave another happy little bark and jumped up, chasing his tail in a puppyish display of delight. Magnus let out a short bark in a half-hearted attempt to pull the young wolf back under control. I swear, if wolves could roll their eyes, Magnus was doing it. But it was good-natured.

Andrei really was a good kid and his joy at being included in this adventure lifted everyone's spirits. In his mind, it was all fun and games. *He* couldn't get hurt. *He* couldn't die. I hoped nothing on this trip dissuaded him from the latter notion, although I wouldn't be upset if he learned a little caution from the former.

Sloane inched forward slowly with her torch outstretched and touched the flame to the bristly fur spiking along one of the spider's spindly legs. The dead creature went up as if doused in kerosene. Sloane moved quickly to the other side, touching the torch to the end of each leg. Even the mangled, bleeding ones.

Soon, the corpse was burning merrily in front of us. Luckily, the ground and surrounding grasses were so wet with blood and venom that the fire didn't spread. I turned my back on the thing, not wanting my night vision destroyed any more than it already was.

"We should move," I said to the other three. "I don't like being backlit by a bonfire in the middle of the night."

Fire was the ultimate way to dispose of zombie corpses. Unfortunately, a large fire might also draw in creatures that would be better left lost to the Fae night.

Sloane cleared her throat. "I agree, but where are we going to go? It's not like we can find somewhere else safe to camp in this area tonight. There's no way I'm getting back to sleep, anyway. Not now." A shiver shook her tiny frame.

"I agree," I said, keeping my back to the fire. I tipped my head toward the dead monster behind me. "Let's see if that thing has any friends, then let's get the hell out of here."

Sloane nodded her agreement and put her back to the blazing monster. She stood shoulder to shoulder with me. We watched the darkness as Magnus and Andrei faded into the long grass, scouting for any additional trouble.

Luckily, zombie corpses burned quickly. The spider-tiger collapsed into smoldering ash in under three minutes. Sloane and I hurriedly kicked loose dirt over any embers that we found, so we didn't accidentally start a prairie fire. After all, it was Smokey the Bear who said, "*You and only you can prevent flaming zombies*", right?

Chapter 3

We collected the gear that had been tossed around the campsite during the fight. When we were ready to go, I sent another low whistle quavering into the night. Magnus seemingly materialized out of thin air a few moments later.

It always surprised me that the gigantic wolf could move as silently as he did. I supposed that was a werewolf trait, but it was still unsettling. Magnus was fast proving himself an excellent fighter and fantastic partner to have at my back in this strange land. We'd learned to fight together like a Pack. We'd had to. Fae was no place for the weak. This was no weekend away; glamping in a curated forest. This was a savage daily battle for survival in the bloodiest arena I'd ever heard of, much less been a contestant in. I had a whole new respect for gladiators and a whole new desire never to be one.

A black shape dashed around Magnus. Andrei yipped happily and wagged his tail with such exuberance that I had to smile. Despite his developing skills, the kid had a good heart and decent instincts. Everything he had learned until this point had been at his daddy's side. After a week in Fae, that was changing fast. Fundamentally, there was nothing wrong with learning by sparring against opponents in training. However, in Fae, no one was going to wait for you to catch your second wind, grab a drink, and try again. They were just going to kill you as dead as they could. There was no pretty in the fighting here. No posing, no pretense. Just mayhem and death. And the kid was thriving in the middle of the madness.

Secretly, a tiny part of me loved it too. I tried to keep that part of me tightly under wraps, but that was getting harder by the day. It was refreshing to have a place where I could cut loose and test out my newly discovered powers.

I eyed the heavy bag regretfully before shouldering it with a sigh. I'd been planning on trying to visit Barqan again once everyone had fallen asleep. Now that I'd had a taste of what my magic could do beyond hiding me from prying eyes, I was desperate to learn more. Barqan was the only being I knew of who had an insight into my strange shadow magic. As long as I was in a strange, magical realm, I might as well contact my strange, magical tutor, right?

The rational side of me knew that regularly contacting a mysterious Supe wasn't a great idea. That was the same part of me that dreaded having to face Damon and tell him that his little boy had gotten a crash course in killing while visiting one of the most murderous realms imaginable. I'd tried to quash that thought by finding some other zombie minion to slaughter. That usually made the little voice of reason inside of me shut up for a while.

The young werewolf was adapting to this place more easily than the rest of us. His skills and instincts sharpened almost by the minute. It was as if this place was changing him from the sweet, gangly kid I'd first met in New Orleans. He was growing more in touch with his primal nature; more wolfish. I just wasn't sure if that was a good thing.

I crouched down, so that I was eye level with Magnus. To be fair, I didn't have to crouch far. "Look, I think it's probably best if you and Andrei stay in wolf form for now. Traveling at night is a bad idea, but staying here and waiting for another ambush is worse."

Magnus bobbed his head in agreement, then nosed at the packs lying on the ground. He met my eyes meaningfully.

"I agree," I replied to the wolf's unspoken question. "We need your noses out there. Besides, Sloane and I can handle doubling up with the packs for a little while. Right, Sloane?" I asked the petite leprechaun, glancing over at her.

"We've got this," Sloane assured Magnus. "You just make sure nothing else attacks us while we act as your porters across Fae."

Magnus let out a snort and flicked his tail in irritation.

Sloane ignored him and dug into one bag. She fished a couple of pieces of fae flatbread out. It was the ultimate traveling food. Even a small piece could keep us energized most of the day. Sloane cracked it into bite-sized pieces for the wolves. They snapped the fae bread out of the air as she tossed it to them. I didn't know what it was made of, but whatever it was kept me going long after my energy would've normally petered out.

"We need to keep up our strength if we're going to keep up with wolves on no sleep," she said as she waved the other piece at me. Dark circles smudged the pale skin under her eyes. Sloane was tougher than she looked. Nevertheless, the lack of sleep was catching up with her. Truth be told, it was catching up with all of us.

"Agreed. Make sure you eat some of that, too."

"What do you think this is for?" Sloane said with a smile. She waved a piece of bread at me. "We'll share it as we walk."

It took some clever re-wrapping of straps, but eventually Sloane and I were ready to go. She looked tiny, with two large packs strapped to her, but there was no way around it. The werewolves couldn't carry their gear in wolf form, so Sloane and I would have to do it.

I adjusted the straps on my two packs, settling them more firmly against my back as we started towards the northwest. A little white mouse scampered out from a pocket in the pack. I'm glad he'd made it through the scuffle with the spider-tigers. I smiled down at him. Goliath was a reanimated familiar that I had inherited when...

I swallowed, pressing down savagely on the memory, and shifted the packs on my back again. I was careful not to disturb the tiny mouse as he settled into his usual spot on my shoulder, the same spot he'd claimed whenever he rode with Ben.

Sloane silently handed me half of the flatbread as we walked.

"You read my mind." I took the food gratefully and ate a large mouthful, swallowing almost before I'd chewed it. The morsel filled the gnawing hole in my belly almost immediately. Tolkien didn't know how close he'd been to the rejuvenating properties of his Elven rations. Or perhaps he did. Who knows? The famous author may have, in fact, crossed over into Fae and his fantastical stories may really have been a firsthand account of his adventures with some strategic name changes. I smiled at the notion, feeling a kinship with the author as I imagined him plodding along with a pack of dwarves on some epic journey.

An idea popped into my head. "Hey Sloane?" I asked. "Any idea where we could find a hobbit?"

Sloane glared at me. "What are you saying? Are you implying I am hobbit-like?"

"Well, you are a vertically challenged creature who loves an excellent beer and who most people would classify as coming from legendary tales. The only major difference I see between you and a hobbit is that you have fancier shoes."

Sloane looked at her worn and mud-covered sneakers and then back at me. "They don't even wear shoes!"

"My point exactly. Yours are Cinderella's slippers by comparison."

Sloane rolled her eyes and huffed, "You're infuriating!"

I wagged a finger at her. "But not wrong."

She glared at me but couldn't find a retort to counter with. Instead, she blew out an annoyed breath and stomped away in her very un-hobbit-like shoes. I grinned and followed her, careful not to voice any more opinions about her height or feet until she'd calmed down.

Chapter 4

It didn't take long for me to get bored. I liked the outdoors, but never saw the point in lugging gear through rugged terrain for miles on end. Why would I work so hard to have a delightfully pleasant house to just go outside and live out of a thin, worn tent? I mean, hiking was one thing, but full-out camping for days on end? Not my idea of a good time.

"Where do you think we are, anyway?" I asked Sloane as we walked.

She bobbed her head back and forth. "It's hard to tell exactly. Borders in Fae have always been fluid. They shift with the seasons, the current power balance, and whoever is fighting. Not to mention that it's been an awfully long time since I lived here."

I looked at her, aghast. "So, you're telling me we're lost in Fae?"

"No, I'm telling you, I don't know precisely where we are."

I shook my head and felt Goliath latch on to a strand of my hair just behind my ear for balance. Sometimes I forgot he was there. "That's the same thing, Sloane," I pointed out.

"Cut me some slack! It's been years! I never liked all the intrigue and the murder and the shit that happens here."

"Which is why you moved to New Orleans and became my best friend? Because I have a calming influence on everyone around me?"

Sloane snorted. "Yeah. Right. That sums you up. You know what? You should teach yoga and meditate on the beach every morning."

"No offense, but that sounds boring."

"It sounds peaceful," Sloane said a little wistfully.

We walked in silence for a few minutes, lost in our own thoughts, before she spoke up again. "I know this must seem like some wonderful adventure that you can brag about years from now, but I *lived* this already. Give me my bar, some music, and a lively crowd. I'll take that any day of the week over this insanity." She waved her hand vaguely.

"All the more reason to catch up to Kroxius and kill him so we can get you back to New Orleans," I said with more confidence than I felt.

"And to save all those fae he infected with that parasitic death curse," Sloane reminded me. "Speaking of what did Letitia say yesterday when you spoke with her? Any updates?"

I instinctively fingered the small stone in my pocket that Letitia had enchanted so we could communicate at a distance. "Nothing good. We're running out of time. Are we sure that killing him will stop the magic from eating them from the inside out?"

"Pretty sure. Most magic spells are tied to the caster's life. Kill the caster, kill the spell."

"Still seems strange that death is the cure for a necromantic spell," I said.

Sloane shifted her pack. "True, but Letitia is buying us all the time she can, and she and her people are running out of it. Fast. We need to take care of Kroxius as quickly as we can."

I nodded in agreement. A chilly wind gusted through the grass, making it whisper like dried bones rubbing against each other. I wrapped my arms around my torso and shivered. I wasn't dressed for this weather. My thin pullover was designed for the Louisiana heat, not trekking through the wilderness.

"Is it just me or is it getting colder?" I asked as sweat dried under the cool, caressing fingers of the nighttime breeze.

"It's not just you. We're probably heading towards the Autumn Court. Or maybe even Winter. It's hard to tell in the dark."

"Speaking of that, I've been meaning to ask you. Is the Winter Court always covered in snow and ice? And the Summer Court is always hot or something? I mean, I know the Courts are seasonally based, but what about the weather? Does it change?" I asked.

"It can get confusing, but the short answer is yes and no."

I rolled my eyes. "You would suck at writing tourist brochures."

Sloane chuckled, used to my sarcasm. "Think of it this way. There is an enormous difference between summer in Texas and summer in Northern Alaska, right?"

"Sure," I agreed easily.

"That's how it works here. When the Summer Court is in power, everything in Fae heats up a little. When the power shifts to Winter, everything cools down again, but the changes are relative to that Court."

I nodded along. "Fair enough. So, how long does a Court stay in power?"

"In human years?" Sloane bit her lip as she thought. "I don't know for sure. Maybe a year? It could be as much as twenty or thirty human years, though."

"Thirty years of Winter?" I squeaked in surprise. There were many reasons I lived in New Orleans, but the weather was a positive in my book.

"Well, it doesn't feel like thirty years here. Remember, time flows differently in Fae."

"So, how many years does it feel like?" I asked.

Sloane shrugged. "How many days was the last winter in New Orleans?"

"How am I supposed to know? There was that troll thing in December, then I was busy hunting through the swamps for rare ingredients for potions for the witches and then —"

Sloane cut me off. "Exactly. You were busy living your life. Why would you bother to count the days or the hours in a season?"

"I suppose," I grumbled. Thoughts tumbled through my mind as we walked along. Finally, I asked, "Okay. So, who is in power now?"

"I don't have a clue," Sloane replied.

"Let me get this straight. We don't know which court is in power right now. We don't know where we are, and we don't know where we're headed. As a bonus, there is still a lich out there trying to kill us. Have I got it right?" I asked.

"Yeah, that about sums it up."

"Fae sucks," I muttered.

"And now you know why I left," Sloane said.

Magnus came trotting up out of the grass and sniffed loudly at my hand. I knelt in front of the werewolf, offering him the rest of my fae bread. He licked it up from my fingers, happily crunching down on the crusty flatbread. Andrei trotted over and Sloane passed him a corner of hers. I dusted off my hands and pushed to my feet. I felt a light tug on my hair under my ear as Goliath secured himself against the swaying. It was reassuring. I smiled, taking more comfort than was rational in the little mouse's presence.

I lifted my arm and glanced at the inside of my wrist. The cinnamon-colored tattoo of a compass was magically inscribed on my skin. A blue light pulsed in the middle of the compass in time with my heartbeat. A faint orange dot hovered at the edge of the circle straight in front of us. Manannan Mac Lir, a god from the Irish pantheon, had created the spell for me as part of a bargain. It linked me with the remaining two spirits that had escaped from the Abyss on Halloween and would only fade when they'd been sent back beyond the veil. Or I was.

The orange dot was Kroxius. I still hadn't figured out who the blue dot represented. Whoever it was had gotten trapped in the fragment of a soul-catching gem that was set in the ring that hung around my throat.

I fingered the necklace thoughtfully, running the golden charm through the ring repeatedly. Although I wanted to know whose soul was trapped in the ring, it was a problem we could deal with later. After we killed the lich. For now, that soul, whoever it was, was safely locked away. The ring housing that soul nestled against the Calling Charm I wore on the same necklace, and I tucked both back under my shirt, safely out of sight. The charm had been my mother's before she died. It was now mine and the only way I could contact Barqan. Unfortunately, I didn't have time to devote to either mystery now. I'd have to make time when I got back to New Orleans. If I got back to New Orleans.

Magnus whined, drawing my attention back to the problem at hand. I glanced at the tattoo again to confirm the direction. "He's that way," I said, pointing ahead. "I think we're catching up. Let's push on, but carefully. Magnus, you scout ahead. Andrei, watch our back trail and make sure we don't get ambushed."

Sloane shook a finger at the teenager. "Not like last time."

Andrei mock-growled at her. Sloane ignored him and started walking again. The young werewolf flicked his tail mischievously. Then he leaped up and snapped his jaws right by her ear. Surprised, Sloane gave a little yelp and stumbled back. She almost toppled over as the unwieldy packs strapped to her disrupted her normal sense of balance. I stretched out my hand to steady her.

"Enough of that," I said to Andrei. I stood and adjusted my own bags into a more comfortable position on my back once again. I spoke to

Magnus. "Sloane and I will continue to play pack horses for a while yet, but even with the fae travel bread, we'll need to find a place to rest soon."

"Are you sure that's smart?" Sloane asked.

"I don't want to stumble across Kroxius when we're all sleep-deprived, tired from walking all night, and in need of a good meal. Do you?"

"I guess not," Sloane allowed, seeing my point. "But only a quick stop, okay?"

Magnus bobbed his head and sent a rumbling growl in Andrei's direction. The young wolf sank to his belly in the dirt under the older wolf's stare, but his wagging tail gave his excitement away.

I sighed, ignoring the pup. "Track the spider's scent if you can. Maybe we'll get lucky, and it will lead us to the lich. But make sure you stay alert for any signs that Kroxius might have left. I have a feeling that he won't be far now and will watch for us on his back trail. Knowing him, he's probably left us a nasty surprise or two along the way."

Sloane nodded. "We need to take care of him. Fast."

"Let's get going then," I said, setting off at a brisk pace.

The wolves disappeared into the night, doing what wolves did best: hunting their prey.

Chapter 5

Sloane and I pushed through the meadow's tall, dry grass. It slapped at our legs and sliced at our hands as we plodded north slowly while the wolves ranged around us, sniffing out threats. By the time the gray fingers of dawn brushed the horizon, fatigue dragged relentlessly at my muscles.

My mind drifted to thoughts of a cold beer at the Forge back in New Orleans or maybe walking to Mama's house for my morning sugar-fix or maybe just curling up in a soft bed with a good book and reading until my eyes were too heavy to stay open anymore. I might have moaned under my breath as the thoughts jumbled together into one amorphous idea of home. A soft bark from Magnus cut through my haze of exhaustion. My head snapped up from the walking doze I'd slipped into. I implored my tired feet to bear my weight just a little further as I fought the slow blink that was a precursor to sleep long enough to stumble out of the long grass onto the bank of a stream.

Magnus sat waiting for us at the side of the burbling water, scratching his back against a tree sporting violently bright orange foliage. When he saw us, he jumped up, circled a few times, then lay on the ground, closing his eyes.

I nodded my understanding, verbalizing for him, "I agree. This seems like a good place to get some rest. It's been a long night." That wasn't the half of it. I was so tired I wasn't sure if I was awake or asleep on my feet and dreaming the whole thing. Magnus opened his eyes wide and nodded his shaggy head at me.

Two heavy thumps sounded behind me as Sloane dropped her bags and stretched the kinks from her back, a yawn cracking her jaw. "I hope he means sleep for all of us and not just him," she said.

I smiled. "Let's get a quick camp set and catch a few hours' rest. What do you say?"

Sloane nodded, jerking her thumb at her chest. "I call last watch for guard duty."

I groaned, but nodded. "I'll take the first shift. The guys can divvy up the middle."

"Great," Sloane said over another yawn as she shook out her blanket, curling up on a soft stretch of grass. She fell asleep as soon as her head hit the ground.

Andrei raced into the clearing and took one look around. Rather than shifting, he curled himself into a ball at Sloane's back, tucking his snout under his tail. Snores soon rose from both of them.

A throat cleared behind me, and I spun, shadows already pooling in my palms. Magnus stood there in human form, with his hand out-stretched, waiting expectantly. And he was naked as the day he was born. He looked almost as dangerous in human form as he did in his wolf form, with all those muscles silhouetted starkly in the gray morning light.

Heat rushed up my face as I tried not to stare. I turned my back and struggled to disentangle myself from the straps of the packs without dislodging Goliath. It was awkward, but I managed it. I handed Magnus his bag, working hard not to let my eyes drift, but it was difficult with the werewolf right in front of me. The ripped, dangerously handsome, naked werewolf.

Why couldn't he shift behind a tree or something?

"Thanks," Magnus said, sifting through the bag, searching for his pants and oblivious to my struggle for control.

"No problem," I replied, examining the sky intently as he yanked them on.

I'd learned quickly that the werewolves shifted wherever and when-ever they wanted to, seemingly unconcerned about their nudity. Sloane ribbed the guys about it, slipping easily into locker room banter. Not me. Something about seeing Magnus's sculpted chest and lean but powerful muscles sent bolts of electricity shooting through me, shorting out my brain and lighting up other parts of me. Parts of me that were delightfully distracting in a place where I couldn't afford a single mistake.

"What are you looking at?" Magnus asked. He kept his voice soft so as not to wake the others.

"Um, just checking for rain. I thought I heard thunder, but it looks all clear now," I muttered, peeking to see if Magnus had finished getting dressed.

Magnus tugged his shirt on, sliding it down to hide the muscular expanse. Suddenly, I found the cool morning air slid more easily in and out of my lungs.

"I didn't hear anything," he said, glancing up and then back at me.

Was that a smirk I saw dancing around the corners of his eyes?

"Good. No need to set up anything else then," I shrugged, attempting nonchalance. "Are you okay with second watch?"

"Sure," Magnus said easily, reaching into his bag and pulling out his blanket. It must be getting colder. Magnus usually ran warm, opting to forgo the blanket altogether, regardless of his form.

"Great. Wake you in an hour." I turned, searching for a place where I could keep watch that was just uncomfortable enough to keep me awake.

Magnus cleared his throat behind me. "Cam, are you okay?" I heard the ring of suppressed sympathy in his voice. As if he wanted to help but didn't want to push me to the brink.

I closed my eyes and took a deep breath, pasting a smile on my face as I faced him. "Sure. Tired, but I'll last another hour. Get some sleep."

"You know that's not what I mean."

"I'm fine." I tried not to bite the words off, but wasn't entirely successful.

"It's been days and you still refuse to talk about Ben's death."

I bit the inside of my cheek, battling the swell of grief and anger threatening to overwhelm me. "Let's just get some rest, okay?" I squeezed the words out past the lump in my throat.

"You can't keep your emotions bottled up forever. You'll explode if you try. Trust me, I know." Compassion and concern flowed out of him as he placed a comforting hand on my shoulder. "I haven't ever told you how I joined Damon's pack, have I?"

The question was rhetorical, and we both knew it, but I shook my head anyway.

He took a deep breath and focused on a spot on the distant horizon. His voice was quiet when he spoke. "You know I was a maverick when I came to New Orleans with Damon and his crew, right? A rogue seeking to join a new pack? Well, I wasn't a loner by choice. I'd been part of a pack in upstate New York for about five years. Nothing as big as what Damon has. Just some friends who ran together. There were four of us to start. During the day, we worked on our tech company and by night we got to turn into werewolves. Best time of my life."

He paused, his eyes flicking over the skyline like he was replaying memories in the cinema of his mind. I touched his arm lightly. "What happened?" I asked softly.

He shrugged and chuckled sadly. "Mostly what you would imagine. One by one, my friends settled down. Colin found a nice witch who wasn't bothered that he was furrier than most men and married her. Rolf mated with a werewolf from a neighboring pack. They'd just told us that Susi was expecting twins. They were so thrilled. And Louie's fiancée, a nice human girl named Maria, was preparing for the change. She wanted to become a werewolf. The Alpha from Susi's pack was going to help, to make sure everything went smoothly. But she never got the chance." He clenched his jaw hard, biting off the words.

An icy fist closed around my heart. "Why?"

He sucked in a deep breath. "It was the vamps," he said, bitterness turning his voice brittle. "Some of the older power players from the city were on a retreat or something. Somehow, they heard about our plans and didn't like the idea of a pack of werewolves forming so close to their territory. It didn't matter that there was and still is an enormous pack of werewolves already in New York City. I don't know. Maybe they were bored. Maybe one of the guys said something in the bar that night. Who knows? We were out, the seven of us, celebrating Susi and Rolf's news and Maria's impending change. A problem came up at work. I told them I'd take care of it. All the other guys had their girls out with them. It would only take me thirty minutes to clear it up. I'd be back in no time." He covered his eyes with a hand. "That was the last time I saw any of them alive. When I got back, there was so much blood. It was everywhere. My friends were dead. Ripped to shreds. The vamps had even stabbed Susi repeatedly in the stomach. I guess to make sure there was no hope of their babies surviving. It didn't matter that she was still in her first trimester. The vamps slaughtered my friends and their wives, but that wasn't the worst of it. They took Maria. It took me a week to track them down, but by then it was too late. They'd turned her. Made her into a vampire against her will and then starved her. It made her feral. Lethal and unpredictable. And then they released her into Susi's father's territory. He had no choice but to kill her before she could kill innocents."

Tears welled up and an unreleased sob clogged my throat. I squeezed his arm in silent sympathy. Magnus wiped at his eyes with the back of a hand. "I went to a dark place. Revenge consumed every waking moment and different, violent scenarios of how I could make those vamps pay filled my dreams. I'm not proud of the person I became or the things I did." He blew out a breath and turned his head to meet my gaze. "I don't want to see you make the same mistakes I did. My desire to make them pay ate away at my soul. I don't want that for you."

I drew in a jagged breath. "Maybe I deserve it." I looked away, fighting the fiery burn of tears welling up in my eyes. For Ben. For Magnus' friends. It was all so unfair!

He reached out, weaving his fingers through mine, and *squeezed*. "You don't. Ben didn't deserve what happened to him, but I don't think he'd want you to become obsessed with a bloody cycle of revenge. Just talk to me. Open up just a little. Let the pain out."

My breath hitched sharply as wave after wave of emotion slammed into me. I don't know how long we sat there as I struggled for composure. It felt like I'd just calm down enough to open my mouth when another memory would suck me back under in a riptide of guilt. Ben's smiling face blurred as tears spilled down my cheeks.

"I... Ben... He... I just can't," I finally choked out.

Magnus' voice was soft. "Don't keep that pain all inside. It will eat you alive."

I bit my lip. "I just can't. Not now."

He squeezed my fingers. "Ok. I get it. Just know I'm here. Whenever you're ready."

My lips tightened in a hard line. I nodded sharply once. Just once. It was all I could bear. Out of the corner of my vision, I saw Magnus close his eyes and bob his head, accepting my terse response. I pulled my hand away, a wash of guilt and shame sweeping over me. He didn't touch me again as I spun and strode away. Before I clambered up the tree with the painfully bright orange foliage, I tested the leaves with a fingertip. They were safe. No razor-sharp edges to slice me into little Cameron ribbons. I hoisted myself up, hoping it would provide me with a good vantage point for my hour's watch.

What I couldn't verbalize to Magnus or to anyone else was that Ben's death was *my* fault. I had failed him. I should've been faster, struck harder, fought better. I should've been able to stop Kroxius from killing the old necromancer. From killing my friend. I should have been able to save him.

But I couldn't and didn't. And Ben had paid the price for my failings.

I banged the back of my head against the rough bark of the tree. I needed a distraction. I fished the small stone Letitia had given me from my pocket. I activated it by tapping it three times like she'd shown me and whispering her name.

"Letitia?"

The stone in my hand vibrated gently as her voice drifted up to my ears. "Cam? Is everything ok?"

"Yes. Kroxius tried to ambush us last night with multiple spider-tiger zombies," I said.

"Oh, my gods!" Letitia exclaimed. "Are you ok?"

"Everyone is fine," I reassured her. "How are your people?"

Her tone was somber. "Not good. We lost another one. That makes three dead since we crossed over and no visible improvement in anyone else."

I read between the lines. Letitia's people weren't the only ones suffering from the lich's death magic. His parasitic curse had also infected her. Which meant there'd been no improvement for her either.

"Letitia, I'm so sorry..." I said.

"Don't," she cut me off. I heard her sigh. "It's not your fault. Just find that lich as soon as you can. My people are depending on you."

"I will," I said. "Letitia, I..." The connection ended with a little pop. It hadn't lasted as long as yesterday's conversation. Letitia had warned me that the spell would fade. I just hadn't expected it to fade today of all days.

I groaned and let my head thump back against the tree trunk as my throat closed up. I tried to hold back the tears for as long as I could. All those fae. Ben. Pointless deaths, every single one. I felt Goliath creep along my shoulder and lay his furry little head against my cheek, patting me gently with a paw. It was like he knew his master had died and he shared my sorrow.

Who knows? Maybe he did.

We sat there silently. Together yet separate, grieving in our own way. The wide expanse of grassy meadow blurred as the sun finally crested the horizon, spilling golden light across the Fae plains just as the tears spilled down my cheeks. I made no sound as sobs wracked my body. I cried until I had no more tears left, sitting alone in my tree, and watching the sunrise over this strange, hostile land with a tiny mouse as my only companion.

A mouse that was here with me only because of my utter failure to protect his master. My friend. Ben.

The hour was an eternity of self-recrimination. My mind refused to stop churning as a single thought kept replaying in a torturous loop.

It's my fault he's dead.

Chapter 6

It felt like I'd barely closed my eyes when a piercing shriek ripped through the air. I jerked awake even as Magnus yanked me roughly into a sitting position. Sloane slid down the tree, breaking branches in her mad dash for terra firma. Andrei stood in the center of our small camp in human form, his head whipping back and forth between Sloane and a distant thundering dust cloud rolling over the grasslands. His eyes were a little wild around the edges, and I thought I saw fur bristling out of the backs of his palms.

"What is it?" I shouted, letting Magnus pull me to my feet. He spun and rushed to Andrei, whispering harshly in the kid's ear. The teenager panted heavily but seemed to listen to the older werewolf.

"Centaurs!" Sloane yelled as she skidded to a stop next to me. "It's a herd of centaurs heading this way and fast! I don't know if they picked up our trail or if we're just that damned unlucky. Either way, we have to get out of here!" She lurched towards the bags and threw hers on her back, fumbling with the straps.

"What do you mean?" I asked, rushing to grab my bag. I disentangled Goliath from his place under my ear. I tucked him securely in a pocket in the bag before hefting it onto my back. I didn't want the little mouse to lose his precarious perch in a mad dash. Fae was still new to me, but I trusted Sloane. She knew the dangers here better than I did, even if she'd been gone for years. If she was running, I'd better run too.

The guys slung their packs over their shoulders simultaneously and loped after us in human form even as Sloane slid down the bank, splashing into the stream.

"Centaurs love chaos. It runs in their blood, and the ones who live in Fae are the *worst*. They're barbarians of the most destructive kind! Conan has nothing on these guys!" Sloane was halfway across the stream when the rest of us hit the water. We were out and on the other side in a heartbeat, dodging into the tall grass. It reminded me of ducking into a cornfield in August. The grass was high enough to hide even Magnus.

Sloane held up her fist as soon as we were all well within the overgrown grass. We pulled to a stop. I understood instantly. Sloane didn't dare rush through the soaring fronds and give our presence away with the swaying movement. She held a finger to her lips as the centaur herd stampeded onto the bank of the stream we'd just vacated. One look at the half-horse, half-human creatures and I knew Sloane had probably saved our lives with her quick thinking.

Hideous scars covered each centaur's human torso, no doubt caused by the primitive weapons the creatures waved at each other. Heavy clubs decorated with stone spikes thumped menacingly against lean flanks as the herd galloped up to the stream. A large, scarred male stopped underneath the tree that had been my lookout perch. He scanned the surrounding area alertly as the rest of the herd knelt and drank from the crystalline waters.

His eyes slid over our hiding place without a hitch. I felt Sloane's fingers clutch at my hand. I gave her a return squeeze. He hadn't seen us.

Suddenly, the guard's head jerked up. His nostrils flared. He yanked the club from his back, letting out a guttural shout and pointing upstream with the massive weapon. Sloane's fingers jerked spasmodically. I followed her gaze and saw a large log drifting lazily downstream towards the herd.

No, not a log. A *head*.

The centaurs responded instantly to the warning cry, grabbing for weapons and turning to face the threat swimming their way.

I felt Sloane's breath tickle the back of my neck as she whispered, "It's a croc. We've got to go. Now."

Slowly, carefully, the four of us moved backwards through the tall grass, trying to disturb the waving fronds as little as possible. I kept my eyes locked on the tableau in front of me, unwilling to turn my back on two different dangerous predators.

The herd of centaurs threw themselves at the crocodile with such abandon that I knew Sloane had been holding back on us when she said they were violent.

Centaurs were battle-hungry maniacs. They attacked with such merciless ferocity that I'd already written the crocodile off in my mind, wishing it the best of luck as the newest fashion accessory for the trending centaur ladies. Suddenly, the creature pushed itself out of the water, letting out a mighty roar and shaking water from its furry body in a torrential spray. I realized that I'd grossly overestimated the centaurs' vicious attack. It seemed entirely justified once I saw the hideous mashup thrashing in the water.

"That's no croc! That's a fucking bear! With a crocodile's face!" I hissed at Sloane. I stumbled backwards, suddenly desperate to put more distance between us and the monster in the river. The beast had the powerful jaws and deadly tail of a crocodile, but the body, claws, and massive teeth of a prehistoric bear. One that could've tangled simultaneously with mammoths and saber-tooth tigers and won.

"It's a croco-bear, and they never travel alone! Hurry!" Sloane hissed back.

I couldn't tear my gaze away. Two more croco-bears surfaced in the deceptively deep stream. The trio roared their intentions at the herd of centaurs racing towards them with preternatural speed. The centaurs screamed their own bone-chilling battle cries as the entire herd splashed towards the trio of croco-bears in a deadly rush.

I hesitated, caught by the violent beauty of the moment. If I'd had an ounce of artistic ability, I would've committed the scene to memory, intending to paint it with wild abandon in the future. I'd undoubtedly be celebrated for my creative imagination throughout fantasy circles everywhere when I was just painting a horrifying reality.

The hesitation cost me. Sloane tugged urgently at my arm, not realizing I'd stupidly stopped. She pulled me off my feet, sending me crashing painfully into the hard-packed dirt. I watched in horror as the centaur guard's head whipped towards us. His gaze locked on mine through the crushed grass.

"Run!" I screamed, scrambling to my feet and sprinting away from the rumbling of charging hooves behind us. Sloane, Magnus, and Andrei followed my lead. We crashed blindly through the tall grass, dry stalks lashing painfully at our arms as we tried unsuccessfully to protect our faces in a mad dash away from the centaurs.

I couldn't get enough speed to outdistance them. The thundering sound of an angry stampede drew closer. I didn't dare risk looking over my shoulder for fear of breaking stride and falling. Suddenly, I felt the air grow chilly. Then frigid. A moment later, it felt as though someone had slipped a knife made of pure ice into my lungs and let it expand. I pressed a hand to my chest, gasping at the freezing sensation spreading through my torso. I was so distracted by the cold that I didn't notice the grass thinning until we burst through the final straggling line of broken stalks.

I slid wildly on an unexpected thin layer of ice under freshly fallen snow. My feet went out from under me, and I flailed my arms in a futile effort to regain my balance. No such luck. I landed hard on my tailbone. Ice-coated weeds under the dusting of snow cracked as I rolled, slipping and sliding as I tried to regain my footing.

What the hell? Where did the ice come from?

Looking behind me, I saw the line where the grasslands ended, and snow drifts started. The two distinct terrains butted up against each other as though a giant had cut through the two biomes with a dull knife and then smashed the two contrasting halves together.

The thunder of rushing hooves grew louder by the moment. I pushed myself backwards, sliding on my ass away from the grass on the slick snow. The centaurs broke through the tall grass like a tsunami, threatening to crush us under an inescapable wave.

I held my breath, bunching my muscles to prepare for what I knew would be a futile attempt to escape the centaurs' rush. Even if I dodged their heavy clubs, there was no way I'd avoid all those hooves. They'd trample me, grinding my bones into the snowy expanse of this strange land.

The centaurs charged, screaming an ululating battle cry, and waving their spiked clubs. I grabbed for my shadows. Before I could force the insubstantial blades into existence, the entire herd shifted as one. They started running parallel to the wispy line of snow-kissed stalks bordering the grassland. I flinched as their screams of frustration rose in pitch, but not a single centaur crossed the line into the strange snow-coated land.

I heard a low, relieved chuckle from behind me. Andrei was laughing nervously. Magnus elbowed the kid, but he looked just as confused as I felt.

I scrambled to my feet and pointed at the centaurs ranging along the snow line and shaking their clubs angrily at us without setting a hoof on the snowy ground. "It's not just me, right? That's weird, even for Fae."

"It's weird," Sloane confirmed.

"No, it's Winter," a voice said behind us, enunciating the last word slowly and clearly.

Sloane and I whirled as one, reaching for whatever weapons were at hand. We shouldn't have bothered. About a dozen soldiers ranged in a rough semi-circle behind us. They were all tall, pale, and well-armed. If I hadn't been in Fae, I would've sworn they were human. Haughtily beautiful, fur clad humans. Based on that, I guessed they were probably High Fae. The only things that differentiated High Fae from humans were their slightly pointed ears and magical abilities. Although, in this case, the fae were also wearing sensible winter clothes.

Warm furs varying in shade from cozy brown to deep purple swathed their lean bodies. The fae looked like beautiful barbarians from a long-forgotten ice age, but the wickedly gleaming elegant weapons coated in hoarfrost pointedly showed these fae were anything but primitive. They also outnumbered us three to one.

A tall man armed with a well-used but immaculately kept bow stepped forward. He held an arrow to the string but kept the tension loose. His stance told me he was ready to draw it in an instant if need be.

The clamoring ruckus of the centaurs behind us fell silent as soon as the man stepped forward. The fae man ignored the centaurs, speaking directly to us.

"There is no welcome to trespassers in Winter. Especially manlings. Speak your business or return to Autumn," he said.

The temperature of the small clearing dropped another ten degrees. Literally, not figuratively. I shivered at the sudden chill. The man jutted his chin towards the trampled grasslands to show where he meant for us to return. The centaurs let loose a guttural cheer. A haughty smile crossed the man's features. "Although it looks as though your welcome on that side of the border won't be any warmer than it is here."

I took a slow step forward, careful to keep my hands wide of my body and offer no threat to the archer. "We have no quarrel with Winter," I said, keeping my voice low and calm. I tried to suppress the shivers shaking my shoulders, but it grew harder with every moment we stood in the cold.

I heard the rest of my small party shift slightly behind me. I waved my outstretched hand at them to stop any foolhardy actions. The last thing I needed was an impetuous teenage werewolf pushing this situation from tense to fucked up.

"Why are you here then, manling?" The tall fae cocked his head to the side, but didn't raise his bow, which I took as a good sign.

"We are tracking a dangerous criminal on behalf of the Spring Court," I replied.

A frown creased the fae's brow. "Why would Spring entrust their business to you? Have they fallen so far that they must rely on manling mercenaries to handle their disputes?"

My fingers started to burn with the cold, but I fought against the instinct to clench them into fists. I didn't want to antagonize the Winter fae. "The criminal we seek is a dangerous sorcerer. Although he once was human, he no longer is. He has become a lich and we must bring him to justice as soon as possible."

"Why should I care?" The fae leader's tone was impassive.

I kept my tone neutral, not wanting to provoke the archer. "He ambushed us. Many of the members of the Spring fae we were with were grievously wounded."

"Sounds like a smart warrior," said a voice from the crowd of fae.

The leader spoke over his shoulder without breaking eye contact with me, "Shut it, Henryk."

"You got it, Cap!" came the cheeky reply before silence settled over the crowd of fae once more.

I shifted my weight uneasily. "The Spring fae were in no shape to chase after the lich. My friends and I volunteered."

The captain blinked once. "Volunteered? Are you stupid?" His tone was crisp with condemnation.

I shrugged, praying I read the man right. "Perhaps. Perhaps not. Only time will tell."

The Winter archer cocked his head, considering my words thoughtfully. He eyed me up and down, ignoring my three companions. I kept my gaze steady and my mind far away from the creation of shadowy weapons, even though I was itching to grab them.

"And do you have any proof of your claims?" he asked.

I nodded slowly. "I have an enchanted stone that I've been using to communicate with the leader of the Spring fae. However, the magic is fading. I can try to use it to reach her, but I'm not sure it will work."

The archer considered me and then stuck out his hand. "Give me this stone," he commanded.

I moved slowly so as not to arouse any suspicion from the Winter fae. Behind me, the centaurs bellowed in anger. I fished the enchanted communication device out of my pocket and carefully passed it over.

The leader rolled the stone between two fingers and then held it up to his eye. Finally, he nodded to himself, apparently having reached a decision. "I believe this comes from a Spring fae, so there is at least some truth to your story." He passed the stone back to me and casually added, "I also believe I know where the man you seek is."

My eyes widened, but before I could open my mouth, the fae captain interrupted me. "The Winter Lady is most interested in new and interesting creatures. You may join our party as our *guests*." From the way he twisted the last word, I knew what he meant.

Prisoners.

Although I didn't want to go back to Autumn with a load of bloodthirsty centaurs mere feet behind me, I wasn't about to roll over and agree to being arrested by the first fae who came along. "I am sure that the Winter Lady would like to hear the news we bring from the Spring Court. Lady Letitia's business is quite urgent." I wasn't above name dropping if that helped smooth over the situation.

The captain nodded thoughtfully. "If you are who you say you are, the Winter Lady will gladly receive you as honored envoys of the Spring Court. However, if we discover that you have not spoken the truth, you will have wished you'd chosen the centaurs. At least your death would have been quick at their hands."

Chapter 7

The Winter fae led us through the deepening snow. Ice coated the stark, leafless trees. Fluffy snow covered the landscape in a downy blanket of white flakes—one that was exhausting to walk through.

The fae navigated the snow with unbelievable speed. Even though they broke the trail for us, I found it difficult to keep up. It was like slogging through quicksand. Cold, damp quicksand that dragged at my feet and clung to my clothes. The cold burrowed under my thin clothes and seeped into the very marrow of my bones. I reached into the pocket of my pack where Goliath had taken up residence and coaxed the little mouse out. I tucked him under my shirt, wrapping a careful hand around his tiny body. I didn't know if the reanimated familiar needed to stay warm, but I wasn't about to let this last little piece of Ben freeze to death.

Luckily, we didn't have far to go. About fifteen minutes after leaving the centaurs at the border, we broke through the trees and into a campsite in a small clearing. The site was compact and obviously built for efficient use rather than comfort. The hard-packed snow crunched softly underfoot, making it easier to walk in the camp than it had been on the trail here. One large cooking fire crackled in the middle of the clearing, ringed by soot-stained stones. The fae had strung large leather tarp-like blankets to act as windbreaks between trees. Tents ringed the edge of the camp. Other than those few necessities, the site was barren.

By the time we stumbled into the camp, I was simultaneously sweating and shivering. That would probably be a big problem if I couldn't get warm soon. I looked over my shoulder, raising my hands to my mouth one at a time to blow on my numb fingertips. Sloane didn't look much better than I felt. The tips of her pointed ears were turning the faintest shade of blue. At least Magnus and Andrei looked capable of doing more than shivering. I knew they ran hotter because of their alter egos, even while in human form. I was more than a little jealous of that fact now.

We stood awkwardly in the middle of the camp. I inched closer to the fire. The heat washed over me, and my shivering lessened. Goliath even poked his head out of the neckline of my shirt. Andrei walked up to Sloane and threw an arm around the tiny leprechaun, tucking her close against his side. The kid even rubbed her exposed arms for good measure. I nodded at him with a faint smile. Andrei winked at me. He had a good heart.

The captain of the Winter fae moved swiftly through the camp, shouting orders. His men jumped to obey, swiftly breaking down the remains of the camp. One guard approached and tossed some worn, smelly fur jackets at us. I grabbed mine and struggled into it gratefully. As soon as I had it on, the guard shoved a handful of fae travel bread into my hands and marched away.

I passed the bread out to my friends silently. We all wolfed the food down as quickly as we could. Magnus moved to stand beside me while we ate. He didn't touch me, but I could feel the heat radiating off him even through the second-hand coat. Part of me wanted to take refuge in his arms and the promise of warmth, but I didn't dare. Not when we were still on shaky ground with our escorts-slash-captors. But at least my stomach wasn't growling, and I wasn't shivering anymore.

Magnus shook snow out of his hair, using the movement to hide his whispered words. "What do you think? Make a break for it?"

I shook my head, keeping my voice low as well. "No. If they really know where Kroxius is, this is our best chance to find him and finish him quickly. Letitia and the rest of the injured fae are depending on us dealing with him as fast as we can."

Magnus nodded, grabbing his own jacket, and slinging it on. "I'll be honest; I wasn't sure we could manage an escape, anyway. Not in this terrain against people better equipped and more familiar with the elements. What's the plan then?"

Sloane and Andrei moved closer, wrapped in their own borrowed furs. The blue tinge was fading from Sloane's ears. That was a good thing, at least.

I kept my voice low but acknowledged them with a jerk of my chin. "Nothing's changed. The plan is still the same. We need to find Kroxius and kill him as quickly as possible."

"How are you gonna do that? Isn't killing him going to upset these guys?" Andrei asked, jerking his thumb at the fae hurrying around the campsite.

"Maybe. Maybe not. We're going to have to figure that out quickly because we've got people's lives hanging in the balance. A lot of people," I replied.

But one less than should be here. I kept the thought to myself.

Magnus spoke up again, "Kill now, apologize later?"

I bobbed my head in agreement. "If needs be. I just hope that these fae have stronger ties to Spring and their own kind than to Kroxius."

Andrei raised his hand like he was in school. "Yeah, but *how* are we gonna kill him? It's not like these dudes are gonna just let you walk up and stab the guy."

I winked at him. "I'm going to do what I do best, pup. Improvise."

"I'm not a pup!" Andrei protested reflexively. I ignored him.

Sloane snorted. I glared at her. "What?" I asked.

She held up her hands in protest. "No offense, Cam, but you could have said anything else there, and it'd be true. Drink. Fight. Swear. Stab things. But *improvise?* Whenever you do that, things go to hell in a handbasket, but with uncontrollable fireworks." She folded her arms over her chest.

I rolled my eyes. "Not helping. Besides, my improvizations always work out. In the end. Somehow."

Sloane raised a sarcastic eyebrow.

"Hey! We're still alive, aren't we?" I demanded.

Sloane put her hands on her hips. "Barely. Do you remember that thing with the kelpies?"

I waved my hand dismissively. "Your hair grew back."

"Eventually!" Sloane exclaimed.

I continued, as if she hadn't interrupted. "As did that teeny tiny piece of your scalp."

"My *head*! It wanted to bite off *my head*, Cam!"

"But it didn't. Because I improvised," I pointed out.

Sloane sighed and rolled her eyes in a way that would have made any tween girl green with envy. "Hold on to your panties, boys. Shit is going to hit the fan. I don't know when or how, but get ready to duck and cover. It's the only way to stay intact whenever Cam says she's going to improvise. You've been warned."

Before I could retort, the captain of the fae strode up to us briskly. I looked around, surprised to note that the only evidence that remained of the campsite was the stones that had ringed the campfire and footprints in the snow. Judging by the fat flakes drifting through the trees, even those would be covered soon.

The captain spoke to us in a commanding tone. "We're moving out. Our main camp is deeper in the woods. We'll stop there this evening. If this weather holds, we should be able to reach the Winter Lady by mid-morning tomorrow at the latest."

"If she's so close, why not push through?" I asked.

The captain's gaze cooled noticeably, and he leveled it at me like a weapon. "Because this is Fae and in Fae, you take precautions or you don't survive long, *manling*." The sneer in his voice turned the word into a pointed rebuke.

"Cameron," I grumbled back at him. In my heart, I knew he was right. Fae was a dangerous place. In the short time we'd been here, that lesson had been hammered home repeatedly.

The captain tossed us some small water skins. "Keep up and don't cause trouble." His lip curled slightly into a sneer before he added, "*Manling*."

I rolled my eyes, but caught the skin, taking a long drink of frigid crystalline water before passing the skin to Magnus.

I wiped the back of my hand across my mouth. "Lead on, *fae*." Antagonizing him probably wasn't a great idea, but I bristled at the way he said 'human'. Like it was a dirty, disgusting word.

The captain narrowed his eyes at me but spun on his heel without another word to us. Snapping orders at his men, the captain whipped the guards into a frenzy of organized chaos. In moments, we'd fallen into the middle of a pack of armed Winter fae. The captain led us deeper into the snow-covered forest.

Sloane shot me a nervous glance as we started walking. I shrugged back. We didn't know what dangers lurked behind the drifting snow, but

I had a feeling the most dangerous thing in this forest held a bow and was leading our party. That didn't make me feel any better.

My legs were cramping by the time we waded through the final windswept drifts and into the main camp about an hour later. The captain stood in the center of a much larger clearing than the first. Where pine trees grew close, supple branches were cleverly woven together, catching the drifting snow and forming a natural wind block. It had the added benefit of reflecting some of the heat from three large blazing fires back into the clearing. Tents ringed the campsite, lending an extra layer of protection from the freezing winter wind. I wouldn't call the set-up cozy, but it was better than hiking through the snowy terrain.

More fae poked their heads out of tents or stopped in preparations for the midday meal as we filed into the camp. The captain barked orders to his men. The Winter fae jumped to obey, falling into the camp preparations with an ease that told me that this was hardly their first time in the woods. Several members of our party greeted those in the camp with hearty handshakes and good-natured teasing.

An unusual flicker of movement on the outskirts of the camp caught my eye amid the busy fae hurrying around the camp. My eyes twitched toward the right, but I didn't turn my head, using my peripheral vision to scan the area.

There it was again. Just a faint flash of orange light from inside a tent.

Without being consciously aware, I was halfway across the clearing, my hands curling into claws. An iron grip clenched my arm, spinning me around. I regained my balance to see the captain standing firmly between me and my target. I glanced over my shoulder. A group of armed fae surrounded my friends. The soldiers didn't precisely have their weapons drawn, but they weren't far off.

I whirled back to the captain, rising on my tiptoes to peer over his shoulders.

A familiar figure brushed the flap of the tent aside and stepped into the clearing. My breath caught and blood pounded deafeningly in my ears, even though I knew we'd catch him eventually.

Kroxius. Ben's killer. He was here.

Chapter 8

The lich looked better than when I'd last seen him. Besides throwing zombie creatures in our path, he must have been draining the life force from whatever he met as he fled through Fae. Hell, as far as I knew, he might have drained energy completely from the monsters and then hurled their reanimated corpses at us.

Whatever method he'd used, Kroxius had regrown a layer of skin and muscle since I'd seen him last. He still looked like he could use a month of six hearty meals a day, but at least he wasn't a literal walking skeleton anymore.

Kroxius looked around, scanning the crowd of returning Winter fae curiously. His eyes lit on me and flashed an unholy orange in recognition.

"*You*," he snarled, taking a step toward me. Orange magic crackled to life around his fingertips. Silence blanketed the clearing. Fae guards materialized at his sides, weapons drawn. He sneered at them but let the magic flare brightly once more before allowing it to crackle out of existence.

I pointed my shaking finger at the undead sorcerer smirking at me behind the fae captain. "You're protecting a *murderer*," I said, fighting to keep my voice even.

The captain chuckled, the dark sound dancing through the camp before spreading through the rest of the fae like cracks spreading over thin ice. Laughter rolled around the Winter fae, doing nothing to dissipate the tension climbing my spine. As the promise of conflict slowly diminished with each passing heartbeat, the fae resumed their chatter and daily tasks.

The captain folded his arms, looking down his nose at me. "You say that like it's a bad thing."

I bit the inside of my cheek until I tasted blood. "He killed my friend," I finally growled.

Condescending mutters ran through the crowd of fae. Popular opinion was obviously not on my side. Kroxius's smirk deepened. The bastard winked at me. My fists clenched, ragged nails scraping at my flesh even as the sniggers rubbed my last nerve raw.

The fae captain shrugged, but kept his attention locked warily on me. "You're approaching this with your weak human sensibilities. This is Fae. Death is part of life here. Accept it or get consumed by it."

I opened my mouth to respond, then snapped it closed, not sure how to voice the storm rolling through me.

The captain jerked a thumb over his shoulder at a fae guard in faded blue furs standing near Kroxius with a wicked-looking short sword. "See him? He killed my cousin," the captain said calmly.

I spluttered, my eyes bugging out of my head as the fae in question raised his free arm in acknowledgment and gave a little wave, obviously overhearing our conversation. "And you, what? Just fight beside your cousin's murderer?!" I hissed.

The captain looked perplexed. "Of course. He's proven himself the superior warrior."

I shook my head at the cold logic of the statement. The captain's face was devoid of emotion. The guard flapped back his faded blue cloak, striking a ridiculous, faux-heroic pose, jutting his sword into the air at his captain's small kernel of praise. His friends jostled and chortled at his posturing.

"I swear, I will never understand that. How can you go from cousin-killer to confidante just like that?" I snapped my fingers, drawing the attention of the nearby fae.

The captain shook his head, speaking down at me like I was a child, "Don't be stupid. I demanded satisfaction first."

"And he got it too. Hell of a fighter, our captain," the guard said. He ran a callused finger along an old scar that sliced from his ear to the tip of his nose meaningfully. "I'm just glad that he chose first blood rather than death, or I'd be a very pretty corpse."

A hoot from his fellow guards sounded behind him, followed by some good-natured ribbing.

"Pretty is a word not even your mama used to describe you!" a soldier shouted.

Another added, "I don't know, maggots climbing out of your nose might be an improvement."

"Maggots wouldn't even touch something that ugly!" Jeers and cheers rose from the onlookers.

"I'd be willing to help you out if you wanted to try the corpse look. You know, as a personal favor," offered another fae.

Raucous laughter rolled through the guards as the banter continued. The large guard threw mock punches at his colleagues. The men jostled each other. Friendly jokes flowed easily as they headed towards the fires and the promise of food. Kroxius moved with them, obviously familiar with the fae in the camp, but I noticed he stayed on the edges of their camaraderie and didn't join in the banter.

A flush of anger burned away the numbness in my fingertips as I glared daggers at the sorcerer across from me. Kroxius must have sensed my scowl. He glanced over his shoulder as he drifted away with the fae. He endured my glower easily, letting it slide off his emaciated form as he pursed his thin lips and blew me a kiss.

My heart thundered in my chest. A vein in my temple throbbed. My vision tunneled, darkness framing the sorcerer like an old vignette portrait. I wanted nothing more than to set that picture on fire and laugh as the winter wind scattered the ash to the four corners of the world. A fragment of the captain's story tugged at my thoughts. I grinned darkly.

"Satisfaction." My voice was menacing. The frigid tone made the wintry clearing look like an island paradise.

The captain jerked, looking at me. "What did you say?" he asked, keeping his voice low. The guards didn't hear me. They continued towards their meal with jovial camaraderie. Kroxius had heard me, though. He jerked to a stop, letting the fae flow around him. He met my eyes and ran his tongue over his lips, looking at me hungrily.

I stared back without flinching and raised my voice. "I demand satisfaction." My words carried clearly through the frigid air.

A hush settled over the campsite. Fine flakes of snow drifted lazily down to coat the still figures in the clearing as if they were statues in a garden instead of living beings. The only sound was the snap and crackle of snowflakes dying in the fires' heat.

The captain of the fae blinked slowly. His voice was quiet when he spoke, meant for my ears alone. "Are you sure? Once the challenge is issued, it's binding. The challenge will be resolved with your blood or his."

I met his eyes coolly, not dropping my volume one iota. "Sat-is-fac-tion." I spoke slowly, over-articulating every syllable. Behind the captain, Sloane jerked as if I'd slapped her with each crisp consonant.

The captain's mouth pinched and drew downwards. He raised his arms, turning in a small circle to address the clearing, his voice snapping through the campsite like a gunshot, drawing all eyes towards him. "Attention!" He pointed at me and then at Kroxius. "This manling demands satisfaction from that sorcerer for the death of her friend." The captain raised an eyebrow, checking to see if he had his facts straight. I gave him a terse nod.

The captain turned to Kroxius. "Do you dispute the charge levied against you?"

Kroxius leered at me. He spoke to the captain, but kept his mocking gaze locked on me. "I do not. I killed him and would do it again without hesitation. The weak, old fool."

My vision darkened, and the remains of my heart cracked wide open at the casual dismissal of the kind soul Ben had been. Rage bubbled inside of me like red-hot magma rising under pressure. Something snapped. Too late, I tried to slam a lid on my emotions, but didn't have the strength to force the anger back into its shattered shell. The fire within me crackled and blazed brighter with every breath I took, threatening to burst through my fragile control. And I wanted to let it.

Kroxius sneered, reading my emotions as if I were a picture book. "Ben was a nothing necro. I possess more power in my little fingernail than he had in his entire miserable life. I gave him a gift by allowing him to feed my magic, although I don't know why I bothered. He was barely worth the effort of draining him."

My face flushed and my hands shook. A guttural roar ripped through my chest and shook the snow from the very heavens, making it fall faster and harder. I threw myself forward, trying to form shadow blades so I could slice Kroxius's brand new flesh from his bones.

The fae captain caught me, holding me in a steely grip. The shadows skittered away from me before I could use my magic to create my weapons. I raged and flailed as Kroxius smirked at me from a safe distance. I knew he was riling me up for precisely this reaction. However, logic had no place in my heart right now. I just wanted revenge.

My mind locked on my purpose. Laser-focused, I was suddenly calm. I relaxed in the captain's arms until he finally released me. The cadence of my heartbeat slowed. I knew my goal. I knew my target. The only thing that remained was playing the hand fate had dealt me. For the cursed fae. For Letitia. For Ben.

Ben.

I carefully set thoughts of the kind old necromancer back in their little box at the back of my mind. Grieving him could wait just a little while longer. I crossed my arms over my chest and focused on breathing deeply. I needed to be ready. When facing someone as dangerous as Kroxius, I couldn't afford to make a stupid, emotional mistake.

The fae captain waited a moment more to see if I was going to fly off the handle again. I gave him a tight nod, encouraging him silently to proceed. My heartbeat sped up as he returned the nod and raised his voice to be heard clearly by everyone nearby. "It looks like we're going to have a show before dinner. Let's set the stage."

Chapter 9

The fae soldiers cleared the center of the camp, drawing a rough circle in the packed snow under the captain's watchful eye. Kroxius disappeared into his tent amid the flurry of preparation. I glared after him, not sure what he was doing, but one hundred percent positive I would not like it.

Magnus grabbed my arm and pulled me aside. "What are you doing?" he whisper-shouted at me.

I shook free of his grip and started stretching, focusing on my legs. The walk through the snow had been hard. Cramps were creeping up my calves. I carefully leaned into my stretches, feeling the glorious pain of used muscles. "This is our best shot to kill him, Magnus. You've got to see that."

"The hell it is!" The werewolf's eyes burned, focusing on me with the hyper-awareness of a predator.

"You and I both know that he has to die. The faster we can kill him, the more of Letitia's people we can save." I kept my voice low, even as I massaged the worst of the kinks from my right calf.

"I know! But why did you have to call him out right now when everything plays to his advantage?"

"Time isn't on our side. Who knows when I'll get another shot at him?" I asked, shifting my focus to my quadriceps.

"So, is this about saving people or something else? Avenging Ben, for example?"

"Does it matter?" I shook my head. "Why can't it be both?"

"Because revenge is a jealous mistress that doesn't share. She gobbles up all your emotional reserves and still wants more. So, which one is it?

Are you pushing the matter because you want to save lives, or is it about Ben?"

"It's always been about Ben!" I closed my eyes and rubbed my hand over my face. "Yes, I want to help those people. To stop the death curse that is eating away at Letitia and her fae. But he *killed* Ben. I can't just ignore that."

Magnus shook his head fiercely. "A hunt is one thing, but revenge is never so simple. I've seen someone walk this path before and I can tell you, it's never enough. Make sure you've got your head on straight or the aftermath of this will eat you alive."

I glanced up at him with a soft snort. "Not the conversation I imagined from you. I thought you'd try to talk me out of this."

Magnus shook his head slowly, never looking away. "I know you better than that. Just want to make sure you come out intact. And I don't just mean physically."

Sloane rushed up, interrupting our conversation in a breathless whirl. "What the hell are you doing? You've seen what that lich can do! You've *felt* what he can do. One of his spells nearly killed you!"

I grunted, moving to massage my other leg. "Yeah, but it didn't." I didn't want to elaborate that the only reason it hadn't was that I'd made a deal with a goddess of death.

The leprechaun put her hands on her hips and stomped her tiny foot at me. Part of me wanted to laugh, but I wasn't suicidal.

Andrei sauntered up behind her, looking torn between concern and excitement. I ignored them both. I couldn't afford to get drawn into an argument with my feisty best friend or waste energy on the pup. Not now.

When she couldn't get a rise out of me, Sloane rounded on Magnus. "Aren't you immune to magic? Can't you fight him?"

I shoved to my feet before Magnus could answer. "It's my fight, Sloane. There's no way the fae will let Magnus take my place. Not when I've issued the challenge. No, you know what? There's no way *I'll* let Magnus take my place."

"Why?"

"You know why."

Sloane glared up at me, lips pinching into a thin line and tears welling in her eyes as I met her gaze stubbornly. With a huff, she whirled to

Magnus. "We can't let her fight him. She's not even fully healed from that fight with the bizarre monkey things from the forest three days ago. What are you going to do about it?"

Magnus looked over Sloane's head, taking my measure in a single glance. I shivered. I felt like he'd stripped me naked with a single glance and not in the good way.

Slowly, he shook his head. "Me? I'm not doing a damn thing."

"*What?* Why?" Sloane screeched in the most terrifying whisper I'd ever heard.

Magnus never looked away from me as he spoke to the leprechaun. "Because she's got this."

A rush of warmth flooded through me at his words. Not because I needed his approval or anything. Magnus had stated his belief in my abilities with the same calm conviction that he would've said that water was wet, winter was cold, or authors who took over a decade to finish a book were the bane of readers everywhere. Simple truth rang through every syllable.

Sloane's mouth opened and closed like she was a fish gasping on a riverbank to burble out her last argument, but it died on her lips before she could verbalize it.

The fae captain's voice rang through the clearing, drawing our attention back to him. "The challenge is issued and accepted. Winter doesn't wait to settle scores."

A cheer rose from the gathered fae as they formed an irregular circle around the roughly drawn battle ground. Andrei grabbed Sloane and dragged her to an empty spot, wrapping an arm around her shoulders. I wasn't sure if it was to keep her warm or to keep her in place. Regardless, I was grateful to the young wolf.

Magnus stood for a moment longer, considering me carefully. He spoke so softly that I barely heard him over the excited mutters of the crowd. "Just be sure that you walk out of this in one piece, Cam."

"Don't worry. I intend to win," I said grimly.

"I have no doubt, but that's not what I meant," Magnus said.

I nodded at him once and slid out of the heavy fur. I handed it over, along with my pack. As much as I hated the cold, the bulky coat would just get in my way. I lifted a hand to my shoulder. Goliath scampered out onto my palm. I gently passed the mouse over to Magnus.

Magnus placed Goliath on his shoulder and nodded at me once. Then he spun and strode purposefully away. The crowd parted before the big man on instinct. I watched as he leaned against the trunk of a tree at the edge of the clearing, folding his arms over his chest and settling in to watch the proceedings, his eyes flashing darkly like his wolf had just scented blood in the air.

The captain's voice interrupted my thought once again. "As the accused, you have the choice of weapons," he said to Kroxius.

The sorcerer spread his hands wide, orange fire crackling to life and licking up his forearms. "I'm not a monster. Let's use whatever we have at hand."

He leered at me. He knew I had shadow magic because I'd used it against him before. I met his gaze coolly. I'd learned a trick or two of my own since the last time we'd met. I didn't need to boast about it now, though. Better to keep my skills under wraps than to divulge valuable information by engaging in unnecessary trash talking. He winked and blew me a kiss. I narrowed my eyes at him and folded my arms over my chest.

A dark chuckle from the crowd rumbled through the glade. I heard someone shout odds, taking bets on the outcome of the fight. I shut out the sounds of the crowd as the captain turned to me.

"As the accuser, you have the choice of fighting to first blood or death," he intoned, looking bored. "If you choose first blood..."

"Death." My voice was clear and firm. Silence rolled through the small clearing, the single word quenching the murmured conversations.

The fae captain jerked upright in surprise. He considered me carefully before nodding in acceptance. "Finish your preparations. We will begin in five minutes."

"Why the delay?" I asked, tension creeping up my shoulder blades. I didn't enjoy waiting.

"Entertainment has been scarce while on patrol at this outpost. I can't deprive my people of some fun and they haven't finished laying their bets."

I snorted. "If I knew your name, I'd curse at you for being an asshole."

He grinned at me. "If you survive, I'll tell you."

"That's a shitty reward," I observed dryly.

The fae captain shrugged and fished a small gold coin out of his pocket. "A bet then. My name and the gold if you win."

I stuck out my hand. "Deal." The captain nodded once and clasped my hand tightly. A *whoomph* reverberated through my chest. I knew from experience this happened whenever I made a deal and no one else seemed to feel a similar sensation. I'd heard horror stories of Supes who broke their word and was determined not to become a warning for someone else. However, in this case, it wasn't too much of a problem. Split the winnings or die. Either way, it would be easy to fulfill my end of the bargain.

The captain met my gaze steadily. In that instant, I saw past the hard exterior. I peered into the eyes of a kindred soul. A fighter, sure. A badass. Someone who probably carefully cultivated a lack of social skills so his men could pull together in grumbling admiration of their leader. What I saw impressed me. I'd enjoy having a drink with the captain someday. After I killed Kroxius.

I rolled my shoulders back, trying to stay loose in the interminable five minutes. Kroxius sauntered over, the magic in his hand extinguished. It took all my self-control not to leap at him right there, but from the expression that crossed the captain's face, I knew it would be an epically poor decision to start the fight before he gave the signal.

I leaned down, working through a limbering-up routine I'd practiced irregularly since I was a teen. It looked like Tai Chi, but nothing about it was relaxing. I flowed through a variety of fighting moves that were slowed down to an exasperatingly sluggish speed. The premise was that if you could perform each move perfectly with the slowness of molasses in winter, you could do it better in a fight. I hoped that proved to be the case today.

Kroxius put his hands on his bony hips, considering me. "Why?" he finally asked.

I looked up at him, clenching my jaw hard. I exhaled and flowed into the next move, my leg extending in a low lunge ever so slowly. "Why what?"

"Why are you chasing me all across Fae?"

I froze, my jaw hanging open as I blinked at him in bafflement. "You *murdered* my friend. You murdered *countless* others. Even though you are miles away, you are *currently* murdering others through your death curse."

"And who are you to judge me?"

I abandoned my routine, straightening abruptly to look him in the eye. "What are you saying?"

"Death is a part of life. People die all the time. Only the strong survive and that is only because they trample on the weak to ensure their survival, as well you know."

"What do you mean, 'as well I know?'" Indignation swelled within me.

"You've killed to get what you want. I watched as you cut Aldrich Kingsley's throat. Admittedly, from the other side of the veil, nevertheless," he let out a long sigh, "it was *so* satisfying to watch the life fade from his eyes. I hadn't seen that delicious look of terror in years."

"That was different! It was self-defense!"

Kroxius held up his hands at my words. "I wasn't criticizing. I was impressed, actually. However, I don't see how our situations are different."

I blew out my breath in surprise. "You can't see how murder and self-defense are two different things?"

"All I see are obstacles. We both removed the obstacles from our paths, and we used the same method. Why does that make me a villain and not you? Either we are both responsible for the same crime or we are both blameless."

Too late, I saw the move he was making. He didn't give a damn about the semantics of our situations any more than he felt remorse for killing Ben or any of those other people. Kroxius had just started the fight early. The worst part was I'd fallen into the trap headfirst. Thoughts swirled around in my head as doubt took root.

Was I the same as Kroxius? He was right; we'd both killed to get what we want.

I shook myself, pulling hard on my anger, burning away the seeds of doubt the sorcerer was coaxing to sprout inside me. "Kingsley wasn't Ben. Ben was kind, caring, generous, and loving. He's a hundred times the man Kingsley was. He's a thousand times better than you are."

"Was. He can't be more than I am. He's *dead*, remember?" Kroxius's tone was cutting and full of condescension.

I stared at Kroxius as he smiled cruelly back at me. Scenes of my life in New Orleans flashed behind my eyes. Coffee with Ben at Mama's big kitchen table. Sneaking the old necromancer an extra sweet behind her back. Biting back chuckles as Ben attempted to garden. Ridiculous little kindness the old necromancer had sprinkled through the life of a lonely newcomer to the Big Easy.

And the lich smirking at me had erased all of Ben's potential for goodness from the world.

I'd make him pay for it.

The fae captain's voice rang through the clearing once more, calling for attention. Voices hushed and the circle of onlookers drew in tighter.

Our final five minutes were up.

The captain spun in a slow circle as he addressed the crowd. "The terms have been set, and the weapons chosen. If either of the combatants wishes to find an alternate solution to their disagreement, speak now." He ended his spin, looking expectantly at us.

Neither Kroxius nor I said a word.

The captain continued after a brief pause, "Very well. The matter between you is in the hands of the gods now. They will mete out rewards and punishments according to their infinite wisdom. For the loser, I wish you peace on your final journey. Know that we will lay your bones to rest in the icy embrace of Winter."

Kroxius grinned widely and pointed a finger at me. "I hope you like the cold!"

A cheer rang up from the fae, the ones who'd bet on the sorcerer supporting their champion. I narrowed my eyes, ignoring all of them. I couldn't afford to get distracted. Or more distracted. Not when I was this close to my goals.

The captain raised his arm as if he held the starting flag at a midnight drag race on the back country roads near the bayou. He slowly backed away from the center of the circle, leaving me facing Kroxius. A faint crackle of magic tinged an icy blue-white dome sprang up along the boundary inscribed in the snow. I didn't know if it was meant to keep us in or keep everyone else out. Not that it really mattered now. I'd chosen my path. Kroxius smiled, orange magic crackling to life in the palms of his skeletal hands. I ignored his mocking expression, focusing on his hands. That's where the threat would come from. The sorcerer held death cupped in his palms.

The captain dropped his arm and shouted, "Begin!"

The world flared orange.

Chapter 10

Kroxius attacked as soon as the captain began forming the word, but I was already moving. I pulled on my shadows and threw them around myself in a cloak to obscure my form. I knew from experience that they would distort my image, making me look as though someone had dripped murky water onto a fresh watercolor painting, fading out the colors and smearing the shapes.

An orange bolt crackled and snapped angrily, barely missing me as I threw myself into a tumbling roll. I'd learned the hard way that my shadows didn't grant true invisibility unless I was standing motionless and in a dark area, neither of which would help me win this fight.

"Oh, ho!" Kroxius chortled. "You've picked up some tricks! But one wonders, what are you going to do without your fancy knives?"

He flared an outstretched hand in my direction and sent a spray of tiny needle-like bolts of magic hissing through the air towards my obscured form. I dove again, dodging the bolts. However, I wasn't quite fast enough. I felt one of Kroxius's needles lance through the edge of my shadows with a tugging sensation. It even burned a small hole in the darkness. The smell of ozone tickled my nose.

Oh, that can't be good.

I pulled on the shadows again, forming a shadow blade even as I rolled to my feet. Desperately, I focused. To my surprise, the sword hardened in my hand almost instantly. However, I felt a heavy weight drop onto my shoulders. It felt like wearing a velvet cloak heavily embroidered with lead rather than one made of shadows. Uh oh. The clock was ticking. I couldn't simultaneously maintain my semi-invisibility and the sword for long if I already felt the drain on my magical stamina. However, I held on a little longer as I dodged and wove through the hail of magical bolts Kroxius threw my way.

The lich threw his head back, laughing with glee as he flung bolt after bolt my way. The orange light lit up his thin face, illuminating the caverns carved into his features as he drew on his own life force to power his spells. Madness lurked in his eyes. The dark irises lit with orange flame every time he sent a bolt crashing my way.

My pulse thundered in my ears and my breath came fast. I tried to dodge another volley of bolts, rolling away again and springing quickly to my feet. It was a mistake. I'd underestimated the power in my enchanted boots. My foot slipped on the packed snow, sending me sliding awkwardly as I flailed my arms, trying to regain my balance.

But a moment was all Kroxius needed. The lich flung his hand out, spraying another blast of magic from his fingertips at me as I struggled to regain my footing on the slick surface. I knew I couldn't dodge all those needles of death magic flying my way.

I gritted my teeth, dropping to a crouch to minimize the target I presented while simultaneously slashing with my sword on instinct. I braced instinctively against the expected pain, knowing that if even one of those deadly bolts hit me, I was a goner. Maybe not immediately, but eventually. Kroxius would finish me by pricking me to death with his needles of orange magic until I spilled my life's blood across the pristine snow.

During the questioning of my life choices, my concentration broke. The fragmented pieces of my shadowy cloak skittered out of my grasp. My form wavered fully into view as the shadows fell away like morning mist disappearing with the rising of the sun. Without the shadowy cloak faintly blurring the world, I saw the speeding bolts of magic race towards me. My heart thundered in an electric staccato as panic froze my muscles. Without my cloak, what chance did I stand?

The triumphant smirk on Kroxius' told me his thoughts on the matter. With a dramatic flourish, he drew his arm back and thrust it forward, unleashing the largest crackling bolt of magic yet.

The answer to my question thrummed in time with my racing pulse. What chance did I stand? Zero. Zero. Zero.

Desperately, I did the only thing I could think of. I raised my blade, bracing for the impact and then the inevitable annihilation as Kroxius' death magic tore straight through me. I sucked in a breath and tried not to wince away, but to meet my end bravely. To be the fighter Ben would've been proud of. To be the person I'd be proud of. Not that it would matter.

A shudder reverberated down my arm as a bolt of death magic pinged off my sword blade. My eyes flew to the sword, and I stared at the blade in surprise. Not a mark was on the dark surface. My gaze snapped up to Kroxius, thinking he was toying with me before making the kill. His mouth hung open and his eyes were wide with shock. A beat of stunned silence fell between us, pregnant with the new possibilities this opened.

Kroxius recovered first, diving to the side in an impressively swift reaction as his own crackling orange bolt of magic came flying back at him. He leaped out of the way, feet tangling over themselves at the unfamiliar movement. I guessed that he'd grown so used to attacking from a distance that he hadn't kept up with his physical fighting abilities.

My training kicked in and I sprang forward, leaping across the distance between us as my enchanted boots super-sized my leap. I crashed down onto the hard-packed snow, toes digging in to keep my momentum going. If I tried to stop too suddenly, I would slip and end up flat on my back like Kroxius. The sorcerer scrabbled away from me, sliding along the snow on his backside. Quickly, I closed the distance. I got within striking distance and raised my shadow blade. Kroxius met my eyes, a wicked grin curling his thin lips. He flung his hands forward repeatedly, one at a time, hurling magic with every flick of his wrist.

Rather than throwing myself out of the way, I stood my ground, deflecting the orange blasts of magic Kroxius hurled at me. Barely. My breath came fast and harsh as I struggled to match his speed. Although I withstood the ferocious barrage, I couldn't press my advantage any further. Ever the opportunist, Kroxius used the precious moments his onslaught bought him. He scrambled to his feet, still throwing magic at me. My only advantage now was that I had time to parry bolts back at him in addition to simply blocking or dodging his attacks. Every time I turned away one of his bolts with my blade, I tried to redirect it back at him. I wanted to force Kroxius to break up his assault by playing defense.

Slowly, as if wading on tiptoes through deep water, I pressed forward, forcing him to fall back. I closed the distance between us one hard-fought footstep at a time.

Sweat beaded on Kroxius's face. He was digging deep into his magical reserves. I grinned, swiping my blade through the air with a shrill whistling tone, deflecting another bolt back towards him. He yelled and threw himself to the side to dodge his own reflected attack.

Dimly, I heard the roar of the crowd every time my blade deflected one of the magical bolts, but I tried to tune out the cheers and jeers. I couldn't afford to slip up by getting distracted.

Kroxius prowled around the edge of the circle as he tried to put space between us. I spun the magical projectiles off my shadow blade in all directions. The lich's magic sputtered and died on contact with the blue-white barrier. The crowd fell back as we moved closer to them, even though the protective barrier kept them safe.

I grimaced, twisting my wrist to drive another streak of screaming orange magic back at the lich rather than letting it fizzle and die. Kroxius threw both hands up simultaneously. He sent a rippling, crackling bolt of orange lightning right at my chest.

I lunged to the right, squatting low and leaning my head almost to the level of my knee as I dodged. I pushed off my bent leg, thrusting myself forward with all the coiled power in my muscles. My left boot landed on a smooth piece of thin ice that had coated the surface of the packed snow. It had been hidden by the soft fall of fat snowflakes. Although I didn't fall, I slipped. I had to do a sliding quick step as I fought for balance on the treacherous terrain.

Kroxius took advantage of my misstep, flinging another flurry of bolts as he put more distance between us. I gritted my teeth, seeing him escape out of my reach. With no better plan, I resumed my slow but steady progress through the lich's magical attacks. My muscles burned, but I kept up the pressure as I parried another bolt back at his head.

Kroxius leaned his head to the side, allowing the errant bolt to sizzle past his ear. "Just give up," he taunted with a confident smirk. "There's no way you're walking out of here. Not alive, that is. Why prolong your torment?"

My lips tightened, and I swung my sword, parrying another pair of projectiles into the barrier surrounding us. Unfortunately, he wasn't wrong. I'd reached the same conclusion a moment before. If I couldn't close the distance to get within sword's reach, Kroxius would just keep dodging until one of his bolts slipped through my defenses. I didn't like my chances if this devolved into a battle of stamina. If I caught even one of his death curses, I was likely a goner.

I whipped my blade up, deflecting another flurry of magical missiles. The crowd hissed in dismay as some attacks ricocheted towards them, but I had eyes only for Kroxius.

My thoughts churned. I needed to break the stalemate, and fast. My blade whirled in my hands, leaping back and forth between the magical attacks as if it had a mind of its own. Sifting through my options quickly, I scrambled to buy myself an advantage.

I wished I had my karambits. Or a throwing knife. Or five. Anything that I could use to attack from a distance. Unfortunately, my shadow blades, while cool, had undeniable limitations. Namely that they dissolved as soon as I lost contact with them, so trying any long-range attack wouldn't work unless I could maintain contact with the blade somehow while it was flying through the air. Talk about impossible!

Another blast of orange bolts crackled across the circle, forcing me to dodge to the side. Sweat beaded on my forehead and dripped down my temple. I blew a breath upwards, sending an errant strand of hair flying out of my eyes as I whacked two successive missiles directly back at Kroxius. I tried for a third, but it pinged off to crackle against the barrier before flaring out of existence.

My mind churned in time with my sword. If I couldn't win, I needed to change the game. How could I turn this situation to my advantage before he tired me out? Another ping reverberated down the dark blade in my hand. Kroxius danced out of the way of the bolt as it came zinging back at his head.

A crazy idea wormed its way to the front of my mind. A ghost of a smile brushed the corner of my lips. Kroxius must've noticed the minuscule shift in my expression because his brow furrowed in confusion. Another bolt of sizzling lightning snapped out of his palms. I threw myself upward and sent two more bolts ricocheting back at him as he tried to blow me out of the sky mid-leap.

Reaching out with my mind, I pulled some shadows across my body as I fell, letting them blur out my form as I crashed back to the snow. It was hard work, but I managed it. Kroxius blinked in surprise. A look of confusion danced under the mad orange flames in his eyes. I pursed my lips and blew him a kiss as I pulled and released my shadows as fast as I could.

I knew what he had seen because I had tried it out on Sloane during our trek through the forest once when I was bored. The way she described it was like I was blinking in and out of existence in a disorienting, shadowy version of strobe light.

Based on the look on Kroxius's face, he was witnessing something similar. One second, I was in front of him with my shadowy sword raised. The next moment, I blurred out, only to snap back into focus again. Kroxius's magic projectiles paused. I wondered if he'd ever seen a strobe light before. After all, he'd been dead for nearly sixty years.

"Focus, Cam," I admonished myself. I took advantage of the momentary reprieve and sprang forward. I yanked hard at the shadows, pulling and releasing them again in a fast, erratic succession as I sprinted across the distance separating us with great, bounding leaps.

It didn't take Kroxius long to recover. He tracked my movement, trying to anticipate the haphazard flashes of movement through my shadows. His hands snapped back up, spurting wide orbs of magic at my distorted form this time.

However, I'd bought myself precious inches. I was almost within arm's reach of him when he let loose with a sizzling crack of orange lightning. This one grew and forked into multiple branches as it came towards me. The spell was bigger than any he'd released yet. I threw myself out of the way to avoid incineration. Kroxius back-pedaled hurriedly. I clenched my jaw as I lost the proximity I'd just fought so hard for.

I threw myself forward and slid under his next volley. I tucked my head and rolled over my left shoulder. It was a good thing I'd practiced the maneuver in training back at home or I might have cut myself on my sword. I'd learned from experience that the shadow blades were razor sharp and hard to break unless I lost my concentration or my grip.

Another wild thought sparked. I almost dismissed it as impossible, but Kroxius danced even further away, cackling with glee. If I couldn't fight my way closer, I needed to try something else, and fast. I reached my free hand behind my back, hoping to pull off a miracle.

Kroxius grunted as he flung another fistful of magic my way. I dodged, spinning away, and sliding slightly on the frozen ground. "I'll admit you intrigue me," he said, skittering back as I feinted at him.

"How so?" As I pretended to gasp for air, I added an extra hitch to my voice. I didn't have to work too hard to appear exhausted. I needed to end this soon. The fingertips of my hand wiggled underneath the layers behind my back.

Kroxius paused with his hands up and ready from halfway across the circle, but the orange bolts didn't fly as he spoke. "I would prefer to take you alive. To dissect you piece by piece while you screamed in order to learn more about your magic. Sifting through your blood and reading the power in your entrails would bring me great joy. Magic pulses in your veins. I want to see your heart pump its last and sample your dying breath as you fight for one more second of precious life."

"Do you say this to all the girls, or am I just special?" I panted.

He ignored me. "It's been my experience that magic degrades as the body does. It is best to keep the subject breathing for as long as possible. However, it looks like I will have to settle for less than optimal experimentation conditions with you. My apologies for that but have no fear. I do plan on resurrecting you. I'll study your magic until it fades from your living corpse. Once you are no longer of interest, I will send you as a single-minded assassin to kill all your friends and bring me their heads. Starting with her." Kroxius flung a claw-like hand towards Sloane, who flinched on instinct, despite the protective barrier separating them. Kroxius threw his head back, letting a bone-rattling chortle shiver through the air.

I shuddered in revulsion, trying to focus on my plan. It was hard. The lich was fighting on two fronts. His words were worming into my head just as his death curse would burrow under my skin if I couldn't maintain my defenses against his magical onslaught. Both weapons could be deadly if I wasn't careful.

"What now?" he taunted. "No witty remarks? No snarky comebacks? Nothing left to say now that you face your demise?"

I held up a single finger on the hand gripping my sword, silently asking for a moment as I sucked in a lungful of air.

Would my plan work?

"Sure, I've got a question," I said, readying myself to move as fast as I'd ever done. I couldn't afford to falter. Speed and concentration were my weapons to counteract his magic and psychological warfare. I only hoped they were enough.

"And that is?" the lich sneered, dropping his hands fractionally. He was like a predator instinctively sensing weakened prey, and he was cocky. After all, I was standing about five yards away from him, armed with a two-foot sword. What could I do from this distance?

Kroxius tipped his head curiously to the side, allowing me a momentary reprieve to ask my ultimate question.

"I just want to know…" I said, adding a dramatic gasp for air as if I were more winded than I was. My fingers finally brushed against the skin at the small of my back. Cool winter wind tickled my spine. Goosebumps spread across my exposed flesh. I grinned. Kroxius raised an eyebrow.

"I just want to know how many liches it takes to get to the center of a Tootsie Pop?" I asked, whipping my hand out from behind my back as I spoke.

I saw Kroxius's brow furrow, and his mouth turn down at the unfamiliar modern-day candy reference after being locked in the Abyss for decades.

I shut out that part of my brain, focusing on the small shadow knife with the entirety of my concentration and will. I'd never been able to maintain a shadow blade for more than a few seconds once it left my grip. The thin, perfectly balanced shadow knife in my hand tore a thin line of pain along my lower back. I felt the blade harden in my grip for a split second before I sent the knife hurtling in a desperate, underhanded throw. I'd practiced the same throw innumerable times, but only with actual knives, never with my shadow blades. All my hopes rode on that blade.

I focused all my will, intention, and concentration on the small, bloody shadow blade with a fierceness born of my desire to rain revenge down upon Kroxius's bony head. I didn't know if this would work, but something Kroxius had said sparked my creative, destructive juices.

Blood. Part of me. My magic and blood mixing to deadly effect.

I willed the knife coated in my blood to hold its shape as it flew through the space separating us. I infused every emotion I held into that tiny blade like it was my final lifeline, whipping through the air towards the lich.

Kroxius still looked distracted by my confounding question. He didn't see the small, dark blade fly through the frigid air until it was too late. His eyes widened as he finally recognized the shard of darkness for what it was. He brought his hands up from where they had dropped. Orange light crackled to life. The sorcerer was too slow. Unformed, unrealized magic dripped through his fingers as the shadow knife thudded sickly into his chest.

He looked down in shock. He tried to grasp at the hilt of the small blade sticking out of his chest, but it finally melted under his touch. Kroxius's hand brushed right through the hilt, and it blew away like crumbling ashes in the wind. Bloody shadows dripped slowly down his chest, mingling freely with a small trickle of blood that swiftly turned into a gush and then a torrent.

Kroxius looked up at me and then back at the wound in his chest. His lips formed words, but an unintelligible gurgle spilled past his thin lips. He tried again. "Power!" he gasped. "Your blood. So much power," he gasped. A bubble of blood puffed over his lips and then popped with a fine, misting spray.

I strode forward, feeling like an avenging angel. I imagined the cheering specter of Ben riding on my shoulder. But the necromancer wouldn't have done that. He would have cautioned me about the dangers of killing another being and the stain it would have on my soul. My eyes narrowed. Ben might have said something like that if he had still been alive.

But he wasn't. Because of this motherfucker.

Kroxius pressed his hands to his chest. Faint sparks of orange magic crackled and sputtered under his hands. I clenched my jaw. I strode forward, readjusting my sword to clasp it in a powerful two-handed grip.

Kroxius glanced up with a panicked look as I marched towards him, crunching snow heralding my approach. More orange sparks sprang out of his hands and danced across his chest. He flung one hand at me. A few weak bolts flew sluggishly at me, but I deflected them easily back at him. He tried to dodge but ended up sprawling in the snow. Red and orange streaks stained the white battlefield as he pushed himself away from me.

Bitterness welled up inside me. Anger at the lich for taking Ben away. For forcing me to fight my way through the Fae wilderness to track him down. For stranding my friends in this hostile land. But mostly for stealing such a beautiful soul from the earth before it was his time. I would have given just about anything for just one more day with the gentle necromancer.

Kroxius raised his skeletal hands, his magic sputtering out as he tried to draw on his own life to power his spell. "Wait!" he cried. "Wait, can't we talk? We could make a deal! I can offer..."

"The time for talking is done," I growled.

I swept my blade up. The razor-sharp edge of the shadow hardened, and the sword took off his head with a single clean swipe.

Kroxius's head spiraled through the air, a weak spray of blood creating a gruesome Pollock-esque spatter in the snow. The lich's head tumbled towards the ground, its orange eyes lighting the winter scene like a macabre jack-o'-lantern. The head hit the snow and slowly spun as the orange light finally faded from its eye sockets.

A small tune from one of my favorite childhood movies jangled in my head unexpectedly. I smiled grimly, humming along under my breath.

Ding dong, the lich is dead.

Chapter 11

Anger still bubbled inside me. I marched over and kicked the lich's head, watching the orange light flicker and die in his eyes for the last time. The head rolled across the clearing and crashed into the embers of a cooking fire, sending sparks curling into the air. They hissed and fizzled out as they touched the magical dome of ice magic still surrounding the battle ground.

A little piece of my heart hardened. It wasn't enough. The bastard had killed *Ben.* He'd deprived the world of the old man's kindness. He'd deprived *me.* Whatever torments were waiting for Kroxius in the Abyss, they would never be enough. Not ever.

I glanced up from the skull as the skin tightened and pulled in the heat of the fire, searching for something else to destroy. A dark figure at the edge of the clearing caught my eye. Magnus was still leaning against the tree with his arms crossed, watching me intently. I was too far away to see his eyes, but the echo of his words reverberated through my mind, dousing my anger. Without my rage buoying me, my legs turned to jelly. I collapsed to my knees. I didn't have the emotional stamina to meet Magnus's cool gaze, so I settled for watching the thin skin on the skull scorch and peel away in the heat of the fire. A sudden thought occurred to me. I glanced down at the magical tattoo on my wrist. The orange dot had vanished, leaving only the blue dot hovering in the middle of the compass. Two souls returned and only the trapped escapee remained on this side of the veil.

The mood of the clearing shifted as whispers filled the glade at the sudden, vicious end to the fight. I ignored them all, staring into the fire and thinking of all the ways I would've liked to extend Kroxius's punishment.

I don't know how much time passed, but when I finally looked up, the circle of fae had dispersed, resuming their regular duties. Sloane and Andrei stood near one of the other fires, shooting me concerned glances. I blinked slowly, staggering to my feet. That's when I caught sight of Magnus. He hadn't moved from his place against his tree. The werewolf was still considering me carefully. When he was sure I was watching, he raised a single eyebrow. I knew what he was asking.

Is it over now?

I turned away without giving him the answer he wanted.

I finally relinquished my tight grip on my shadow blade, and the sword disintegrated. Shoving to my feet, I staggered as the blood rushed back down to my feet. The prickles of returning circulation tingled up my legs. The slight burning sensation made me do a little jig as I headed towards Sloane and Andrei.

Sloane let out a sigh of relief and wrapped me up in a giant hug for such a tiny leprechaun. "You had me worried," she said, her voice muffled as she squeezed me tightly.

I wrapped my arms around her and squeezed back. "I was worried myself for a moment there, but it's okay. Everything's going to be okay now."

I felt her nod on my shoulder before she pushed away. Sloane swiped at her eyes and gave me a hard, bright smile. I nodded back. We'd been through our share of close calls. Someday, fate would conspire against us, and we wouldn't be the ones walking away. Luckily, today wasn't that day.

Andrei sidled up, waiting to be sure we'd finished with our female bonding ritual before interrupting. The pup wasn't dumb. I looked up and smiled tiredly at him. The events of the past two days were finally catching up with me as the adrenaline seeped out of my system.

"That was awesome, Teach!" Andrei gushed, handing me my borrowed fur coat. I slid into it gratefully. Goliath stuck his tiny head out of the pocket. I tickled a finger over his soft fur.

Andrei continued, "I can't believe it! You were like *fwip, fwip, fwip* and he was all, *pew, pew, pew.*" He made the sound effects as he mimed swiping imaginary bolts out of the sky with an invisible sword.

"Stop calling me 'Teach'," I said, but I couldn't help smiling a little wider. His enthusiasm, while misplaced, was infectious.

Andrei leaned in, mischief glinting in his eyes. "I guess you could say that you got ninety-nine problems, but a lich ain't one."

I groaned. "How long have you been holding on to that one? Wait, were you even alive when that song came out?"

Andrei puffed out his chest. "Yeah, it dropped the same year I was born. Jay-Z is my boy." He thumped his chest with his fist to emphasize the point.

I stifled a laugh but didn't have the heart to tell him the famous hook had been written over a decade before he'd been born. Sloane didn't have my restraint. She grabbed the young werewolf's arm, wheeling him away. I didn't envy the pup. Sloane took her music seriously and had no problems "educating the unenlightened". Her words, not mine.

The captain of the fae guard walked over as Sloane launched into a history of rap for her unwilling student.

"Frost," the captain said, sticking a hand out.

I gripped it on instinct, but the strange greeting confused me. "Um, thanks? Frost to you too," I tried, not sure if he was offering some sort of bizarre Winter congratulations.

He pumped my arm briskly just once. "No. That's my name. Frost. Captain Frost, if you're being formal."

"Oh. Right. Nice to meet you, officially. Cameron Blaze," I stumbled over my tongue as a chill crept up from my hand. I jerked it back, making a fist and raising it to my mouth to blow warm air over icy fingers.

Captain Frost shrugged. "Apologies. Occupational hazard. Speaking of, are you sure that you don't have a little Winter in you? The way you handled yourself in that fight, I'm pretty sure you've got some ice in your veins."

I narrowed my eyes at him over my fist as I blew noisily into my palm again, warming my fingertips.

The captain raised his hands in self-defense. "No harm meant. It's a compliment."

"Right," I drawled, unconvinced.

"Truly spoken!" He fished in his pocket and withdrew the gold coin. "Your winnings," he said, handing it over with a slight bow.

I took it, somewhat surprised. I'd forgotten about the bet in the after haze from the fight with the lich. "What?"

"You didn't think I'd make good on my end of the bargain? Deals are important here in Fae, Cameron Blaze. It's something that humans know very little about. Humans break promises at the slightest provocation. Not so in Fae. We honor our word here."

I opened my mouth with a sharp retort burning on the tip of my tongue when I felt a warm hand close over my shoulder. Magnus's voice rumbled behind me. "Is everything okay?"

"Fine," I said shortly. "Captain Frost was just introducing himself."

Magnus stuck out his big hand. "Glad to meet you, Frosty."

A haughty look shadowed the captain's eyes, and the surrounding temperature dropped noticeably. He gripped Magnus's hand tightly. "Just Frost." Ice crackled under their feet, spreading outward from the captain.

Magnus smiled easily, apparently unaffected by the cold radiating off the Winter fae. "You're going to have to try harder than that if you want to play domination games with me, Frosty."

I heard the fae grind his teeth and tried to stifle a smile. Magnus might not win a diplomacy award, but he certainly was a contender for prize shit-stirrer.

"Excuse me, please," I said, hoping to break the tension. I fished Letitia's stone out of the depths of my pocket and held it up. "I need to let the Spring fae know what happened."

I took a few steps away, finding the closest thing to a secluded spot in the busy campsite. I tapped on the stone and called out her name. The stone flared to life and then sputtered slightly. I heard Letitia's voice crackle in and out. I shook the stone. "Letitia, are you there?"

"Cam? Can you hear me?" Her voice sounded far away.

"We got him. Letitia! Did you hear me? We got him!" I exclaimed.

"You got him?" Disbelief warred with hope over the tenuous connection.

I sighed in relief. "Yes. Kroxius is dead!"

"Cam!" Her voice crackled in and out like she was on a cell phone with poor reception. "I can't belie..."

I shook the stone again, hoping it might jar the dregs of whatever magic powered the stone. It must've worked because her voice came through more clearly.

"Can you make it to the Spring Court?"

I looked around at the Winter fae camp. "I don't know. It might be tricky, but we'll do our best."

"Get to...Court...meet you there...back to New Or..." A weak sputter of purple sparks fluttered up from the stone, and Letitia's voice cut out completely. I shook the stone again. Nothing. Not even the faintest glow of purple.

Well, at least I'd done my part. Letitia and the other injured fae had a fighting chance to recover. A sense of relief washed over me. I stuck the stone back in my pocket and walked back over to where Magnus and Captain Frost still stood. Now to try and figure out a way to get to the Spring Court, Letitia, and our ticket back home.

The werewolf's head jerked up as I neared, but his attention wasn't focused on me. Something was out there in the woods. His nostrils flared as he sniffed audibly at the winter breeze rattling through the leafless branches, gusting through the fresh snowfall. "Smells like we've got company coming," the werewolf growled, turning to the north.

A moment later, I heard a faint jingle drift through the trees. Captain Frost turned as his ears caught the faint noise, too.

"What does *he* want?" Captain Frost muttered, moving to the center of the clearing. He faced towards the tinkling sound and folded his arms with a scowl.

The jingling of what I could now tell was bells grew louder. I strained to see past the captain into the dark, wondering what sort of creature made that distinctive sound. It was like Santa's sleigh being pulled by a gaggle of octopuses, clenching pleasantly harmonizing handbells in each tentacle.

A blur detached itself from the shadow-darkened woods and sped into the camp. The Winter fae let out a deafening cheer that surprised me so much that I jumped slightly. Well, more than slightly, given my enchanted boots. But no one noticed as a bizarre figure burst through the tree line and into the well-lit clearing, circling the welcoming fae with a booming laugh and a wave.

I blinked, trying to focus on the curious visage. A team of four pure white dogs pulled a small sled over the crusted snow. The team yipped and barked in excitement. They were beautiful, with pointed little snouts tipped in pink noses and dark eyes that looked mischievous and intelligent. Each one sported a pristine white coat of luxurious, thick fur that made me envious of the built-in warmth. But the most striking thing about their appearance was their tails. Each animal had two puffy white tails streaming in their wake.

"What kind of dogs are those?" I breathed to Magnus.

"Not dogs. Foxes," he responded just as quietly.

"Good eye," Captain Frost interjected. "They are the royal winter foxes, and they serve the Winter Lady, Lady Estaria, by providing the swiftest transportation in all of Fae."

"Foxes?" I asked. "I've never seen a fox with *two* tails."

Captain Frost explained, "Apparently, the Teumessian fox got frisky with a kitsune once upon a time and these fabulous creatures were born."

"Yeah, I didn't understand anything but 'frisky' there."

Captain Frost huffed out an exasperated breath. "Humans and their lack of mythological memory!" He scrubbed a hand over his face and then tersely elaborated. "The Teumessian fox was one of Dionysus's magical creatures."

"Like the Greek god of wine?" I asked.

"Precisely. He sent it out to prey upon the citizens of the ancient city of Thebes. Legend has it that the Teumessian fox was destined to never be caught. Naturally, the Greeks, being Greek, sent a magical dog who was destined to catch everything. It chased to catch the Teumessian fox, thus creating the first paradox."

"Sounds like that would blow Zeus's freaking mind," I said.

"Kinda like the chicken and the egg situation?" Magnus asked curiously.

"Yes, but with canines. And a lot more destruction," Captain Frost replied.

"I knew I liked the Greeks," Magnus whispered to me.

I jabbed an elbow at his side, speaking to Frost over the werewolf's grunt of surprise. "What's a kitsune? That doesn't sound Greek."

"It's not. Kitsune are native to Japan on Earth. Kitsune are wild, unpredictable fox spirits. Some tales tell of the kitsune as messengers for the gods, while other stories claim they are tricksters and shapeshifters who delight in causing chaos."

"You know an awful lot about different pantheons from Earth," I said guardedly.

Captain Frost waved a careless hand. "Of course. It used to be mandatory that anyone wishing to serve in the royal guard do a tour of duty on Earth to better understand manlings and their beliefs. Not so much these days, but that was the practice when I was coming through the ranks."

"Wait, you lived on Earth?" I asked.

He waved his hand dismissively. "Briefly, but that's by the by. Anyway, these beautiful creatures fled to Fae, found refuge in Winter, and have served the Winter Lady ever since as her personal transportation."

"You're telling me that the Winter Lady is *here*?" I hissed, trying to straighten my torn and burned clothing.

"Unlikely. She regularly lends the royal foxes to her emissary, especially when he needs to travel quickly."

A shrill whistle burst through the clearing. Captain Frost raised an arm and took a few steps forward to meet the fox-drawn sled. The team slid to a stop, spraying the motionless form of the captain with a shower of fresh snow. I snorted a laugh, but quickly covered it with a cough. Magnus didn't bother to hide his amusement. He threw his head back and roared with laughter. The captain ignored us as he brushed the loose flakes from his furs with a disdainful flick.

"Hemlock," the captain said coldly.

A compact figure wrapped from head to ankle in white fur leapt spryly from the back of the small sled with a bright tinkling sound. The creature skidded across the packed snow to a halt in front of us and bowed deeply. It was only then that I realized just how short he was. The creature barely came up to my waist. When he rose, I got my first good look at the Winter Lady's emissary.

My first impression was that he looked like someone had crossed a gnome with a yeti. A fine dusting of snow covered the creature from head to toe, and a long beard dangled nearly to his knees. I saw the source of the peculiar tinkling sound as soon as he stood. Icicles coated his beard and played a merry tune whenever the little creature smiled. Judging by the wide grin and deep laugh lines near his eyes, I guessed that music followed this Hemlock wherever he went.

The creature turned toward us, and his eyes sparkled with interest. "Oh! Newcomers! How exciting!" He had a strange burr to his accent that I couldn't quite place. Irish? Scottish maybe? Something in between? Whatever it was, I wanted to listen to him talk all day. "I am Hemlock of the barbegazi, at your service," the emissary said, extending a hand towards Magnus.

"Barbie-what-now?" Magnus asked, pumping the little man's hand, and returning his warm smile.

"Bar-bee-gah-zee," Hemlock said slowly, before throwing his head back and letting out a belly laugh accompanied by a sweet tinkling from his beard. "I know, I know. It's too big of a name for such a wee creature." He slapped his little round belly and roared with delighted laughter.

I smiled back at the jolly creature despite myself. His merriment was contagious. Hemlock offered his hand to me. When I looked down, I saw bare toes poking out below his long beard. "Oh! It looks like you lost your shoes." I said, pointing down with my free hand and looking around, hoping to find the missing footwear before Hemlock suffered any permanent damage from frostbite.

"Ah, kind of you, very kind indeed. But I didn't lose them. I never had them!" Hemlock held up one enormous foot and wiggled his hairy toes in my direction. "Shoes impede me in the snow. They get in the way of skiing, don't you know? Besides, who needs help when you've got stompers this huge?" The emissary let loose another roar of burbling laughter. For a creature so small, he had a cheerful disposition that filled up the surrounding space, making him seem bigger than he was.

Captain Frost cleared his throat as he brushed the last of the snow spray from his jacket. "What are you doing here, Hemlock?"

"Word came on the winter wind that there was an honest-to-goodness lich in Winter. Is it true? Tell me it's true! Lady Estaria is very excited to meet him. As am I, if truth be told," Hemlock clapped his hands excitedly, looking around at the fae gathered by the fires. "Where is this fellow, then?"

Well. This is awkward.

Chapter 12

I tucked my hands behind my back as if that would hide all evidence of the lich's demise. I shouldn't have bothered. Captain Frost pointed towards the fire, where the lich's skull still smoldered.

"There's your man," the captain said.

The barbegazi looked around, searching futilely for a walking, talking person. "Where? I don't see him... oh." Hemlock's eyes fell on the scorched skull. "Oh dear. I see. I take it this your doing, Jacky, my boy?"

"Captain Frost," the fae corrected coldly.

"Of course, of course," Hemlock said, waving a hand dismissively in the air. "You know, I never liked the formalities. Give me a flagon of ale and a raucous crowd out in the wild singing dirty limericks around a campfire any day. Am I right, Cap? I mean, *Captain.*" The small emissary puffed out his chest and gave a mock salute.

"Not my scene," Captain Frost said coolly.

Hemlock snorted, sending his massive mustache dancing. "Naturally. I forgot you hate all the fun things in life. Not me. This is perhaps the *fun*-damental difference between us. See what I did there?" Hemlock grinned up at Captain Frost. When the captain didn't respond, Hemlock shuffled closer, framing the wrong side of his mouth with a hand and loudly stage-whispering. "Did someone not hug you enough as a child, Captain?" Hemlock threw his arms wide, wiggling his fingers. "Bring it in! I'll fix that hole in your cold, ice-crusted heart."

Captain Frost pointedly folded his arms over his chest and glared down at the barbegazi stoically. Hemlock waited a moment more, waggling his bushy white eyebrows towards the captain like two jovial caterpillars. "Going once. Twice? Alright, your loss, Cap. Tell me what happened here then." Hemlock pointed a stubby finger at the blackened skull in the fire.

Swiftly, Captain Frost filled him in, glossing over the details in favor of the briefest sketch of events. "We found both the lich and these strangers," he gestured widely at the four of us as Sloane and Andrei rejoined our group. "They were all wandering in the woods on the edge of Winter. We planned on escorting them to the Court. Apparently, there was a prior dispute between them and the lich. He wasn't as deadly as he thought."

Hemlock chortled, "A lich. *Deadly*. Good one, Captain!" Captain Frost just stared at the little emissary as Hemlock used his tinkling beard to wipe tears of mirth from his eyes. When he'd regained control of himself, the emissary looked around our party, examining us carefully. He pointed a finger at Magnus. "I'll bet it was you who took out the lich. Am I right or am I right? A big fella like you would have smashed a puny sorcerer into jelly, I have no doubt."

I heard Sloane open her mouth, but Magnus interjected before she could speak. "Not me. Her." He jerked a thumb my way.

Hemlock turned towards me in surprise. His beard twitched as his mouth opened and closed, at a loss for words. "You? Well, I suppose... You must be a powerful sorceress in your own right? Perhaps a witch?" He tipped his head to the side, considering me thoughtfully. I saw a glimmer of shrewd intelligence surface behind the good humor in his eyes.

"Nope," I said, leaving it at that.

Hemlock widened his eyes, encouraging me to continue. When I didn't, he let out a sigh, followed by a small chuckle. "A mystery. I like it. There are too few genuine mysteries left in our world these days. However, I must warn you that while I enjoy a mystery, our Winter Lady does not."

"Fine. I have no intention of meeting with her. We did what we came to do and now need to get back to the Spring Court as quickly as possible," I said.

All good humor fled from Hemlock's face. He hissed at Captain Frost, "When did Spring start sending assassins to Winter?"

"What? Wait!" I nearly shouted.

"We're not assassins!" Sloane exclaimed simultaneously.

"Seriously?" Magnus asked, unimpressed, as he folded his arms.

"Cool," Andrei said, bobbing his head with a goofy grin. Sloane elbowed him in the side.

"We are not assassins. We are—" Sloane said.

Hemlock held up a stubby finger, cutting her off as a chill breeze blew through the clearing. He cocked his head to the side as if he were listening to something beyond my hearing. He nodded once, then twice. Finally, the emissary muttered something, sending his beardsicles jangling discordantly. The breeze whipped around his head and swirled off into the trees with a rustle and crack of frozen branches.

Hemlock clapped his hands, rubbing them briskly. "Right, where were we? Oh, that's right, the assassins. Pardon, I mean, the *not*-assassins. We'd best get you to the Winter Lady. She will know what to do with you."

"And if we decide not to go?" Magnus asked belligerently.

Hemlock shook his beard, icicles tinkly sorrowfully. "Above my pay grade, I'm afraid. What do you say, Captain?"

I glanced over to see that the fae captain already had an arrow nocked in his bow. I hadn't realized he still had the weapon with him. And he looked ready to draw at the slightest provocation. The friendly bustle of the fae in the camp fell silent. I saw more than one hand drift towards weapons.

I placed a hand on Magnus's forearm and squeezed. Hard. "We would be happy to accompany you to meet the Winter Lady," I said loudly. Magnus shot me a dark look. A chill settled at the base of my spine. If Magnus started something now, I didn't like our chances. I flicked my eyes meaningfully toward the surrounding fae. The werewolf understood instantly. He relaxed and gave the barest of nods. Out of the corner of my eye, I saw Captain Frost also relax minutely.

"Excellent!" Hemlock said, his good cheer returning in an instant. He clapped his hands briskly. "Break camp, my good fellows! We are bound for the glory of the Winter Court!"

A crack of ice sounded. Hemlock glanced guiltily over at Captain Frost. "Apologies, apologies, Captain. I will leave you to sort out the camp to your heart's desire while I see to Winter's newest guests, shall I? To each their own, as it were?"

The captain glared at the emissary a moment longer and then whirled, shouting orders at the gathered fae. They jumped to his commands with practiced efficiency.

A whisper of a breeze blew through the camp again and Hemlock froze in place, tipping his head to the wind. He nodded once, and the breeze fled through the woods once again.

"What was that?" I asked.

"What can I say? Winter is enigmatic and Lady Estaria is more so than most," Hemlock said with a small shrug. A bright smile lit his jolly face. "Now that we have a moment alone, let's have some proper introductions without Captain Stuffypants breathing down my neck."

I smiled in return, opening my mouth to explain to the charming little man precisely what we were doing in Winter. In full detail. Sloane cut me off, a warning flashing in the blue depths of her luminous eyes. "I'm Sloane. This is Magnus, Cameron, and Andrei," she said, pointing at each of us.

Hemlock nodded, smiling widely. He paused, waiting for Sloane to continue. Her smile was on the brittle side as she stared down silently at the small emissary.

His smile faded, dimming under the leprechaun's stony silence. He cleared his throat. "Well, then. After those rather brief introductions, I suppose we could consider ourselves friends. And as a friend, is there anything that I can answer or do for you to make your transit in Winter more comfortable?" Hemlock asked courteously.

Andrei raised his hand. Hemlock's grin returned, creasing his rosy cheeks. "Yes, lad?"

"Why are you called Hemlock? Isn't hemlock, like, super poisonous?" Andrei asked in a rush, as if it had been an effort to hold back the question for so long.

"Why yes, lad, it is. On Earth. But hemlock doesn't grow in Fae. Me mam didn't know that it was poisonous until she'd given me my name and trained me to answer to it. She just thought hemlock was a pretty wee plant with wee white flowers that she stumbled across in some book or another. She used to tell me I was the same size and color as the hemlock flowers when I was a babe. Now, for better or worse," he shrugged, "it's all I answer to."

Magnus jerked his chin up. "I've got a question. Why do you work for Winter? You seem like a nice guy and everything I've heard about the Winter Court—well, it sounds terrifying."

Hemlock chuckled. "Winter has that reputation, doesn't it? It's not all that bad here. Barbegazi can live anywhere, you know. Some of my kin like the Summer Court because of the hibernation we do in the warmer months. Although, just between us, it is usually the elder barbegazi who opt for Summer. For me, I find Autumn is home to too many strange things and Spring never quite knows what it is. Winter is simple. You survive or you don't."

"Sounds harsh," Magnus said.

"Oh, I don't know. I almost prefer it that way. Pass or fail. Live or die. Less ambiguity. Besides, where else could I go skiing as part of my job?" Hemlock held his arms wide and spun in a circle, chuckling and trying to catch a fat snowflake on his tongue as he whirled. It got stuck in his beard, which made him laugh all the harder, his beardsicles chiming merrily.

"Hemlock!" Captain Frost's voice cut through the chaos in the clearing.

The little barbegazi slowly spun to a stop, looking annoyed at the summons. However, by the time he faced us again, a regretful smile adorned his face. "I beg your indulgence for our brute of a captain. Someday, I'll smooth those rough edges of his, but it's a task that is taking me longer than expected to complete." He waved a hand in farewell as he bounded away on his enormous feet.

I looked after the strange, good-natured emissary with bemusement. Sloane grabbed my arm and wheeled me around. She tugged the werewolves into a close huddle, whispering urgently. "Look, Fae is always a dangerous place, but Winter is the worst of the lot. Watch your step. Don't volunteer more information than is required. Be careful of your words. You don't want to accidentally acknowledge that you owe someone a debt for something like, I don't know, getting you a glass of water or something and then you end up serving them as a cupbearer for the next century."

"Wait. That doesn't actually happen, does it? That's just a fairy tale," Andrei said, voicing my own thoughts.

"In case you hadn't noticed, you're in Fae. Your fairy tales are our reality here, but not the happy-fluffy-everything-ends-well stories you see in animated movies. These fairy tales are more like those the Grimm brothers told, but bloodier. It's probably best practice to assume that everything terrible you've ever heard about Fae is the absolute gospel truth," Sloane said seriously.

I heard the young werewolf gulp.

Sloane held up three fingers, ticking off warnings. "Most beings in Fae can't lie, but that doesn't mean what they say is the whole truth. Luckily, leprechauns are exempt from that little rule, thank all the gods. Take nothing from a High Fae without first establishing there will be no obligations if you do. Also, avoid any sort of bargain, gambling, or deals. High Fae are sly and think it's a game to wriggle out of obligations on a technicality at the most inopportune times." Sloane tapped the last finger. "And never, *ever*, make a sworn promise to a High Fae."

"Why not?" Andrei asked, his question coated in hushed excitement.

"Because that's a great way to end up dead. Or worse. Let's focus on getting back to Spring so Letitia can open a portal and send us back home," Sloane said sharply.

I sidled closer to her as Andrei started chattering excitedly at Magnus. "Are you going to be, ok? With all the High Fae around?" I asked under my breath.

"I don't have to like them. My goal now is to get back to Letitia as fast as possible so I can get home. If that means I have to play nice with a couple of the High Fae, I can do that," Sloane whispered back.

"Yeah, but will they play nice with you?" I asked.

She lifted a shoulder and let it drop. "My kind aren't common in Fae anymore, and we look pretty similar to some types of elves. Wood elves, in particular. I should be able to get by without too much fuss."

A shout rang through the clearing, interrupting our impromptu huddle. A few moments of confusion later and we fell into the middle of a line of Winter fae. We crunched through the snow, marching towards the Winter Court. The darkest, coldest part of Fae and the seat of the Winter Lady's power.

A wickedly chilly breeze swirled around us as we tramped into the woods, heading north. I shivered, feeling the cold settle into my bones once more. I was sure it wasn't just from the icy wind. My gut was telling me something evil lurked on the horizon. I set my jaw. We needed to get back to Letitia and the Spring Court as soon as possible so she could send us home to New Orleans. The fastest way to do that was heading straight into the heart of winter. I pushed my bad feelings to the side with the vague hope my gut was wrong.

I should've known better.

Chapter 13

Despite my misgivings, the trek to the Winter Court was quick and uneventful. The fae pushed hard through the snow, breaking the trail for those of us with less experience slogging through the frigid landscape.

Hemlock alternated between riding on top of his well-packed sled and gliding along the icy crust on the snow. He hadn't been kidding. His feet worked better than any pair of snowshoes I'd ever seen. He kept up the amiable chatter, and the time passed pleasantly enough. He didn't even seem put off by the limited responses he received from us.

The combination of the barbegazi's pleasant company and maintaining a grueling pace through the snowy terrain meant we reached our destination sooner than I could've anticipated. Captain Frost called a halt at the bottom of a sloping cutback trail winding up the side of a small mountain covered in snow. I craned my neck to get a good look at the path as the tail end of our party caught up.

"What's this then?" I asked Hemlock.

"The seat of Winter Court! We're almost there! Just up this trail and down the road!" cheered Hemlock, dancing a small jig of delight on top of the deep, wind-blown drifts.

Captain Frost called back to the emissary, "Do your job then and go announce us!"

"I've never been happier to follow a grumpy order!" Hemlock said. He stroked his long, jingling beard and whistled a merry little tune. The four foxes who'd been dragging the heavily laden sled near the front of the group and helping to break the trail whipped their heads up, all eight tails wagging. The team wheeled and sped back to Hemlock. He leaped up to his seat on top of the bags tied onto the sled.

"Adieu, my friends. Duty calls, but I'm sure we will have the pleasure of each other's company again soon!" He gave us a cheery wave and then the foxes zipped off up the switchbacks, sending the sled careening wildly from side to side, seeming to almost tip Hemlock off his precarious perch with every turn. I held my breath until the sled crested the hill and dipped down out of sight.

"Nice guy," Magus said.

"I just hope he doesn't fall. That trail looks dangerous," I replied.

Captain Frost's voice rang out from the front of the group. "Well, at least he's broken the path. Drinks on me once we get to the Court!"

A cheer rose from the fae. They stomped forward with renewed energy. Even I felt my spirit buoyed by the promise of a drink and the possibility of a long sleep in a proper bed.

I puffed for breath by the time we crested the top of the hill. The slope had been steep, but the view spread out before me was worth the climb. A palace glimmered with welcoming lights sat nestled among evergreen trees. Even the trees twinkled merrily at us as fairy light reflected off snow and ice. The palace's massive gates were thrown wide in welcome. The setting looked like a photographer's dream for a winter wonderland.

My eyes took in the rest of the valley, noting the tactical advantages. The mountain slopes sheered steeply away from the palace as if a giant's hand had carved the valley out of the living rock. Given that this was Fae, I wouldn't be surprised if that had been the case. The mountain rose steeply up on three sides, making the switchback trail we'd climbed the only viable means of approaching the palace. Anyone who wanted to attack the Winter Lady would have to be suicidal to attempt it here.

Captain Frost led the train of fae straight towards the glittering palace. Attendants dressed in dark purple livery rushed out to meet the entourage. Frost shouted directions over the noise and confusion, sorting everyone into their respective duties in short order.

For a moment, the four of us were left alone. Sloane beckoned us towards an alcove and out of the way of the flurry of chaos in the courtyard as the massive gates of the palace swung shut.

Sloane held up a cautionary finger. "Remember what I told you. Don't take anything, eat anything, or promise anyone *anything*," she whispered.

"Oh, come now," a chiding voice said. We turned to see Hemlock approaching, his eyes twinkling merrily. "It almost sounds like you don't trust us."

Sloane opened her mouth, but I laid a hand on hers, cutting her off and changing the subject. "I don't know about the rest of you, but I need a bathroom in the worst way. Being a woman while walking miles through snow isn't the easiest. You either deal with constantly needing to pee or a frostbit butt." I clenched my knees and did an anxious little dance that was only partially an act. I hated the cold. "Hemlock, can you show me where the bathroom is, please?" I asked.

Hemlock performed a small but elegant bow. "Right this way, milady."

The little emissary led me through the small hallways next to the main gate. He chattered cheerfully at me, but I mostly tuned him out, examining the layout of the palace as we walked with Hemlock through what looked like a guards' barracks. The rooms looked orderly and well-stocked with weapons, but empty of life for the moment. That was no doubt because of the bustle in the courtyard. If the steep climb and defensible position hadn't been enough, one glance at the barracks was enough to tell me that this palace wouldn't fall easily if it were ever attacked.

Hemlock pointed me towards a small door at the back of the barracks. I slipped in and did my business. I hadn't been lying about fearing frostbite on my more delicate parts. I don't know how Sloane did it. I finished up and washed my hands in the basin of water provided when a surprised shout followed by a thump and a groan outside startled me. Instinctively, I pulled shadows around me and crept to the door.

I peered through the crack to see a hairy monster holding Hemlock by the neck. It pinned the barbegazi to a wall. Hemlock's feet kicked wildly in midair as he grasped at the monster's arm. The creature looked close to six feet tall and was covered in dirty, matted fur.

The door to the bathroom creaked as I eased it open to get a better look at the thing. It must have heard me because it whipped its head around. Two curved horns protruded from the monster's forehead. Large fangs that didn't fit in its mouth caused it to pant. A long tongue lolled awkwardly over its lips. Frosty blue eyes darted around the room. As they slid over me, I held my breath. I was immensely thankful that I'd cloaked myself before opening the bathroom door. I was just about to fling it completely open and dash through to save Hemlock from whatever Winter demon this was when the little emissary's voice rang out.

"Krampus," Hemlock said, gripping the monster's clawed hand with both of his smaller ones. "To what do I owe the pleasure?" He didn't sound as terrified as I thought the situation demanded. The incongruity made me pause.

The monster took a couple of deep sniffs, its large nostrils flaring on each inhale. I held my breath but called up my shadow blade. It formed slowly, and I had to focus intently on its creation. However, if the creature took a swipe at Hemlock, I wanted to be ready to attack. Briefly, I wondered if the monster was male or female. Nothing about its appearance gave me a clue as to its gender. Finally, the monster snorted, sending a snot rocket flying across the room to *splodge* wetly against the opposite wall.

Gross. Definitely a dude.

"Hemlock. I knewed I smells poison in the air," Krampus finally said, turning back to the squirming barbegazi in its grip.

Hemlock sighed and rolled his eyes. "How many times do I have to tell you that 'Hemlock' is my name? It's not like I'm made of the stuff!"

Krampus sniffed again and swayed slightly on his feet. I noticed then that one foot was a cloven hoof while the other was a large, hairy human foot.

Man, Winter is weird.

The creature paused and snorted, sending another bullet of snot rocketing out of one large, extremely hairy nostril. Hemlock squirmed to the side, narrowly avoiding the disgusting projectile. "Are you surer?" Krampus asked, uncertainly.

"That I'm not a plant? Yes. I'm sure. How much have you had to drink?"

"A barrels of ale. Or was it twos barrel of ale. I has dinner with it," Krampus said defensively, failing to suppress a massive burp. It rumbled out of him, straight into Hemlock's face. The tiny emissary grimaced and tried to wave the stench away.

"What did you have for dinner? It stinks!" Hemlock exclaimed.

"Rotting goat-ses. Delicious!" Krampus said with a shrug that lifted the barbegazi up and down on the wall.

"And you say I'm the poisonous one. Put me down, you big oaf!" Hemlock demanded. Krampus complied immediately. The emissary slid to the floor with a crashing tinkle of beardsicles.

"Things are happening. Bad things. Wild fae are rising. Castles are crumbling. People is dying. Worse and badder. Baddest things. Badder than baddest," Krampus muttered, trying to brush wrinkles free of Hemlock's clothing.

Hemlock slapped at his shirt, straightening his clothing with affronted dignity. "You're always focused on the bad, Krampus. I know that's part of the job, but try looking on the brighter side of things once in a while. Besides, we were all wild fae once upon a time," Hemlock admonished.

"A storm's coming. I can smells it, I cans. Then youse turn up," Krampus pointed a finger at Hemlock, swaying again. The move was apparently too much for Krampus. He stumbled, tripping over his uneven feet and crashing into a sturdy wooden table.

Hemlock sighed and tried to help pull Krampus back to his lopsided feet. "I'm an *emissary*. It's my *job* to travel. Besides, I've just escorted Captain Frost and his entourage back to the Court and..."

Krampus let out a whimpering snort and whipped his head, searching the shadows in the corners of the room with something akin to terror lighting his eyes. "Frost!? He's here? With his big pointies?" The massive beast attempted a whisper, but it came out closer to a bellow than anything discreet.

Hemlock patted the huge hairy arm, smiling up at the creature in a way meant to calm irate drunks and irrational toddlers. "Not *here* here, big guy. But yes, he's back."

Krampus let out a sigh, his shoulders sagging. "Maybe he brings the storm. He scares me, yes, he does." The creature's hairy nose wrinkled as he snuffled the air twice before sneezing directly in Hemlock's face. The force of it sent the barbegazi's beard jangling. I winced when I saw a thick, bluish mucus coating Hemlock's once pristine whiskers.

Krampus wiped the back of his paw across his nose and sniffled. "I is sorry. Not nice to sneezes on you, but nasty smells..." Krampus trailed off. Slowly, he refocused on Hemlock, who was attempting to wipe monster snot out of his beard. "Is it Captain Frost that bringes the stormes? He makes my furs prickle," Krampus's voice dropped to a conspiratorial whisper as he looked cautiously around the room.

Hemlock reached out and took Krampus's paw, patting it gently. "I know that Captain Frost can rub people the wrong way. He's, well..." Hemlock paused, seeming to search for a diplomatic way to phrase his thoughts. Finally, the emissary added, "Well, he's brusque, isn't he? Quite an abrupt man, to be sure. I can understand why he wouldn't be everyone's cup of tea, I surely can." Hemlock laid a knowing finger alongside his nose and nodded his head meaningfully.

Krampus let out a little moan. "He scares me, he does. Just glareses at me all the time. All I done was eat a sheeps no one wanted anymore! Is that a baddie thing?"

"Hardly, my good fellow!" Hemlock exclaimed. "But all that being said, I can't help if you're smelling things on the wind." Hemlock leaned in and took a deep sniff of Krampus's arm as he helped the hairy monster to his feet. The emissary grimaced and waved a hand significantly in front of his nose. "Hate to break it to you, big guy, but that thing you are smelling? It's you."

Krampus lifted his arm and took a deep whiff. "I don't smells anything," he said, confused.

Hemlock patted Krampus' hairy hand and lowered his voice to a whisper, "Then trust me. You could do with a bath. And maybe a haircut. When did you last let someone comb through that fur of yours?"

Krampus brushed a hand down his matted fur, self-consciously. "It's been a whiles," he muttered.

"My point, exactly!" Hemlock exclaimed. "What about this? Have a bath, take a rest, and find one of those lovely little pixies who will comb out your fur for you. You'll come back feeling like a new Krampus!" Hemlock beamed brightly up at the monster.

"You is right, you is," Krampus muttered, swaying as he moved towards the door across the room. He almost crashed into the wall, but caught himself just in time with a clawed, furry hand.

"And lay off the winter ale!" Hemlock called after him. The emissary put his hands on his hips, watching the monster stumble away. Krampus muttered something indistinctly as he disappeared into the darkness.

With the crisis averted, I let go of my shadows, let my sword dissolve, and walked out into the main room. "What was that?" I asked, padding up behind Hemlock.

The little emissary jumped and whirled, hand clutching at his chest. "Oh! Oh my! I didn't see you there! Shall we return to your friends?"

I pointed down the hall where I could still hear Krampus muttering. "What was that?" I repeated.

"Oh, just one of the Winter fae. We get all sorts here. Krampus is a good fellow, but drinks more than his fair share when he's not working," Hemlock said.

"What's a Krampus?" I asked.

A brilliant smile bloomed on Hemlock's face. "He's not just *a* Krampus, he's *the* Krampus." At the confused look on my face, Hemlock elaborated. "Think of Krampus like the anti-Santa Claus. His job is to scare all the wicked children onto the straight and narrow any way he can."

I stared after the dying echoes of the departing monster. "Looks like they hired the right guy for the job. He'd scare me into behaving," I said with a slight shiver.

"Yes, he is rather perfect for that line of work, isn't he?" Hemlock beamed in the general direction in which Krampus had stumbled off.

"But I thought Santa left coal for the bad kids."

"No, he outsourced centuries ago. Too much on his plate, you know? And he isn't the young man he once was, is he?" Hemlock said as winked at me over a good-natured smile.

"What did Krampus mean, 'smelling something bad on the wind'?" I asked, despite the inclination to ask about Christmas traditions coming to life.

"Who knows? Focusing so much of his energy on the baddest apples of the bunch wears on him, I think. He sees wicked things wherever he goes, even when they aren't there. Or smells them, in this case. I think that's why he spends so much time on his own or at the bottom of an ale barrel. He tries to hide away from the things he sees while on the job, poor fellow," Hemlock said, shaking his head remorsefully.

Thoughts were churning in my mind, and I'd just opened my mouth to ask another question when the little emissary clapped his hands together, interrupting any further inquiry. "Well, all refreshed, are you?

Good! We wouldn't want to keep the Winter Lady waiting, would we?" Hemlock smiled and marched off down the hall with a cheerful yet somehow gooey tinkle from his blue-snot-covered beard.

I paused, considering the darkened doorway before heading after the barbegazi. Although the emissary's dismissal of the confrontation was entirely logical, something about the encounter between Hemlock and Krampus set my nerves on edge.

I had a feeling not all was not right in Whoville. But in a land of Krampuses, how did you find the Grinch?

Chapter 14

Hemlock led me back through the twisting corridors until we popped out into the courtyard. Sloane, Magnus, and Andrei stood in the middle of a much quieter space with an impatient-looking Captain Frost. They were all wearing different clothes. The captain had ditched his well-worn furs for a resplendent deep purple jacket decorated with many medals and insignias. He'd tucked thick woolen trousers into highly polished boots. A rapier encased in a tooled leather sheath gilded in silver rode on one hip and a long dagger with a matching sheath was on the other. The ensemble looked rather distinguished on the taciturn captain.

My friends all wore woolen blue tunics and thick leggings with high furred boots. An envious shiver rippled down my back. They looked warm and toasty while I still battled the chilling breeze in my New Orleans ensemble topped by a smelly, borrowed fur.

"Took you long enough," grumbled the fae captain.

"Now, what kind of welcome are you offering our guests if you won't look after their comfort?" chided Hemlock, shaking a finger up at the captain. I noticed he didn't mention the confrontation with Krampus.

Captain Frost snorted and tossed a compact bundle my way. I caught it easily, fingering the blue cloth curiously. It was soft, but sturdy. "For you, with no expectation of return or obligation. Get changed. Lady Estaria awaits," Frost said curtly.

Given that my friends already wore their own sets of Winter gear, I assumed the clothes were safe for me to accept. I nodded briefly once in acknowledgment. "I'll just go put these on then," I said, turning back towards the barracks and the bathroom.

"Do you know where you're going?" Hemlock called after me.

"No worries!" I shouted back, hurrying down the corridor. Not bothering with returning all the way to the bathroom, I ducked into the dark, empty hallway and pulled on the surrounding shadows. I changed quickly, trying not to shiver as the icy wind kissed my exposed skin. I thankfully slid out of my dirty, worn gear and into the clean, warm tunic and leggings. I tucked my necklace with the Barqan's charm and the ring carefully inside my tunic to keep them both as safe as I could. However, I ignored the furred footwear, opting to keep my boots instead.

Captain Frost raised an eyebrow as I jogged out of the hallway with the crumpled ball of my old clothes under one arm, but that was all the comment he gave on my speedy change. He jerked his chin towards Hemlock as he spoke to me. "Give your old things to the emissary. He'll see they get to the right place for a clean before they are returned to you." The captain spun on his polished booted heel and spoke over his shoulder as he marched towards the interior of the palace. "Follow me. Lady Estaria does not like to be kept waiting."

Hemlock snorted after the departing captain but held out his arms towards me. "He's not wrong. Give me the lot, lass, and I'll see to it all. Best hurry along now. I've heard that they've upgraded dinner to a feast on short notice and a Winter feast is something wholly unique," the emissary said with a bright smile.

I almost murmured a 'thank you' but caught myself in time. Instead, I handed him the bundle with a warm smile and a nod. Then the four of us rushed after Captain Frost. He led us through a series of corridors and up a flight of stairs before pausing in front of an enormous set of double doors made of ornately carved opaque glass. I peered closer at the intricate carving. It took a moment, but when my mind made sense of the stylized figures, I could easily read the story of a bloody battle decorating the doors. I shivered. This wasn't the type of welcome I'd expected, but then again, we were in Winter.

"Follow me. Do not speak unless spoken to," the captain ordered tersely. Before we could answer, the doors swung wide to reveal a breathtaking sight.

Hemlock hadn't been kidding when he said a Winter feast was a thing to behold. A herald stood inside the double doors. He wore lavender velvet livery trimmed in silver and held a large wooden staff topped with a bright sprig of holly in one hand. He banged the stick loudly on the floor as we entered.

"Captain Frost and guests," his voice boomed through the massive hall.

The captain ignored the herald and marched down a long indigo carpet towards a dais at the other end of the hall. Fae of all shapes, sizes, and descriptions craned their necks to peer at the newcomers. There were many High Fae. However, they weren't the only creatures I saw in the stark hall. There were also small pixies whizzing through the air, pixies serving drinks, stocky dwarves knocking beer mugs together, a couple of barbegazi playing cards, lean and elegant elves were arm wrestling among a group of shouting fae, three trolls were engaged in what looked like a spitting contest, and what looked like a half-giant snored noisily in a corner with his mouth wide open. It looked like someone had combined frigid minimalism with a tavern from medieval times, added some furs, and threw a party.

A flash of dirty white fur in a recessed alcove caught my eye. I turned in time to glimpse Krampus as he ducked into a darkened hall and out of sight as the captain strode purposefully in front of us. I looked around, my eyes wide, drinking in my first sight of the heart of the Winter Court.

Semi-opaque columns stretched up towards a high arched ceiling. Each column was carved with sharp edges and glimmered dangerously, like they could cut you if you bumped into one at the wrong angle. My eyes continued the journey upwards, where twinkling lights like stars were embedded in the deep blue of the ceiling, sending fragments of icy blue light dancing over the crowd. I nudged Sloane, jerking my eyes upwards as a smile lit my face.

"That's so cool," I breathed.

"I forget sometimes that you've never been to Fae before. Magic is a part of life here and way more likely to be used for everyday things," she whispered back, shooting a glance at the ceiling.

"I feel like I'm eleven years old and just got the owl admitting me to Hogwarts. A kind of scary, loud, cold Hogwarts, but still," I said, trying to take everything in.

Sloane snorted. "Trust me, this place is nothing like Hogwarts." She tipped her head to the side. "Except perhaps for the constant threat of death or horrible maiming."

"How did they whip up a feast in such a short time?" I asked.

"How else?" Sloane said, waving her hand through the air. "Magic."

The large double doors closed with a heavy thud behind us, and I flinched at the sound.

"Looks like the only way out is forward," Magnus said softly.

"Are you offering life advice now?" I quipped.

"Survival advice, more like," he returned. We shared a wry smile.

The herald cleared his throat softly behind us. "If I may, you'd best catch up with the captain," he murmured under his breath. "The Winter Lady doesn't suffer disrespect, real or imagined." The herald flicked his eyes towards the hall meaningfully. I looked over my shoulder, down the path Captain Frost had carved through the turmoil of the great hall, then back at him. The herald stood with his eyes glued straight ahead and didn't acknowledge us further.

I tipped my head to my companions. "Well, at least there's a roof over our heads tonight. If we play our cards right, we might get to sleep in a bed."

"I'd kill for a hot bath," Sloane groaned, setting off at an impressive speed for someone with such tiny legs.

"I don't care about baths. I just can't believe I'm in the Winter Court. The guys back home are gonna flip when I tell them!" Andrei said, spinning in circles as we hurried towards the dais.

"Eyes straight ahead, boy, or you're going to trip over your own feet," Magnus murmured, but I saw a smile tugging at the corners of his eyes. Andrei's enthusiasm for, well, *everything*, was hard to dismiss.

I reached out to drag my fingers along one column as we passed, impressed with the glass work. I'd never seen carved glass used for an immense structure like this. It was brilliantly marbled with swirls of ice blue, deep indigo, and white twisting around in abstract swirls underneath the surface. It was stark, but somehow stunning. In an unnerving, primitive sort of way. My fingertips brushed the smooth face of the nearest column. I jerked back. That wasn't glass. That was *ice*. I knew this was Winter, but *damn*. It must have taken a lot of magic to build the palace of ice, let alone keep the ice pillars from melting in the middle of a packed room.

I looked over at Sloane with wide eyes. She nodded. "We aren't in Kansas anymore, Dorothy."

"Yeah, I guess not," I breathed.

Captain Frost reached the bottom of the stairs leading up to the dais. He clicked his polished heels together sharply, pulling my attention back to the front of the hall. We hurried to catch up as he executed a sharp bow to the figure seated on the immense, austere ice throne. As he stood and stepped to the side, I got my first good look at the Winter Lady.

The pale, slender, High Fae woman who sat on the throne of carved ice inclined her head graciously towards Captain Frost. Her long white hair was streaked with shades of blue ranging from sky to brilliant azure. It was intricately braided back from her face, revealing her sharply pointed ears. A small, icy blue tiara spiked out of the braids, sparkling with crystalline designs that were echoed in the beading of her elegant gown. Her makeup was expertly applied, transforming her beautiful features into something exotically alien with crystals forming shimmering designs on her porcelain skin. At least, I think it was makeup. It might have been magic. Or just her.

Lady Estaria extended a perfectly manicured hand to the captain, her fingertips sparkling blue and silver. Captain Frost bounded up the steps as quickly as decorum allowed, bending low to brush his lips against the back of the Winter Lady's hand.

A cool smile touched the edges of her lips as Captain Frost stood. "It's good to see you again, Captain. It has been a while since you've graced the Court with your presence," Lady Estaria murmured softly.

"Too long, my lady," he replied, just as softly. I saw his thumb gently caress her fingertips before he rose and moved to stand by her side. Captain Frost faced us and clicked his heels together crisply. "I present Lady Estaria, our gracious monarch of the Winter Court, and the Winter Lady of all of Fae. My lady, may I present our esteemed travelers who have journeyed far to make your illustrious acquaintance?"

Her gaze fell on us. Suddenly, I wanted to squirm. Her cool gaze bore into me as if she had harpooned my soul with an icicle. It felt like she took my measure with the merest look and found me not only wanting but also mildly disgusting. My breath hitched as I realized my utter lack of training in addressing royalty. It had never been a problem before, but now it seemed like an egregious oversight in my education.

Sucking in a breath, I stood taller and executed what I hoped was an acceptable tiny bow. In the middle of the movement, I remembered I was, in fact, female. I tried to morph into a curtsy, only to realize to my utter horror that I wasn't wearing a skirt. At which point I decided bowing was the better option. I ended up looking like a fish flopping around on dry land as everyone else simply bowed. A condescending snort drifted down to me from the Winter Lady. A rush of heat flooded my cheeks.

Before I could say anything to mitigate my flapping and flailing, the Lady's voice rang through the hall, bouncing strangely off the ice pillars. "Captain Frost, I was told you were escorting a powerful sorcerer to our Court. A lich, I believe. Where is he?" She made a show of stretching her elegantly long neck to peer over our heads in search of the invisible sorcerer.

Captain Frost cleared his throat and looked as though he wanted to run a finger around his suddenly too-tight collar. "Unfortunately, he could not complete the journey. We had to bury him at the outpost."

Lady Estaria arched a delicate eyebrow as she scanned us from head to toe. "Oh? And why is that precisely?" she asked, acknowledging his words, but not looking at him.

Captain Frost waved a hand at me. "That one demanded satisfaction for a quarrel that happened outside of Winter."

"Ah, satisfaction. An ancient tradition that must be honored, to be sure. It is important that our customs are upheld, even in the wild stretches of the realm," Estaria said, absolving the captain of any malicious whispers. He inclined his head, acknowledging her words.

The Winter Lady turned to face me. Her face was a composed mask of curiosity that looked so perfect that it felt faked, but there was nothing artificial about her condescending tone. "I find I am overwrought with curiosity. How was it *you* bested a lich? Do you possess powerful spells that outclass a resurrected undead sorcerer?"

I bristled under the patronizing tone. "I possess a faster sword and better fighting skills. He was a one-trick pony. Take away his spells and he had nothing left to fall back on." Sloane elbowed me hard, and I quickly added, "My lady."

"I see you've learned an important lesson about men who become liches. They fixate on raising hell but can never keep it up long enough for one to be fully satisfied," Lady Estaria said, smirking.

A roar of laughter erupted from the Court behind me. Lady Estaria rose and gracefully descended the short flight of steps as the crowd rumbled, sharing the Winter Lady's remark with those at the back who might have missed it. She stopped in front of us and tapped a long, blue fingernail against her lips. Slowly, she circled our party as the crowd continued to murmur with titters and chuckles.

Magnus stood silently at my side, eyes straight ahead. Sloane turned her head to follow Lady Estaria's progress as she moved around us as though she were a dangerous snake. Andrei didn't know what to do and spun with her, always keeping her in front of him.

"An interesting group," said the Winter Lady as she stopped in front of me. Her words were lost to the still chuckling crowd, but I heard them clearly.

Raising her voice to be heard over the remnants of laughter reverberating through the hall, she addressed me. "It was kind of Captain Frost to bring you to the palace with such haste to offer you succor and respite, don't you agree, lich slayer?"

"We are here—" Sloane started to say.

"Know your place and speak only when spoken to!" The Lady's words cracked through the room like a thin layer of ice on a lake fracturing dangerously underfoot.

I felt Sloane's fingers brush against my hand in warning. Not that I needed it. As a child, I had read tales of the fae entrapping humans with clever word tricks, often enough to recognize the ploy. I needed to choose my next words *very* carefully. I clenched my jaw, weighing my choices before speaking. "The captain was kind. The company was enjoyable. But I am sure we would've managed on our own without his help," I stated carefully. It felt like I was walking a tightrope between acknowledging the courtesy without implying that we owed the Winter Court a favor or being rude.

"Indeed," Estaria said, clasping her hands in front of her, "and after such a long journey, I imagine that you and your companions are famished." She clapped her hands, raising her voice. "Prepare some food for our..." she paused, her cold gaze slowly scanning me before meeting my eyes, *"guests,"* she finished slowly. It sounded as though we could interpret her words as something more menacing if we were so inclined. It was eerie how closely Lady Estaria's words reflected those of Captain Frost when we first met him.

I hid my nerves behind a gracious smile. "I appreciate the offer. However, my companions and I have just eaten. Therefore, we couldn't possibly infringe upon your hospitality."

The Winter Lady's eyes hardened, and I saw for the first time that there were flecks of molten silver dancing in the deep blue.

"Indeed," she repeated coolly. "Well, as guests of the Winter Court, allow me to invite you to enjoy our hospitality with no risk or obligation. You are free to partake in all of Winter's offerings without fear of reprisal or recompense for as long as you shelter within our hall."

"What? That was too easy," I heard Sloane whisper from behind me.

I ignored her and nodded my head deeply at the Winter Lady to avoid the awkward bow-curtsy-bow conundrum. "Stories of your gracious hospitality were not overstated," I said, choosing my words with the utmost care. Sloane squeezed my fingers as Lady Estaria turned towards Captain Frost. I let out a silent breath, glad that I had passed the verbal sparring. Give me a sword over words any day.

"Captain, see that our guests are looked after," the Winter Lady said as she glided back to her throne. The captain courteously offered her his arm as she sat. She placed her hand on his sleeve. I was close enough that I saw her squeeze, digging her blue talons into his thick formal jacket. Their eyes met and a silent message passed between the two of them. Captain Frost withdrew respectfully as Lady Estaria elegantly raised her hand. "Let the feast begin," she said, her voice ringing through the icy hall like a clarion bell. A cheerful smile hung on her lips, but when she looked at us, I saw only cold calculation lurking behind the cheerful façade.

Chapter 15

After the Winter Lady's dismissal, Captain Frost led us to the side of the hall and an empty table with short narrow benches made of dark, rough planks. I bit back a sigh as I sank onto the uncomfortable, uneven seat. It had been a hard few days, and I'd been hoping for a comfortable reprieve. Apparently, Winter was not the place to find such succor.

Two Winter fae in lavender livery materialized as soon as we sat down, bearing a large, steaming pot of what smelled like stew. A third dumped an armful of bowls and spoons haphazardly on the table. Another slammed a platter of dark, heavily seeded rolls down on the table so hard that he sloshed broth out of the pot. I barely dodged in time to avoid getting splashed. The server glared at me as if I'd caused the spillage. Or maybe he was mad that I'd gotten out of the way in time. I would've glared back if my stomach hadn't rumbled loudly as the scent of savory vegetables and meat wafted up to me. It's hard to look intimidating when your belly is talking loudly enough to be heard over a room full of boisterous fae.

I tapped Sloane's shoulder and then leaned over to whisper in her ear. "Are you sure this is okay? I don't want to end up trapped here for years owing my soul to the Winter Lady just because I ate some soup and bread or something. I don't want a sort of freezing reenactment of the Persephone–Hades' relationship. That would suck. I wasn't built for snow six months out of the year."

Sloane whispered back, "Didn't you hear her? Don't worry about the food. Everything here should be fine."

Captain Frost nodded, obviously following our conversation despite our attempts to keep it discreet. "She's right. You do not need to fear reprisals for filling your stomachs in Winter's hall. Please, enjoy your meal."

It might have just been me, but the cynical part of my brain filled in the last part: *For it may be your last.*

Before I could voice my hesitation at the captain's words, the two werewolves fell upon the food. Between them, they shoveled away steaming bowls of the stew, scooping up the bigger chunks of vegetables with hunks of bread torn from the dark rolls with no care for formality or decorum.

After days of gnawing on anything just for the calories, I focused my entire attention on the simple meal. The bread and stew were the most delectable things I'd tasted in days. Warmth swelled up from my belly, radiating to my extremities as I filled the hole in my middle with the humble but delicious meal. It was only after I'd pushed back from the table a second time and had a thick mug of dark beer pressed into my hand that I noticed the volume in the hall had risen from a comfortable murmur to an excited buzz.

I craned my neck to see what was happening. A man in a long, brown cape sparkling with heavy gold and shimmering orange embroidery swept through the hall on a wave of excited murmuring. The man looked out of place next to the furred and furry Winter fae. He jumped up on a small stage off to the right of the Winter Lady's throne at the front of the hall. Someone must have erected the stage while I'd been engrossed in my meal because I didn't remember it being there before. The man turned to the crowd and held up an instrument case shaped like a bizarrely smooshed guitar. The crowd of fae creatures roared their approval as he pumped the case up and down.

"What's going on?" I asked Sloane as the cheers rose to a deafening level.

Sloane put her lips near my ear. "It's a bard," she raised her voice over the din.

"Wait. They have bards here? Like the traveling singers from olden times?" I asked, my brain a little foggy from the combination of exhaustion, a full belly, and the strong, dark beer.

Sloane gestured at the room. "In case you hadn't noticed, this is 'olden times'. At least by your standards." She used air quotes to emphasize her point. I never knew air quotes could carry such a nuanced level of sarcasm, but Sloane managed it somehow. "What do you think people do here for entertainment? It's not like you can plug a TV into the ice or click on a snowflake to watch the daily news. Books and live music, that's where it's at."

I nodded thoughtfully, conceding the point. All things considered, not a bad way to spend one's leisure time. Hell, there were people back on Earth who would kill to have their evenings occupied with live music. Or books. Or both.

The bard strummed delicate fingers across the strings of his strangely shaped instrument. He sat in an armless chair and leaned a careful ear closer to the strings. Carefully, he twisted the pegs at the end of the squat neck, checking the tuning. He fiddled with the pegs until they satisfied his precise musician's ear, which gave the crowd time to settle and find seats.

The buzz faded to a murmur as the bard sprang back to his feet, a welcoming smile lighting up his tanned features. He ran a hand through his short blond hair, giving it a roguishly disheveled look while he winked at a woman in the front row. With his hair sticking out in all directions and his long limbs, the bard reminded me of a scarecrow brought to life. He struck a shimmering chord and the image of a straw-stuffed puppet faded. His fingers danced over the strings with an elegant precision no scarecrow could have managed. The bard continued to play the cheerful little ditty until the crowd quieted.

I leaned over to Sloane again. "What kind of instrument is that? I've never seen anything like it before."

"A fae lute. It's like the human version, but with twenty-seven strings instead of the normal thirteen or fifteen. They're very rare, not only because of the skill needed to play the instrument, but also the skill to make it. A fae lute can only be made of yrash wood that has been aged at least fifty years. Besides, the tree is native to Summer, which makes the fae lute even more rare. Besides, you must have delicate fingers and incredible speed to play with any success. Although, if one can master it, the fae lute is the most incredible instrument." A wistful note entered her voice, and a sad smile flitted across her lips. I wondered what it felt like to return to Fae after she'd fled all those years ago. She didn't talk about it much, and I wondered if I should press her for details about her previous time in Fae. Before I decided, Sloane shook herself and continued, "But if it's played badly, it'll make you want to carve your eardrums out with a spoon."

I bobbed my head in understanding. In my elementary school, there'd been a girl who was learning violin, and she loved to practice at recess. Every time she picked up the aural torture device, it sounded like she was slowly murdering cats. I spent a lot of time finding places as far away from her as possible on the enclosed school playground. And that was on an instrument with only four strings. I shuddered at the memory, imagining learning the lute was exponentially harder given its number of strings.

Sloane continued her whispered narration, oblivious to my internal dialogue. "It takes years of apprenticeship under one of the few master musicians to train on the fae lute. They aren't often seen. Even in Fae. Let alone in a different realm. It's been more years than I care to admit since I've heard one and I've never heard a master bard play a fae lute before. This is a real treat."

Sloane gripped her mug of beer tightly in excitement and leaned forward as the bard's fingers hit one last hard chord, drawing the attention of the settling crowd. The living scarecrow of a man whirled his embroidered cape off with a dramatic flourish and tossed it to a young woman at the edge of the crowd. She caught it deftly and tucked it under her arm. She bore a striking resemblance to the bard, but her hair was so long that it nearly fell to her waist. Both were much darker-skinned and noticeably taller than the pale, slender High Fae in the crowd of Winter fairy-tale creatures.

"They don't look like they belong here," I whispered to Sloane, trying not to let my voice carry.

"That's because they don't," Captain Frost responded.

"What do you mean?" I asked curiously.

Captain Frost nodded towards the bard on the stage. "Brio Amber-meadow is the Autumn Court's master bard. Bards travel from court to court as a combination of a diplomatic emissary, news-bearer, and entertainment. The courts rotate their bards as a sign of good will, a way to communicate between courts, and to spy on each other."

He said the last so casually that it took me a moment to comprehend his meaning. When I did, I sat upright in surprise, almost knocking over my wine.

"If you know he's a spy, why do you allow him to come?" I asked, not caring that my confusion was obvious.

"Because he's good. One of the best, in fact," Captain Frost said easily.

"At spying or playing music?" I scoffed.

"Yes." Frost folded his arms across his chest, eyes narrowing at the bard and refusing to elaborate further.

I widened my own eyes at Sloane, hoping she'd fill in the blanks for me. She sighed and leaned over, dropping her voice as the hall quieted. "There's a certain beauty to the games the creatures in Fae play," she explained. "Everyone here seems to delight in clever manipulations and turning the tables on an opponent. There is nothing better than knowing someone is trying to trick you and turning the trick back on them. The High Fae of the courts love to engage in machinations. It is an open secret that the bards and their entourages spy on the neighboring courts, returning with useful information while simultaneously trying to sow false flags. It has become an open secret. A game for the opposing courts to weave in deceptions, so that the bards never know for sure what is truth and what is fiction."

I blinked slowly and rubbed my forehead. "That sounds stupid. And confusing. Why not just shut the bards out? Or, I don't know, lock them in a tower until they have to perform? Or, Gods forbid, people actually just tell the truth," I muttered under my breath.

Sloane shook her head. "It doesn't work like that in Fae," she said. "Most creatures here are long-lived. They look for entertainment differently than humans do. Remember? There are no soap operas or scripted reality TV here. Instead, we create our own dramas. It is so much more engaging to be involved in the plot thickening than to be a mere spectator on an overstuffed couch."

Magnus interjected unexpectedly into the conversation. "To be fair, it's not just the High Fae. Werewolves enjoy creating their own entertainment too, but they do it through overly complicated territorial games," he whispered.

Before I could respond, the bard sent another shimmering chord dancing over the now silent crowd before turning to face the Winter

Lady. He allowed his melodic voice to ring clearly through the hall. "Lady Estaria, I am Brio Ambermeadow, master bard of the Autumn Court. With your permission, I would gladly entertain your court for an hour or two." The bard raised his hand over the lute, pausing dramatically for Estaria's approval.

All eyes landed on the Winter Lady. She smiled graciously out at the crowd without moving, letting the tension build. Finally, Estaria raised her hand, waving a delicate permission for the bard to continue. As one, the audience sucked in a breath, anticipation mounting to see what sort of entertainment the bard had in store this evening. I craned my neck to get a better view of the musician. Within minutes, the music swept away me with the rest of the crowd.

The bard struck another forceful chord, refocusing all the attention back on himself before speaking in clear, ringing tones that effortlessly carried throughout the entire hall. I knew little about music, but his voice was strong, clear, pleasant to listen to and seemed to be complimented by the sweet tones of the lute.

"Listen now, for I have much to tell.
Too long since I've fallen under Winter's spell.
The ice is clear, the women fair,
The monsters sleeping in their lair..."

Brio the bard hit another chord, and I lost myself to his music.

I couldn't tell you how many songs the bard sang, but he seamlessly alternated between sharing recent events and tales of the past. He wove through his repertoire with the ease of long years of practice, all the while accompanying himself flawlessly on the fae lute. Sloane hadn't exaggerated. Even to the musically inept such as myself, the bard's skill on the instrument was remarkable.

An indiscernible time later, the Autumn bard sent a hard chord jangling through the crowd, waking the audience from their musical daze. Brio raised his arm. Mutters and protests erupted, but Brio spoke, his clear tenor voice ringing easily over the noise of the dismayed audience. "My good people, I'm not leaving you just yet. I merely need a moment's respite to wet my throat with some of your excellent ice wine. However, do not despair! My charming journeyman and student, Jazria, will entertain and delight you in equal measures until I return. Please, my friends, welcome her to the stage!" The bard enthusiastically led the applause as the young, tanned woman who'd caught his cloak replaced him on the stage. Instead of a lute, she held a violin. I tried not to wince.

As she ran a bow over her violin strings to check the tuning, I saw Captain Frost make a surreptitious circling motion with one finger. Guards appeared at the edge of the stage as if by magic. They restrained the crowd from thronging after the departing Autumn bard as he escaped to a vacant table and his promised ice wine. A little, cynical part of me wondered if that's truly what they were doing or if they were keeping the bard away from the people instead of the people away from the bard. After all, it was difficult to spy if you couldn't talk with anyone.

The bard was obviously familiar with this game. He brushed by a guard with a friendly pat to the shoulder, pushing past with more strength than I would have credited to the slim musician. The bard embraced his audience with open arms. The Winter fae crowd swirled him off to a crowded table in an instant. Brio settled himself in the center of attention, reveling in the fawning adoration of the audience with a heavy mug of beer. Conversation burbled around the room as the sweetest sounds of a violin floated above the jovial rumble, punctuated occasionally by a boisterous laugh.

The audience seemed content to mostly ignore the journeyman musician. Conversations resumed, filling the hall with a pleasant hum. Some fae took the break to stretch their legs or to relieve themselves as the young Autumn violinist sent her light music lilting through the air. Even with my limited understanding, I could tell she played well, but perhaps without the flair the bard had shown on his lute.

"She's good," I said, leaning over to Sloane.

"Very good," Sloane said.

"Yes." The captain offered his unsolicited opinion while nodding thoughtfully. "It will be interesting to see how she progresses. She might be good enough to make it to master status. After all, Brio doesn't take many musicians into his tutelage and brings even fewer to tour the courts with him. Unfortunately, we cannot stay to witness her endeavors." Captain Frost dropped his voice, and I had to lean closer to hear him.

"What do you mean?" I asked.

Captain Frost nodded discreetly towards the throne. Lady Estaria stood and swept grandly from the hall, followed closely by some ladies of the Winter Court. None of the women cast a glance in our direction.

"Lady Estaria demands an audience," the captain said. "Whatever you do, don't anger her. Winter is growing in power as the yuletide season nears. I would hate for anything untoward to happen to a guest in this hall."

The violin music shifted into a lively jig. Winter fae sprang to their feet, obviously recognizing the tune. Soon, the entire hall was stomping and clapping along as they madly whirled in a swirl of fur and laughter. One overweight High Fae gentleman had indulged in too much alcohol and overestimated his ability to keep up with the spritely jig. He spun out of control, knocking two stocky dwarves to the floor in his careening. Laughter erupted as the other dancers reached out to guide the drunken dancer to safer territory.

The captain made the most of the distraction. He ushered us to a side door as the hall erupted once again in shouts and laughter. Despite the cheerful atmosphere, a chill settled in my bones. Whatever reason the Winter Lady had for commanding a private audience couldn't be good. Captain Frost led us quickly through the darkened doorway and through a confounding labyrinth of tunnels and hallways.

"I'm confused," I said to Sloane, feeling like I should make that my mantra during my visit to Winter. "What did he mean we should be careful now that the yuletide season is approaching? Why does it matter that Christmas is coming?"

"He means that the balance of power tips in Fae depending on the season. Seasons in Fae aren't solely tied to those on Earth, but they draw power from seasonal events on Earth," Sloane explained, as we hurried after Captain Frost down the dark, chilly hallways of the castle.

"That's just confusing," Andrei piped up from behind us, echoing my thoughts.

Sloane tipped her head back and forth as she walked. "It is, and it isn't. Time progresses differently in Fae. Think about all those stories about kids disappearing into Fae and stumbling out a century later without having aged a day. Or a young man vanishing for an hour and reappearing as an ancient version of himself. That type of thing. But even though time flows differently here, Fae is still unequivocally connected to Earth and draws power from human beliefs, celebrations, and events."

Magnus interjected softly for behind me, "So, the seasonal courts are in power for an indeterminate amount of Earth time because they operate according to Fae time?"

"Yes, and they also get power boosts from humans based on Earth's timeframe, regardless of the season in Fae," Sloane responded.

"Doesn't that mean there's an ever shifting and evolving power balance?" The werewolf looked slightly discomforted by the notion.

"Sounds complex. And dangerous," I added.

Sloane spread her arms wide. "Welcome to Fae." She shot a maniacal grin at all of us for emphasis.

"So, what does that mean for us? Right here, right now?" I asked.

"Apparently, Winter is in season. That means that the Winter Lady holds more power now than the other courts and that's only likely to grow in the coming weeks with the upcoming winter celebrations on Earth," Sloane explained. She dropped her voice into a hushed whisper, slowing to put more distance between us and Captain Frost. "And I overheard some soldiers talking on the way here about how Estaria is new to the role. Apparently, her brother had been the Winter Lord for years, but he died in a mysterious accident a few months ago." She waggled her eyebrows significantly, implying that it might not have been an accident at all. "Estaria has always been a somewhat reclusive figure in the Winter Court. No one thought she'd ever inherit and now, no one is sure how she is going to handle her new role with the upcoming power surge."

The captain halted in front of an ornately carved double door made entirely of opaque ice. Our little party fell silent as we drew even with him. The captain held up an admonishing finger. "Don't forget what I said. Do not anger Lady Estaria or we all may well regret it."

Before I could give voice to the curious questions burning on the tip of my tongue, Captain Frost spun and pounded twice on the door. An echoing boom resonated eerily through the empty hallway. A female voice from inside the room called softly in response.

"Keep your wits about you," Sloane murmured as the heavy ice doors swung open silently and Captain Frost led us into the Winter Lady's private chambers.

I had a sudden premonition that, despite all the monsters we'd encountered in our journey through Fae, the most dangerous creature yet sat just inside that room. And she was wearing a crown of ice.

Chapter 16

Inside, the room was filled with harsh, minimalistic edges. The furniture had the pale blue sheen of conjured ice I was starting to recognize as inherent to Winter magic. There wasn't a cushion or a carpet in sight that could have mitigated the chill or provided an unspoken welcome to a guest. Everything in the room looked chilly and inhospitable. Glancing ahead, I wasn't sure that the group waiting for us across the room was going to change my opinion of this place any time soon.

The Winter Lady lounged on a bench of pure ice that would have frozen my ass off in seconds, looking entirely comfortable eating partially frozen berries from a crystal bowl, while her ladies-in-waiting perched around her on the hard, slick ice chairs and tittered amongst themselves.

"Captain Frost," Lady Estaria said as we entered. "Your speed at bringing our guests here is to be commended." She waved a hand at the guards standing watch just inside her chamber doors. "You are dismissed. I will be safe enough under Captain Frost's watchful eye. Please go enjoy the feast." The guards marched briskly from the room.

"You too," the Winter Lady said to her ladies. She popped berry after berry into her mouth, staining her lips a dark wine red. The crunching of the semi-frozen fruit filled the room as the ladies gathered their things and swept from the room with a soft rustle of furred cloaks. The heavy doors banged shut with a dull thud, cutting off the noise from the outside world and leaving us alone with the Winter Lady and her agenda.

Estaria threw the remaining berry she held into the crystal bowl at her side with a soft *ting*. "Finally," she said with an exasperated sigh.

She waved a hand at her elegantly beaded dress, and it morphed into a body suit that hugged her lithe curves but sported the same crystalline designs. Even with all the beading, it looked infinitely more comfortable than the elaborate court gown. I was jealous of the outfit change, though. I saw now what Sloane had meant about magic being used as an everyday tool.

Lady Estaria approached, prowling around the four of us as she had done in the crowded hall. This time, I felt a chill creep up my back that had nothing to do with the cold of Winter. It was more primal than that. Like being stalked by a wild animal on the brink of starvation.

Lady Estaria completed her circuit, coming to stand in front of us once more with her hands on her hips. Her gaze was so intense that I felt like my secrets were being stripped from me one at a time without my consent.

"Oh yes, they'll do nicely, don't you think, Captain?" she purred.

"I still believe we can handle this matter internally, my lady. There is no need to involve outsiders in your private affairs," the captain spoke formally, clasping his hands behind him and staring just above our heads. If I hadn't been watching so carefully, I would've missed it, but I saw his eye twitch twice before he smoothed an impassive expression across his face.

Why was he nervous?

"I disagree, my Captain. These interlopers are exactly the people for the job. They will serve Winter nicely," Lady Estaria said, her expression hardening as she continued her scrutiny.

"No. No way in hell are we working for you!" exclaimed Sloane, pushing past me to glare up at the taller woman.

"Oh, no?" Lady Estaria snapped her fingers and four wickedly pointed icicles each the length of my arm appeared in midair with a *crack*. One hovered in front of each of us and slowly floated menacingly forwards.

I held up my hands in protest. "Look, we don't want any trouble. We just want to get back to the Spring Court and then home to New Orleans."

Estaria smiled grimly and the icicle hovering in front of me darted forward. The wicked tip pricked the palm of my right hand, drawing a bead of blood.

"Ow!" I shouted, throwing myself to the side. The icicle swerved as though equipped with a homing beacon locked on my chest.

"Hang on! Wait a second!" I shouted, wiping the blood on my borrowed leggings as I backed up. The icicle followed me but didn't attack again.

"I don't think you understand. I wasn't *asking*," the Winter Lady growled, an intense gleam lighting her eyes. She pressed her hands slowly forward, shoving the icicles of death forward again.

"Guest right! You promised us guest right!" Sloane yelled from off to my left as she dodged the glittering projectile. Her icicle swerved with her, locking on Sloane once more as she darted away.

"While you were in the *hall*. Tell me, does this look like a hall to you?"

Sloane's eyes widened as the verbal trap snapped closed on all of us.

Estaria continued ruthlessly, "And even if you make it out of the castle, I doubt you will survive Winter. It is beautiful, but deadly. Just. Like. Me!" Lady Estaria's frosty smile was predatory as she pressed her outstretched hands forward, throwing more magic into her deadly icicles.

"I told you that was too easy!" Sloane hissed at me.

Before I could formulate a plan, I heard a shout that morphed into a snarl, accompanied by the sound of shredding cloth. A dark blur darted past me and leapt toward Lady Estaria, followed closely by a long shard of ice.

Shit! Andrei!

I was moving before he'd fully bounded past me. Without considering my plan, I threw myself forward, scrabbling at the young werewolf's hind legs. I caught hold of his waist as he completed his shift, and I was suddenly holding an angry werewolf as he snapped and snarled at the Winter Lady.

A sharp, freezing pain dug into my upper shoulder. I'd just intercepted the icicle pursuing Andrei. Desperately, I tossed myself to the side before the icicle could burrow deeper. The thing was as sharp as one of my knives, but not as durable. It cracked and shattered as I rolled to the floor with a snarling werewolf on my chest. I groaned in pain as I rolled over the broken icicle. My grip slackened and Andrei wriggled free.

Magnus was there in a moment, wrapping his arms around the teenage werewolf, even as the strength in my injured arm gave out.

He hauled the younger wolf back to the edge of the room, snarling in Andrei's furry ear.

I shoved to my feet with a groan. I gritted my teeth and glared up at the Winter Lady. "That wasn't very nice," I ground out.

She shrugged, unperturbed. "My castle, my rules." I glanced down to see that spiked icy talons had erupted from her nails. Captain Frost was at her side with his hand on the sword at his waist. If Andrei had reached her, I'm not sure he would have survived the encounter. A droplet of cold sweat spilled down my spine. If I didn't bring the Alpha's son home to New Orleans, I wasn't sure I'd survive *that* encounter.

Good Lord, that kid is going to take years off my life!

Captain Frost cleared his throat and slowly, meaningfully, released his grip on his sword, one finger at a time. "Perhaps you might explain your job offer, my lady," he said mildly. "They cannot work for you if you kill them, after all."

Estaria closed her eyes, taking two deep breaths. The ice talons retracted slowly until it revealed her glittering manicure, restored to its former luster. "Fine," she drew the word out.

The Winter Lady whirled, marching angrily back to her ice bench as her gown morphed back into existence to cover her body suit. The feminine flare of fabric looked decidedly out of place after the violent explosion of magic. The icicles still hanging in midair clattered to the ground and shattered on impact.

Sloane tore a strip of cloth from the hem of her long tunic and passed it over to me. "It doesn't look too bad. A deep scratch is all," she said.

I accepted the make-shift bandage and pressed it firmly against my shoulder, mopping up the seeping blood. It didn't even hurt anymore; it just felt numb under the bandage. "Just a flesh wound," I responded. We shared a smile.

My flippant words belied my true feelings about the injury. It was already numb, but the blood hadn't stopped. If I hadn't reacted and shattered the icicle, would it have continued to burrow into my shoulder? Would it have gone straight through me? Magic was a funny thing. I didn't know if fae magic reacted differently than the magic I'd encountered on Earth.

I turned to face the Winter Lady. "What the hell is wrong with you?" I said angrily.

Her eyes flashed dangerously at my words. Frost spread up her hands, and ice claws descended from her fingertips again.

Captain Frost sprang between us. "Stop!" His shout echoed loudly in the chilly room. He lowered his volume. "My lady, please. Stop this. Just explain what has happened. I'm sure that reason will work better than force."

The Winter Lady nodded slowly, and the ice claws retracted once more. "Your advice is sound as always, my Captain."

I moved to speak up again, but Sloane laid a warning hand on the small of my back. I looked at her, then shut my mouth with a snap.

Lady Estaria said, "Being new to Fae, you might not be aware that I have not always ruled the Winter Court. My brother, Etienne, was the Winter Lord before his death..." her voice trailed away, and she stared off into the distance.

I glanced at Sloane as the silence stretched. The leprechaun shot me a confused look and shrugged to show she had no additional information. I cleared my throat softly. "You have our condolences."

The Winter Lady shook herself and came back to the moment. "Yes. Indeed. However much I appreciate your condolences, I would prefer answers. Which is why I was ecstatic when there were rumors of a lich in Fae."

"No offense, my lady," Magnus said from the back of the room where he kept a firm grip on Andrei's ruff, "But there is nothing to be excited about regarding Kroxius. Except perhaps that Cameron did you a favor and killed him before he could cause trouble in your court."

"Perhaps," the Winter Lady said. "However, death magic is not a gift given to the fae. I hoped he could use his powers to help me uncover answers."

"Answers to what?" I asked.

"Answers about the cause of my brother's death," Lady Estaria snapped.

Captain Frost cleared his throat. The Winter Lady looked at him and then raised her hand in silent apology before continuing. "My brother was thrown from the royal sleigh when he supposedly lost control while accompanying the Goblin King on the Wild Hunt. Etienne broke his neck." Her voice caught on a suppressed sob, but she met each of our eyes fiercely. Conviction vibrated through her entire being. "My brother was a fine huntsman. Too well practiced to lose control, especially when the sleigh was pulled by the royal foxes. They have served my family faithfully for hundreds of your human years."

I had to ask. "What do you think happened?"

She met my gaze. The force behind her words nearly bowled me over. "My brother was assassinated. His death made to look accidental. For what purpose, I do not know, but I know in my heart that his death was no accident." She pounded a fist on her chest as she spoke. Then she pointed at us. "Since you killed the only person who has entered Fae in decades who could contact the dead, you are going to help me find out who was behind Etienne's death or, I swear on his grave, you will not leave Winter alive." Estaria conjured an icicle the size of a spear between one heartbeat and the next and leveled it directly at my heart.

Chapter 17

Instantly, I grabbed at the shadows with my magic, pulling them from the deepest corners of the room to blanket Sloane and me. I had to hope that Magnus and Andrei could take care of themselves for the time being.

"Wait!" I said desperately, a memory tickling its way to the front of my brain. "Isn't there a way for fae to contact each other from beyond the grave?" It was something that Aldrich Kingsley had said to me just before Halloween, but the strange custom had stuck in my mind.

A tendril of icy magic spiraled through the shadows, searching for us. "Yes, but only at certain times. Arranging for communication across the veil is Autumn's domain and only the gods know when their court will rise to power again." Estaria sent another questing tendril of magic through my shadows as she spoke. I felt it brush across my skin and yanked harder on my shadows even as Lady Estaria gripped her spear and held it, ready to attack. I held my breath, but no attack came. She couldn't see us, but if those tentacles of magic could find us in the shadows, maybe she could, too. I kept a tight hold on the shadows but spread them out as far as I could to cover a wider area even as I focused on forming a blade. I sweat beaded on my brow at the effort of holding on to so many shadows at once, but I felt the sword finally solidify in my hand.

"Enough of this!" Estaria exclaimed. I don't know if she sensed some stir in magical energies, but she suddenly threw a hand forward and a frosty blast of winter wind gusted through the chamber. The magical wind tugged at my shadows and, try as I might, I couldn't maintain my grip on them. They disappeared, blown back to the four corners of the room. At least I still held my blade. I raised it to a guard position.

"Assassin!" Estaria shrieked as she saw the naked shadow blade in my fist. She drew her arm back and flung the spear at me from a mere ten feet away. At that range, I doubted I could dodge it, even with my supernatural speed. I gritted my teeth, readying for impact.

Impact that never came.

Captain Frost was faster than me. Somehow, he'd manage to both draw his blade and insert himself between the Winter Lady and me. He smashed the spear down with his sword as it hung in midair. It crashed into the stone floor and shattered into a thousand needle-like fragments. I danced backwards to avoid getting cut on the shards. Frost leapt at me, crunching down on the icy fragments. He held his fancy rapier at the ready. I read the grim determination in his eyes.

"Jack! Get out of the way!" Lady Estaria screamed as she formed another crystalline spear out of glittering ice.

I whipped my blade forward, attacking before Frost could strike out. His blade flowed like quicksilver to meet my dark sword in a parry. The jolt of contact jarred me to my shoulder. I disengaged and rotated my arm, coming up under his guard and trying to force him back. His blade stoically met mine again. I reversed my attack, slicing at his open side, but again, his sword met mine with a dull ring in a strong parry.

But nothing more. No counterattack, not even a mild shove to get me out of arm's reach. Just one lightning-fast parry after another. Conscious awareness took back control of my brain. I kept my sword up and ready, but took a small step backwards.

Captain Frost met my eyes as I disengaged, but he made no move to attack. He just stood in front of the Winter Lady, protecting her from me.

Or was he protecting me from her?

Something else finally registered now that I had a moment to think. "Jack?" I asked softly. I remembered then that Hemlock had called him Jacky. "As in Jack Frost? *The* Jack Frost?" I hadn't put two and two together until this moment.

He dipped his head slightly. "At your service. I'm also the Captain of the Winter guards and the Winter Lady's personal bodyguard. Please. She means no harm, but is trying to cope with her unbearable, unrelenting grief at losing her brother and the new reality of becoming the most powerful being in Winter. Possibly in all of Fae. He was her only family."

I snorted in response. His eyes bore into mine, pleading for understanding. "Please. Lower your blade. I swear to you on my power, no harm will come to you while you are in my lady's home."

I sucked in a breath. The captain had just put his very essence on the line to convince me that I was safe in the presence of his arguably unstable ruler. I considered the consequences of believing him or not believing him. Tension mounted and invisibly vibrated like a taut string as everyone waited to see what I would do. My actions would dictate if we spoke with words or with swords.

Finally, I let my shadow blade dip, but didn't release my hold. "I believe you, Captain Jack Frost, and accept your oath. However, Lady Estaria has already attempted harm against my party, so I will keep my blade. Although I promise that I have no intention of using it unless hostile action is directed at me or mine."

Jack Frost met my eyes and nodded once. "Acceptable." He dropped his own blade out of his ready stance, but also maintained his grip on the rapier.

"Jack?" Estaria asked again, but this time her voice held an uncertain quaver. I looked past the captain's shoulder. She was staring at the second ice spear in her hand in shock. "What's this? What has happened?" She dropped it to the floor as if it had burned her and stumbled back to collapse on her bench as the spear shattered on the floor to join its predecessor.

Frost held up his free hand to me, palm outwards in a silent implication to wait. He didn't move until I gave him a slight nod. The cautious captain backed up slowly. His sword was still lowered in what could have been called a relaxation of his guard. However, I'd witnessed his speed in our limited clashes. His stance was likely to put me at ease than because he was actually relinquishing an ounce of his awareness.

"Do not worry, my lady. A small misunderstanding is all," Captain Frost said coolly as he glided to her side. When he saw I didn't make a move, he sheathed his sword and pressed a goblet of wine into Lady Estaria's hands.

Estaria whispered so softly that I almost missed it. "The power. It grows. It *hurts.* Help me, Jack!"

She leaned her head against his side as she gripped his arm like a lifeline. The captain froze for a moment and then stroked her hair gently.

"My lady," he murmured. "We have guests." He put his hands on her shoulders and forced her to sit upright.

She passed a hand over her face. "Oh, yes. Yes, of course. My apologies." Estaria looked around the room at us. "Forgive me. I hadn't realized. It is a pleasure to meet you all. I trust you had an enjoyable journey." She dipped her head graciously.

Sloane shot me a confused glance. I shrugged my puzzlement back at her. My shoulder twinged painfully at the movement, and I winced.

Estaria noticed. "Captain, one of our guests appears to be injured! How has this happened? And under my roof, no less?" The rebuke was as sharp as her ice spear from a moment before.

Captain Frost dipped his head. "I will see to it at once, Lady Estaria."

Estaria looked aghast. "And why have you not provided sustenance for our travelers? Is not the feast still joyous in the great hall? Surely, they must be hungry after their long journey." There was a slight reprimand in her tone.

Jack Frost straightened his spine, reverting to his mask of blank impassivity. "Of course, my lady. I will see that their needs are met. However, you requested an urgent audience with the human travelers. You thought they might be of assistance with..."

"With Etienne's death," Estaria said, as though was piecing parts of a jigsaw puzzle together. When her eyes met mine, she sounded like a lost little girl. "Will you? Will you help me find out who murdered my brother?"

The helpless, childlike nature of her plea struck through my cynical defenses, yanking on my heartstrings. I felt Sloane's fingertips brush the small of my back again. I slammed my will down on the emotions. Estaria was obviously unstable. We needed to get out of here and meet up with Letitia.

I cleared my throat uncomfortably. "I am truly sorry for your loss. I also know what it feels like to lose your only family in the world.

However, my friends and I have pressing business in the Spring Court, and we must travel there as fast as possible."

Estaria tipped her head to the side, looking even more like a small child as her eyes lost focus. "Spring? Wasn't there something about Spring? Some warning? Some... thing?"

Captain Frost stepped in. "As the new Winter Lady, it is customary that you visit all the Courts to formally introduce yourself in your new capacity, but we have been delaying the traditional diplomatic visits."

Estaria pressed two fingers to each temple and rubbed in small circles. She closed her eyes. "Remind me why that is, Captain?"

Frost looked uncomfortable as he glanced around the room at us, obviously not wishing to discuss delicate matters in front of strangers.

"Captain." There was more steel in her voice, making the single word a command.

Duty won out, and the captain leaned over, whispering in her ear. Despite his attempt at discretion, I was close enough to hear the murmured words. "Because you fear that whoever killed your brother will come after you next, my lady."

"But I must visit the other courts! If we don't maintain our strong ties across the realm, Fae will crack and sunder into smaller courts or, heavens forbid, no courts at all! It would spell disaster for all who live here!"

Captain Frost shook his head. His voice never rose in volume, but I heard each word. "Need I remind you that you are the last of your line? If you die without an heir, Winter will consume itself. Without the balance Winter brings, the rest of Fae will fall into anarchy. Death, blood, pillaging. These are all happy daydreams compared to what will happen to Fae if you die without an heir. Tense diplomatic relations are by far the lesser of the two evils. We must protect your life at all costs until you name an heir."

Estaria gripped his arm tightly. "No, I must go to Spring! I must warn the other courts. Someone might be plotting against them as well!"

"You have, my lady. You sent your emissary to all the other courts to bear a warning. But accidents happen..."

"It was no accident!" Her voice trembled, but whether with rage or tears, I couldn't be sure.

Captain Frost patted her hand consolingly. "As you say, my lady." He sounded unconvinced, even to my ears.

Lady Estaria looked up at him with glistening eyes. "I must go to Spring," she said, her voice sounding more confident than she looked.

"I'd advise against it," Captain Frost whispered, a hint of impatience cracking his perfect soldier façade. "The wiser option would be to name an heir before engaging in such an undertaking."

"Perhaps not having an heir and the consequences my death will have without one is the only thing keeping me alive. Have you thought of that?" Estaria hissed back.

"Well, no, but…"

"Then it is a good thing that I am the Winter Lady and not you."

Estaria rose abruptly and shouted, "Guards!" They entered with a clatter. She pointed an imperious finger at us. "Take my guests to their chambers for the evening. Ensure that their every need is met. Then ready my entourage. We leave for Spring in the morning!"

Chapter 18

Captain Frost silently led us through the confusing twists and turns of the castle before depositing us in a suite of rooms. Somehow, he maintained his impeccably blank expression, but I had a feeling a veritable storm was raging under the blank, composed expression he wore.

The captain spun on a heel in front of a door guarded by two well-armed Fae soldiers. "This is your suite for the evening. I trust you will find everything you require within. Although you are guests in Lady Estaria's home, I would suggest that you do not wander about the castle on your own this evening. I would hate for anything untoward to happen to you. If you need anything, my men have the strictest instructions to see to your every comfort."

The stony-faced guards had obviously learned a thing or two from their captain regarding expressing their feelings. Neither betrayed a single emotion as they swung the doors wide for us. One guard handed a small amber jar stoppered with a cork to the captain. Frost nodded curtly as he accepted it and led us into the room.

As soon as the doors shut, he turned and extended the vial to me. "Please accept this with my apologies on behalf of my lady. Few people can form ice weapons. Even fewer can make weapons that can actually inflict any sort of damage. I am told that the frostbite one incurs from one of our ice weapons is extraordinarily painful. This ointment will help heal your injury." He gestured upwards towards my shoulder with the jar. "It's best to apply it liberally to the wound before the numbness wears off."

I accepted the jar, surprised at the captain's kindness and just as much at the idea of getting frostbite from a weapon. "Thank... I mean, I accept your kind gesture," I murmured sincerely.

Captain Frost nodded briskly, then whirled and marched out of the room, letting the door slam with a dull thud behind him.

"Not the most talkative of men, is he?" Sloane asked.

"You can say that again."

"Not the most talk—" Sloane repeated.

I cut her off. "Just because you can, doesn't mean you should, smartass."

"Well, I told you to watch your words," she countered. I shook my head at her and turned my attention to the suite.

Just beyond the entryway was a gorgeously appointed sitting room filled with tasteful but serviceable furniture in pale creams and sky blues. Everything was edged with ornate silver swirls and decorated with crystalline snowflake designs. A blazing fire crackled merrily in the hearth, lighting the room with the buoyant feeling of a warm embrace from an old friend. I sighed, feeling tension drip out of my muscles, and caught the barest hint of a scent in the air. Evergreen mixed with, what was that? Cinnamon? Whatever it was, it reminded me of the holidays and happiness.

The lock on the door to the suite clicked loudly behind me, and I jumped. "How much do you want to bet that Frost told those guards not to let us out of here unless the castle was on fire?"

"I'm not sure we'd qualify for release, even if that was the case," Magnus observed drily.

Sloane put her hands on her hips. "Well, I've been in worse jail cells."

"Wait. You were in jail?" I screwed up my face in confusion. I'd never heard Sloane talk about jail before.

"A story for another time," she waved a hand in dismissal. I wasn't about to let her off that easily. However, Sloane cut me off before I could get my questions out. "More importantly, what are we going to do now?"

Andrei, still in wolf form, lunged for the silver-and-cream-colored couch. Magnus caught him before the teenage werewolf could shed black fur all over the pristine furniture. "I think I'm going to take the kid to get changed. Maybe give him a good talking to at the same time."

"No arguments here," I said.

Magnus jerked his chin at a discreet wet bar in the corner. "I wouldn't say no to a whisky if you can find one. The faster I can get to sleep tonight, the better. Sounds like we got a big day tomorrow."

I gave him a half-hearted mini salute. "You got it. I'll play bartender anytime if it means I don't have to deal with teen wolf over there."

"*I'll* be the bartender," Sloane said, waving me off as the wolves headed towards the door on the left of the sitting area. "You go take care of that shoulder," she ordered, pointing to the door on the right.

"Probably for the best," I admitted, faint flares of pain flickering through the cold in the deep scratch on my shoulder.

I ducked through the door and slid out of my ruined tunic. Without a mirror in the room, I couldn't get a good look at the injury, but by twisting around, I glimpsed a dark purplish-black bruise on the back of my shoulder. It looked nasty and would probably feel much worse once the numbness wore off. I worked the cork loose on the jar Captain Frost had given me. The smell of pine and wood smoke undercut by something sharply medicinal assailed my nostrils. It wasn't exactly unpleasant, but I doubted I'd be able to find the scent at any perfume shop in New Orleans.

I took Frost's advice and smeared the viscous unguent liberally over the back of my shoulder. The ragged edges of the shallow wound felt cold under my fingertips but burned with a throbbing ache as soon as I touched them, like circulation returning with a painful swell to a limb too long unmoved. Despite the discomfort, I covered the entire cut before re-corking the jar.

I looked around the room, spying a wardrobe in the corner. A quick rummage revealed a series of tunics similar to my ruined one. I figured if there were this many, the Winter fae wouldn't mind me dirtying another with the smelly healing goo. I yanked a clean one out and tugged it on as I headed back to the sitting room.

I dropped onto the sofa with a sigh. It was as comfortable as it looked, welcoming me in with a downy soft embrace. Sloane handed me a tumbler filled with a generous pour of amber liquor over ice with a cherry and a slice of dried orange. She retrieved a second tumbler from the wet bar.

"How's the shoulder?" Sloane asked.

I rolled it tentatively. "Better, I think. Whatever was in that jar seems to work. I'm glad that Frost thought of it. It had gone numb, and I'd almost forgotten about it entirely."

"Winter ice frostbite isn't something you want to mess around with. Or so I've been told."

"Speaking of messing around, what is this bizarre concoction?" I asked, eyeing the drink in my hand. I carefully sniffed at it. Fruit and smooth smoke over notes of wood spice. Interesting.

"Brandy old-fashioned," Sloane explained. She sipped hers and sighed in contentment.

I looked at it suspiciously. "Why brandy and not bourbon?"

Sloane toed off her boots and curled into a corner of the sofa. "One, this is how folks up in Wisconsin make it. A tourist showed me once, and I figured, if anyone knows about dealing with the cold, it's those Wisconsinites."

I couldn't fault her logic. I sipped my drink, then eyed the glass in appreciation. It was good. "You said one. What's the second thing?"

"There was no bourbon."

I chuckled and raised my glass. "Here's to improvising!"

Sloane smiled and clinked hers against mine. We sipped in contented silence. I felt the combined comfort of the crackling fire and the strong liquor warm me like I was cuddled under a weighted blanket on a snowy winter night.

"So, do you think she's telling the truth?" Sloane asked. "Lady Estaria, I mean."

"About her brother getting murdered?" I asked.

Sloane nodded. "It all seems dramatic, if you ask me. Then add in the way she was acting with the micro-amnesia? I don't know if I believe her. What about you?" Sloane asked.

I shook my head slowly. "I'm not sure. But there's no doubt in my mind that *she* believes someone killed her brother."

Sloane shifted her weight. "Okay, so either she's crazy, and it's all in her head, or someone really killed her brother, and she might be next. Which do you think it is?"

"Oh, there's no doubt in my mind on that point," I said.

"She convinced you already?" Sloane was incredulous.

"That she's crazy? Sure. Didn't take much. However, the brother-assassination thing? I'm not so sure. Who would stand to benefit?"

"Well, the obvious answer is Estaria," Sloane said. "But she was so torn up about her brother's death that I doubt she had anything to do with it. That is, if it is some nefarious plot and not just a horrible accident."

I nodded. "I agree. But if not Estaria, who else benefits from killing the Winter Lord?"

Sloane shrugged and sipped on her drink. "I guess it could be anyone else that benefited from her rise to power. Someone riding on her coattails?"

"Sounds plausible. Anyone specific spring to mind?" I asked.

Sloane shook her head. "I couldn't give you specific names without poking around some more. It's been too long since I've been in Fae. Besides, I never spent much time at the Winter Court, even when I lived here. To be honest, I tried to stay as far away from court intrigue as possible. I couldn't speculate on current court politics with any accuracy."

"Yeah, I'm not sure I follow all the political complexities of Fae either. I mean, I know the basics about the four courts. Each named after a season, that they rotate power to maintain balance, all that jazz. But I don't know much else. Is there anything you think might be important for me to know? Like how the courts came to be in the first place?"

Sloane nodded. "I'll do my best." She gathered her thoughts and then spoke. "Keep in mind I wasn't alive when all of this happened, but fae are usually excellent storytellers. I'd guess most of this is close enough to the truth for sketching out a basic history." She took another sip of her drink and cleared her throat. When she spoke again, her voice dropped subtly.

"Three hundred fae years ago—and don't ask me what that is in human years because I don't know—Fae was a lot wilder. It was a terrible, primal place with little order and less civilization. Power spiraled and magic swelled throughout the realm. The strong took both at will and wielded them against their enemies. The weaker fae creatures were fodder to feed their wars. People died. Livelihoods were destroyed. Cities burned. Despite the desire to embrace the wild magic of Fae, things were getting out of control. Even though the fae reveled in the wildness, there were rumors that the constant fighting would break Fae. Sunder the realm completely."

"Wait. What?" I asked. "How could Fae break apart? I don't get it."

Sloane shrugged and sipped her drink. "I'm not sure I do either. But remember, this happened centuries ago. Who knows what is fact and what is embellishment after all these years?"

"Fair enough. So, what happened next?" I leaned forward eagerly.

"Well, to cut a very long story extremely short, the Fairy Queen and Goblin King united under one banner. Together, they fought, bribed, coerced, and threatened the rest of the fae. One by one, the major players either joined or fell. Together, the Fairy Queen and Goblin King brought peace and order to the land."

"How so?"

"Well, Titania and Oberon..."

"Wait!" I interrupted. "Like *the* Titania and Oberon? Like from Shakespeare? Swapping people's heads for donkey heads or whatever?"

"Precisely. Although the real Titania and Oberon wouldn't have returned anyone back to normal. But that's by the by. It was their plan for Fae that found a balance between the innate nature of the wild fae and developing a civilized realm. Or at least a realm populated with creatures who agreed to suppress their darkest desires for the greater good."

"Yeah, that doesn't sound like any of the fae I've met so far. Remember that troll who went mud-bathing in the middle of the Mississippi? Or that pixie at the beer festival who swapped all our powers?"

Sloane shook her head. "Those were mere child's pranks compared to what used to go on in Fae before the courts. Nowadays, well, think of the courts as a series of built-in, but highly confusing, checks and balances." She tapped a finger against her lips as she searched for an apt analogy. "Have you ever been to the circus and seen someone spinning plates? Fae is kind of like that."

I nodded, mulling over the information. I'd never heard of a country or realm being described as an ever-shifting imbalance of power. Geopolitical power, sure. Economic power, fine. But seasonal power was a new one for me.

Sloane continued. "Think of Fae like a delicately balanced spinning plate. The balance of power is always tipping one way or the other with the seasons. Summer bleeds to Autumn, which spins into Winter that eventually fades to Spring and then back to Summer. So turns the axis of power within the Fae realm."

"Fine. I get that. Mostly. But what about these power surges or whatever from the human realm?" I asked.

Sloane set her drink on a small end table and interlaced her fingers, palms almost touching. "At one point, Fae and Earth were like this. It was easy to pass between the realms, and each grew stronger for it. Fae fed off the humans' belief in the supernatural and Earth benefited from fae magic."

I made a face at her, and Sloane quickly amended, "Okay, okay. *Sometimes* benefited from fae magic. But we already established that the fae were in a violent, primal circle of death. You can hardly expect them to be all murderous backstabbers with each other and super benevolent to the humans."

"I suppose," I allowed. "So, what happened next?"

The side door snicked open, and Magnus slipped into the room. "The kid's asleep already. Sometimes, I wish I had the superpowers of a teenager," he observed. Magnus helped himself to the drink Sloane had left him on the wet bar and he slid into a chair. "What are we talking about?"

"Fae history," I said. "Sloane was explaining how Fae and Earth are connected." Magnus nodded and turned his attention to Sloane, listening attentively.

Sloane slowly pushed her palms apart until her fingertips were barely touching. "Over time, Fae and Earth drifted further apart. No one quite knows why. Was it the rise of organized religion, the Industrial Revolution, or the increased influence of science? Maybe a combination of all three? Or maybe it was something else entirely. Regardless, humans' belief in the supernatural faded. The fae were reduced to mere stories humans tell their children to illustrate proper moral choices or some such tripe. Fairytales. The reduction in belief drained Fae of its surplus of power, increasing the bloody conflicts to an insane degree. No one was safe."

"Until Titania and Oberon?" I asked.

"Exactly. They stepped in and ended the fairy wars. But it wasn't all smooth sailing after the wars ended. They knew they couldn't enforce the hard-won peace on their own, so they set up the courts and placed the High Fae in their positions of power."

I shook my head. "I'll be honest, I still don't understand the ever-shifting power thing."

"I do," Magnus spoke up for the first time. "It's all about domination games."

"Isn't everything about domination games with you werewolves?" I quipped.

Sloane smiled and shook her head at me. "He's not wrong. The constant ebb and flow of power means that no single court can establish a firm enough footing to make a power play for all of Fae. That, and they spend so much time with small skirmishes or elaborate spying efforts that, by the time they are ready to solidify their power base into something stronger, the power has shifted to another court. Or there's a power surge from Earth."

"It's a clever way to balance the power or, more appropriately, to keep it perpetually unbalanced. Titania and Oberon developed this system?" Magnus asked.

Sloane nodded. "Or so the stories go. It's not perfect, but it's kept relative peace in a hostile land for centuries, at least."

"Okay, that explains the what. Now let's talk about the why. Namely, why did Estaria seem so unstable?" I asked.

Sloane rubbed at her forehead. "My best guess? She wasn't ready to be a conduit for Winter's power. Add in the upcoming surge from Earth, and I'll bet she's finding it difficult to maintain a constant grip on the heart of the Winter Court's power. It can lead to unstable behavior. Blackouts. Loss of control. That type of thing."

"And this power all transferred to her immediately upon her brother's death?" Magnus asked.

"Sure. It happens with every leader of each court. Although fae deaths are few and far between if they occur from natural causes," Sloane allowed. "Violent deaths are a far more common occurrence, unfortunately."

"What happens if Estaria dies?" Magnus pressed.

"Her heir succeeds her. Same as she did with her brother," Sloane said.

My throat tightened, thinking of what I'd inadvertently overheard. "And if she doesn't have an heir?"

Sloane's eyes widened. "The balance of power would crumble. Without someone to hold Winter's portion, that spinning plate falls. The entire system would crash and shatter. Power would run rampant, waiting to be used by whoever could harness it." Her voice dropped to a hoarse whisper. "The fairy wars would start all over again."

Chapter 19

A knock at the door interrupted our conversation. I glanced at the door curiously. Magnus sprang to his feet. A low growl rumbled out of him as it swung wide without invitation.

Captain Frost slipped in and closed the door swiftly behind him. He held up his hand, palm outwards. "Peace, wolf. I just want to talk."

Sloane, ever the hostess, offered drinks all around. The captain demurred, but the rest of us gladly accepted another round.

Magnus spoke as we all settled on the comfortable furniture in front of the fire. "What brings you here, Captain? Visiting your prisoners?"

Captain Frost shook his head. "Hardly. I am here to extend Lady Estaria's formal invitation to accompany her to Spring in the morning."

I raised an eyebrow. "Invitation? Not command?"

The captain looked uncomfortable, fidgeting with the hem of his heavy ceremonial jacket. "Yes. A cordial invitation. It is always safer to travel in larger groups and you said that you wanted to contact your friends in the Spring Court as soon as possible."

"Hmm," I grunted, unconvinced.

Frost tipped his head slightly. "And Lady Estaria was concerned that she didn't present the best first impression during your meeting."

Sloane snorted derisively and hid it poorly behind her drink. Magnus lifted a lip in a silent snarl. I harbored similar sentiments but didn't want to upset the most powerful woman in the court by being disrespectful.

Good Lord, help us when the burden of tact falls on my shoulders.

"We accept your offer, Captain. We would welcome the company on our journey to the Spring Court to reunite with our friends," I said.

There. That should avoid any issues with who owes who debts or obligations or whatever.

The captain nodded, fidgeting with his jacket again.

Sloane shot me a discreet look and jerked her chin at the captain. I dropped my head in the smallest of nods. "Umm, Captain? I can't help but notice that you seem to have something else on your mind. I don't want to piss you off or anything. Crossing swords with you once today was more than enough. And today has been going on for over a week now. What do you say we cut through all this fancy talk and just speak plainly?"

The captain lifted his eyes to the ceiling and sighed. "I didn't think I was that obvious."

When we didn't answer, he sighed again and sank into a chair, leaning his forearms on his legs. "I need to ask a favor of each of you. One that I'd be willing to formally swear, if that would help."

"I'm listening," I said, curiosity sparking inside me.

"What you witnessed today in the lady's private chambers? Well, it would be best if that stayed between us."

Magnus shook his head. "Uh-uh. If you want to bargain for our silence, the only thing I'm interested in is the truth. Why was she acting so crazy? Is she a danger to everyone, or were we just special?"

Captain Frost dropped his head to his hand and scrubbed his clean-shaven cheek. "If I answer your questions about Lady Estaria, will you swear to keep your silence about your meeting with her and its ramifications from all but each other?"

I looked at Sloane and Magnus, who were already bobbing their heads in agreement. "Looks like you got a deal, Frost. Spill the tea." A *whoomph* resonated through my sternum like I'd just gotten the wind knocked out of me. I made a mental note to keep my word, as I didn't want to incur any nasty magical repercussions. It shouldn't be too hard. When we made it back to New Orleans, who would believe me anyway?

Captain Frost wrinkled his brow. "Very well. The abbreviated version is that she is finding the transfer of the mantle of power following her brother's death extremely difficult. They trained him to be the Winter Lord, to take control of the court's magic upon the death of the former Winter Lady, their mother. Lady Estaria is the second born. She received no such training, nor did she ever show the inclination to learn once her brother became the Winter Lord. I think she just assumed he would marry and sire an heir as quickly as possible."

"And that didn't happen?" I asked.

"It did not." The captain's response was terse, cutting off any further questions on that topic.

"Why?" Sloane asked.

Frost squirmed deeper into his chair. His voice was low when he spoke, and he refused to meet our eyes. "She does not yet have an heir. She is so set on finding out the answer to the conspiracy theory she has fabricated around the death of her brother that she refuses to even consider marriage or children."

"Isn't that, you know, dangerous?" I asked.

"Extremely." Frost leaned forward slightly. "I wish she could just reach closure over her brother's death. I'm convinced that this would help her adjust to holding the might of Winter's mantle of power more quickly."

Magnus spoke up. "So, you don't believe that the former Lord was murdered?"

Frost shrugged. "I'm a soldier. I do my duty. That's all. I leave the power struggles and conspiracy theories to others."

Sensing an opening to pry, I took it. "Have you always been a soldier?"

Frost skewered me with his penetrating gaze, but slowly shook his head. "I was assigned to be Lady Estaria's personal bodyguard when she came of age. Upon her ascension to the role of Winter Lady, she generously made me the Captain of the Royal Guards."

"Quite a promotion," Magnus said blandly.

"It has been observed," Captain Frost returned with a wry twist to his lips.

I cut to the quick of the matter. "Okay, Captain. For argument's sake, why would someone want to assassinate the Winter Lord?"

Frost shook his head. "I can hypothesize, but any such guesses would be unsubstantiated."

I shrugged. "Indulge me."

He met my eyes intently. "If someone killed Lord Etienne, my assumption would be that they're making a play for control of Winter. One option would be to control Lady Estaria, like a puppet master tugging her strings. However, in my time as her bodyguard, I don't think it's too forward to say I'm accustomed to how Lady Estaria's mind works. Anyone who thinks they might control her will be in for a rude awakening."

"She's independent?" Magnus asked.

Captain Frost didn't quite smile. "One could say that, yes."

"Okay, so what's the play? If not to control her, what is the outcome of this supposed conspiracy?" I asked.

The captain didn't blink. "Winter. The entirety of Winter."

"But to do that, they'd have to get Lady Estaria to name them as heir and then kill her," Sloane breathed.

Frost nodded grimly. "That's the point she has made repeatedly to me since her brother died. Which is one reason she refuses to name an heir; in case she inadvertently plays into the hands of the plotters she is sure are behind her brother's death. However, until she names an heir, it isn't safe for her to travel through Fae."

"Why?" I asked. "I mean, if she doesn't name an heir, doesn't that act as a kind of insurance for her?"

Frost tipped a hand back and forth in a balancing gesture. "Maybe. Maybe not. But if she was killed without an heir, her death would send unprecedented fractures throughout the realm. Which is why I've advised against traveling to Spring. We can control the situation much better here than on the road or in a strange court."

"Flush out the culprit," Sloane mused.

"If there is one," Frost returned.

I raised my hand. "Human here. Or manling. Whatever, never mind. What are these 'unprecedented fractures' that happen if the Lady Estaria dies without an heir?" At the stricken look on the Captain's face, I hurried to add, "Gods forbid, of course. This is purely hypothetical."

Frost nodded at my words, but swallowed hard. "In the first case, chaos. Until Queen Titania and King Oberon could temporarily take control of the Winter mantle. Once that happened, they'd assign a new Winter Lord or Lady."

"Then what?" I pressed.

"Who knows? It would depend on Titania and Oberon's allocation. Those two have never been predictable." The captain looked uncomfortable at the turn the conversation had taken. He clapped his hands on his knees and pushed to his feet, obviously intent on ending the meeting as quickly as possible. "So, I can count on your silence regarding your audience with Lady Estaria?"

Sloane nodded silently, and Magnus jerked his head in the affirmative once. I drummed my fingers on the side of my glass. "You have my silence already, but I have one more question."

"Which is?" Captain Frost looked like he wanted to bolt from the room.

"Who did it? Hypothetically? I mean, assuming that the Winter Lady is right, and someone murdered her brother while hunting, who had the motive and the opportunity?"

Captain Frost's spine was ramrod straight as he stood. "I'm sure I do not know. There are many monsters in Fae, and more than our fair share in Winter. However, I am not convinced that a conspiracy is the answer here."

"Because deaths just happen, right?" I pressed.

The captain's lips tightened. "Unfortunately, that has been my experience. Now, if there are no further questions, I have pressing duties to which I must attend before we leave in the morning." He marched crisply to the door, the steel in his spine not relaxing a single iota. He spun on a heel to face us. "Your continued silence on the matter is much appreciated." The threat behind the courteous words hung in the air even after the captain eased the door shut.

Sloane, Magnus, and I finished our drinks in short order. Sloane and I headed for the room we'd share, and Magnus slipped into the opposite one he'd share with Andrei. The lure of a comfortable night's sleep was too tantalizing to ignore. However, despite the exhaustion tugging at my soul, sleep eluded me. The events of the day played on the cinema screen of my closed eyelids. I'd always been a sucker for murder mysteries. I didn't care if it made me an old lady. Agatha Christie was my hero. She kept me on the edge of my seat every time.

As I lay in the luxurious bed with Sloane snoring softly next to me, part of me enjoyed the fantasy of playing Hercule Poirot in my mind. But without a ridiculous mustache. And in Fae.

Until I remembered that there was an actual dead body out there. Not some scribbles on a piece of paper, but an actual dead person. A life cut short.

Suddenly, the draw of playing detective lost its charm.

I was almost asleep when a jarring thought jerked me awake. If Estaria was right and someone had killed her brother and if Captain Frost was right and Estaria was too independent to be manipulated into puppet-hood, then that meant that there was a very good chance that the murderer would finagle his or her way into the company bound for Spring.

Hypothetically, of course.

That thought didn't make sleep any easier to find.

Chapter 20

The next morning came too swiftly for my liking, especially on the heels of a night spent tossing and turning. A banging on the door jerked me out of a bizarre dream featuring a variety of fairytale creatures in a Battle-Royale-fight-to-the-death scenario. When I woke, the giants were almost obliterated, and the pixies were winning. Yeah, it surprised me too.

The pounding on the door turned out to be a delivery service. Not only were our clothes returned, but the Winter Lady had thoughtfully equipped us with gear to travel swiftly to Spring. It wasn't anything fancy, but was serviceable and warm. Apparently, she didn't wish to delay the diplomatic mission. We pulled on the borrowed traveling clothes gratefully. I made Goliath a little nest in my pack. The little mouse snuggled in gratefully to his cozy traveling abode and promptly went to sleep.

After a quick, cold breakfast, a guard came to retrieve us. He led us to the courtyard where we were assigned a rather large sled pulled by creatures who would've been the prehistoric ancestors to wolves on Earth if they'd survived that long. Although I was dying to talk to Sloane or Magnus, I didn't want to be overheard, so I opted to stay silent. Sloane and Magnus engaged in banal small talk, so I assumed they had reached the same conclusion.

Hemlock wandered up to our sled as the fae driver was doing a last check on the harnesses. "This is all rather exciting, isn't it? Going out for an adventure through the wilds of Fae," gushed the barbegazi, rubbing his hands together. "I mean, it feels like an age since Winter has opened her borders. Officially, that is. It's the start of something new. I can almost sense it on the wind, can't you?" The hairy little man performed an exuberant twirl, accompanied by a cheerful jingle of his beardsicles.

I bit the inside of my cheek to keep from smiling. "Sure. I mean, I've been in Winter less than twenty-four hours, so the borders seem pretty open to me, but I get your meaning."

Hemlock shot me a wide grin and a cheeky wink. "Well, I'm happy. Never did well shut away in one stuffy old court or another. Built for travel and adventure, I was!" The barbegazi craned his head around me, apparently seeing someone he knew. "I've got to dash. Grax looks like he's having a rough time getting my foxes hooked up." Hemlock leaned towards me and cupped his hand around his mouth as he dropped his voice. "If I could offer a word of warning? Go easy on the water. I don't think the Winter Lady looks like she fancies a slow journey today."

The barbegazi's words turned out to be prophetic. Lady Estaria set a brisk pace with the royal two-tailed foxes breaking the trail for the rest of us. Captain Frost and Hemlock accompanied her. Hemlock drove the royal sled at a brisk speed throughout the day. It was all our poor, relatively normal team could do to keep up. But the barbegazi was right. Travel with the Winter fae was cold travel bread in the back of the sled, muttered conversation, and, when that gave out, the whisper of runners over snow. The caravan halted when absolutely necessary and even then, only for the briefest time possible. Otherwise, I doubted Estaria would've waited for us if we'd indulged in any superfluous pit stops. Not that I wanted any more than truly essential. After the injury to my shoulder, having a frostbitten butt didn't sit well with me, no pun intended.

Although the journey wasn't unpleasant, due in part to Hemlock's timely warning, it was long. By the time Estaria called a halt for the day, evening was creeping dangerously close to twilight. I uncurled myself from my corner of the sled and happily helped collect wood for a fire. It took a while, but by the time it was blazing merrily, my legs no longer felt like compressed, frozen jelly. Magnus, Sloane, Andrei, and I settled around the fire, trying to stay out of the way of the busy Winter fae as they whipped a camp together out of pine branches, twine, and snowflakes. Well, that's what it seemed like to me, at least.

Hemlock came strolling over, his hands stuck into an oversized, fur-lined jacket. I glanced at his feet. Still bare. I shivered. I was thankful for my borrowed clothing, especially the two pairs of heavy wool socks I wore inside my enchanted boots.

The little emissary cleared his throat and spoke loudly, "Lady Estaria has invited you to her tent for dinner." His eyes twinkled merrily. "Unless you prefer sitting out here in the cold."

"Nope!" Sloane sprang to her feet, rubbing at her arms through the heavy fur jacket she wore.

I shot her a look. Sloane gave me a little shrug in response. I spoke directly to Hemlock. "We would be honored to join the Lady Estaria this evening."

"Wonderful! Her Ladyship hoped you would accept," Hemlock said, gesturing towards the center of the camp where the bustle of activity was the densest.

I looked around at my little party, but everyone was already gathering their things and following Hemlock without discussion. I shrugged and fell in line.

The little barbegazi led us straight to a large tent dyed a deep violet color and heavily embroidered with silver snowflakes. "The Lady Estaria bids you welcome," he said, performing a little bow. Two guards stood on either side of the tent flaps and opened them wide for us as we approached.

When I ducked into the Winter Lady's tent, I didn't know what I was expecting to see. I mean, I figured there wouldn't be sleeping bags on top of waterproof mats over hard packed snow, but the grandeur of the interior almost took my breath away.

The Winter Lady's tent was more ostentatious than our suite of rooms had been back at the castle. Thick rugs woven with ornate designs carpeted the floor to protect Lady Estaria's toes from getting cold. Glowing braziers threw out enough heat that I knew I'd be sweating if I didn't shed some layers soon. Cushions littered the floors, inviting the Winter Lady's guests to partake in the delicacies laid out on low tables around the perimeter of the tent. Lamps set with colored glass illuminated the entire area in flickering shades of purple and blue. Estaria's tent put the term "glamping" to shame.

"That's it," Sloane whispered to me, obviously reading my mind. "She's ruined camping for me."

"Me too," I whispered back.

Estaria turned as we entered and threw her arms wide. She was dressed much like the rest of us, in heavy leggings and a tunic. She'd already taken off her long fur coat and fur-lined boots. Not that I blamed her. The tent was almost a sauna compared to the freezing weather outside.

"How lovely of you to join me! Please, make yourselves at home. My cooks have been busy preparing a marvelous dinner for us. Help yourselves to whatever you like. No obligation, of course." She gave us a warm smile and waved a hand at the food behind her. I saw nothing of the violent ice queen from the day before in her demeanor.

Andrei and Magnus wasted no time. They fell on the food ravenously. To be fair, the only reason they beat Sloane and me to the food was because they had longer legs and we stopped to shrug out of our jackets. After a long day with nothing much to eat besides some winter apples and tough jerky, I wasn't about to turn down an invitation like this.

"Hemlock, your service is impeccable, as always. Please ensure to look after the rest of the party as well." Estaria spoke kindly, but the dismissal in her voice was obvious.

I snuck a glance at the hairy barbegazi. He didn't appear the least perturbed. He executed a small bow accompanied by a warm smile that made his beard jingle merrily before exiting the tent without another word.

Estaria stood in the middle of the tent, staring at the tent flaps for a moment or two more. "Are we alone?" she asked.

I looked around, confused. Captain Frost stepped out from behind a screen that I'd assumed was part of the structural integrity of the tent. "We are my lady."

"Good," Estaria said. She waved a hand and a chill wind swept through the tent, making the embers in the braziers flicker. I shivered as Winter magic brushed my exposed skin with chilling efficiency.

"What was that?" I blurted out, rubbing my upper arms briskly. The chill dissipated almost immediately.

Estaria waved a hand. "Just a minor enchantment to ensure our conversation remains private. No one outside the bubble will interrupt our conversation without my permission." She strode over to us briskly and settled on a large cushion, popping a small, round shortbread topped with cream into her mouth.

"Why the precautions?" Magnus asked, wrapping his hands around a large wooden mug. I grabbed a mug and inhaled deeply. A heavenly mixture of cinnamon and nutmeg comforted me on a drift of fragrant steam.

Lady Estaria met each of our eyes directly. "Captain Frost informed me you witnessed one of my, shall we say, *episodes* and have graciously agreed to keep this matter between us."

"Your business is yours alone," I said earnestly.

Estaria leaned forward. "What would it take to convince you to make my business your business?"

I heard Sloane suck in a quiet breath. Even without the almost inaudible signal, I knew I needed to tread carefully. "What do you mean?"

"Someone murdered my brother and, if my captain's worst fears come to fruition, I am this murderer's next target."

"Just the captain's fears?" Magnus asked softly.

Estaria looked at the werewolf. "My captain would prefer I didn't speak this plainly, but yes. We are both confident that I am the next target."

Magnus met my eyes briefly. That wasn't the impression Captain Frost had given us back at the castle. Perhaps this was another side effect of Estaria's rocky adjustment to her newfound power? Before I could figure out a way to probe politely, Estaria spoke again.

"My Captain disagrees with pursuing an investigation into my brother's death, but I must know what happened. To that end, this excursion is twofold. On the public front, I am completing a necessary diplomatic duty that has been ignored for too long. However, I am also putting myself out there as bait to draw out this murderer, get my satisfaction from him or her, and put my brother's soul to rest."

Captain Frost looked uncomfortable at Estaria's words but made no move to gainsay her. I had a sudden flash of insight that she didn't mean to draw first blood for her satisfaction the way he had with his cousin's killer. She wanted the person responsible for her brother's death dead.

"Why ask us?" I blurted out. "You could have anyone in Winter work for you. Possibly anyone in Fae, if you asked nicely enough. What can we do for you that they can't?"

Estaria met my eyes, and they were stark pools of lucidity. I could see now the difference between the powerful Winter fae who had attacked us in the castle and the woman in front of me. She wore her pain openly, but unabashedly. It wasn't something to shrink from, but a crucible that would either consume her or she'd come out the other side stronger.

"You are the only beings in Winter that I can guarantee *didn't* kill my brother. Possibly the only creatures in all of Fae that I can trust had nothing to do with Etienne's death," the Winter Lady said firmly.

"Because we weren't in Fae when he was killed," breathed Andrei, his eyes wide and shining in excitement. If he'd been in wolf form, his tail would've been thumping an excited staccato on the carpeted floor. No doubt the young werewolf thought this was all some big adventure.

"Precisely. Travel between the realms is severely curtailed and scrupulously managed. Besides, you're also less likely to be subsumed into a fae plot."

"Why's that?" asked Magnus.

Estaria lifted her shoulder. "Some of my kind assume humans are less intelligent, less crafty than we are."

"And you don't?" I asked.

"I know better." A slight smile teased at the corners of her mouth, but she refused to elaborate further.

Silence stretched. Estaria sat there considering each of us without speaking. Tension crept down my neck and into my shoulders with the infallibility of an avalanche.

Finally, I broke the silence. "Umm, I don't think that we can. I mean, we're going to the Spring Court to meet up with our friends. Then we need to get back to Earth as quickly as possible, what with the time misalignment between the two realms."

Estaria waved a hand. "Of course. I wouldn't dream of keeping you here longer than you wished to be." The faintest downturn of her lips had me questioning if that hadn't been her true ploy.

Sloane interjected firmly. "If we decide to look into the matter for you, we can't be held to uncovering the culprit before we leave."

This time, the Winter Lady actually frowned before pasting on a brilliant smile. "Of course not. But anything you could uncover regarding my brother's death during your remaining time in Fae would be appreciated. However, please do so discreetly. I would hate for my... condition... to become the subject of campfire gossip."

"Or for any more lives to be endangered," Captain Frost added swiftly from across the room where he stood sipping from his own heavy wooden mug.

I looked around at my friends, trying to gauge their individual states of mind while giving nothing away to our hostess. I started to say, "Well, I think we will have to talk ab—"

Hemlock burst through the tent flaps, screaming at the top of his lungs. The little barbegazi tripped over his enormous feet and tumbled headfirst across the carpet. He landed in a sprawl at Lady Estaria's feet but sprang up with alacrity. "Wassets!" Hemlock panted past his eerily jangling beard. "Snow wassets are attacking the camp!"

"What? They should still be in hibernation!" Captain Frost shouted. He was out of the tent in a single bound with his sword in his hand. The captain was so quick I hadn't even seen him draw. A small *pop* pressed on my eardrums as the captain dashed outside, like I'd just equalized to a pressure change in an airplane.

"Wassets? Are you sure? They don't attack camps!" Estaria's voice cut through the mayhem building outside.

"You take it up with them!" Hemlock said, urgency and terror coating his words in equal parts.

Spears of ice materialized in Estaria's hands. "Stay here," she snarled, marching towards the entrance.

When she pushed through the heavy flaps, I saw chaos raging in the campsite. Small dark shapes darted in front of the campfires, flinging themselves at the fae defenders. From the brief glimpse, they looked to be about the size of a medium-size dog, but they flowed through the frigid night air with the ease of a mermaid's mane in the ocean. If the mermaid wanted her hair to strangle you and drag you down to a cold, watery grave, that is.

I felt the hard grip of a shadow blade slap comfortingly into my palm before I realized I'd even called on my shadow magic. "Hemlock! What in all the realms is a snow wasset?" I shouted, keeping my eyes locked on the tent flap.

"They're like weasels on steroids," Sloane gasped, scrabbling through the cushions, searching for a weapon. She grabbed two sharp knives from the table, wheeling to face the tent flap as well.

"Okay. We can handle weasels," I said, feeling a sense of cool aware-ness that preceded a fight settling over me. I didn't know how good of a homicide detective I was, but I knew I was a damn good fighter. I spoke over my shoulder to the werewolves. "Better shift, guys. You can snap their little weasely necks if they make it in here."

Hemlock shook his head furiously. He grabbed a heavily embroidered cushion and used it to form the worst start of a barricade I'd ever seen between himself and the door of the tent as he said, "No, you don't understand. Snow wassets are *vampiric* weasels on steroids. If you let them get close enough, they'll either rip your throat out or sink their teeth in and suck you dry." He shrugged, piling another couple of pillows up to almost reach his chin. "It's about a sixty-forty chance."

"Lovely," I grimaced.

At the same time, Andrei said, "Which one is the sixty?"

I shot the young pup a dirty look. He held up his hands in surrender. "Just a kid trying to learn here on the hard streets of Fae."

The heavy flap of the tent rustled and billowed ominously.

"Less talking, more shifting," I whispered as my palms started to sweat. "We've got company."

Chapter 21

Five dark shapes slid into the tent between one breath and the next. My knees convulsed into a quivering mass of terror at what I saw.

The snow wassets were sinuous creatures. They moved like furry snakes, but on six legs instead of their bellies. Each looked about two feet long and weighed between fifteen and twenty pounds. Their fur was almost blue-black but faded to white at the tips of their tails and paws. It made them look like they had the worst balayage hairdresser in history. It also made them damnably difficult to track.

The deadly grace with which they crept silently towards. The strange shadowy shimmer of their coloring emphasized the sinuous grace of movement. They looked like smears of oil coating dark water, and with teeth. I tried to keep tabs on all of them, but felt like I was going cross-eyed.

I wasn't overly concerned until I glimpsed their eyes. They were bloody, hellish red. Not just the iris, either. The. Entire. Fucking. Eye. It even looked like one was crying rivulets of blood.

That is, before it opened its maw and snarled at me past needle-sharp teeth the size of small daggers. Blood coated its mouth and dripped from its overly large incisors. I shuddered. The thing wasn't crying. It had been *feeding*.

A yell and a shout drew my attention back to the opening of the tent as a mangy white wall of fur tore through the flapping fabric with a harsh ripping sound.

"Don't just stands there!" Krampus roared at us. He flung a clawed hand out towards the closest snow wasset. Ragged shards of ice materialized, shooting out of his talons like the best-slash-worst-finger-gun ever. I had no desire to be on the other end of friendly banter with the Krampus when he was in this mood, if you get my meaning.

Apparently, neither did his target wasset. The creature dodged the first two ice projectiles and slapped the third out of the air with a front paw. But it wasn't fast enough to slink past all of Krampus's icy bolts. The fourth drove straight through the wasset's hind leg, making it a stationary target for the fifth and final bolt. It took the wasset straight between the eyes, driving deep into the creature's brain. In a split second, Krampus turned the dead wasset into the most bizarre unicorn hybrid I'd ever heard of. The wasset slumped to the ground, still pinned in place. Krampus whirled with a roar to find another target. Which reminded me to get my ass in gear. The time for watching was over.

My empty hand flashed to the small of my back on instinct before I remembered I had lost my karambits back on Earth. Gritting my teeth, I imagined the familiar small, curved blade with the retention ring looping around my index finger. It took a few moments, but I felt the blade slap into the palm of my hand. Unfortunately, it was time I shouldn't have spent making a close-quarters blade when I already had a sword in my hand. By the time I reoriented on the surrounding fight, a wasset had slipped past Krampus and the wolves. The shimmery, greasy creature was midair and headed right for my face.

I batted at the thing with my blade instinctively but couldn't manage a killing blow. It twisted unpredictably in midair. I don't know if I was getting slow, or the wasset was just really that fucking fast. It landed on my shadow blade with its two front paws, using my ever-loving sword as the tiniest of trampolines to perform a weaselly front handspring and somersault towards my face.

No way was I letting that thing attach itself to any part of me. I mean, it looked like a rabid squirrel had done the dirty with a flying boa constrictor.

I reversed my momentum, swinging my newly made karambit around with as much force as I could thrust behind the movement. The wasset tried to dodge again, but apparently had used all of its midair power-ups. The karambit drove through the meat of its shoulder and down into its chest. I fell to my knee, forcing the knife through the thing's body. It writhed and moaned on the lush carpet, smearing blue-black blood everywhere.

Without hesitation, I decapitated the creature. The wasset twitched twice and then lay still, oozing oily blood onto the Winter Lady's once beautiful rug.

I looked around. The other wassets lay strewn in pieces around the tent. Magnus and Andrei had each taken care of one creature, and Krampus took out the last. I glanced at Sloane. She stood between Hemlock and the snow wassets, her dinner knives at the ready. She was breathing hard, but not a drop of blood was on her.

Hemlock popped his head up from behind the barricade of brocade. "Did you get them all?"

"Looks like it," I said, working my karambit free. I wiped the blood off on the creature's fur out of habit before realizing there was no way the blood could cause my shadow blade to rust.

"Comes on, then!" Krampus roared. "No time to waste!" He scooped up a dead wasset and bit the creature's head off. The horned Krampus chomped merrily, spraying blue-black blood all over his chin and chest as he gestured outside. "More killings! More eatings! Good times!" He lunged out the ripped doorway, running on his lopsided feet and using the knuckles of his empty hand for stability, much like a gorilla might. He continued to munch loudly on his wasset snack as he disappeared.

I tried not to gag. I wasn't the only one. The sound of retching made me turn. Hemlock had a fist pressed to his mouth and another to his stomach as he dry-heaved his way back to control. A small ice knife peeked out of his lower fist. I was glad the little barbegazi hadn't impaled himself on it by accident.

I snapped my fingers. "Andrei, you and Sloane guard Hemlock. Magnus? You're with me."

Andrei whined in protest. The massive silver wolf growled low in his throat at the younger werewolf. The teenager hung his head and slunk to Sloane's side. She patted the ruff at the back of his neck, careful not to nick him with a blade. Whether it was to keep him there or for comfort, I didn't know, and I didn't have time to find out.

I rushed through the opening in the tent with Magnus close on my heels. As soon as we hit the chaos outside, I pulled shadows around us. Campfires had spread to a couple of tents, which were blazing with vicious efficiency. Some of the fae were attempting to put out the flames, while others guarded their firefighting colleagues. However, the sparks and fires were doing a number on everyone's night vision. Everyone except the wassets.

And Lady Estaria apparently.

She stood like a warrior goddess in the middle of a ring of dead wassets. The lower part of her outfit was liberally spattered with greasy blue-black blood. She snapped her fingers and another spear of ice materialized out of thin air. She tracked a wasset as it scampered between two tents, dragging a misshapen object after it. A familiar head covered in what looked like straw poked out under the tent.

"My lute! Bring that back, you nasty mongrel!" Brio, the Autumn bard, shouted. It shocked me to see him here, but it didn't startle Estaria in the least. She hurled her spear at the pilfering wasset. The creature let out a shriek of agony that clawed painfully at my eardrums. Estaria immediately formed another spear of ice. The creature's dying screams ended abruptly as she nearly decapitated the thing with her second strike.

Brio scrambled out of his tent inelegantly. "You saved my life, my lady!" the bard shouted over the din of battle.

"Save your gratitude," I heard Estaria mutter before she raised her voice. "I promised you protection on your journey to Spring and I hold my word sacred, Bard Brio." She formed another spear out of ice and threw it. It whistled through the air, right past the bard's head, and impaled a wasset leaping at the back of his neck.

"Umm, yes. Quite. I think," Brio stuttered.

"Get into my tent. You'll be safe there until the danger has passed," Estaria shouted, forming another spear, and searching for her next target.

Brio muttered something and scooped up his lute case. He picked his way across the snowy field littered with wasset corpses. His journeyman poked her head out of the tent a moment later. When she saw her mentor saving his precious instrument, but not her, a look of dark resignation crossed her face. She disappeared back into the tent, only to reappear a moment later under the enormous weight of what looked like several instrument cases. She staggered after her mentor and towards relative safety.

Magnus snarled at my side, drawing my attention to more pressing matters. He lunged forward, catching a wasset around the throat. The creature hadn't seen us hidden in the shadows. A look of surprise crossed its face before Magnus tossed his head back and forth viciously, snapping the snow wasset's neck. I sliced another one in half as it attempted to avoid the Winter Lady's icy extermination tactics.

Suddenly, a flood of snow wassets seemed to pour out of every tent and wagon in the entire camp. They all fled into the woods as if controlled by one vampiric-weasel-hive-mind. Captain Frost leapt into the royal sled, shouting at Estaria. "Estaria, the foxes!"

She seemed to read his intent. She flung a hand out in a dramatic gesture, as if backhanding a giant on a stage in front of an audience of thousands. I'm surprised she didn't dislocate her shoulder at the violent motion. The winter wind gusting out from her caught the royal foxes from their makeshift kennel and blew them to the sled, where Captain Frost stood with his bow in one hand. Chains of ice formed around the two-tailed team and hardened into a harness.

Captain Frost shouted a guttural command at the foxes. They instantly leapt off in pursuit of the fleeing wassets as Captain Frost formed arrows of ice out of thin air. He fired shot after shot at the wasset-shaped smudges, using only the wavering light from the moon to locate his targets. He disappeared into the night as a tent collapsed into embers and sparks. Flames jumped from the ruins of one tent to another as a gust of winter wind fanned the fire in the wrong direction.

With a curse, I looked around in consternation. One enemy was gone for the night but had been replaced by another. If the fire consumed our supplies and, more importantly, our shelter, I wasn't sure we could survive the freezing Winter night. I let my shadow blades dissolve and got to work.

Chapter 22

Unfortunately, that wasn't the last we saw of the wassets. They seemed to haunt our every move through the wild forests of Winter. More than one fae grumbled about the irregularity of the wild snow wassets' behavior, but we fell into a familiar, if somewhat bloody, pattern.

Lady Estaria refused to turn back. The entire caravan pushed hard throughout the day, trying to outrun the wassets. Every night, we posted extra guards for safety. A ring of fires surrounded each night's camp, and everyone took their turn at guard duty.

The precautions kept us mostly safe from the relentless nightly attacks, but they were draining. We couldn't travel as far each day because the extra fires required so much wood to burn all night. No one got a decent night's sleep or enough sleep, because of the rotating shifts and dying wasset cries.

Sloane, Magnus, Andrei, and I occasionally indulged in guarded, whispered conversations in the back of the sled as we traveled over the snowy terrain.

"So, are we going to help her?" Andrei asked as he happily worked a large wad of jerky between his jaws.

"I don't see why not," I said.

Sloane spoke at the same time. "I don't think we should." She glared at me. "Why do you *want* to get pulled into murderous fae politics?"

"Well, I don't. Not when you say it like that. But Lady Estaria might be right. Every day we fend off unseasonable, irrationally violent snow wasset attacks. Why? Unless someone is egging them on somehow. Why would someone do that?" I asked.

Sloane folded her arms over her coat and glowered at me, but I was too tired to keep my snark in check. "Oh, that's right!" I continued without waiting. "To kill the Winter Lady. And if someone has it out for her, chances are slim that her brother's death was 'an accident'." I added two fingered air-quotes just in case anyone missed my sarcasm.

Sloane's response was a nuanced one-fingered salute overly spiced with heavy sarcasm and baked so long in the depths of sleep deprivation that it stood straight up, seemingly of its own accord.

Magnus put both hands up between us. "Okay, ladies. Let's call it there. You don't need to bite each other's heads off when the little wasset bastards are already trying to do that nightly."

Sloane ignored him. "Well, who do you think it could be, Nancy Drew?"

I rubbed at the back of my neck, where a burgeoning headache was threatening to burst into full bloom. "I don't know. But what I do know is that this is all too much of a coincidence. We need to keep our eyes and ears open."

"You got it, Teach!" Andrei piped up.

I shot him a dirty look. His smile was broad and unrepentant, paired with an innocent, wide-eyed expression. I didn't like it.

Sloane shook her head stubbornly, speaking up before I could address Andrei's cheek. "You can't trust anyone here. If someone is truly trying to assassinate the Winter Lady, they won't hesitate to kill a measly human like you."

I nodded seriously. "Right. We only trust each other. Always move in pairs. Watch each other's backs. Keep an eye out for clues."

"Until we find Letitia and go back to New Orleans," Sloane added fiercely.

I hesitated, not liking the sound of that. Going back to New Orleans meant that I'd have to face the truth. Something I'd been studiously avoiding thinking about ever since I killed Kroxius. Ben was gone. He'd never come back. I dug my fingers into my pack and stroked Goliath. The little mouse had made himself at home in my bag, no doubt finding it preferable to riding on my shoulder. I was a lot more violence-prone than his previous master. The only things Goliath had needed to worry about when hitching a ride on the necromancer's shoulder were Ben tripping over his own feet or flinging dirt everywhere in his attempts at gardening.

Ben.

A hard lump formed in my throat as thoughts of the necromancer danced in my mind's eye. I caught Magnus looking at me sympathetically, and I hurriedly brushed the back of my hand across my eyes.

"Yeah," I muttered. "Until we find Letitia and head back to New Orleans."

Sloane nodded once in satisfaction and settled back with her arms folded over her chest for warmth. I busied myself mulling over potential murderers capable of regicide in the diplomatic party from the Winter Court. Anything to keep myself distracted from the thoughts of Ben.

Other than that single fraught conversation, the entire journey turned into a blur of bizarre routine. Wake up. Gulp down a cold breakfast of jerky and fae traveler's bread. Slide over the hard-packed snow while my legs cramped and my ass grew numb. Make camp. Eat. Stand guard. Kill wassets. Sleep. Stand guard. Kill more wassets. Repeat. At least I had the chance to rest while on the back of the sled.

Eventually, I got so used to the motion of the sled that as soon as I sat down on the furs, I fell into a waking coma, not really registering what was going on around me. I felt sorry for our driver. He looked like he'd aged about ten years over the course of the week it took us to reach the border of Spring.

The change between Winter and Spring was almost unnoticeable at first, like a gradual thaw. Ice floated down flowing rivers, making them more difficult to cross. Snowdrops and daffodils fought through the crust of ice, splashing color against the otherwise stark, white scenery. They changed the runners on the sled out for clever wheel attachments that were better equipped for the new terrain. I slowly shed layers until I was down to a light woolen tunic and leggings and was still sweating.

The best thing to come out of the week of travel was that the wound in my shoulder had healed up. It was still a blotchy, angry red under newly mended skin, but at least it didn't hurt anymore. The dark purple frostbite at the edges had healed completely as well, thanks to the unguent Captain Frost had given me. I'd carefully wrapped the small bottle in an extra shirt and tucked it in my bag. Mostly to save the remaining ointment, but also to protect myself from the smell. A week of the Winter medicine as my only perfume was more than enough for my olfactory tolerance levels.

Midmorning on the seventh day, we broke through the wild terrain and stumbled onto a hard-packed dirt road surrounded by lush green trees alternately decorated with fragrant white blooms and the faintest dusting of frost. Our taciturn sled driver let out a sigh of relief. "I didn't want to say it until now in case I jinxed us, what with all the wassets plaguing our every step, but welcome to Spring!" A relieved smile lit his face as a warm breeze lightly scented with wildflowers tickled the small hairs framing my face.

I craned my head to look around the driver's shoulder. A shining castle covered in flowering vines stood at the top of a distant hill. I briefly closed my eyes and let my head fall back against the hard wood of the sled as I heard Sloane let out a long exhale of relief. Within the day, we'd be off the road, away from bloodthirsty wassets, and able to enjoy a bath and a bed.

The driver pointed at the castle. "That's the Spring Court," he said unnecessarily. "We'll be safe once we reach it."

If only we'd known then how wrong he was.

Chapter 23

Estaria called a halt just as the sun crested its zenith. Glad to stretch my legs, I jumped out and headed off to find a private place to do my business. When I came back with a much relieved bladder, it surprised me to find two large tents standing amid a flurry of activity.

I sidled up to Sloane. "What's happening? Usually, we barely get enough time to pee when we stop and now there are tents?"

Sloane passed over a small sandwich made of crusty bread from last night's dinner, stuffed with a large wedge of crumbly cheese that tasted faintly of nuts and apricots. "We're traveling with the fae equivalent of royalty. It doesn't do to just rock up at your destination covered in road grime, sweat, and gods know what else."

"But we could just grab a shower or bath or whatever once we get there, can't we? I mean, they *know* how long travel takes from one court to the other, don't they?"

"Appearances matter." Sloane leaned close to me and sniffed audibly. "And so do smells." She wrinkled her nose and waved a hand in front of her face dramatically.

"Hey!" I swatted at her.

Sloane chuckled as she dodged. "Besides, I don't know about you, but I'll be glad to change into something a little lighter," she said, tugging at the woolen tunic.

"You've got me there," I replied, feeling sweat bead and drip down the backs of my knees.

One woman stuck her head out of the smaller of the two tents. She shaded her eyes from the midday glare, intently searching for someone. When her eyes landed on us, she gave an impatient wave.

"That's our cue," Sloane said before popping the rest of her sandwich in her mouth. I gulped down my sandwich quickly as I followed her inside.

Estaria sat in the single tub in the middle of the tent with fragrant bubbles up to her chin. I didn't know how the fae had managed such a feat as a bubble bath in the middle of a makeshift camp. It *had* to be magic.

While the Winter Lady enjoyed the luxury of a long soak, we rushed through a quick sponge bath. The fae women basically stripped Sloane and me out of our travel clothes as soon as the tent flap swung shut. My necklace caught on my tunic, and I had to convince my overly zealous helper to allow me to disentangle it before she choked me to death. I carefully unsnagged the necklace. She looked like she wanted to take the necklace as well, so I made a point of settling the chain with the oblong gold charm and silver ring carefully back around my neck. The fae woman huffed, but scampered away with my dirty clothes under one arm.

I grabbed a towel from a passing servant and wrapped it around myself. Sloane chuckled. "You're not self-conscious, are you?"

I whispered haughtily. "No. I mean, not usually. But they're all freaking fae! Being gorgeous is in their DNA so deep that they'd have to be rotting corpses before their genetic dominance faded."

"Wow. Morbid much?" Sloane shook her head. "Besides, you've got nothing to worry about in the looks department."

"Says you," I grumbled, folding my arms over the towel.

"Yes. Says me. Now, just sit back and relax. Think of this like a day at the spa."

The woman who'd taken my clothes came back with a bowl of steaming water and a small, clean cloth. She dipped the cloth in the bowl before silently tugging on the towel I had firmly clamped around my body.

I tugged back, looking wildly around at Sloane as another servant started washing her back.

"Sloane!" I hissed.

She looked over at me and laughed. The leprechaun chortled at the fear in my eyes. "I've seen you look less scared when you were ready to tackle a nest of vampires almost single-handedly!"

"That's because I knew what to do! The pointy end of my sword goes into the other guy. But here? I... No... I mean... what is she..." my voice trailed off as Sloane let loose another boisterous guffaw.

She wiped her eyes. "Just a day at the spa, Cam. It's just a day at the spa," she reminded me through her giggles.

"And this is why I don't go to the spa!" I snatched the bowl and tugged at the cloth until the servant let go. I took my prizes and headed towards the most secluded corner of the tent. Then, I washed the worst of the dirt off. Alone. By the time I was finished, the servant woman had laid out a new set of clothes for me and disappeared again.

A sky-blue dress with slits almost up to my waist on either side fell to my knees over thin lavender leggings. It wasn't an ensemble I would've picked for myself, but it was comfortable and easy to move in. I'll admit, the supple, light brown leather boots that accompanied the ensemble would've looked a lot better than my black and red ones, but I wasn't about to stuff my boots into a bag just because it clashed with my dress, appearances be damned.

Sloane strode up as I was trying to tug the laces of the dress into place. She wore a matching ensemble and looked traveler-chic. However, she'd found the time to smooth on a bit of makeup and run a brush through her hair until it gleamed while I was still fighting with my dress.

I stared at her. "How? Just how?"

"Like I said, think of it as a day at the spa. But with pixies. Which you should use. You've got a little something." She licked her thumb and wiped away the offending smudge on my cheek.

"Hey! Stop it!" I said, rubbing the back of my hand along my cheek. "When did you become a middle-aged mom?"

"Since you can't look after yourself. But seriously. Go see the pixies before we break camp."

"Why? I look fine," I protested.

"Maybe from the neck down."

"Hey!"

She glanced down at my feet. "And the ankle up. Seriously? *Those* boots?"

"They're custom!" I huffed.

Sloane pointed towards the glowing mass of pixies flittering around Estaria. The Winter Lady wore a long violet dress that billowed in the breeze every time the tent flap opened. Amid the flickering, flying mass of sparkly beauticians, Estaria looked every inch a fae princess.

Sloane gave me a little nudge. "Seriously, Cam. Pixies. Now. Go."

"Fine," I grumbled, but headed off to my first trip to the fairy-run day spa. In a tent. In the middle of nowhere.

I'd rather fight a troll.

Chapter 24

I learned two things about pixies at the most random day spa in all of Fae. One, they are extremely bossy for beings that are so small they can sit on the palm of my hand with room to spare. Two, I was sorely tempted to step on them once or twice. Accidentally of course.

Sloane pulled out a handheld mirror for me when the pixies had finished. I barely recognized the person who stared back at me from the silvery surface. Sure, I mean, it was *me*. The face, the hair, the eyes were all me, but somehow *more*. My skin had that dewy fresh look only found on social media with a buttload of prep time plus filters. My hair gleamed and curled, giving me old-fashioned movie star vibes. Whatever the pixies had done to enhance my eyes was nothing short of magic. The gold depths twinkled with alluring mystery, drawing me into my reflection in the mirror.

Whoa. Note to self. Don't drink the water.

"See? Look what a little time and effort does?" Sloane said primly.

I mentally apologized for even thinking of stepping on the fairy beauticians. "Do you think they make those pixies in travel size?"

Sloane smacked me lightly with the mirror. "Shh, they'll hear you!" She chuckled past the finger in front of her lips.

"I mean, seriously? They're already teeny, but a travel-sized fairy would be so awesome. But how would you take one on a plane? Do you think they're less than three ounces?" I eyed one speculatively as it flitted by. "They've got to be, right?"

Sloane dragged me away as silent laughter shook her body.

Magnus and Andrei found us a little while later. They both wore similar outfits to ours, but their blue shirts were tucked in and hidden behind silvery waistcoats. Okay, I'll admit it. Magnus looked drop-dead handsome in his new clothes. He'd even found time to shave off the beard that he'd sported by the time we arrived in the Winter Court. Andrei, on the other hand, kept running a finger around his collar and tugging at the waistcoat. He looked like he wanted to shift and run as far away from the confining clothes as he could manage.

Sloane rolled her eyes. "Come here, pup. I'll get you sorted." She stood on tiptoe and started fussing with the laces on his shirt. Andrei looked over her head desperately.

"Sorry, kid," I grinned unsympathetically. "You're on your own. I know better than to fight with her." I gestured at everything from the hair to the outfit. "This is what she does. Just be glad she doesn't turn you over to the pixies," I said with a wicked wink.

Andrei looked ready to bolt, but Sloane was muttering darkly as she pulled and readjusted his borrowed clothes. I sidled away before I could get pulled into her crazy. Magnus drifted along with me.

"If that is what Sloane does, she's in the wrong profession running her bar," Magnus said, his voice pitched low and for my ears only.

My cheeks warmed. "Don't tell her that. She'll take it personally."

Magnus chuckled as we strolled towards our converted sled. "I've been around her long enough to know that, at least." His expression shifted into something gentler. "How are you doing?"

I was about to run a hand through my hair before I remembered the styling. I ended up flapping it around in midair as I spoke. "Confused still. I mean, between all the wasset attacks and now arriving in the Spring Court, I haven't seen or heard anything that might point to Estaria's conspiracy theory other than the supposition the wasset attacks might be linked somehow. Maybe Captain Frost is right. It's all in her head. But then again, maybe there *is* a murderer, and she is just biding her time. Or he. Or it. I don't know which pronoun to use with all these fae creatures around."

Magnus put his hands on my shoulders, stopping my rambling. "I meant, how are *you* doing? We haven't really had time to sit down and talk since you killed Kroxius."

I heard was he was saying between the words. *We haven't really talked about Ben.*

My eyes burned, and I looked away, furiously blinking back tears. "I'm fine. It's fine. Everything is fine."

His thumbs stroked comforting circles on my shoulders. I saw him nod out of the corner of my eye. "Well, when that 'fine' cracks, I'm here."

I managed a small nod before Sloane and Andrei joined us. The caravan started its slow roll towards the Spring Court. We quickly jumped into our converted sled before we could get left behind.

Goliath clambered out of my bag and reclaimed his place on my shoulder. Apparently, he deemed it much safer now that the dangers of frostbite and snow wassets had faded. He seemed excited as we moved at a properly sedate pace towards the home of the Spring Court. He was constantly patting my cheek or tugging at my hair to get me to look this way or that.

I wondered if the little mouse behaved the same way when he rode on Ben's shoulder. If so, I had more sympathy for the necromancer, always appearing distracted. It was like always having a nearly invisible partner with you. I'd have to be careful, or I'd start talking to the little creature, too.

The procession rolled up to the waiting contingent from the Spring Court. I studied the crowd of fae curiously until I saw someone I recognized. Hemlock was waiting for us. His snowy white beard and purple livery stood out amid the cheerful, smiling Spring fae dressed entirely in shades of green and pink. The barbegazi's frosted white beard stuck out like a ghost in the middle of a garden party. His magic must extend to his beardsicles because they jangled merrily in the Spring sunshine.

"How did he get so far ahead of us? Didn't we eat dinner with him last night?" I whispered.

"The royal foxes, remember?" Sloane whispered back. "With their speed, he can get almost anywhere in half the time it would take the rest of us."

"He left late last night," Magnus chimed in. "I assume that's how the Spring Court knew we were coming?" The lift in his voice made it a question.

I smacked the heel of my hand against my forehead. "Of course. No phones. No email. No instant communication. Sorry, that's still taking some getting used to."

Sloane nodded. "Fae tried using homing pigeons for a while. Or the fae equivalent, which of course, came with a lot more teeth and claws. Some nasty venom too, now that I think of it. However, they kept disappearing. Everyone assumed they got eaten."

"Sounds like unreliable communication," I said.

"It was. But even with all that, the birds were better than using pixies. Every so often, someone tried to convince the pixies to convey messages between courts or wherever. But pixies are a lot more fickle than the birds ever were. They kept getting distracted by shiny objects or the rain or the clouds or sometimes just by their own thoughts."

"Sounds like somebody I know?" I said, playfully elbowing Andrei.

"Hey!" he said. "Umm, what're we talking about?"

I chuckled. "My point exactly."

Sloane tried to rein us in. "Alright everyone, best behavior. Try not to mess anything up. Don't make promises. Don't drip wine down the front of your shirt."

"She's talking to you there, not me," said Magnus to me out of the side of his mouth.

"I've done nothing of the sort!" I protested.

"Yeah. Today. Give it time," Sloane muttered.

"See?" Magnus said with a wink. The werewolf's cheeky grin made him even more attractive than he had any right to be. My heart gave a little flutter. I had to look away quickly.

Sloane ignored us. "And keep your eyes and ears open for anyone acting shady."

Andrei glanced at her. "Like the trees?" he asked, attempting to be funny.

Sloane maintained a serious expression, but her eyes twinkled. "Don't be ridiculous. This is Spring. Here, the trees are all best buds. They only start getting shady in Summer."

Andrei groaned at the terrible pun. "Really?"

"You're not the only one who can stir the pot, kid," Sloane said.

Andrei shook his head, choosing to redirect the conversation back toward serious matters. "Has Cam finally convinced you into thinking that Estaria might be right? That there is some sort of murderer traveling with us?"

Sloane tipped her head to either side in a silent equivocation, but I spoke up before she could. "Worse comes to worst, the only thing we waste is a little time while we are waiting for Letitia to open a portal for us."

"In your scenario, that means that the best case is that we track down a dangerous killer," Magnus pointed out.

I shot him a glare. "Don't go getting all logic-y on me now. You know what I mean. If we've got nothing better to do, we might as well do some casual snooping."

"I can think of loads of things better to do than hunting down a murderer, fictitious or not," Magnus replied. "Eating. Drinking. More eating. Sleep. More drinking. Followed by some more eating."

"Good Lord, I wish I had your metabolism!" I exclaimed.

Sloane leaned over. "He's not wrong. I mean, how often are you in Fae? Come to think of it, how often are *any* humans in Fae anymore? Think of all those delicacies to sample. If the Spring Court is anything like it was when I lived here, they are the reason humans in fairy tales always ended up stuck here. The food is exquisite. Spring is known for its fresh produce, the best chefs, and the most exquisite feasts. Trust me, we're in for a real treat."

"A feast like the feast at the Winter Court?" I asked, dubiously. While the stew and hard bread had filled the gaping hole in my stomach left by a week of hard travel, it hadn't been anything extravagant.

"Nothing like that," Sloane assured me. "Again, it's been years, but Spring always was the place to go if you wanted delicious food, better drinks, and fantastic parties. Spring kicks Winter's butt in everything but skiing, sledding, and Christmas. Although, I wouldn't be surprised if a Spring Court Christmas outclassed a Winter Court Christmas just on the food alone." Sloane waved a finger under my nose for emphasis.

My mouth watered, but before I could probe for more delicious details, Lady Estaria raised her arm at the front of the caravan.

A flurry of shimmering snowflakes danced from her fingertips in all directions, spiraling through the air with a sparkle of silver and brilliant white magic. I jumped in surprise when a veritable explosion of pixies sprang to life from their respective parts of the caravan as if on signal. Except for helping with camp setup and making my hair look red-carpet-worthy, the little beings had mostly kept to themselves, but now they sprang into action with twinkling exuberance. The entire contingent from Winter performed aerial acrobatics in such an array of intricate patterns and colors that the living firework display dazzled my eyes.

"They may not be the smartest of creatures, but they know how to put on a show," Sloane observed.

"Yeah," was all I managed as I tried to watch everything at once.

The pixies from the Spring Court leapt into the sky, not to be outdone by their Winter counterparts. Soon, the clearing in front of the castle was lit by pirouetting, sparkling pixies throwing what looked like glitter everywhere.

Our driver cursed softly under his breath. I jumped. I hadn't heard him speak more than was absolutely necessary. He brushed hastily at his arms and ran a furious hand through his hair. He caught me staring and frowned. "Pixie dust. I *hate* pixie dust. It gets everywhere and doesn't come out for days!" With that said, the taciturn driver turned his grumpy expression back to the road.

I turned wide eyes to Sloane as the glitter settled in her hair. "Pixie dust? Like Peter Pan? If I think happy thoughts right now, can I fly?"

"Yes, yes, and it's probably best not to try right now," Sloane whispered to me.

I matched her volume. "Why is that?"

"Because the Winter Lady is officially meeting the Spring Lord and Lady for the first time and you flapping wildly in midair before crashing on their heads probably wouldn't make a good first impression."

"How do you know I'd crash?"

Sloane looked at me like I was an idiot. "Because everyone crashes the first time."

My jaw snapped shut, but I filed that away along with the myriad of other questions that sprang to life for a better time. Over the throng of the gathering courts, a familiar face appeared. It was the one person I'd been hoping to see.

Letitia.

Chapter 25

The train of cleverly converted vehicles surrounded Estaria as she dismounted from her sled. I noticed that the two-tailed royal foxes stood proudly in front of the Winter Lady as she moved to greet her Spring counterparts.

I muttered under my breath to Sloane. "Wait. I thought Hemlock took the foxes when he left last night?"

"Well yeah. They returned," Sloane whispered back. "They're really smart, you know."

Something clicked into place for me. "And we're just supposed to believe that they threw the Winter Lord in such a way that he broke his neck?"

"Cam, this is so *not* the time," Sloane murmured, barely moving her lips as she widened her eyes in a silent appeal for me to *shut the fuck up already.*

I persisted. "But it doesn't make sense."

Magnus cupped my elbow and leaned close. His breath tickled my ear. "You are drawing the wrong kinds of attention right now."

I glanced around. Several of the Spring Court were staring directly at me. I wouldn't go so far as to say they were glowering, but it wasn't far off. I shut my mouth.

The Spring Lord was a stern-looking man with olive skin and dark features. He wore a formal jacket of brilliant, new-leaf green, heavily decorated in elaborate golden swirls. If there was any doubt of his rank in the court, a gold crown made of curling vines and artistically placed gold flowers sat regally on his dark hair. If I'd met him almost anywhere else, I would've called him menacingly powerful, and it still probably wouldn't have been enough to describe the sudden shivers dancing up my spine.

On the other hand, his lady was all bright laughter to his dark smolder. Her blonde hair was like spun gold, cascading over her shoulders to her waist. Brilliant green eyes dominated her face, drawing me in with their intelligent sparkle. A crown of delicate pink blooms nestled in the luxurious tresses and perfectly matched the color of her gown. A blonde girl who looked to be in either late childhood or early teens stood behind the Spring Lady. I noticed she had the same intense eyes as the woman. I wondered if it was a family trait. Perhaps this was the lord and lady's daughter? I wracked my brain, trying to remember if it had ever been mentioned.

Estaria turned to face us. I'd obviously missed the formal introductions. She gestured towards us with a gentle flick of her wrist. "This is the party from the human realm who graciously accompanied us from Winter. I believe they know a member of your Court."

Letitia slipped around the blonde child. She looked pale and worn. There were hollows in her cheeks that hadn't been there the last time I'd seen her, and her simple gown of pink embroidered with curling green leaves hung off her gaunt frame. I stared in shock at her frail state. She smiled at me fiercely, and I nodded in acknowledgment of her unspoken words. I was thankful the lich's curse had been reversed in time. Letitia would be ok. She was a survivor, and she would recover from Kroxius's death curse too. Now that he was dead.

Seeing that she was alive and working her way back to health brought me an unexpected sense of relief. I guess I knew Letitia was in danger, but it had never really occurred to me she might succumb to the curse. Looking at her, I had a sudden realization of just how close she'd come.

Letitia dipped in a perfect curtsy, flaring her pink and green gown dramatically. "Yes, my Lady Estaria. Cameron and her companions have done all of Fae a great service by ridding us of the lich who attacked our Embassy without provocation and unlawfully invaded the Fae realm. They have saved countless lives through their swift and decisive actions. Including mine."

"Are they okay? The rest of the injured, I mean. Are they going to recover?" I blurted out. I garnered looks of surprise and dismay at the interruption to the formal proceedings, but I couldn't help myself. I needed to know.

Letitia chose her words carefully. "The healers have been able to save everyone who survived the journey to the Spring Court."

My heart clenched. *Everyone who survived.* But that didn't mean everyone. I wondered if any more had died since the last time I spoke with Letitia through the stone before the magical connection fizzled out.

Estaria turned and pretended to study us carefully. "What a marvelous thing to ride with such esteemed company! They have kept the tale of their exploits rather close to their chests." She waggled a reprimanding finger at us teasingly. Titters from both the Winter and Spring gatherings erupted at her words.

I had to admire her verbal tap dancing. She knew precisely what we had done and why, but very few others did. I wondered if dancing close to the truth without revealing all of it was a common trait among all fae or if it was unique to Estaria.

The Spring Lord cleared his throat. Letitia stepped back, providing introductions in a firm voice that belied her frail appearance. "This is Lord Treston and Lady Aubrette, of the Spring Court. My lord and lady, allow me to introduce Cameron Blaze, Sloane O'Shea, Magnus Donovan, and Andrei Lykaios."

We all bowed to the Spring Lord and Lady. I was pleased when I didn't perform a repeat of the awkward flailing that had occurred when I met Estaria.

"Ah, these are the ones, are they? The humans who assisted in the battle at your Embassy in New Orleans?" Lord Treston rumbled in a deep bass.

"Indeed, my Lord," Letitia said.

Lady Aubrette laid a delicate hand on her husband's arm and looked up at him through her lashes. Her eyes were a stunning green. She obviously knew how to wield them to their full effect. "Dearest husband, should we not throw wide the gates of Spring and welcome in these travelers as the heroes they are?"

"I mean…" Lord Treston started.

Lady Aubrette caught her husband's hand in her free one. "I agree, my Lord. We owe them so much. The lives of our people. The life of our niece." She gestured at Letitia. My gaze snapped to Letitia. The faintest pink tinge crept up her cheeks as she avoided my eyes.

"Of course. I mean… if… well…" Lord Treston stuttered to a stop as he looked down into his wife's imploring eyes. He let out a long sigh and patted her hand. In that moment, I had no doubt that the crown might rest on Treston's head, but Lady Aubrette was the neck that turned the head. By the way he looked down at her with amused resignation, I think he knew it too.

"You are right, of course, my lady." Lord Treston turned to us. "We owe you a great boon, but until it can be repaid, please consider the Spring Court your home for the duration of your visit to Fae, with no expectation of obligation or return."

Sloane sucked in a breath. I did better at hiding my surprise. The Spring Lord had just openly admitted that he owed us. In front of witnesses. My mind spiraled into thoughts of what I could ask for. Images of an enchanted cornucopia that produced whatever was asked of it, or magical clothes that morphed into anything the wearer could imagine, or mythological weapons that possessed mysterious powers all danced in front of my eyes before I reined my mischievous subconscious back under control.

When no one else spoke, I reluctantly stepped forward. "It was our pleasure to assist a friend such as Lady Letitia, my Lord," I said simply and ducked my head in a bow again.

With that bit of business sorted, I could almost see Lord Treston mentally dusting off his hands and moving on to the next thing on his to-do list. He raised his voice and spoke to the entire Winter contingent. "Please be welcome in our home. With the help of our friend, Emissary Hemlock, we have prepared a sumptuous feast for your party to enjoy, Lady Estaria, with no expectation of obligation or return for any food or hospitality for the duration of your stay with the Spring Court."

"Except for the hope of continued peace and prosperity between our two courts," Lady Aubrette added with a brilliant smile as she parted the fae of the Spring Court with a slight wave of her hand to allow us entry into the castle.

The head and the neck indeed.

Chapter 26

My first sight of the Spring Court stole my breath away. Vines crawled up the walls and flowers exploded in a riot of colors against a thick backdrop of leaves. The Spring gardeners weren't content to keep their craft confined to the ground, it seemed. Attendants seemed to magically appear from what I eventually discerned as cleverly hidden doorways in the foliage. The attendants rushed around in a flurry of activity, pressing welcome drinks into our hands, and offering silver trays piled high with sweets.

I glanced at Sloane, not wanting to make a misstep. She caught my eye and whispered, "Lord Tristan gave us a free pass for as long as we are in his court. No fancy wordplay like Estaria did. Don't worry." To emphasize her point, she plucked a small, sculpted chocolate flower from a passing fae's tray and popped it into her mouth.

I blew out a relieved breath. "That's good news. I wasn't looking forward to having to turn all this down," I said.

Sloane chuckled. "I've always liked Spring the best out of the Courts."

"I can see why! No frostbite and snacks? Sign me up!" I selected a plump purple berry from a passing attendant and popped it into my mouth. The tart sweetness made my lips pucker and my hips to a happy wiggle.

"Hush!" Sloane swatted at me. "Don't say that where one of the Winter fae can hear you!"

I swallowed. "You're right. Frostbite from magical ice weapons sucks. I don't want to endure that again if I can help it. However, the truth was the truth."

"No arguments here," Sloane said as one of the liveried Spring fae approached and led us to our rooms. We shared a silent smile as he led us and the two wolves to our accommodations.

The opulent apartment for my sole use was five rooms of lavish comfort. I assume that Sloane and the werewolves were shown to similar accommodations as Spring fae led them to identical doors off the same corridor. However, I got so lost in exploring my rooms, I didn't even check. My bedroom had a massive four-poster bed that was big enough for at least five people. It was piled high with a mountain of cushions that beckoned to me with downy whispers of slumber. I had a sudden urge to launch myself into the bed and sleep for days. Goliath must've had the same urge because he detached himself from my hair as soon as he saw the bed and curled up on a small, pink pillow near the head of the bed. The tiny mouse was fast asleep in no time.

I chuckled as I watched his cute little nose twitch in his sleep. I was tempted to join him when a sharp rap sounded on my door. I opened it to find Sloane. I let out a low whistle. Somehow, she'd changed clothes already and looked amazing in a mid-length dress of azure blue trimmed in deep fuchsia and covered in abstract splashes of tangerine orange, buttery yellow, and merlot red. Her knee-high boots were a brilliant pistachio color. I knew that if I'd tried to wear that ensemble, I would've looked like a clown trying to escape cosmetology school, but somehow, she pulled it off.

She held out a hand in shocked dismay as she pushed into my room. "What are you doing? Why aren't you ready? Didn't you hear them? There's a feast waiting for us! Something other than fae traveler's bread and jerky. The guys have already gone down! What's wrong with you? C'mon, let's go!" She clapped her hands at me as she headed for the wardrobe. I chuckled and followed along. I'd been friends with Sloane too long not to recognize the signs when she was on the verge of becoming hangry.

In a whirl of hunger driven efficiency, Sloane plucked a floaty Tuscany yellow dress shot through with splashes of soft apricot from the closet along with matching embroidered slippers. She shoved the ensemble into my arms with an order to get changed. Surprisingly, it looked better on me than it did in the closet. It also fit remarkably well. So well, in fact, that I wondered if there wasn't some sort of tailoring magic at work. The absolute best thing about the dress, though, were the pockets hidden along the seams.

"What's with the colors?" I asked, spinning around in front of the mirror. "I look like an escapee from a paint sample shop."

"You do not!" Sloane exclaimed, swatting at me. "Besides, this is Spring. Everything is brighter here. Now, hurry up already. I'm hungry!"

"Are you sure I can't wear my boots?" I asked, as she linked an arm through mine and tugged me towards the door.

"Positive. They clash with your outfit and trust me, they will judge you for crimes against fashion," Sloane assured me.

"What if I tell them the boots are enchanted?" I asked, shooting one last plaintive look over my shoulder.

Sloane snorted. "This is Fae. Everything here is enchanted."

A Spring guard stood outside my door, waiting to escort us to the feast. If the Spring feast was anything like the Winter feast had been, I was distinctly over dressed and possibly should have searched my room for extra rations before leaving.

The doors to the banquet hall were flung wide and a herald in bright green livery announced us in a booming voice. Suddenly, I didn't feel so out of place in my bright dress. As I looked at the lavish display of the Spring Court flexing its incredible might, I lost my ability to words the form. That is, speak the letters. I mean, word the sentences.

Ah, screw it.

The Spring banquet hall was a riot of color and texture where Winter had been sparse and cold. Creatures of all shapes and sizes moved through the room with an air of joyous frivolity. Someone had cleverly maneuvered living walls of vines and flowers throughout the hall to create a variety of unique rooms. Each nook was filled with delicacies to sample. An array of complimentary drinks lined a discreet alcove in each room. Sloane snagged two tiny crystal flutes filled with a brilliant green liquor that tasted citrusy with a fresh, almost minty finish. It made me feel awake, alert, and ever so slightly buzzed after just a couple of sips. Sloane winked at me knowingly and clinked her glass to mine.

I continued my wide-eyed examination of the Spring Court's feast as I sipped carefully from the flute. There were even secluded dining areas off the grand primary thoroughfare that could seat anywhere from two to twenty people. The Spring fae had carpeted the entire floor with lush moss and rose petals that seemed to magically retain their vibrancy, no matter how many feet trod on them.

I quickly noticed that each section of the hall seemed to be color-coded by the flowers that formed the partitions. I nodded to myself in appreciation. That bit of knowledge made it much easier to navigate the massive hall.

Sloane got roped into conversation with some elves almost as soon as we entered. They looked like they might be related to Rudolph, the wood elf bartender Sloane employed at the Forge. I'd expected Sloane to be more uptight as the elves chatted away at her, but eventually she started cracking a joke or two of her own that had the others laughing uproariously and slapping their thighs. Sloane never spoke too highly of Fae when we were in New Orleans. Or since we'd been in Fae. In fact, as long as I'd known her, Sloane had actively sought to avoid returning here. However, she seemed to be loosening up. Maybe she had indulged too quickly in the citrusy green liquor. I chuckled to myself at the thought as I drained my glass.

I set the empty flute on a passing server's tray and quickly decided I needed to investigate the various other offerings the Spring Court had hidden throughout the hall. I shot a discreet look at Sloane before wandering on my merry way, but she waved me off with an amiable smile. She looked more comfortable here than I'd seen her in the entire time I'd been in Fae. I took that as a good sign and set off to explore.

I meandered through the hall; the sights, the sounds, the smells, the Spring-i-ness of it all making me nearly giddy. After all the turmoil of the last few weeks, it felt glorious to let my mind go blank and just enjoy the moment.

I glimpsed what looked like a swarm of determined little pixies flitting all over Krampus. The anti-Santa looked like Spring had sprung all over him. His matted fur was now a pristine white. It even glistened with sparkling fairy dust when he shifted uncomfortably. Elaborate braids of fur decorated with flowers and brightly colored ribbons stuck out in all directions. Krampus looked a little wild around the eyes, twitching as though he wanted to make a break for it, but was too scared of squashing one of the tiny pixies flying around his head. I chuckled and wondered what he would look like when his makeover was complete.

Letitia appeared out of the crowd and held out a glass of wine to me. I smiled and accepted it. "How are you doing, Letitia?" I asked.

She shrugged a too thin shoulder. "I've been better, but I'll heal, eventually."

"Good. I'm glad to hear it. What about the rest of your people?"

Letitia smiled sadly. "About a third survived."

My stomach dropped. Only a third?

Letitia read the dismay on my face and reached out, squeezing my hand. "You saved a lot of people, Cam. The survivors from the attack on the Embassy owe you their lives."

"If only..." I paused, not really knowing what else to say. Letitia nodded sadly. We stood there in silence, trying to make sense of a needless tragedy brought about by one man's desire for power. The Spring fae swirled around us, enjoying the festivities spread throughout the hall. I raised my glass to Letitia, who clicked hers against mine. We sipped. I was grateful that we had both lived long enough to be here this evening.

Music flooded the hall. I turned to see Brio, the Autumn bard, strumming his lute from a small stage across the hall. Cheers erupted as the bard struck a sharp, short chord on his fae lute. Seeing him reminded me of the first time I'd seen him play in Winter. Just after I'd killed Kroxius. The man who'd killed all those people, including...

Ben.

My thoughts skittered back from memories that threatened to drag me under, but I wasn't quick enough.

"I don't get it," I muttered darkly, half to myself.

Letitia leaned closer. "Don't get what, Cam?"

"How can you be this okay? With your people dying? I mean, just last week they were alive and running around New Orleans. And now?" I trailed off as it became impossible to talk past the constriction in my throat.

Letitia eyed me strangely. "We're not okay, Cam. *I'm* not okay. But this is how we deal with death in the Spring Court. Everyone has different ways of dealing with death. This is ours." She gestured with her goblet at the party. "Rather than focusing on our pain at losing our loved ones too soon or feeling sorry for ourselves, we focus on their lives. We celebrate all the wonderful things they did and the joy they brought into our world. We share stories, drink to their memories, and honor their contributions. That is what this party really is. It's not just for you or the Winter Lady. It's partially for the survivors of the death curse, but more importantly, it's for *them*. My people. The ones who didn't make it." She choked out the last words past the tears pooling in her eyes. She hid behind her wine glass, stealing a moment to compose herself as Brio started a sad, slow song.

A hush fell over the crowd. Brio took us on a musical journey, honoring those who had fallen. With the deft skill of a lifetime musician, he blended the end of the lament into a melody laden with hope for the future.

Letitia and I stood side by side, lost in our own thoughts even as the bard finished, and his admirers pulled him into a fawning crowd of adoration. Neither of us moved, not ready to talk yet.

A sharp, unexpected shove in my back broke the spell Brio's music had cast over me and sent me stumbling forward. I spun, already grabbing for my shadows. An insubstantial karambit formed in the palm of my free hand. I was a hair's breadth away from trying to pull it into sharp focus when I saw who my attacker was.

A child. An *angry* child, but a child, nonetheless.

Chapter 27

The shadows gathered in my palms dribbled through my fingers like fragments of a barely remembered dream.

A tickle of memory brushed against the back of my mind as I stared down at the beautiful blonde child glaring up at me. She was petite. The top of her head barely reached my shoulders. Her heart-shaped face was surrounded by a luxurious fall of thick golden hair. There was every sign that she would be breathtakingly beautiful in a few years. However, a mild air of awkwardness clung to her that could only be erased with time. The same aura of uncertainty that hovered around all newly minted teens. But this was Fae. She might have been a hundred and this could all be a glamour. The thing that really convinced me she was likely as young as she looked was the unexplained rage snapping in the depths of her brilliant green eyes. The same stunning shade as the Spring Lady's. I suddenly remembered wondering if they were related. If so, how had I made the daughter of the Spring Lord and Lady this angry at me already?

The girl thrust out her arms to shove me again. However, she telegraphed the move plainly. I dodged. She went lurching past me. The girl flailed for balance as she nearly careened into a rather rotund dwarf's backside as he sampled sweets from a server's tray. The fingers of her outstretched hand caught my necklace as she fell. I stumbled forwards. The chain dug into my neck while she fought for stability, but they didn't design the delicate piece of jewelry for such abrupt tension. Under the unexpected pressure, the thin chain snapped. The charm and the ring both fell, almost getting lost in the moss underfoot. My heart stuttered as I watched both spiral towards the ground.

Letitia suddenly appeared at my side, smoothly taking my wine glass, and placing it alongside hers on the tray of a passing server. The girl regained her balance and whirled on me. A mask of rage contorted her beautiful features into something ugly.

Letitia's calm voice arrested any movement from the girl. "That wasn't very nice, Blythe. We wouldn't want to cause a scene." Letitia folded her hands in front of her demurely and forced a brilliant smile. She looked serenely out over the crowded room, as if she didn't have a care in the world.

"Do you know who she is? What she's done? How can you stand to be around her?" The girl's voice was trembling, but whether with anger or something else, I couldn't tell. Before I could figure it out, Letitia narrowed her eyes and leaned over to whisper urgently in the child's ear. I took advantage of the brief respite to retrieve the charm and the broken chain from where they'd fallen in the moss. I shoved both into a pocket of the dress and immediately felt better. The charm had been my mother's, and I didn't want to lose it. It took me a moment more to find the small pink quartz ring in the thick layer of moss. The glint of silver amongst the green caught my eye. I was relieved as I plucked it from the spongy ground and tucked it into the opposite pocket of my dress.

Just before I had tumbled into Fae, I had figured out that the pink quartz was really a fragment of a magical relic that could hold an un-housed soul. I was fairly confident that the azure light flickering deep within the stone was such a soul, but in the chaos surrounding the pursuit of Kroxius and then the travel to Spring, I hadn't given myself the time to explore that mystery. What I knew was that I didn't want the ring to fall into someone else's hands while it might still contain a malevolent soul.

With both items back in my possession, I could finally focus on what Letitia had said. She'd called the kid Blythe.

Blythe. Why did that sound familiar?

The older fae woman stepped back, obviously concluding her whispered admonitions. Rather than being cowed, the girl named Blythe looked enraged and slightly wild around the eyes.

"You bitch!" hissed the girl as she took an aggressive step towards me.

My eyes widened in surprise. "Look, kid, I don't know who you are or who you think I am, but..."

Letitia interjected, "Blythe, really, you must calm down. Think about your godmother. Would she appreciate this type of behavior in the middle of her feast?"

The girl's gaze was so venomous that it surprised me Letitia didn't wither on the spot. "I don't care," Blythe spat out. She curled her hands into claws, green magic coalescing slowly in her palms. "You know what she did! She killed my father!" Magic coiled around her fingertips and forearms, glowing stronger with each passing heartbeat.

"Blythe! No magic! Not in the hall! You know you still can't control it!" Letitia hissed, what little color there was draining from her gaunt features.

Blythe raised her hands, more magic curling around her hands. Her brilliant green eyes snapped to mine, and I saw more than a hint of madness in them. This child was broken inside and had enough magic coiled in her palm to do some real damage. Before I could decide whether to attack or defend, Letitia sprang forward and grasped Blythe's hands firmly within her own. The older woman's smile never faltered. I'm sure to anyone observing, it looked like Letitia could've been the girl's doting older sister. However, I was close enough to see Letitia's own magic crackle to life. Hers moved much faster than Blythe's, encasing the girl's hands in a shimmering, almost transparent bubble and preempting any magical attack.

Letitia's voice was low under her unperturbed smile. "Not in your godparents' home. Besides, there is more to that story than you know. Calm now, remember your breathing exercises. You are in control. Don't give way to the chaos within."

The silent battle for magical domination raged, unbeknownst to the rest of the partygoers. In the meantime, I desperately fought past the pleasant, alcohol-induced haze I'd been enjoying and wracked my memories.

Who was Blythe? And more to the point, who was her father?

Just as Letitia's bubble of suppression magic hardened, things finally clicked into place. No wonder Blythe looked familiar. I'd seen her picture before. In Aldrich Kingsley's office. Just before I killed him.

My mouth hung open. As soon as I understood who she was, a part of me wanted to protest. To explain the situation. After a moment, my jaw snapped shut with a resigned click. No matter what I said, Blythe wasn't wrong.

I *had* killed her father.

Chapter 28

My mind whirled. Blythe's father was Aldrich Kingsley, the former fae ambassador to New Orleans. I doubted she knew that he'd kidnapped both Sloane and me to use as human sacrifices to bring his dead wife back from the Abyss. Blythe's mother. Letitia had said her mother's death had broken her mind and sent her spiraling into the depths of madness. Not that I blamed the kid. If I'd lost my mom when I was that young, I'd have gone a little crazy too. Hell, I did lose my mind when I lost my mom and I had been a lot older than Blythe appeared to be.

But the fact of the matter was that Aldrich Kingsley had been more than willing to trade Sloane and me for his wife's return, and I had disagreed with the arrangement. The truth probably didn't matter to her right now. I don't know if it ever would. All she knew was that I took her father away from her. I'd killed him before she had the chance to bring home a boyfriend, or sneak out of the house for a party, or come home a little too drunk for the first time, or whatever it was fae kids did to rebel against their protective parents.

Guilt stalked the heels of horror as I realized she might actually think that I'd taken away *both* her parents. Her mother had died in the human realm over a year ago. A victim of a drunk driving accident. However, apparently, there was a way in Fae for the deceased to come and visit their living relatives. I wasn't clear on the details, but I'd been told that visitation rights only worked if the person had died in Fae. Which is why Aldrich had been so intent on trying to pull his wife's soul out of the Abyss in that bloody ritual on Halloween. If he'd been successful, Blythe would have both her mother and father right now. Sure, Sloane and I would've been dead, but looking at the angry fae girl, I doubted she cared.

I swallowed hard. "You're Aldrich Kingsley's daughter," I said. I took a cue from Letitia. I kept my voice low and a pleasantly mild expression on my face, even though a storm of emotions roiled inside me.

"You aren't fit to say his name," Blythe snarled. She spat at me and tugged wildly against Letitia's grip. The older fae woman smoothly pulled the girl forward without releasing her hold on Blythe's hands. Letitia tucked Blythe firmly against her side. I was struck by how similar they looked. They were cousins, but they could've passed as sisters.

"Blythe," Letitia murmured in a low, warning tone.

"How can you stand to be around her? After what she did?" Blythe turned her vitriolic attack on Letitia. "Who knows? Maybe you were in on it too. You always were jealous. A power-hungry, ugly, jealous little *bitch*," Blythe spat out.

I saw Letitia's lips tighten, but that was the only outward sign that Blythe's jab had hit a nerve. An apology danced on the tip of my tongue but died when I saw hatred and madness sparking in Blythe's eyes as she struggled against her cousin's hold. An explanation or even an apology from me would make no difference to her state of mind right now. Maybe not ever.

I tried a different tack. "Look, I get that you're angry. If I were in your place, I'd be angry too."

"Yeah, but you're not in my place, are you?" Blythe snapped, redirecting her rage my way.

"No, I'm not. But I've been some place similar."

"What? Your parents got murdered, too?" Blythe bit off each word with such sarcastic precision that it felt like she punched me in the kidney with each syllable.

I kept my tone calm. "Something like that."

Blythe looked at me sharply. I don't know what she saw in my face, but the fires of all-consuming hatred in her eyes dimmed slightly, taking away a fraction of the madness too.

I took that as a good sign. I doubted we'd ever be anything close to friends. But at least I'd given her pause. Maybe my words had shaken her enough for her to see me as something other than just a killer. I opened my mouth to tell her the truth. All of it. There were too many similarities between Blythe and me. I didn't want her living with the unknown the way I'd been forced to do.

Letitia rubbed her hand over the younger girl's shoulder, cutting me off before I could make a start. "I know you are angry, Blythe, but now is not the time or place. Perhaps later…"

"Just stop it!" Blythe hissed. I saw tears pool in her eyes. She wriggled free of Letitia's hold and shoved roughly by me. I nearly lost my balance again as she jostled me in her haste to leave. Blythe disappeared into the crowd a moment later.

Letitia touched my elbow lightly. "I'd like to apologize on her behalf. She was apparently doing much better over the past few months. That is until…" Letitia paused and then spoke again. "Well, things have been understandably difficult for her. Ever since her mother passed, something hasn't been quite right." Letitia waved a vague hand around her head, obviously uncomfortable discussing her cousin's mental health.

I waved my hand tiredly. "I don't blame her. In fact, I kind of sympathize. Fate dealt her a shitty hand and it just got worse when her dad's killer, aka me, knocked on her front door. If she *didn't* react this way, I'd be worried. I just hope that she gets the help she needs."

"Well, that is very understanding of you," Letitia said diplomatically. She linked her arm through mine and gently steered me in the opposite direction. Away from Blythe and away from the whispers cascading in our wake. Apparently, we had attracted more attention than I'd thought.

Letitia spoke as we walked. "Blythe really is a sweet child. It hurts me to see her like this, especially when I don't know how to help her when she goes to that dark place inside."

"Just keep being present for her. Show up. Listen. Do your best and she'll eventually see how much you love her."

Letitia quirked an eyebrow at me. "That is…surprisingly kind of you."

"What? I can do kind. It's kids I find challenging."

The fae woman snorted lightly. "Kids. You can love 'em like crazy and they can still drive you to drink. Speaking of, I could use another glass of wine," Letitia said, pulling me towards a long table filled with promising-looking bottles.

Something Letitia had said bubbled past my confrontation with Blythe. "Speaking of kids, what did you mean when you said 'godparents'?"

"Blythe was officially adopted as a ward of the court by our aunt and uncle, the Spring Lord and Lady, when her father refused to come home from the mortal realms. They figured she needed a stabilizing influence in her life during this traumatic time and it seemed to be working. She was getting better." Letitia glanced over her shoulder again at where Blythe had disappeared. A worried frown creased her brow. "Until now."

"Give it time. It seems like she's got a good setup here with people who love her. If she's anything like her cousin, she's stronger than she looks," I said as we continued our slow stroll through the crowd. Letitia shot me an appreciative look. I decided to change topics, "But speaking of family, you got some 'splaining to do, Lucy!" I said, poorly affecting Ricky Ricardo's heavy accent.

"What? My name is Letitia, not Lucy. Just how much have you had to drink?" She peered at me critically.

"What? No. It's a TV show. Famous red head always getting into trouble... you know what? Never mind. What's this about you being the niece of the Spring Lord and Lady?"

"Oh. Yes. Well. Umm, surprise?" Letitia looked as flustered as I'd ever seen her.

"Good Lord, you can say that again! Buried that lede a little deep, didn't you?"

Letitia shook her head. "No, you made your assumptions. I just chose not to correct you. Besides, a girl can have more than one uncle, you know."

"Yeah, but not every girl's uncle is basically royalty," I argued. Then I paused, a sudden thought striking like lightning out of a clear blue sky. "Wait. Does that make you an actual fairy princess?"

A deep red color flooded her cheeks. "I'm a long way from a princess."

"But you told me to call you, and I quote, 'Lady Letitia.'"

"Yes, but only in the human realm. Things are... different here," Letitia said, grabbing two glasses at random from a nearby table. She led me out onto a spacious veranda lit by glittering fairy lights. A warm breeze tickled the loose tendrils of hair at the nape of my neck as she walked towards a secluded bench and took a seat.

"Well, you can tell me about your family or explain how we're getting home," I said, sitting next to her.

"Oh, returning to Earth is easy. The portal we came through should be recharged by the time we make the journey back there, but that will take at least five days. However, my uncle has access to a more private portal that opens into a small, rarely used embassy in South Carolina. If you don't mind a flight back to New Orleans, that is."

"Don't get me wrong, I'd love to stay here and enjoy being pampered for as long as you'll have me. But the only problem is that I don't know how long that will be in the human realm."

Letitia nodded. "I understand. We won't wait for New Orleans. We'll head to South Carolina as soon as I can apprise my uncle of the situation."

"Yeah, about that. I'd like to circle back to that minor matter of your family now, if you don't mind."

Letitia sighed. "You're like a bulldog."

"What? Adorable and everyone loves me?"

"No. Tenacious and slightly slobbery," she replied, flicking a finger at the corner of her mouth meaningfully.

I surreptitiously tried to wipe away a droplet of wine attempting to escape. Letitia chuckled. I dabbed at my lips carefully as I spoke. "Look, not that I don't appreciate a good stall tactic. I do. But I'm not letting this one go."

"Fine," Letitia tossed back her wine as if she were steeling herself for battle. "Let's make this short. Aubrette and Aldrich are—*were*—twins. My mother, Breena, is the youngest sibling. Aubrette, the eldest, was always praised for her beauty, poise, and grace. She grew up and caught the eye of Treston, the future Spring Lord. They got married. Aldrich was the clever and cunning one. The way my mother told it was that Aldrich constantly felt as if he were compared to Aubrette and never quite measured up. Eventually, he met and married Carina, a fae woman who was as cunning and clever as he was. For a while, he was deliriously happy."

"Until she died," I breathed.

Letitia nodded somberly. "Her death rocked my family."

I nodded, contemplating her words. After a pause, I asked, "What about your mother?"

Letitia sighed. "My mother has always been a free spirit. She'll go anywhere the wind takes her without a second look at what she's leaving behind." There was more than a trace of bitterness in Letitia's tone. More like years of compounding anger and hurt born out of neglect.

"And your dad?" I asked softly.

"He died when I was little. I don't remember him. Aunt Aubrette talks about him sometimes. I wonder if the memories of him keep chasing my mother away from the court." She waved a hand, trying to brush away the pain of abandonment in the careless gesture, but I saw through it. Her mom. My dad. I knew that pain well.

"Anyway, Mother left me here so often that I sometimes feel like Aunt Aubrette is a more maternal figure than my own mother."

I nodded in sympathy. "But at least you were here, with family. Surrounded by cousins, I'll bet."

"Sadly no. Aubrette and Treston's son, Niall, died in an accident about a year ago. He was an only child, just like Blythe and me. I think that's why Aubrette was so keen to take Blythe in."

"At least you got to grow up with all this," I gestured at the castle. "I mean, this is as close to a fairytale princess as I can imagine." I tried to find a positive spin, but Letitia wasn't having it.

Her lips tightened. "And what about fairytales make you think it's all sunshine and candy? Think hard, Cam. *Really* hard. Those darker versions of the old stories tell the true nature of the fae, not the happy-go-lucky cleaned up modern tales."

"I haven't seen anything like that here," I protested. Thoughts of chasing Kroxius through the wilds of Fae sprang to my mind. I amended, "I mean, once we got to the Courts, that is. Everyone has been charming and wonderful." A memory of the Winter Lady almost killing Andrei popped into my mind. "Well, almost everyone," I finished lamely.

Letitia smiled wryly, her wan features looking even more drawn and pinched. "If that has been your experience, then it's because you're new and everyone wants to see how they can manipulate you, your presence, or the *idea* of your presence to their advantage. Give it a day or two and I'll bet you that someone tries to pull you into some maniacal scheme or another."

I thought back to how Estaria had tried exactly that almost instantly. But Letitia looked like she could use some levity along with a week's worth of sleep and several hearty meals, so I said, "I'll take that action.

Starting from today, I won't get drawn into any schemes while we are still in Fae. What are we betting?" I stuck out my hand and waited.

Letitia paused, considering, then grinned wickedly. "I get to take you shopping."

I jerked my hand back and stared at her skeptically. "Wait. You win and you want to take *me* shopping? I don't think you understand the concept of betting."

"And I don't think you understand the concept of psychological warfare. It starts with the premise of 'know thy opponent'. You hate shopping and my shopping trips take *days*. Days where I get to watch you squirm."

Shit. Impressive. Scary, but impressive. I always underestimated Letitia. Which was probably her superpower.

I stuck out my hand again. "Fine, shopping it is. And if I win?"

Letitia gripped my hand, the bones of her hand painfully apparent as she shook to seal our bet. "Don't worry. You won't."

I felt a *whoomph* of silent reverberations vibrate through my chest as the deal was magically sealed. There was no backing out now. Unless I could figure out some way to win. I didn't hold out a great deal of hope for myself.

Chapter 29

Voices drifted to us on the soft spring breeze. Letitia stiffened. I sat up straight, peering into the darkness and grabbing at shadows, readying them to make a blade. Three figures walked onto the veranda in the middle of a heated conversation.

Andrei was speaking. "No offense, but without monsters to kill or sparring every night, hanging out with adults all the time is *boooring*." He dragged out the last word until he almost ran out of air.

Sloane glowered at him. "Offense very much taken, pup."

I smiled, stood, and walked up to the group. Letitia followed close on my heels. "What's up?" I asked.

Sloane pointed at Andrei. "He called us old."

Andrei shook his head. "No, I called you an adult," he argued stubbornly.

"I know what you meant," Sloane shot back, putting her hands on her hips.

"I don't want to argue. I just want to go talk to someone born in this millennium," Andrei said in exasperation.

"Good luck with that here," Sloane snorted.

Andrei ignored her and turned to direct his plea at Magnus. "Can I go? Please?"

Magnus folded his arms over his chest and fixed the teen with a stern look. He waited until Andrei squirmed before relenting. "Fine. You want to go hang out with the kids or play video games or whatever kids do in Fae? Go for it." The older werewolf held up a finger. "But absolutely no shifting."

Andrei nodded enthusiastically and backed away, sensing victory.

"Keep an eye out for anything out of place," I said loudly as he slid closer to the door leading back into the hall.

Andrei gave me a cheeky wink and a small salute. "You've got it, Teach."

"Don't piss anyone off. Absolutely no fights!" Magnus raised his voice to be heard as Andrei opened the door to the banquet hall and the noise of a very merry crowd spilled onto the veranda.

"And don't make any promises!" Sloane shouted after the teenager as he disappeared into the crowd of merrymakers.

I shot an amused look at Sloane and Magnus. "I don't know about you, but I think we make some pretty fine parents. What do you say?" I raised my glass in a self-congratulatory cheer.

Sloane snorted and almost choked on her wine. "Yeah. Right. Come and talk to me after you've done the nighttime feedings, diaper changes, and potty training. For a frickin' *werewolf.*"

"Okay, okay. We make excellent babysitters." I enthusiastically raised my glass a little higher.

They both stared me down without moving.

I rolled my eyes. "*Fiiiine,*" I dragged out the word. "We make a passable imitation for somewhat responsible adults who just happen to be teenager adjacent."

"And there you go," Magnus chuckled, clinking his glass against mine. Sloane followed suit. We all enjoyed the wine in a moment of blissfully silent, teenager-free peace.

Letitia cleared her throat behind us. "I'd toast to that as well, but I seem to have misplaced my wine and it's bad luck to toast with an empty cup."

Sloane tossed the rest of her wine back easily. "You know what? I'm facing the same dilemma."

Letitia nodded sagely. "A tragedy, to be sure."

"But one we can easily remedy," Sloane replied.

"Then let us do so before our situation turns dire!" Letitia exclaimed.

"And in doing so, we will no doubt save the world!" Sloane raised her glass like it was a sword and she was a general, leading a tiny group of ragtag soldiers straight into the maw of overwhelming odds.

Letitia linked her arm through Sloane's. "I'll show you where they keep the good stuff," she said with a wink.

"You know what? You're ok! For a fae," Sloane said with a wink.

Letitia smiled. "I'll take it."

Sloane turned on me, wagging a finger in my direction. "I'll only be gone for a moment now. No shenanigans, you hear me?"

I held up my empty hands in protest. "I have no intentions of any shenanigans, Nanny Sloane."

She narrowed her eyes at me. "I know all about you and your so-called intentions. You can intend any which way you want. Just make sure there are none of your usual hijinks."

Letitia tugged at her arm with a laugh before I could answer. I watched in amusement as they charged back into the hall. In the most decorous way possible, of course. Because, after all, Letitia was a fairy princess.

Yeah, it still felt weird to even *think* that sentence.

Through the open door, I saw Captain Frost standing in the middle of a crowd of Spring fae women, looking uncomfortable. One woman linked her arm through his while a second tugged on his other sleeve. A third offered him a glass of wine and a fourth held up a plate piled high with sweets while batting her eyelashes at him. The good captain looked like he wanted to bolt, but couldn't figure out which way to run without treading on toes or egos.

"Someone's made new friends," Magnus chuckled, his gaze having followed mine.

"We'll have to see if they're all still friends by the end of the night," I said, as the door swung silently shut. Leaving me alone with a very handsome man. In Fae. While I was a little tipsy.

Magnus smiled softly down at me. A warm breeze swirled around us suddenly. My dress floated dangerously skyward. I almost stumbled, trying to keep the fabric from defying gravity and exposing things I'd rather not have seen in the middle of a party.

"Whoa, careful," Magnus said as he wrapped an arm around my waist.

Suddenly, I was pressed against his chest and staring up into his eyes while the mischievous breeze faded to stillness. Heat rushed up my cheeks and my heart thundered in my chest. I was close enough to see Magnus's eyes dilate as he stared down at me.

Moving slowly, as if approaching a skittish animal, he raised a hand and brushed an errant strand of hair back into place. I bit my lip as

I looked up at him. His breath caught raggedly in his chest. His arms tightened around me, and I felt him try to fight for self-control.

Suddenly, I knew. I knew, deep in the center of my very essence, that I wanted him. Realization welled up and spilled over the walls I'd built inside to contain my feelings.

Self-control be damned.

As I soaked in his warmth, I closed my eyes and leaned against his hand. I felt him freeze, unsure of what to do next. Slowly, I opened my eyes and looked up at him.

"Cam," he cleared his throat. "I'm not sure. I mean, we've been..."

I cut him off with a single word. "Please."

It wasn't a request.

His eyes widened. A low growl rumbled out of him as he cupped the back of my head and brushed his thumb across my lips. Then he lowered his head with maddening slowness and replaced his thumb with his lips.

Heat radiated between us, and electricity zipped from my lips to my toes and everywhere in between, making me feel tingly and almost vibrating with energy.

Magnus deepened his kiss, wrapping an arm around my waist and pulling me up to him. I ran my fingers through his hair, wanting to be closer, nearer. Wanting more. Wanting all of him.

Why had I been fighting this for so long?

With that thought, the dam I'd unknowingly built inside me shattered.

Much to my horror, tears formed behind my eyes. Before I knew it, they were trickling down my cheeks. Magnus jerked back, searching my face.

"Cam! I'm sorry. I thought you wanted..." he said.

I buried my face in his shoulder as I heaved with silent sobs. He froze for a moment, then gently wrapped his arms around me. Magnus held me there, swaying gently and whispering soothing words into my hair.

Finally, the torrent of emotion settled into a flood and then subsided into a dribble of snot and tears. Unfortunately, I wasn't one of those women who could cry prettily. Magnus rode the tide, holding me until I gently disengaged.

I sniffled and wiped my eyes. "I swear, that's not how kisses with me usually go. I don't know what happened."

Magnus snorted a soft laugh. "I do. You cracked. And it's about time too. Bottling up intense emotions like that never ends well. I was getting worried that you were going to do something dumb. Or destructive. Or both."

"Don't hold your breath. There's still time for all of that," I said wryly.

Magnus chuckled. He offered me his hand, and I took it. He led me to a bench on the edge of the veranda behind a series of potted plants that created a mini room of living greenery.

Magnus cleared his throat. "I didn't know Ben well, but I don't think he'd want you to be on the warpath or to mourn his memory forever."

"Why do you think this is about Ben?" I asked, my internal defenses rising again.

He raised a skeptical eyebrow. "Isn't it?"

"Well, no. Yes. Maybe. A little?" I rubbed my hands over my face. "I mean, there was the fae who Kroxius had cursed. He was sucking the life out of them, and that was the fastest way to stop him. But then there was Ben, too. And Letitia. And then all of Fae! There's just been a *lot* lately, you know? And I feel like I'm barely keeping my head above water." I let all of it out in a rush.

"Well, if you ever need to vent to a listening ear or a shirt to cry on, I've got both," Magnus said. I glanced at his shirt. It was dark with splotchy patches of tears. Magnus leaned back and stared up at the Fae night sky, apparently oblivious to my rising consternation.

I opened my mouth to apologize, but Magnus interrupted me with his eyes still on the stars. "Like I said, I didn't know him well, but I think he'd like this type of send-off." Magnus tipped his head toward the party in the banquet hall. "You know, everyone getting together, having a drink, and telling stories."

I sniffled again and nodded through a watery smile. "I think you're right. He would've loved that."

"Would he have loved to see you focusing on revenge fantasies, however well intentioned, or hiding away from your friends?" Magnus asked, his voice mild.

Steel straightened my spine. "I haven't been doing that!" I protested.

Magnus crossed his legs at the ankle and stared up at the strange constellations overhead. "Sure, you have," he said easily, neither backing down nor rising to confront. "First with the lich and now with this obsession to find a murderer that no one believes actually exists."

"Estaria does."

"And remind me, just how stable is she, again?"

I opened my mouth to argue, but snapped it closed when I realized I didn't have much of an argument.

Magnus sighed, keeping his eyes on the sky. "Look, Cam. You know I'm interested in you. Hell, from the way you kissed me, I'd say both of us are way past 'interested'. But you should know that I'm not the type of guy to mollycoddle you. I'll always support you, but I'm going to tell it to you straight."

"Like what?"

He met my gaze directly. "Ben wouldn't want you to stay in that dark place in your mind where you've been hiding. He'd want you to let him go. To move on. Not to forget him, of course, but to move forward with your life."

"What would you know about it?" I instantly regretted the sharp lash of my tone, but I couldn't walk it back.

Magnus's gaze grew a little distant and, wait... was that a touch of sadness? "Quite a lot, actually. I've been down that path before and it wasn't pretty. It took me a long time to find my way back."

He shook his head, returning his attention fully to me. "I don't enjoy seeing you in pain, Cam. But I'd hate to see you head into that same dark, emotionless void where I spent years. If telling you the blunt truth of what I'm seeing messes up my shot at something more with you, well, then I guess I'd rather just be your friend and *know* you are okay than try to be something more and *hope* you are."

A spark of indignation flickered to life inside me at the directness of his approach. Quickly, my more rational side sluiced cold logic over the spark before it could become an all-consuming flame. Magnus wasn't wrong. In anything he said. I could even understand the difficulty of choosing to broach the topic now. By doing so, he was placing my well-being above his own desires, even if I chafed under the blunt delivery.

Logically, I could understand all of that.

Emotionally, I wasn't ready to accept it. I wasn't ready to surrender my pain yet, even if it was a mental self-flagellation Ben would never have wanted me to suffer. If I set that pain aside, it felt like I'd be tarnishing his memory. I deserved whatever pain came my way and then some because it was my fault he was dead. Tears burned behind my eyes again.

Damn it! When did I become a woman who cried all the fucking time?

Magnus laid his warm hand on top of mine when I didn't speak. I jerked away. Hurt flashed deep in his eyes as I jumped to my feet.

"I'm sorry. I just..." I looked around wildly, feeling suddenly trapped and claustrophobic on the veranda. "I need to go. I'm sorry." I repeated as I dashed for the door, leaving Magnus in my wake as I tried to keep the tears from spilling over. Again.

Chapter 30

A loud fanfare played on a brash brass instrument as I re-entered the hall. I was wound so tightly that I jumped, thinking for a horrified moment that the musical welcome was for me.

Across the hall, the Spring Lord stood from his seat at the raised table of honor and waved to the crowd. The Winter and Spring Ladies followed suit. Then the three royals swept out of the hall, followed by a retinue of attendants and guards from both courts.

Someone tapped my shoulder. I jumped again as I spun around. Andrei was standing behind me, looking concerned. I pressed a hand to my chest to calm my pounding heart. "Andrei! You should know by now not to sneak up on me!"

"Sorry, Teach." He shot me a quizzical look. "Hey, you don't look so good. Are you okay?"

"I think I ate something that didn't agree with me." I waved a hand, trying to brush it off. Employing distraction tactics, I nodded at the departing royal party. "What's going on?"

"Something about going off to discuss treaties. Sounded important. And boring."

I snorted at the typical teenager response. Andrei focused back on me. "Seriously, Cam. You look upset. Can I do something for you?"

I patted his shoulder. "You're a good kid, Andrei. But seriously, I'm okay. Just too much rich food after the past week. My stomach hasn't caught up yet. I'm going to find some water and I'll be fine."

He didn't look convinced. "Are you sure? I could go get Sloane or something?"

"No, no. Don't worry. I'll be alright. There's no need to bother her. I think I might go find a quiet place to sit and let my stomach settle. Any idea where the bathroom is?"

Andrei pointed a thumb over his shoulder. "Over there, I think. Are you sure I shouldn't get Sloane?"

"No, I'll be fine. Stay here and have fun. No worries. I'll be back in a minute." With that, I beat a hasty retreat.

I hurried out of the hall, needing a moment to collect myself. The wine wasn't making things any easier, but I wasn't about to admit that to the teenager, no matter how mature he was acting now.

The corridor off of the banquet hall was crowded with milling party-goers. I slipped through them, taking one random turn after another to escape the press of bodies.

In a quieter hallway, I saw a pair of guards in green livery. They stood at attention outside of a set of double doors and eyed me skeptically as I approached.

"What are you doing here, manling?" The guard's voice was full of disdain.

I didn't know if I was meant to be in this hall, or if I'd just committed some horrendous faux pas. So, I fell back on the tried-and-successful bathroom dance. I wriggled urgently as I fluttered my eyelashes at the guards. "So sorry! I got lost and I really need to *go.* Can you help a poor girl out?"

The guard who'd spoken first rolled his eyes and pointed down the hall. "Take a right, a left and then it's the second door on the left," he said. His words were polite, but his tone implied that I was the worst kind of idiot.

"Got it!" I said, smiling brightly up at him. I dashed off down the hall as quickly as my dress and slippers allowed me to go.

The guard's voice drifted down the hallway to me as I rounded the corner. "Humans. I can't understand the fascination with them. Every single one I've heard tell of is a moron, a greedy bastard, or a horny fuck."

"Sometimes all three," his buddy chimed in.

"My point exactly. Just kill 'em all and be done with it, that's what I say."

My cheeks burned, and my stomach dropped simultaneously. They must not have known that I was a Supe and could hear their vitriol. Or they didn't care. Regardless, my resolve to leave this place as soon as possible hardened. As far as I was concerned, Letitia couldn't orchestrate our departure fast enough.

I hurried down the corridor, away from the guards. In my haste, I turned the next corner to see two figures huddled together. It took me a moment to realize I recognized them.

Hemlock and Brio stood outside a pair of doors, chatting quietly. They shook hands and Brio clapped Hemlock on the back with a hearty laugh as I awkwardly slowed my headlong approach. Hemlock looked around Brio at me in surprise.

"Oh, you wee lamb, you look upset! Are you okay?" Hemlock asked, concern lighting his kindly expression.

I pressed a hand to my stomach, offering the same excuse that I'd given Andrei. "I just ate something that disagreed with me. Do you know where the bathroom is?"

The door behind them opened, and a trio of fae women giggled past us. I glimpsed a room behind their swishing skirts that was full of other women.

The barbegazi gestured towards the closing door. "There you are, lass. Is there something we can do? I can fetch your friend for you. What's her name? Slade? Spleen?" he offered solicitously.

"Sloane and no, thanks. I just need a minute." I hurried past them and pushed my way into the powder room. It was filled with overflowing vases of flowers and mirrors. Luckily, the women inside were too busy with their gossip and makeup reapplication to give me more than a passing glance. I slipped by relatively unnoticed.

I took my time doing my business and thinking about what Magnus had said. As much as I didn't feel like I deserved to be forgiven for Ben's death, Magnus was right. Ben wouldn't have wanted me to spiral into misery or vicious revenge. Well, any more than I already had. But good Lord, I *missed* Ben, and that was a different aching pain.

As I washed my hands, thoughts of Ben drifted through my mind. Gardening under the New Orleans sun; sneaking an extra treat when he thought Mama's back was turned; offering sage advice cloaked in folksy analogies that took me much too long to understand. The sudden thought crossed my mind, and I smiled. It was the first time in a while that I'd thought of Ben and hadn't wanted to rip something or someone to shreds.

That had to be a good thing, right?

I wiped my hands on a thick towel and pondered my next move. What would Ben want me to do now? There, in that powder room with my damp hands smelling slightly of lavender from the soap, inspiration struck. It was like Ben had somehow communicated to me from beyond the grave.

Ben would want me to make things right with Magnus.

A wide grin split my face. And, since it was Ben, he'd want me to do it with as many sugary treats in hand as I could manage.

Feeling like I had my feet firmly on solid ground for the first time in a long while, I headed out into the empty hallway. My goal was to find a delectable dessert paired with a glass of apology wine before tracking down a werewolf.

My plan was set. A buoyant feeling filled my heart. Things were going to get better from here. I just knew it.

Which was precisely when the screaming began.

Chapter 31

A wretched, choking sob echoed down the empty corridor. I pulled on my shadows as I peeked around the corner towards the previously guarded double doors. A blade appeared in my hand before I'd even realized I'd made it.

The soldiers were gone, but one door stood ajar. I tiptoed closer, wishing I was wearing my enchanted boots, which would have magically muffled the sound of my approach. The cold comfort of my shadow blade in my hand made me feel better as I approached the doors.

I pressed my back to the wall next to the open door as another gut-wrenching scream ricocheted down the corridor. I pulled my shadows around me tighter, hoping to dull the brilliant bloom of my dress. Quickly, I bobbed my head around the door, but couldn't get a clear look at what was happening. The screams had stopped, but soul-deep sobbing had replaced the horrible sound.

I took a deep breath and pushed myself into the room. Two women were near the center of the room. One was lying unresponsive on the floor. Blood stained her elegant clothes and seeped to pool on the floor. The other woman knelt over the injured lady, hands pressed to her wounds as she attempted to revive her. I didn't spare them more than a glance, scanning the room for threats.

Nothing.

I ignored the sobbing woman behind me and instead prowled quickly around the room, looking for the woman's attacker. However, this was a room built for utility. There were few places to hide. Other than an elegant but serviceable table set with six chairs, the room was empty. I did my due diligence, but there was no means of egress other than the double doors through which I'd entered. That meant whoever had attacked the bleeding woman on the floor had left the room just before I arrived.

With the location secure, I turned my attention to the ladies. No. Not ladies, Ladies with a capital L. As in the Spring and Winter Ladies. Aubrette lay in a growing pool of her own blood, gasping faintly in a struggle to work air into her lungs. Estaria crouched over her, sobbing, as she pressed a wad of cloth that looked like it was torn from her gown against the other woman's chest. Blood seeped from under the makeshift compress. Estaria turned bloodshot eyes dripping with tears towards me.

"Cameron, you must help her! Help me help her!" Estaria shouted.

I flew to Estaria's side, landing hard on the unforgiving wooden floor. Something sharp and cold bit into the exposed skin of my knee under my dress with a familiar icy burn. I hissed and brushed the fabric aside to get a better look. Blood welled around a minor cut and the torn skin was already darkening to a dull bluish-black at the edges as angry, red blood pulsed out of the wound. I'd just knelt on ice. Magically hardened ice. This was the start of Winter magic induced frostbite.

My eyes snapped up to Estaria. "What did you do?" I whispered in horror.

Estaria shook. "It wasn't me, Cameron. I swear it. At least, I don't think it was me."

Aubrette's green eyes fluttered weakly open as she fought to draw in another breath. Her hand twitched, then fell limply back to her side. Her eyes closed, shutting away that intense green gaze as a grimace of pain clouded the Spring Lady's features.

I tightened my grip on my shadow blade.

"The Spring Lady was just stabbed with an ice weapon. You're the only one in the room. You want me to believe you had nothing to do with this? I know that you fae don't think highly of us humans, but c'mon," I scoffed. "I was born at night, but not last night."

Estaria shook her head firmly, keeping up the pressure she held on Aubrette's wound as she spoke. "It wasn't me. I would never hurt Aubrette. We've known each other for years and although we've never been close, I didn't want her dead. You must believe me!"

"Why?" I shot back, leveling my blade at her throat.

Estaria sucked in a breath. Her hands clenched on the wad of bloody fabric, but she didn't release the pressure. "If I wanted Aubrette dead, which I most certainly did not, I wouldn't have killed her with anything that could so obviously be tied back to me. Nor would I have committed the crime in the depths of the Spring Court, in her very castle, where she is strongest, and I am at a disadvantage." Estaria's voice turned pleading. "Cameron, believe me. There are a thousand more subtle ways to orchestrate someone's demise. Why would I act so obviously? So openly? Then stay here and try to save her?"

I frowned. She had a point. "Well, if it wasn't you, who was it?" I kept my sword up just in case this was a ruse to get me to lower my guard. Estaria bit her lip, hesitating. Approaching footsteps rang dully through the open door. I glanced at the door, then back at the pair on the floor. "Estaria, look. If you want me to believe you, tell me the truth. What happened?" I asked.

She followed my look towards the door, then spoke in a rush. "I wanted to discuss opening an investigation into my brother's death, but Treston started pressing me about trade routes instead. I grew angry, which makes me more prone to one of my blackouts. So, I made my excuses and left as quickly as I could. However, I barely made it back to the banqueting hall when a guard came after me to tell me that Aubrette wanted to apologize for her husband's behavior. I returned to find her like this." Estaria's voice caught in the back of her throat. "With that ice knife sticking out of her."

I glanced at the ice shards on the floor that were rapidly melting into tiny puddles. A few minutes more and all evidence of the weapon would've disappeared. I clenched my jaw, considering her words. Based on the sounds coming from the hallway, I only had a moment to deliberate.

I met her eyes. "Swear to me you didn't do this," I whispered fiercely at her.

Estaria met my gaze firmly. "I swear to you on my brother's grave. I had nothing to do with this or any plot against Aubrette."

I held her gaze. Estaria met my evaluation calmly. I'd seen enough liars in my time to read the signs, especially when the situation was so tense. If she was somehow skirting the truth, she was damned good at it, but there was very little wiggle room in her statement. A little tickle in the pit of my stomach told me she wasn't. It was hard to fake sincerity in the face of an attempted murder without giving *something* away. Besides, she was right. It was all just a little too convenient.

I let my shadow blade dissolve. "I believe you. For now," I murmured, leaning down to feel for a pulse in Aubrette's neck. It thrummed weakly under my fingertips, but it was there. I let out a sigh of relief. Something caught my eye. I leaned forward, examining the front of her dress. There, snagged on some of the elaborate beading, were two coarse, dirty white hairs.

I reached out to examine the incongruous addition to Aubrette's attire when the doors slammed wide, crashing with an ominous *crack*. An irate Spring Lord stood framed in the open doorway surrounded by armed guards.

Treston pointed a finger at Estaria and screamed, "Murderer! She murdered my wife!"

"I did no such thing!" Estaria protested loudly.

At the same time, I shouted, "She's not dead!"

Treston's roar of anguished outrage drowned us out. Swords sprang out of the guards' sheaths. I kept my hands far away from my body and made no threatening moves as I glanced up at the nearest guard. He skewered me with a freezing stare. I swallowed hard. There were no allies for me here.

Treston wrenched a sword from a guard's hand and charged across the room. "You will pay for what you did to my wife!" Spittle flecked from his mouth as he raised the sword above Estaria's head.

She made no move to defend herself. Instead, she just bowed her head, keeping her hands firmly pressed on the wad of bloody cloth. I understood instantly. Estaria was afraid that if she released the pressure on Aubrette's wound, the Spring Lady would succumb.

In the moment of Estaria's inaction, I made up my mind. A guilty woman would've let her target die as she tried to save herself from the Spring Lord's righteous rage. But Estaria was trying, even in what might be her last moments, to prolong Aubrette's life. That was enough for me.

My shadows slapped into my palm and hardened slowly as Treston began his downward swing. I braced, hoping my magic worked fast enough to stop him. It did, but barely. His blade crashed against mine in a shower of sparks. Surprise lit his face at the sudden appearance of my sword. Treston gritted his teeth with a primal growl and pressed down. I swayed under the pressure and struggled to keep the Spring Lord's blade from separating Estaria's head from her shoulders.

"I said, 'She's. Not. Dead.'" I forced the words out, a bead of sweat forming at the effort of holding his blade in place. "But if you kill Estaria, we might all be dead in short order. You included."

His eyes locked on mine for an interminable heartbeat, the fate of the Fae balanced on his sword's edge.

Chapter 32

*H*ow did I seem to get pulled into crazy shit even when I was trying to keep my head down?

I paced anxiously around Estaria's suite of rooms. It was a luxurious jail cell, but a jail cell nonetheless. Guards were stationed at every door and a roving patrol passed frequently below the second-story window. Once Treston realized his wife was still alive, he'd diverted all his attention to her. He'd ordered us to be placed under house arrest for the time being.

That was an hour ago. I'd already exhausted all the escape options. If I'd been wearing my enchanted boots, I could've used them to jump from foothold to foothold up the vine-covered walls of the castle to the roof with a little of luck. However, I didn't know what might wait for me up there. Without the boots, my opportunities to break out were much more mundane and none of them were even remotely good.

Estaria seemed to have reached this conclusion before me. She sat on the sofa with her knees drawn up to her chest, rocking gently as she stared into the middle distance.

She will not be of much help right now. It's all up to you, Cam, I thought.

I flopped into a chair and rested my head against my hands. Talking to myself probably wasn't a good sign, but if I couldn't force my way out, maybe I could think my way out. Time to put on my Sherlock Holmes hat and hope for the best.

"Nothing like a crash course in detectiving," I muttered at the floor.

"That's not a word," Estaria said dully.

"She speaks!" I crowed, raising my head. The Winter Lady refused to look at me. I rubbed my hand over my forehead. "Help me figure out what's going on here."

"Why?" Her voice cracked hopelessly on the single syllable.

"I don't know? Because you're confident that somebody is setting you up? Because you're innocent? Because Treston wants to kill you, which could send the whole Fae realm spiraling into chaos and war? Because I'm on the hook for being your accomplice, simply because I walked into the wrong room at the wrong time? Because we've got nothing better to do? Take your pick!" I threw my hands up and flopped back in the chair.

"So, you believe me? That I didn't kill her?" Estaria pulled her gaze away from staring into oblivion and met my eyes.

"I mean, logic says you'd have to be a special kind of stupid to try to save the woman you just tried to murder instead of making your escape."

"Did you just call me stupid?" Frost spilled out from her fingers and coated the arm of the sofa.

"No. Never." I waved my hand. "Not the point. The point is that you're *not* stupid, and by sticking around to help Aubrette, you proved you didn't do it. To me, at least." I glanced down. The frost had stopped spreading over the upholstery but didn't dissipate. I took that as a good sign. "But if *you* didn't do it, someone is going to great lengths to make it *look* like you did. If we can figure out who or why or even how, maybe we can talk our way out of this mess."

"And you think Treston will listen to talking as his wife lays dying?" Estaria scoffed. "Truly, you are like a babe in the woods and you're about to get eaten by hungry wolves." She leered at me fiercely, but I could see panic dancing at the edges of her expression.

"So, we'll have to be fucking convincing. C'mon! Like you said, you're not stupid. Prove it." I was taking a risk speaking to her like that. I pulled on my shadows, ready to leap out of the way of ice shards if they appeared.

But the verbal slap to the face seemed to snap Estaria out of her panic. "No one speaks to me like that," she said, tendrils of ice creeping across the frost onto the sofa cushions.

"And I'll bet no one frames you for murder, either. It's a big ol' day of firsts for you. Now stop that before you ruin the furniture," I said, pointing at the ice inching towards me.

Estaria looked down and blushed. She waved her hand ashamedly at the couch. The ice faded without leaving a trace.

I cocked my head to the side. "Wait. Do that again."

"What?" Estaria sounded confused.

"The ice. The non-melting-melting thing. Do it again."

Estaria looked baffled but complied. Ice coated the hardwood floor under her feet. She waved her hand, and it faded. Not melted but faded. Nothing was left. No water damage, no puddles. Nothing.

I pointed at the floor. "Who else can do that?" I demanded.

"Absorb their ice? Everyone who can make it. Why?"

I lifted the hem of my skirt to show the ragged cut on my knee. The bleeding had stopped, but the edges of the cut were still a dark purple fading into an angry, blistered red, like the wound on my shoulder I'd incurred in the Winter Court. It was still numb now, but who knew how long that would last until the pain set in? "Whoever attacked Aubrette purposefully left behind evidence of their crime. Evidence that would point directly back at Winter."

Estaria peered critically at the cut. "You got that from kneeling on the ice shards?" She looked perplexed.

"Well, it wasn't like it was intentional. I didn't see them and was slightly distracted by the woman bleeding out on the floor," I retorted, rubbing at my knee.

Estaria shook her head. "Not what I meant. It means Winter magic was at play. Regular ice wouldn't have given you frostbite on contact. It's an extra defense mechanism used to injure enemies of Winter. It's unique to conjure ice weapons that only a select number of the Winter fae can manage."

"No offense, but Winter sucks," I grumbled. Then I paused as something she said sank in. "Wait. Only *some* Winter fae can make this kind of ice magic?"

Estaria nodded. "It is extremely difficult to manifest an ice weapon of any size or shape, let alone infuse it with enough power that it maintains its form after leaving the creator's grip. For you to be cut on a shard of the broken ice, well," she shrugged. "The creator would have to be incredibly gifted in ice magic."

"Which doesn't look good for you," I observed. My thoughts flickered back to my own difficulties with maintaining my shadow blades' form after they left my hand.

"No, it does not," Estaria agreed softly.

"So, other than you, who has this kind of power?" I asked.

Estaria flung her hands into the air. "In Winter? It would be impossible to track them all down!"

I lifted a finger. "No, not in Winter. In Spring."

Her eyes widened in understanding. "Much less. A handful, maybe," she said in a hushed voice.

"How many? Give me names!"

Estaria ran a hand through her long hair. "Well, me, of course. Captain Frost, naturally."

I snapped my fingers. "That's right. I saw him when the snow wassets were attacking. He's a good fighter. Handled himself well. Is he as competent with magic?"

Estaria nodded. "He enjoys making ice arrows. He claims they are more aerodynamic."

"And you like ice spears. Can either of you make a knife? Something like the weapon that attacked Aubrette?"

Estaria shrugged. "Naturally. Knives aren't as difficult. Besides, once you know how to conjure the ice and have sufficient power, you can form the ice into any weapon you can imagine."

"So, it would be possible for Captain Frost, a military man who is well versed in the martial arts as well as magic, to create and use an ice knife?" I pressed.

A faint blush crept up Estaria's neck. "I suppose so, but I don't see why—"

"He would have?" I asked, cutting her off. "Any number of reasons. He rose quickly through the ranks after your brother's death, didn't he? Went from bodyguard to the heir to one of the Winter Lady's most trusted advisors. What kind of promotion would he enjoy if you died?"

"He would never!" Estaria exclaimed. "I know him! He is—"

"Where exactly?" I interrupted. "For a bodyguard, he actually has to be around to, you know, guard your body. So where is he?"

My question pulled her up short. She frowned. "He was in the hall, talking with some of the Spring guards. I got pulled away."

"How long has it been since you saw him?" I asked, feeling like I was on the cusp of something.

Estaria bit her lip. "I'm not sure. A while, I guess. But I know him. He would never—"

"Hurt you?" I interrupted her again. "But he has the ability, both magical and martial, and the opportunity to attack Aubrette and frame you."

"But he wouldn't!" Estaria protested, her voice rising.

I raised a finger. "I have another question. Where was he when your brother died?"

Her teeth clicked shut. All the color drained from her face, but she shook her head stubbornly without answering me. I didn't need her to. I'd already added Captain Frost's name to the top of my suspect list.

I waved aside the question before I provoked the Winter Lady's anger, choosing to redirect her attention to other suspects. "Okay, who else from Winter can make ice weapons using this magic *and* is currently in Spring?" A memory tickled at the back of my head as I remembered the snow wasset attack. "Krampus? He grew talons of ice and flung them at the wassets. He was deadly with those things. His ice darts or whatever stayed hard even when he wasn't touching them."

Estaria didn't look convinced. "It is old magic. Krampus is an ancient being."

I snapped my fingers as something clicked into place. "His fur! I saw a couple of strands of coarse white hair stuck on Aubrette's dress!"

Estaria shook her head stubbornly. "That proves nothing. He sheds horribly. Anyone who is in his presence for more than a few minutes is likely to have some of his fur transferred to them." She brushed at her own clothes to make her point, pinching a piece of the same coarse fur from her bodice and handing it over.

I frowned at the fur. What I'd taken for a clue could easily be explained away by a cordial greeting between Krampus and Aubrette. Or it could have even been transferred from Estaria's dress as she crouched over the Spring Lady. I cast my mind back, thinking about all of my limited interactions with Krampus. The conversation I'd overheard between him and Hemlock sprang to mind. "Isn't he a little paranoid? Looking for conspiracies and that sort of thing?" I asked.

Estaria shrugged. "Perhaps, but I doubt he would've acted on anything like that. He's usually such a gentle soul."

"Why do you say that? He didn't hesitate when the wassets attacked."

Estaria waved that away. "That's different. I was in danger. Winter was in danger. However, I doubt he would've attacked the Spring Lady."

"Why do you say that? Isn't he the anti-Santa? The robber of joy? The killer of the Christmas spirit?"

"Yes, that is his *job*. That is not who he *is*," Estaria said coldly. "Would you want the essence of your character judged based solely on what you do for a living?"

I squirmed in my seat. Considering that my job often fell on the wrong side of the law and most morals accepted by most civilizations, I could see the difference. "Well, no. I see your point. But what if he thought Winter was in danger somehow? Someone played on his paranoia to convince him that Aubrette was a threat?" That gave Estaria pause. She weighed my words. "Well?" I pressed.

She spoke grudgingly. "I suppose it could have happened that way. But who would have told him Aubrette was a threat?"

I drummed my fingers on my leg, thinking quickly. No suspects came to mind. I blew out my breath. "I guess we'll have to track him down and ask." Mentally, I added Krampus' name to my suspect list, under Captain Frost's. I wasn't sure the anti-Santa would've committed murder, but if he was one of the few who *could*, then it was important not to dismiss him. However, Captain Frost was the more likely culprit in my mind. He had the means and motive. After all, his rank improved significantly when Estaria became the Winter Lady. He might have even been responsible for her brother's death as well. I nodded to myself as things seemed to slot into place. Frost was first on my list of suspects and Krampus was a distant second. "Are there any other people who can do this special ice magic?" I asked, covering my bases in case there was anyone else who could be responsible.

Estaria's eyes flicked back and forth like she was sorting through a mental catalogue. Finally, she shook her head. "I can't think of anyone."

"Ok, so right now we have a suspect pool of three." I held up a corresponding number of fingers. "And if you didn't do it," I folded down one finger. "That leaves two people who could've created the weapon used in the attack. What does your gut say? Who was it? Frost or Krampus? Because I'm betting on Frost."

Estaria's eyes tightened at the corners, and her lips pursed. I could tell she didn't like any of the options. Just as she opened her mouth to respond, the door behind her swung open on silent hinges.

I jumped to my feet, pulling a shadow blade out of thin air as two dark shapes swiftly ducked into the room. My first thought was that Treston had sent assassins to finish the job neatly and quietly. When the first of the two figures met my eyes, I saw it was worse. Much, much worse.

Chapter 33

They say that, aside from humans, the deadliest animals on Earth are snakes and mosquitoes. I'd like to suggest that angry leprechauns should also make the list. In Sloane's case, perhaps leprechauns should top the list.

Sloane stormed across the room as Letitia shut the door noiselessly behind them. Letitia pressed her ear against the door, listening intently.

"What the *hell* is going on?" Sloane whisper-shouted at me, ignoring Estaria. "I told you, no shenanigans!!"

"I didn't do anything!" I protested.

"Well, then care to explain why you are locked up here with her?" Sloane jerked a thumb at Estaria. Her eyes narrowed. "And why she's covered in blood?! What was it about 'No shenanigans and no hijinks' that confused you?"

"Umm, what do you know?" I asked, eyeing the Winter Lady carefully.

Sloane folded her arms across her chest and tapped a foot at me. "Not much. The entire court is in chaos. Lord Treston requested everyone return to their rooms but didn't give any details. He backed up his suggestion with armed guards, so it was less request and more threat. Guards are now roving the hallways to make sure everyone stays put and they aren't answering questions. When I realized you weren't coming back to our rooms, I snuck out and found Letitia. We've been looking everywhere for you! Are you okay?"

"I mean, okay is a relative term. But I'm not dead and I didn't kill anyone, so that's a start," I said, shooting her a double thumbs up.

"If that's your idea of good, what kind of shit did you drag us into?" Sloane hissed.

"Hey! I resent the implication!"

"Am I wrong?" she shot back.

"Not exactly."

"Ha!" Sloane waved an accusing finger under my nose.

"But it's not my fault!" I protested.

"It never is."

"Wait! How did you guys get in here, anyway?" I asked, looking at the door behind them. One I was sure had been both locked and guarded.

Sloane wiggled her fingers. Small specks of gold light danced in the air at her fingertips. "A little of luck goes a long way. I've been saving it up, just in case."

Letitia pushed away from the door, obviously satisfied that their entrance hadn't been detected. "I'd like to think my illusion glamour helped a little."

Sloane ignored her. "What's going on, Cam? I leave you alone for less than an hour and then... well, what the hell happened? How pissed should I be right now?"

I closed my eyes, knowing this would not go over well. "The Spring Lady was attacked. She was alive last time we saw her, but barely." I pointed at Estaria. "Treston thinks she did it and that I helped her."

Sloane's face darkened. I hurried to speak before she could explode in outrage. "But she didn't do it! And then I stopped Treston from killing her, which I think he took personally. Now we're both locked up here. There. You're all caught up."

"What the actual *fuck*, Cameron?! I leave you alone for a hot second and you create an international, no make that *interdimensional*, incident? What the hell is wrong with you?" Sloane barely kept her voice down as she vibrated from her toes to the tips of her spiky hair with frustration and anger.

I held up my hands in protest. "It's not my fault! I just needed to pee!"

"Well, next time fucking hold it!"

Letitia stepped up between us, palms raised in a plea for peace. "Now's not the time, ladies. Cameron, let's sit down. Catch us up on what else has been happening."

I blinked in surprise. "You don't know any of this?"

Letitia shook her head, lips tight. "No. After Treston announced the end of the celebrations, he sequestered himself away. I haven't been able to get in touch with anyone. I think the only reason the guards didn't order me to return to my rooms was because I'm Treston's niece. Now, tell me everything," Letitia commanded, her tone sharp. I could see why the guards didn't order her around.

As quickly as I could, I narrated the events. I ended with the paltry suspect list Estaria and I had brainstormed. Letitia stood when I finished and started pacing in agitation.

"So, you see," I said in conclusion, "I think this was all a clever frame job."

Sloane rolled her eyes. "What are you? Some kind of hard-boiled PI in a black and white movie? No one talks like that." Her tone lashed across my tight nerves like a whip.

"Fine. I don't think she did it. I think she was set up. There. Is that better?" Sloane glowered at me. I glared back. "Look, Estaria may be a lot of things, but she's not stupid enough to get caught in the room trying to save the person's life that she supposedly just tried to kill with a weapon that obviously ties it back to her. It doesn't make sense."

Estaria pushed a hand forward, interjecting it between us. "While I appreciate the vote of confidence in my mental capacity, I dislike being talked about as if I'm not present."

Sloane ignored the Winter Lady and shook her head. "It doesn't matter. This is not our job. It's not our responsibility. We just need to make sure that you get out of here without causing any more problems. Why did you get involved in the first place? Couldn't you have just kept out of trouble for once?"

I glared at her. "What was I going to do? Let them kill an innocent woman because she'd been framed?"

"You *think* she was framed. You don't know," Sloane shot back.

Estaria waved the hand hovering between us. "As a reminder, I'm still here. Listening to every word. Even happy to participate in the conversation, should you so desire."

I ignored the Winter Lady. "I couldn't let them kill her, Sloane. You *know* why. If she dies, then..." my voice trailed off significantly. Sloane's eyes widened in understanding. The color drained from her face.

Letitia interjected from the other side of the room. "What? If Estaria dies, then what?"

Estaria cleared her throat. "I don't have an heir. If I die, there is no one to take the Winter mantle of power."

Letitia's eyes widened in horror. "But a release of power on that scale would be like setting off a nuclear explosion in the middle of the castle!"

"Shit," Sloane breathed.

My mind was whirring at hyper-speed. Fragments of a plan were coming together. "Look, you said you didn't know anything about the attack, right?" I asked Letitia. When she nodded, I continued. "Okay. So that means they're keeping things quiet. I don't know why, but it plays in our favor, and we haven't got much going our way right now."

"What do you mean?" Sloane asked warily.

"Once the attack on the Spring Lady becomes public knowledge, everything will get locked down tighter than a dwarf's vault. We have a small window of opportunity here and we need to take it," I said.

"What in all the realms are you talking about?" Estaria asked.

I started to pace. "Who is higher than the court's Lords or Ladies? The, what did you call them?" I waved a hand by my head, hoping to bring the memories back, but my mind was whirring too fast to recall names.

"Fairy Queen and Goblin King," Sloane supplied.

"Titania and Oberon," Letitia said at the same time.

I snapped my fingers. "Right. Them. If we got them here, they could take control of the situation, right? Overrule whatever emotional decisions Treston might make without knowing the full consequences of his actions?"

Estaria shrugged noncommittally. "Sure. Theoretically. But they'd have to get here first, and who knows where in Fae they are? They might not even *be* in Fae. They could be traveling to one of the other realms."

Letitia held up a finger. "No, they aren't. As soon as the Winter emissary arrived, Treston and Aubrette sent their own emissary to the King and Queen to invite them to celebrate your ascension. They might even be on their way now."

"Perfect!" I exclaimed.

"How is that perfect?" Letitia asked, confused. "If they were at their residence—and that is a big if—they are a hard day's travel away at most."

"How long is that by royal fox?" I asked, turning towards Estaria.

The Winter Lady nodded, immediately understanding my question. "It could work. But Hemlock would have to take the team. Other than me, he's the one who can get the most speed out of them, but he won't leave unless he receives the orders directly from me, and there's no way I can get out of here to tell him to go." Estaria's face fell.

"Write a note with the orders and I'll deliver it," I said, with more confidence than I felt. "Hurry. We don't have much time."

Estaria jumped to her feet and dashed into the bedroom to draft an order for Hemlock.

"Letitia, how good is your illusion glammourie?" I asked.

"It depends. It's not the strongest out there, but with a little luck and some distance, it usually does the job. What do you have in mind?"

"Could you make Sloane look like me?"

"Oh, *hell* no!" Sloane exclaimed.

Letitia bobbed her head thoughtfully, examining Sloane. "As long as she doesn't move or talk too much and the guards stay near the door, it should work."

Sloane shook her head vehemently. "No way. No how."

"Sloane, we both know that I'm the better fighter and I'll be able to slip around the castle a lot easier than you can," I said, relying on logic.

"I got here just fine, didn't I?" Sloane retorted, folding her arms across her chest.

"Luck," I said, pointing at her. Then I pointed at myself. "Near invisibility due to shadow magic." I held up my hands and bobbed them up and down like I was weighing something.

Sloane glared at me, but I knew I'd won. "Fine," she finally acquiesced. She didn't look pleased about it, though.

"Great." I turned back to Letitia. "I need you to run recon. Go find out as much as you can about the attack. Any clues that you can uncover or overhear might be the leverage we need to stop Treston from doing anything stupid."

Letitia nodded. Estaria came back and handed me a note sealed with purple wax with an elaborate snowflake pressed into the cooling blob. I tucked it into the pocket of my dress.

"So, what's the plan after you deliver that?" Sloane asked.

I wiggled my fingers at her. "I'll do what I do best. Improvise."

"Well, shit." Sloane flopped into a chair. "Hold on to your hats, girls. Things are going to get a whole lot worse before they get better. *If* they get better."

I wanted to disagree, but I had a feeling Sloane was right.

Chapter 34

I pulled my shadows tightly around us as Letitia and I slipped out of Estaria's room. Sloane didn't look too happy to be left behind. It was even more disconcerting to see her silently frown using my face. I had to give it to Letitia: her glammourie for illusion magic was pretty damn good despite her misgivings.

The guards were returning to their posts, and they looked angry. I grabbed Letitia's hand and held a finger to my lips. She looked around wildly, able to see the guards through my shadows. She didn't know that they couldn't see us. I felt her suck in a silent breath as the guards marched past us close enough that we could hear them muttering darkly at each other.

Swiftly, I led Letitia down the corridor as the guards resumed their posts. After we rounded the corner, we reversed positions. Letitia led me down the winding castle passageways with the unerring confidence of long experience. Luckily, we only ran into one roving pack of guards. We avoided them easily by ducking behind a colossal statue of an elven archer. I pulled my shadows even tighter as they passed, my heart thundering in my ears.

Letitia leaned close, her breath warm on my skin as she whispered, "Hemlock's room is just around the corner. Third door on the left. Do you know your way back from here?"

"I think so."

"Okay. I must find my uncle."

"Good luck."

Letitia met my eyes seriously. "I don't need luck. Find out who did this to my aunt. I'll buy you as much time as I can, but you need to hurry."

I swallowed hard and peeled my shadows back from Letitia. She nodded at me once, straightened her dress and set off briskly down the hall. With no time to waste, I turned the corner and hurried to Hemlock's door.

He answered on the first knock. I shoved my way inside and shut the door behind me. Only then did I drop my shadows.

Hemlock's beard jangled discordantly as he spluttered, "What's happening here, lass? What in all the realms is going on?"

I shook my head. "We don't have time for long explanations. Here." I thrust the sealed letter from Estaria at the little barbegazi. "The Winter Lady told me to give this to you. She wants you to get the team of royal foxes, find Titania and Oberon, and bring them back here as fast as possible."

Hemlock's eyes widened and his normally rosy cheeks paled behind his beard. He quickly broke the seal and scanned Estaria's letter. He bobbed his head up and down as he read. I bounced on the balls of my feet, not liking the delay. Finally, he looked up and waved the letter at me. "The Winter Lady doesn't give me many details here. Care to elaborate?"

"Lady Aubrette's been attacked and Estaria's being blamed for it," I said shortly.

"What?" Hemlock squealed in surprise. "Is she okay?"

"Yes, both are okay for the time being. Aubrette was injured, not killed, thank all the gods. Estaria is just locked up for the time being. But time is short. Can you do it? Can you get Titania and Oberon here, fast?"

Hemlock stroked his beard. "I'm the best chance you have to find them quickly, but there's a wee problem you may have overlooked."

"What's that?"

"They locked the castle down tighter than a swimming troll's asshole. How do you propose to go about getting to the foxes, hooking them up to the sled, then getting all of us out?"

Rather than try to explain, I yanked hard on all the shadows and swirled them around my body in a small cyclone of magic. The barbegazi's eyes widened as I winked out of visibility and then back into view. His mouth opened and closed once, then twice.

Finally, he squeaked out, "Right you are, then. Lead the way."

I grabbed his hand. "Stay close," I said, easing the door open.

Hemlock stayed on my heels as I peered down the hallway. It was empty still. I retraced my steps, turning right. Hemlock tugged gently on my hand.

"The kennels are this way," he whispered loudly, turning to point. His beard jingled noisily as he waved his arm in the opposite direction.

"Keep that beard quiet! We need to make a stop first," I whispered back, resuming my careful progress down the hall.

Hemlock pressed his free hand to his impressive chin hair, muffling the tinkling sounds. "What could be more important than getting to the foxes as soon as possible?"

My grin was almost feral when I responded. "Wolves."

Hemlock and I nearly made it to the corridor where my friends and I'd been given rooms mere hours before without incident. Just as I was about to turn the corner, Hemlock tugged urgently on my hand. I glanced down at the little creature. He was trying to flatten his beard to his chest and wave his fingers around the corner at the same time.

Rather than laughing at the awkward little dance, I took his warning. I kept my shadows tight around me as I peered around the corner.

Brio stood at the end of the hallway in the middle of a trio of Spring guards. They looked to be in serious conversation, but were too far away for me to hear them clearly.

Suddenly, Brio raised his voice and the angry whine carried clearly down the hall to where we hid. "Well, I don't *care* what is going on. If you won't allow me to seek medical attention, then I *demand* that you send a healer to my rooms. Immediately!"

The guard's response was too low for me to discern what he was saying, but Brio didn't seem to take the news well.

"What are you saying? My hands are my *life*. You get me a healer and you get one right now or I swear to you I will go straight to Lord Treston and report you!" Brio waved a gloved fingertip under the guard's nose.

The Spring guard spread his arms wide and firmly ushered the bard back into the room with the open door behind him. The guard said something short and clipped that I couldn't quite catch and then shut the door. He pulled a key ring out of his pocket and locked the door even as Brio started hammering on it.

The guard's colleagues jostled him good-naturedly as they started walking towards us. I pressed Hemlock back against the wall, but there was nowhere to hide in the bare hallway. I ducked down, trying not to wince at the stab of pain in my knee as the sudden movement tugged my newest frostbite uncomfortably taut. I pulled the shadows tightly around us as the guards' voices became clearer.

"... and what does he think we're doing? Just keeping everyone in their rooms because we hate a delightful party?" the first guard complained.

"Musicians. Dramatic lot, aren't they?" The second guard slapped the first on the shoulder jovially as they rounded the corner. I held my breath as one of them stepped on the end of Hemlock's beard. The little barbegazi's eyes widened in horror as the guard's foot landed. The barbegazi's white whiskers crumpled under the soldier's boot without a sound. Thankfully, the guard missed stepping on an icicle by a hair's breadth. A barbegazi's beard hair, to be precise. The guard kept walking without noticing the extra padding underfoot.

"What is even going on?" The guards' conversation continued, oblivious to how close to a conniption I was.

"I don't know. Nobody tells me nothing."

"You know the Sargent. He's all 'orders, orders, orders'."

"Gods forbid you ever ask a question, or it'll be..."

"One hundred pushups, cadet!" the trio said in mocking unison as they rounded the next corner.

Hemlock shot me a wide-eyed look over the hand clutching his beard. Ever so carefully, he tucked the end of the beard behind his belt. It made him look ridiculous, but I didn't even crack a smile. Instead, I held a finger to my lips. He nodded silently.

I peeked around the corner again for good measure, but the hallway remained empty. Tightening my grip on the little barbegazi's hand, I half-dragged Hemlock down the hall and pulled him into my room, shutting the door softly behind me.

I dashed into the bedroom. Goliath was still asleep on the pillow on the bed. I left the little mouse on the bed. There was no point in bringing him along on what was an already dangerous mission. However, I took advantage of the opportunity to slip out of my party dress and into clothes more suitable for skulking.

I even spent valuable moments digging the small jar of ointment out of my bag and smearing the pungent stuff liberally over the cut on my knee. The numbness was fading. Unfortunately, it had been replaced by a dull, pulsing ache. The throbbing eased almost instantly. I smiled grimly and tugged on my leggings. In less than two minutes, I was wearing a matching set of dark green leggings and tunic, subtly embroidered with budding leaves. I almost sighed in relief when I slipped on my enchanted boots.

"I am never taking you off again," I whispered, running a finger along the abstract, flame-red design.

"What was that?" Hemlock called from the other room.

"Nothing." I hurried out into the main room and headed towards the door.

Remembering suddenly that I'd shoved my broken necklace, the calling charm, and the pink quartz ring into my dress pockets, I spun and grabbed the discarded dress. I dug in the pockets and fished them out. Except the ring wasn't there. Desperately, I turned out the pockets again, just in case I missed the small ring the first time around. Still nothing. This was bad. So very bad.

Chapter 35

Hurriedly, I pushed my sleeve up and looked at the cinnamon-colored tattoo on my wrist. The azure dot that had been pulsing in time with my heartbeat no longer glowed in the center of the compass. Instead, it perched on the edge of the simple, circular design.

"Shit," I whispered, tugging my sleeve back down.

As much as I wanted to look for the missing ring, I had more pressing issues. I filed it at the top of my list of urgent things to address as soon as I finished dealing with the current crisis. Quickly, I stashed the calling charm and broken necklace into a drawer under some loose stationery. It wasn't a great hiding place, but it would have to do. I wasn't about to lose the charm, in addition to the missing ring, because of faulty pockets.

Hemlock eyed me speculatively as I entered the room. "Those aren't wolves. Unless you humans have a drastically different definition of the word," he observed.

"Don't worry. They're next on my to-do list," I muttered, yanking the shadows back around us. We slipped out of my room. There was no response when I knocked on the door across the hall. I was pretty sure it was Sloane's, but I hadn't been paying close enough attention when we arrived. Magnus opened the second door a moment after I tapped lightly on the hardwood. I let the shadows fall to the side as soon as I saw him. His eyes widened, and he jerked us inside.

"Cam! What's going on? Where have you been?" Magnus said. He looked as if he wanted to pull me into a hug, to reassure himself that I was okay. Instead, he awkwardly reached out, hesitated, then patted me on the shoulder. Hemlock snorted softly behind me.

"Things are a little nuts right now, and I need some help."

Magnus nodded. "Sure. Anything. Tell me what you need."

I held up my finger as if something had just occurred to me and turned to the little emissary. "Look, can you run across the hall? We can't leave the teenager on his own. His dad will kill us if he ever found out."

"Are you sure?" Hemlock asked speculatively.

"His dad's an Alpha. I don't want to piss him off, okay?" I snapped.

"Fine. Just make sure I'm not seen," Hemlock said. I pulled shadows around him as he scuttled across the hall to Andrei's room. The teenager opened the door a few moments later with a towel wrapped around his waist and hair dripping steaming droplets onto the hardwood floor. I guessed he must've had a hot tub, too.

A sound tickled at my ear. I cocked my head in confusion before I realized it was the thump of marching feet. I hissed at the pair in the hall and urgently waved my hand at them. Andrei jerked Hemlock inside his room. I saw the toe of a guard's boot at the end of the hallway just before I shut the door to Magnus' room.

Magnus looked confused. "What's going on, Cam?"

"Look, we don't have a lot of time. There's been an attack on the Spring Lady. Whoever did it framed the Winter Lady and the Spring Lord wants retribution. Like, her head on a spike kind of retribution."

Magnus sucked in a breath, "But if he kills her..."

"I know," I said, cutting him off. "Letitia's trying to stall Lord Treston. We need to buy Hemlock time to find Titania and Oberon. Apparently, they're the head honchos here and can help stop a catastrophe from happening. If we can get them here in time."

Magnus nodded, all business. "What do you need from me?"

"You and I are going to track down whoever is responsible for the attack."

"How? There must be hundreds of people here. How are we going to narrow that down?"

I ran a hand through my loose hair, weaving it quickly into a braid as we talked. "The weapon used on the Spring Lady was an ice dagger. A magical ice dagger. There's only three people who can make that kind of weapon in Spring at the moment: Estaria, Captain Frost, and Krampus."

Magnus's face hardened. He reached towards the hem of his shirt and tugged it off in one fluid motion. My fingers paused in my hair as I took in his sculpted chest and shoulders. I shook myself. Now was not the time for ogling. I grabbed a piece of string I'd tucked into my pocket just for this purpose and tied off the braid.

"And you're sure it's not Estaria?" Magnus asked, tossing his shirt on a nearby chair. He crouched and worked his shoes off, obviously readying for a shift.

"Pretty sure."

Magnus snapped his head up to look at me, eyes fierce. "This isn't something you want to be 'pretty sure' about."

"Given the circumstances, I'm willing to bet that she didn't do it."

Magnus met my gaze briefly. Whatever he saw there must've convinced him, because he nodded once. "Good enough for me. Tell me the plan."

That's one of the many things I liked about Magnus. No unnecessary chit chat in the face of an emergency.

"Well, as much as I would like to gather them all in one place and dramatically monologue until I stumble on the right solution, I don't think that's going to fly here."

Magnus snorted. "Probably not. And dramatically monologuing isn't really your style. Maybe a Scooby-Doo mask reveal? But then you need to get someone to do the 'I would've gotten away with it, if not for you meddling kids' line, and I doubt the fae are up to date on their Saturday morning cartoons."

I cracked a smile despite my tension. "Yeah, probably not. Ok, so no monologues or masks. That leaves tracking down the suspects that had the means and see if they had motive and opportunity."

Magnus nodded. "Sounds reasonable. Who are we going after first?"

I bit the inside of my cheek. We didn't have time to waste. Time was of the essence here, which meant it would be best if we split up. I pointed at Magnus as I made up my mind. "I want you to take Andrei, shift, and track down Krampus. I'll go after Frost."

"Not a good idea. I don't like the thought of you running around after a potential assassin on your own," Magnus countered. "Besides, I don't know how the fae would respond to shifters running loose on their turf. Especially during a crisis. I think the kid will be safer here and we should stick together."

"We don't have a lot of time here! Sloane is standing in for me, but it's only a matter of time before they realize I'm gone. And as for you shifting, if the fae aren't used to shifters, they might just assume that you're a big dog wandering the grounds. And the kid will be safer with you than locked up in a castle full of potentially hostile fae," I argued, my hastily thrown together plan solidifying as I talked. "Besides that, I don't have your noses for tracking. No, it'll be faster if we split up."

"Cam, this isn't a simple recon mission. You want us to split up and track down someone who might have just attempted to kill the Spring Lady! Besides, what do you think is going to happen once the Spring fae realize we're gone?" Magnus's voice was tight and low.

"What do you think will happen to Andrei if they find out *you're* gone, and he's still here?"

Magnus clenched his jaw, the muscles in his temple jumping and pulsing. Finally, he grunted out what could charitably be called agreement. "Fine. I'll take him with me, but I still think we should stick together."

"And I'm telling you, I will be fine on my own," I shot back.

He breathed loudly through flared nostrils until he calmed down enough to speak. "Fine. I'll take Andrei and find Krampus. But then I'm coming back for you. And you *will* wait for me before you do anything stupid. Like confronting Frost on your own."

I held up my open hands, placating the perturbed werewolf. "I don't want to confront him. Just to find him," I said, keeping my voice low.

Magnus narrowed his eyes at me, but even he could see that my plan, while not great, was the best one we had. "And you'll wait for me," he said, pointing a finger at my chest. I nodded, not willing to verbalize just how long I was willing to wait. No sense in provoking him further when he was on the brink of doing what I wanted.

Magnus huffed out a breath. "Alright then. Once we find him, what do you want us to do with Krampus?"

I paused, not having gotten that far in the plan yet. "We need to figure out if he was close enough to the banqueting hall to have slipped away for about fifteen minutes after I left you on the veranda." I tried not to blush as I mentioned my hasty departure after our kiss.

"And if he was?"

"Figure out a way to bring him in as fast as possible."

"Alive?" Magnus asked seriously.

"Good Lord! Yes! Alive! We don't need to make this worse than it already is!"

Magnus shrugged. "I mean, if he's to blame, it solves the problem."

"And if he's not, it creates a bigger one!" I exclaimed. "Just track Krampus down. No biting, no killing. Got it?"

"What if he comes at me?"

"Hide! Hamstring him! Isn't that what you wolves are good at? Besides, you'll have Andrei with you. It's probably better not to engage unless necessary."

Magnus grimaced and reached for the waistband of his pants. I spun around quickly when I realized what he was doing. The wall was bland compared to what I imagined was going on behind me, but I wasn't about to sneak a peek. Not after I'd essentially run away from him on the veranda.

"What about you? What's your back-up plan if Frost turns on you?" Magnus asked from behind me.

"I'll improvise," I said.

Magnus growled deep in his throat. "I'm starting to hate it when you use that word."

"You don't have to like it," I snapped back. "But we both know that Andrei will listen to you better than he will to me. Keeping Andrei close to you is the best way to keep him safe right now, don't you think? And tracking down both Frost and Krampus is the best way to keep everyone else safe while we sort this mess out."

"And what's the best way to keep you safe?" Magnus's voice was low. It sounded like he was right behind me. I turned around, careful to keep my eyes up and focused on his face.

"I can take care of myself," I said steadily, meeting his eyes.

"See that you do," he rumbled, the heat from his gaze intense. He held me pinned there for a moment more, then he began the shift. I turned away. I told myself it was to give him some privacy, but I also needed a second to get myself under control.

I was going after a potential killer. I didn't have time to think about whatever was happening between Magnus and me.

But after this was done? I was going to have a long talk with my werewolf.

Chapter 36

I let out a silent breath of relief as I led Hemlock and the two wolves into the building housing the kennels. It hadn't been easy, but I'd kept my shadows wrapped around all of us as we moved through the castle. The effort was making me sweat, but no one had seen us. I was thankful when we slipped inside, and I could release my hold on the magic. I eased the door shut behind us as Hemlock raced to get his team of foxes ready for their desperate mission.

The building was a sturdy stone construction built over heavy beams of wood. Thick vines of ivy crawled up the sides, making the place appear as if it had erupted, fully formed, out of the landscape. There was a sweet smell of fresh straw and a deeper, richer aroma of worn and oiled tack. While the wolves kept watch, I searched in the stashed gear for anything that might have belonged to Krampus.

I finally uncovered a massive blanket covered in strands of dirty matted hair, some glittery dust, and one brightly colored ribbon. A memory of Krampus getting his fur braided by some pixies at the feast sprang into my mind. Dragging it out of the pile, I carried it over to the wolves. "I'm pretty sure this belongs to Krampus. Will this work to get his scent?" I asked. "It was buried in with all those things. Will it make a difference?"

Magnus sniffed, then sneezed. He pawed at his nose and snorted violently.

"I know. If I can smell it, it must be strong. But that should make him easier to track, right?"

Magnus bobbed his massive silver head up and down in the affirmative. Andrei trotted over and sniffed at the blanket before suffering a similar reaction, whining pitifully as he pawed at his snout. However, it wasn't long before both wolves started moving around the building with their noses to the ground, searching for Krampus's scent.

I looked over at Hemlock. He already had the team of foxes hitched up to a sled converted for travel in Spring.

"Do you know where you're going?" I asked as I swung the doors wide.

"The palace of the Fairy Queen and Goblin King is about a day's ride by horseback to the southwest of here. But for us," he flicked the foxes' reins gently, "We can be there in less than half that time. Besides, if what you say is true, they may be on the road already. If that's the case, I'll meet up with them sooner. There's only one road leading from Spring to their palace, so I can't miss them."

"Great," I said. "Find them as fast as you can. Estaria is depending on you to get Titania and Oberon back here and we don't have a moment to lose."

"I know," he replied, flicking the reins again. The foxes trotted out of the building. "And you don't have to worry about us. If we know anything, it's speed!"

Hemlock flicked the reins one more time and he and the sled disappeared in a blur of white and a fading tinkle of icicles.

Behind me, Magnus gave a little bark. I turned to see him racing away from the castle and towards the woods with his nose occasionally brushing the ground. Andrei let out a little yip and tore after the older wolf. They crossed the meadow in front of the castle as two dark streaks, blurring like arrows flying towards their prey.

Something thudded with a dull *thwack* beside my head. An arrow fletched with iridescent purple feathers quivered in the door where I'd been standing. I ducked and rolled on instinct, grabbing at my shadows even as a male voice rang out behind me.

"Stop!"

I faded into the shadowy gloom of the interior of the kennels. The disembodied voice spoke again. "Stop where you are. I don't want to hurt you, but I will if you don't explain yourself."

I crouched behind a trough full of water, searching for the owner of the voice. There! A flicker of movement caught my eye in the faint light sneaking through the cracks in the heavy wooden slats on the roof. A tall, slim man with a bow. And the way he moved was so familiar...

The man hunting me darted from one support beam to the next, using the heavy timber as cover while he worked his way closer to my position. He passed through a thin stream of sunlight and, just for a moment, I saw his face with startling clarity.

Captain Frost.

The man I was supposed to hunt down because he may have tried to kill someone today. Suddenly, I wished I'd followed Magnus' suggestion and waited for the werewolf to return. Unfortunately, waiting was no longer an option.

I focused on making a sword out of shadows, but it felt like I was trying to wade through chest-deep water. The shadows responded sluggishly. Not good. I needed to buy myself some time.

"Why don't you put down your weapons and explain yourself?" I said, ducking behind a pile of burlap bags overstuffed with grain to give myself a little extra cover. An arrow thumped into the trough the second I moved.

"Or you could tell me why you just worked with your friends to steal the Winter Lady's royal foxes," Frost said. I heard the slight crunch of straw underfoot as he prowled closer.

"What the hell are you talking about?" I asked. Desperately, I worked to form a weapon. Ever so slowly, a shadow sword materialized in one hand. I panted slightly from the exertion. But against a fighter like Captain Frost, there was no such thing as over-prepared. In my other hand, I focused on creating a karambit. Just in case.

"I saw the sled depart, pulled by the royal foxes, and then your werewolves a moment later." Captain Frost's tone was accusatory.

"We didn't steal anything!" I protested. The karambit popped into existence much faster than the sword had. "But that's not the point right now, the point is..." A sharp crack interrupted me. A noise that was far closer than it should have been.

Captain Frost's foot landed on something unexpected under the layer of straw on the ground. That was the only warning I had before he spun around the edge of my hiding spot with an arrow drawn back and pointing at my heart.

However, the sound had given me just enough notice. I jumped, putting all the power from my crouch into the sudden movement. I soared over Frost's head, batting the arrow away with my sword as he tried to compensate for my sudden movement. As good as he was, he hadn't expected the speed or height of my jump.

Thank all the gods for Thistle and her enchanted footwear.

I landed without a sound off to his right. Frost was a consummate soldier and recovered quickly. He was already nocking another arrow to his bow when I pushed off the ground for the second time. This time, I propelled myself straight at his face.

I slashed at him with my sword, hoping to get close enough to use the knife I held concealed in my other hand. Frost was fast, though. He drew and loosed his arrow in one smooth motion, forcing me to deflect the projectile into a pile of straw. I brought my sword into line, just in time to keep his bow from braining me. I grunted, catching the crushing blow with my sword. My eyes widened in surprise.

What the hell?

My magical blade did nothing to the wood of the bow. After this was done, I needed to steal some of whatever magical item Fae had birthed to give Frost his bow. The wood was as strong as iron, but as supple as a bow should be. Despite the magically sharp edge I'd given my sword, it barely nicked the captain's bow as he swung it like a club for my head and I countered for a second time.

The jarring impact almost knocked my blade from my hands. The captain didn't give me a moment to recover. He reversed his swing immediately. His attacks were viciously effective. Frost never took two steps when one would do. The power behind his bludgeoning blows threatened to drive me to my knees.

I needed to even the playing field, and fast. Pulling on the shadows surrounding us, I used the quick catch-and-release tactic to create a strobing effect in front of his eyes. I gasped at the effort, not realizing how drained I was from using my magic but gritted my teeth and pushed through. It must've worked. Frost's eyes danced around the room crazily as he saw me blink in and out of existence. Each time, I'd moved just enough that his brain struggled to fill in the blanks that his eyes missed.

He swung wildly at my head, disoriented by the unusual effect. I guessed they didn't have many raves in Fae. I dodged to the side, thankful for the milliseconds my shadow strobing bought me. Taking advantage of Frost's disorientation, I drove my blade up between the wood and string of his bow, hoping to cut the string. If I couldn't damage the wood, at least I could remove the advantage of distance attacks. No such luck. I don't know if he twisted at the last minute or the string was made of something much stronger than bowstring on Earth, but it didn't split under my blade.

With a groan, I twisted my wrist painfully. The move forced Frost to sway with me if he wanted to keep a hold on his bow. I drove my sword into the ground, locking his bow in place with my arm. He grunted, trying to yank the bow loose. But the heavy, unrelenting wood refused to break even when he dragged it against the edge of my sword.

I swung my free hand up, driving my karambit under and upwards. For the moment, I was trying to go for a submission lock on his closest arm. I didn't want to injure or kill him if I could avoid it. Frost flung up one arm without releasing his bow and punched out towards my face. I leaned to the side, which threw off my aim. The karambit scraped along his arm, doing little more than tearing a clean slice in the sleeve of his tunic. The captain was starting to piss me off enough that the dial on my care-o-meter for whether he came out of this intact was dipping dangerously close to I-don't-give-a-fuck.

His next punch landed squarely on the side of my head, snapping my skull around. The ringing in my brain shattered my focus. With a guttural yell of dismay, I watched in horror as my sword dissolved before my eyes. Luckily, I maintained my grip on the karambit.

Frost stumbled forward at the sudden loss of resistance on his bow. His mouth twisted in surprise, and he lost his balance, stumbling forward a few paces before regaining his balance. I used those precious seconds to make another blade. Rather than going for a sword, I opted for another karambit because it was faster and easier to make. By the time Frost slid to a stop and whirled back at me, I held a karambit in either hand. This time, I wasn't about to let him land a blow.

Frost rushed in, trying to use his speed and reach to his advantage. I twisted my wrists, flicking the karambits out in viciously effective flails. Back and forth, back and forth. The knives snapped forward like striking vipers, scoring cuts and slices on every rotation before slapping back into my palm. I felt like the most destructive juggler in the world, and the primal part of me loved it.

Frost tried to dance backwards and away from my attack, but I pressed close. There was no way I was letting him sneak away after he tried to kill me. By his sudden and unprovoked attack, I made a bet with myself that he was the one responsible for attempting to kill the Spring Lady. Otherwise, why would he try to shoot me on sight?

I twirled my left karambit in a whistling arc through the air, capturing Frost's wrist. Remorselessly, I sliced through the tendons. Captain Frost screamed, but I kept moving, jabbing at his shoulder joint. He slid away from the attack. Frost must've been unfamiliar with countering a karambit attack because he left his other side open. I curved my blade into his elbow joint, using my momentum to spin around. In between one short, sharp gasp and the next, I was behind him, holding his uninjured arm aloft while the other blade kissed his jugular.

"Why did you do it?" I hissed in his ear.

Frost held still. "What?" he panted through the pain.

I jerked back on both blades, digging the points into his flesh. "Why did you attack her?"

He gasped. "What are you talking about?" Frost's words were ragged and short.

"Stop lying to me!" I screamed. "I know what you did!"

"I'm not lying! Believe me!" Frost gasped.

An arrow whistled by my head, the fletching brushing my cheek before it thudded into the post behind me.

I stumbled backwards, keeping my hold on Frost as I searched for my newest assailant.

Three figures stood in the doorway to the kennels. They were backlit by the sun, so it was hard to see their features clearly. However, the most important aspect of their identities was all too obvious, even with the poor lighting.

All three were archers. All three held nocked arrows pointed directly at me. Even though I held Captain Frost in front of me, at this range, I doubted all three would miss.

Chapter 37

The archer in the middle took a step forward. "I am Commander Maeweather of the Spring Court and I order you to let him go." The man spoke with the air of someone who was used to being obeyed.

I compacted my body behind Captain Frost, trying to shield myself from his friends. "Not a chance," I grunted back.

"Stand down!" Frost shouted from in front of me at the same time.

The archer drew up short and did a one eighty from aggressive to confused. "What was that, Frost?"

Frost waved his injured arm weakly. "Stand down, you fools! Put your weapons down." When no one moved, he roared, "NOW!"

The three archers finally reacted, releasing the tension on their strings and pointing their arrows at the ground.

"If I may..." the man in the middle started to say as he took another step into the interior of the kennels. Once he was fully inside, I could clearly see the brilliant green and pink of his fancy Spring guard uniform.

"What are you doing with the Spring guards?" I hissed, paranoia flaring. I pulled Frost deeper into the kennels and frantically searched the gloomy shadows for a means of escape.

Frost kept still, pliantly moving wherever I pushed him. "We were having a shooting contest. What's happened?" he asked.

"Likely story," I snorted. I looked around wildly. Despite my best efforts, the only way out of the building I could see was directly behind the three archers.

Shitfuckdamn.

Frost spoke again, keeping his voice calm. "You said someone's been attacked. Who is it?" A faint tinge of desperation colored his voice. "Estaria! Is she alright?"

I blinked in confusion. "You don't know?"

"Know what? Just tell me what is going on up at the castle!" Frost commanded. I could hear the terror behind his words.

"Where have you been?" I asked instead of answering his questions. My mind was spinning. This was not the reaction I'd been expecting. I'd assumed from the unprovoked attack that Frost was responsible for the attempt on Aubrette's life as well. Now, I wasn't so sure.

Captain Frost didn't move, but spoke over his shoulder to me. "Those gentlemen rescued me from the overly flirtatious attentions of some of the more inebriated guests. They suggested a shooting contest."

I jerked back on the knives. "Where? When?" The questions rattled out like machine gun fire.

"About two hours ago. Lady Estaria was eating dinner with Lady Aubrette and Lord Treston in the main hall. The Winter guards were on rotation. I didn't see the harm."

The Spring commander spoke up. "I can corroborate Captain Frost's story. He didn't look to be enjoying himself and we were on strict orders from my Lord Treston to be gracious hosts. Tales of Captain Frost's skill with a bow are legendary, so we thought he might enjoy a friendly match."

"Where?" I demanded.

"The range behind the barracks," Frost said.

All three Spring guards chorused, "The shooting range."

Commander Maeweather continued, "We thought it best not to draw any undue attention. Wine and arrows do not mix well, in my humble experience." He pressed a hand to his chest and dipped his head in a slight bow. I noticed that his gaze never left me, despite the courtly manners.

"How far away is this range?" I pressed.

"At the back of the castle grounds. It's isolated to prevent accidental injuries. It took us about ten minutes to walk back here," the commander said, raising a brow quizzically at my line of questioning.

"And Frost never left your sight?" I asked.

All three Spring guards shook their heads. "No. He seemed to prefer archery to dancing, and so we stayed. Had quite a little contest too," Maeweather confirmed.

"How do I know I can trust you?" I asked suspiciously, although it seemed highly unlikely to me they could have coordinated their stories this tightly prior to seeing Hemlock drive away with the foxes.

Frost and one archer spoke simultaneously. "Fae can't lie."

Frost cleared his throat and continued. "Well, not outright lies. Omission or implications are a different matter."

"It's one reason we rarely speak in absolutes about anything," the lead archer added.

"And I can promise you I had absolutely nothing to do with an attack at the feast today, nor any knowledge of it beforehand," Frost said. Sincerity rang in his voice.

If it had been anyone else, I would've laughed off the words as a lame attempt at convincing me of his innocence. But Frost was fae and, being fae, couldn't lie. There wasn't any wiggle room in his words. Unless, of course, he'd figured out a way around this rather inconvenient little piece of fae lore. But Sloane had told me that originally, and I trusted her with my life. And if I was taking her word on the situation, then, by extension, I had to take Frost's as well.

I tried to put the timeline together and simultaneously assimilate this new information. If Frost had been with these guards for a little over two hours, there was no way he could've attacked the Spring Lady. Even if he had made some excuse and hurried to and from the castle proper, he would've been gone for at least twenty minutes—something these men would've commented on. Add in the not being able to lie part, and all the evidence pointed to one logical conclusion.

Frost wasn't behind the attack. My prime suspect was innocent, and the would-be murderer was still out there.

I released Frost. He grasped at his wounded wrist with a hiss, but when he spun to face me, his face betrayed no pain. "Who has been attacked? What's going on?" he demanded.

I eyed the Spring guards shifting uneasily behind Captain Frost. I held up my hands and let the shadow blades fade away. The guards seemed to relax marginally once I was unarmed. When I spoke, my low voice was for Frost's ears only.

"We need to talk. In private."

Frost nodded just once. "Gentlemen, excuse us a moment," he said, tipping his head towards the back of the building. I followed him. Once we were as far from listening ears as possible, I filled him in on everything that had happened.

Frost was a good listener and didn't interrupt the brief narrative. When I reached the end and described the conclusions we'd drawn regarding the magical construction of the ice dagger, Captain Frost nodded along until I explained my hypotheses that either he or Krampus were behind the attack.

"But you couldn't have been behind it," I said. "The timing doesn't fit."

"So glad to know that it was the timing and not my impeccable character that convinced you," Frost said dryly.

I ignored him. "And if it's not you, it must be Krampus. He's the only other person here who has that kind of ice magic besides you and Estaria." I started looking around for something that I could use to catch up with Magnus and Andrei. "The werewolves are tracking him down now. If we hurry, we might catch up."

Frost shook his head slowly. "No, I don't think Krampus did it. As I was walking towards the barracks, I saw him snatch a goat from the castle pens and lope off across the meadow. The only reason it is so clearly ingrained in my memory is because he was so clean that he almost sparkled."

"To be fair, he probably did sparkle."

Frost shot me a strange look.

"Pixies," I said by way of explanation, waving a hand complete with wiggling spirit fingers to replicate the idea of glimmering pixie dust.

Frost blinked just once.

"Right. Not the point at the moment."

Frost cleared his throat. "If I know anything about Krampus, he was going to find a nice, quiet cave somewhere and enjoy some dinner. After that, he probably slept off the meal."

"And if he left about the same time as you..." I trailed off.

Frost filled in the end of my sentence. "... he's probably still out there, sleeping."

My mind spun. If Frost could be believed, both he and Krampus were too far away to have attacked the Spring Lady. Which meant...

I took off at a dead run, heading straight back for the castle. I ignored the startled shouts of the men behind me as I poured on all the speed I could muster, a single thought playing on repeat in my stunned brain.

Which meant that Estaria had somehow played me, and I had left my best friend alone with a murderer.

Again.

Chapter 38

I gave up all pretense at stealth as I raced through the castle with four confused fae in hot pursuit. Frost and his buddies tried shouting at me to stop, but I ignored them. My breath was better spent on running than trying to explain my train of thought. Every moment counted.

What had Estaria said to me? Were there any loopholes in her words that I'd missed? There had to be. Which meant that Estaria had been playing me this whole time and Sloane was in danger. I'd go through anyone who was stupid enough to try to keep me from reaching my best friend before Estaria could hurt her.

If the Winter Lady hadn't killed her already, that is.

Luckily, I didn't encounter any guards in my mad dash through the castle. A little voice of caution at the back of my skull whispered that this was too good to be true. I ignored it, focusing instead on keeping my lead on Frost and his cohort.

I skidded around the last corner. The pair of green-clad guards standing outside of Estaria's room looked bewildered as I attempted to shove past them.

"You can't go in there!" The closest soldier attempted to grab me, but I ducked and jabbed a fist into his gut. He gasped for breath and weakly tried to grasp at me again. I avoided him, but that made it easy for the second guard to latch onto my arm with a steely grip.

He shook me like a rag doll. I tried to lash out with my free arm, but he dipped his head to the side, caught my wild strike in his other hand. I continued to struggle as he held me by both arms in front of him. The guard's eyes widened in recognition as I tried a futile headbutt to free myself. "Wait! Aren't you *supposed* to be locked up in that room?" His voice was incredulous.

"That's what I'm trying to do, bonehead! To get back in there!" I shouted.

Captain Frost and his three friends came running up behind me.

"Open the door!" Frost ordered. His face was pale. He gripped his wrist with his good hand, blood oozing through his fingers to splatter on the floor. The guard holding me froze in surprise while the other wheezed weakly on one knee.

"Do it," Commander Maeweather snapped from behind Frost.

A moment later, the door swung wide. I wriggled loose from the guard's grip. I was the first one in the room with Frost close on my heels.

"Sloane!" I shouted. "Sloane! Are you okay?"

Sloane's head popped up from behind the sofa. Or rather, my head popped up from behind the sofa because Sloane was still wearing Letitia's illusion glammourie.

"Umm, hi," Sloane said lamely through a mouthful of cheese, wiggling her fingers in greeting.

"Where is Estaria?" Captain Frost roared.

Estaria sprang up from behind the sofa and launched herself at Frost. "Jack! I'm so glad you're here!" She flung herself into the surprised captain's arms. For a few moments, the room erupted in a confused hubbub of anxious voices.

"Snacks? Really? At a time like this?" I asked Sloane in disbelief as Estaria and Frost started talking in hushed, urgent tones.

Sloane shrugged and swallowed. "They offered. I didn't want to be rude."

The lead Spring archer spoke at the same time. "Two of them? What is going on here?"

"Seriously, we can explain this," Sloane said, gesturing between the two of us with a tiny cheese knife. The illusion shimmered, wavered, then disappeared with a soft *pop.* Sloane stood in front of us in her party dress, wearing her face instead of mine. Something about the scene niggled at the back of my brain.

I rushed to Sloane. "Are you okay? She didn't hurt you?"

Sloane shook her head. "No. What are you talking about? We've just been killing time here while you did your thing." She gestured at the low table where they'd been sitting. A paper football sat forlornly in the middle. A couple of plates and a picked over cheeseboard littered the carpet.

I snorted. "Seriously? Not only snacks, but you're playing bar games with her?"

"What? I'm a bartender, not a kindergarten teacher. That's the extent of my arts and crafts ability."

I put my hands on her shoulders, checking her over for injury. "Are you okay? She didn't do anything to you? You're not hurt?"

"Just my pride. She's a quick study."

I pulled her into a hard hug. Sloane wrapped her arms around me, too. I bit back a sudden welling of tears. If I'd lost Sloane, I don't know what I would've done. Something clicked into place in my mind. The last time I'd felt like this was when the snow wassets were attacking. Sloane had been standing with a knife then too. Next to...

"Shit!" I cursed, pounding my fist on my thigh hard enough to hurt. "Stupid fucking idiot!"

"I beg your pardon," Estaria's voice was icy in the sudden silence of the room.

I held up my hands. "No, not you. Me. I just remembered that there was another person who could make ice weapons. One we hadn't even considered."

"What are you talking about?" Frost said, striding forward.

"Hemlock." I turned to Sloane and gripped her arm. "When the wassets attacked the first time, he was standing next to you. I told you to protect him and he had a little ice knife. I remember it because it was a ridiculous weapon for that particular fight."

"Isn't that the little barbegazi? The emissary?" Commander Maeweather asked.

"Yes, Hemlock is my emissary," Estaria said, looking concerned that she hadn't thought of him as a suspect before. "I wasn't aware he could use that kind of magic. I've never seen him do it before. Are you sure?"

"Positive. It makes sense. If you didn't attack the Spring Lady and both Krampus and Frost were outside the castle walls, who's responsible for the ice? Hemlock. He attacked the Spring Lady. It had to be him."

"Not possible," a clear voice rang out from the side of the room.

"What was that?" snapped Maeweather.

"Apologies, sir, but that's not possible. I saw the barbegazi in the banquet hall when the news of the attack came and he'd been there for at least ten minutes beforehand," the guard near the door said crisply.

"How can you be sure?" Commander Maeweather asked. "There were many people crowded in the hall and a lot was happening."

The guard nodded his head assuredly as he addressed his commanding officer. "Yes sir. There were. But I remember the barbegazi because he and a couple of gnomes got into it. Someone insulted someone else's mother or beard or something. Fists were thrown. They knocked over a table and shattered a half dozen bottles before I could break it up. I still have the wine stains," the guard said, gesturing at a splatter of purple fading to an ugly brown on his trousers.

"A barbegazi, you say?" Commander Maeweather asked. "Aren't they rather small creatures?"

"Hemlock is no taller than my waist," Estaria said numbly, dropping to the sofa as if this was all too much for her. "To think he betrayed me. How could he?"

"And yet my guards tell me that the Lady Aubrette was stabbed in the chest. Unless she was bending down, it seems highly unlikely that a *barbegazi* of all creatures could inflict such injuries." Maeweather held up a finger to the room as a guard marched up and whispered in the commander's ear. The room broke out into a quiet hum of conversation as Maeweather dragged the guard outside. Estaria moved over to stand next to Captain Frost and the two began conferring urgently in low voices.

Sloane sidled over. "Do you really think he did it?"

"When you rule out all the other possibilities as impossible, the only thing left must be the truth," I said.

"Sherlock Holmes said it better," Sloane returned.

"Sherlock Holmes was fictional."

"Well, if he wasn't, he'd be sitting here like a pompous English ass explaining how a piece of ash or a fragment of a German word led to a brilliant deduction into means, motive, and opportunity. Hemlock might have had the means, but he didn't have the opportunity. He was in the ballroom, remember?"

"Starting a conveniently attention-grabbing fight. Perfect alibi. Besides, he could've had an accomplice," I whispered.

"And what about motive?" Sloane asked, looking unconvinced.

I shrugged, casting my mind back over the various encounters and conversations I'd had with the emissary. Something snagged at my memory. I voiced the theory before I fully thought it through. "For someone who works for the Courts, he sure mentioned his love of the wild a lot. Maybe there's more substance to the rumors Estaria told us than we first believed."

The door banged open and Maeweather re-entered the room, gesturing for all the guards to fall in around him. They did so quickly, and he whispered hushed instructions that not even my keen hearing could pick up.

"You think there is a deeper conspiracy going on in Fae?" Sloane dropped her voice. "Something that includes killing both the former Winter Lord and the Spring Lady?"

"What would've happened if I hadn't been there and Lord Treston had been successful? Estaria would've died. It's the whole two birds, one stone thing, but with nobility and a knife," I said.

Sloane's face drained of color as the implications of my theory spiraled out in front of her. "If you're right, how do we prove it before this thing gets any further out of control?" she asked.

"I can only think of one way. Find Hemlock's accomplice."

"How are we going to do that?"

Commander Maeweather cleared his throat, drawing the attention of the room. "I've just been informed that Queen Titania and King Oberon have arrived. Their Majesties command all parties involved be brought before them immediately, so the trial may commence."

"Trial? What trial?" Captain Frost said coldly.

Commander Maeweather's face was devoid of expression. "My Lord Treston insists that Lady Estaria be punished for her crimes against his wife. The Fairy Queen and Goblin King want to hear both sides before meting out justice."

"But what about Hemlock and his ice magic?" I asked.

"You mean the barbegazi who was nowhere near the Spring Lady when she was attacked?" Maeweather gaze was stony when it met mine.

"He could've—"

Maeweather held up a hand, cutting me off. "I am not the one that needs convincing. The King and Queen will act as judges in this matter and, if needs be, executioners."

Estaria's knees gave out and Frost caught her before she fell. Spring guards moved to surround the pair, looking grim.

Sloane squeezed my hand. "What are we going to do?"

"The only thing we can. Find Hemlock. Failing that, we need to find his accomplice."

"And if you can't?"

I smiled at her with more bravado than any sort of plan. "I'll do what I do best. Improvise."

Sloane groaned but didn't have time for anything further as we were ushered to an audience with the King and Queen of Fae at sword point.

Chapter 39

The guards surrounded us and led the way into the depths of the castle. Our small group walked stiffly in the middle of the ominously silent Spring fae. I was afraid to speak for fear that I would say something that would cast further aspersions on Estaria, but my thoughts raced to find some sort of logical solution.

Who could Hemlock's accomplice possibly be?

The guards marched us up three flights of stairs as my mind churned. However, by the time we were ushered into an elegant room, I was no closer to unraveling the Gordian Knot that was tightening with inexorable determination around us.

Maybe calling it a Gordian Noose would be a more apt description.

All thoughts of twisted mythological references shattered to fragmented musings as the elegantly carved door swung wide. Treston paced the floor of the large room. He looked torn between overwhelming rage and inconsolable worry. Aubrette lay in a massive bed, looking frail and worn. Her brilliant green eyes were closed. Her breathing came raggedly under a concerningly large wad of blood-stained bandages wrapped around her chest.

Blythe sat at her godmother's bedside, stroking her hand. Tears rolled silently down the girl's cheeks. My heart wrenched at the sight of her. She'd already been through so much. The child didn't need this trauma added to her load as well.

Letitia sat in a chair, just behind Blythe, but she refused to meet my eyes. It was at that moment that I knew. My stomach dropped and a tingle of warning zipped up my spine.

Oh, this was worse than bad. Far, *far* worse. This wasn't just a hearing about an assault. They were treating it as a murder trial even if the Spring Lady wasn't dead yet.

A pair of pixies darted about under the watchful eye of an elven healer. The stern woman wore a high-necked white dress and had her silver hair plaited into a severe braid that added years to her already aged countenance. She directed her glittering minions with an ease that spoke of long collaboration and practice. The healer ignored the commotion as the guards pushed us into the center of the room and took up defensive positions in case we did something stupid.

Soft music tickled at the corner of my awareness. Brio, the autumn bard, sat in the corner looking bored while his journeyman strummed a calming melody on something that looked like the smaller cousin to a guitar. The female musician glanced up. Her eyes met mine, and I saw a touch of wildness at the corners of her countenance before she lowered her gaze to focus on her instrument again.

A pair of people rose from their seats at a low table in the room's corner. My breath caught in my throat. The woman was a tall, lithe fae with sharply pointed tips to her ears. Hers was an elegant but cruel beauty. A crown of silver flowers nestled in her intricately braided hair. The braids cascaded down her back in shimmering silver waves that perfectly matched the glittering embroidery in her ice blue gown. Her blue eyes were slit vertically, like a cat's and, like a cat's, prowled over each of us, silently evaluating whether we posed a threat or were prey.

Her companion was the antithesis to everything she was. Where she was lithe, beautiful, and feminine, he was hulking, wild, and fiercely masculine. He towered above everyone in the room. Muscles rippled and bulged underneath the darkly tanned leather barely held together with a rawhide whipstitch. A wide brown belt circled the man's trim waist and soft brown boots barely whispered against the shining hard-wood floor.

My breath caught in my throat, and my knees turned to jelly when I dragged my eyes upwards. A mass of curling, dark chest hair spilled out of a deep split in his tunic. A coarse black beard faded into a wild mane and framed his menacing eyes. His eyes were intense pools of darkness that flicked over each of us as if analyzing threats. Something about his manner reminded me uncomfortably of a dangerous predator. And on top of his head was a dangerous rack of antlers, each tip tapered to a wicked-looking point that seemed to glitter with potential violence.

Wait. Antlers?

I did a double take. I hadn't been mistaken. Massive, sharply pointed antlers erupted from the man's head. It was a good thing that he was at least a foot taller than everyone in the room, or he could've accidentally impaled anyone who had the misfortune to walk beside him. He looked like a cross between a giant and an angry elk stag who'd indulged in too much hair re-growth serum.

Titania and Oberon had arrived.

Lady Estaria immediately dropped to her knees in front of the pair. Sloane, Frost, and I followed a moment later. I sucked in a breath as the frostbite cut on my knee protested with a silent shriek of agony at the abrupt mistreatment. The numbness and the pain relief from the ointment must've finally worn off.

"My Queen..." Estaria murmured as she rose. We followed suit.

"Silence!" The Fairy Queen threw up a hand, her cat eyes flashing and crackling with raw magical potential.

Estaria's mouth snapped closed. My mouth went dry as I tried to reconcile the fairy queen I'd seen depicted on stage and in cartoons with the elegant, alien monster who commanded the room. She held my fate within her talons. I mean, her glittering manicure. I tried to gulp but couldn't work enough moisture into my mouth to manage it.

Queen Titania lowered her hand. "Lord Treston has told us everything, but Lady Aubrette's injuries speak for themselves." She lowered her voice, glancing at the Winter Lady. "How could you, Estaria? What were you thinking?"

Oberon cleared his throat in a low, barking rumble. "Perhaps she wasn't, my Queen. There have been rumors circulating about Winter since her brother's unfortunate passing."

"What rumors?" Titania turned her calculating gaze on her husband.

"Treason, my queen," Estaria said, her head still bent in deference.

"Lord Etienne's passing, as tragic as it was, was just that—a tragedy." Lord Treston exploded from across the room. He gestured wildly at his wife, lying pale and struggling for breath. "And yet, the Winter Lady is perpetuating the rumor of a treasonous rebellion consuming the realm. Don't fall for her lies! I demand she be held accountable for my wife's death!" His voice rose until he was shouting. Spittle flew from his mouth as he rushed at Estaria and grabbed her hair, jerking her head back. "Her! She deserves a long-suffering death for what she did to my Aubrette!"

"No!" The word flew out of my mouth before I could marshal my rational thoughts.

"No?" Queen Titania raised a supercilious eyebrow in my direction.

Sloane elbowed me hard, but I ignored her. "I meant, no, the Spring Lady is not dead."

The Queen looked over my head, ignoring my words and scanning the room. "Who gave the mortal leave to speak in my presence?"

King Oberon flopped into a chair, which groaned in protest under his bulk. "You know my opinion on the matter, love. Execute any mortals you wish. Or better yet, turn them into hogs and we can have them for breakfast. Or, if that all offends your delicate sensibilities, turn them over to me. My goblins could do with another Wild Hunt." He popped a grape into his mouth from the fruit tray on the side table, munching loudly as he eyed Sloane and me like prized pieces of chattel.

Titania ignored her husband, gliding towards me with sinuous grace. She reached out with long fingers and gripped my chin, squeezing painfully as she turned my face from side to side. Her nails dug cruelly into my skin. She sniffed audibly, flaring her nostrils as if an indescribably offensive odor wafted up to assail her delicate sensibilities.

"A manling? Who invited a *human* to Fae?" Queen Titania kept a firm hold on my chin, but twisted to look around the room, silver sparks crackling at the fingertips of her free hand.

Letitia paled but stood. She dipped into a low formal curtsey and spoke softly but clearly. "My Queen. We didn't precisely invite them. Their presence in Fae is more of a happy accident than a premeditated visit."

"The rules are clear about humans visiting Fae," Oberon rumbled, popping another grape in his massive mouth and chomping down loudly. The skin split with a *pop* and dark red juice dribbled into his beard. It was almost the color of fresh blood.

"Yes," hissed Titania. "Unnecessary manlings are not allowed in Fae without royal decree, which I can assure you, *I did not grant.*" Silver sparks coalesced into a ball of glowing fire in her palm. "But I promise you, I will end the human scourge in our realm right now."

The Fairy Queen raised a glowing fist above my head, holding my chin firmly in place for the deadly strike. I pulled on my shadows, feeling them leap to my hands despite my exhaustion. I'd have to figure out why my magic responded so quickly sometimes and so sluggishly at others. But that was a question to be addressed when an angry fae sorceress wasn't threatening to destroy me for having the audacity to be human. I just really needed a shadow blade *now*.

Shadows pooled in my palm. I focused, readying my will to become the magic whetstone that would birth shadow blades in my hands as quickly as I could. I imagined lunging forward and —

"WAIT!" Letitia's voice rang out like a clarion bell in the enclosed space. The entire room seemed to pause, everyone holding their collective breath.

I felt Titania's nails dig deeper into the skin on my throat and chin as she slowly turned to Letitia. "What did you say to me?" The Fairy Queen's soft voice rang out with reverberating menace in the ominously silent room.

Letitia froze. My eyes flicked towards her, knowing that my future hung precariously balanced on her next words. Letitia looked frozen to the spot, paler than I'd ever seen her. Blythe still held Aubrette's hand, but all semblance of the angry teen had fled. She was just a terrified little girl, hoping that her aunt would wake up soon.

I did a double take, noticing something glittering around the girl's neck. A thin silver chain looped through a small silver ring. One set with a pink quartz stone that danced with a strange, internal light of azure blue.

What the hell!

I quickly reviewed my run-in with Blythe at the feast. She'd bumped into me as she left. She must've used the opportunity to pick my pocket. I doubted she knew what she'd actually taken. More likely, she was just trying to exact her own type of revenge in the moment. However, I couldn't leave that ring in her possession.

One problem at a time. Deal with the Queen who wanted to kill me first. Then I could worry about the teenager. If I failed at the first, the second became moot anyway.

Letitia finally sucked in a noisy breath. When she spoke, her voice was low, but there was no fear in it. I had to grant her that. Letitia wasn't a wilting flower. She rode into battle bravely, waving her banner ever higher. But not all battles were fought with swords and shields. Some were fought with words and tone. The blood spilled, however? Just as red. And I was averse to any blood spilling at the moment, as mine would likely be first.

Letitia's voice was earnest in the silence. "Cameron was not invited to Fae," she started.

"An intruder!" Titania crowed, raising her arm again.

"No!" Letitia shouted, throwing out her arms in protest. Titania furrowed her perfect brow and lowered the crackling ball of silver magic she held cupped in one hand. "No," Letitia repeated, bringing her hands slowly down as if calming a wild animal. Titania mirrored her movements.

Letitia took a deep breath. When she spoke, her voice was clear and calm. "Cameron *accidentally* fell through a portal to Fae as she was trying to protect some members of the Spring Court Embassy in New Orleans. She has tirelessly dedicated herself to finding a lich who was draining my people of their magic and their lives. Courageously, she and her companions pursued this murderous lich across Fae before tracking him down in Winter. Knowing time was of the essence, Cameron challenged the lich and killed him. Because of her selfless bravery, many of my people are still alive today."

Well then.

When Letitia put it like that, I sounded damn near a hero. But I was savvy enough to know that spin was everything and Letitia was practiced at the art of diplomatic double-speak.

Unfortunately, so was Titania.

"Fine. We will deal with the human and her questionable motivations in our realm separately. For now, we must address the murderous rampage of the Winter Lady."

A thin silver cord of magic snaked out of the center of Titania's palm with the speed of a striking viper and wrapped around Estaria. The Winter Lady struggled futilely as magic cords stronger than steel wrapped around her wrists and forced her to back to her knees before Titania. A silvery blade of pure magic crackled to life in the Fairy Queen's hand.

"Or should I say, the former Winter Lady?" Titania snarled, drawing her arm back for a deadly strike. Estaria bowed her head before her Queen, mouthing a silent prayer as the Fairy Queen's magical blade hovered above her head, a breath away from execution.

Chapter 40

I drew on my shadows, throwing myself in front of Estaria. My shadow sword flickered into existence a moment before Titania's silver blade crashed down. Sparks flew and hissed through the air on impact. I gritted my teeth and groaned as my arms burned with the effort of trying to keep the Fairy Queen from separating Estaria's head from her shoulders.

Titania screeched in incoherent rage as she bore down on my shadow blade. I forced all my will into my magic, pouring my belief in Estaria's innocence into my sword. My shadow blade drank in the silvery fire of the Fairy Queen's sword where it crackled and sputtered impotently against the edge sharpened by my determination and sheer grit.

"You. Can't. Kill. Her," I said through bared teeth.

Titania pressed down, using her weight plus gravity to force her blade downwards. "And why not, mortal?"

"You should really ask her," I gritted out.

Titania stepped back fractionally, releasing the pressure on my blade. I almost tipped over at the sudden lack of resistance.

"Why?" Titania asked, raising an eyebrow.

I held my blade ready just in case she was playing some sort of mind game.

"I made a promise and I've already pushed the limits of that today," I panted. "But believe me. You don't want to kill her. For the good of Fae."

Titania narrowed her cat eyes at me, considering me with an air of disbelief. "No, I really think I do." She stepped forward, throwing the weight of her body behind her blade as she redoubled her efforts. I countered and grunted with the exertion of holding off her fresh attack.

Oberon's voice rumbled behind me. "An honorable manling? How quaint. I didn't think any of them knew how to keep a promise anymore. Not without a ridiculous amount of paper and the threat of lawsuits, at least." He chuckled deeply.

The Fairy Queen blinked once at the sound of her husband's voice, then twice. She kept her gaze locked on mine but finally spoke to Estaria. "What is the human talking about? Why shouldn't you I kill you?"

Estaria cleared her throat uncomfortably. Titania snapped her fingers at the Winter Lady. "Come now, I don't have all day."

"I've been experiencing some difficulties with the transfer of power from the Winter mantle. Blackouts. Uncontrolled power surges. I also have yet to name an heir," Estaria said quietly.

The Fairy Queen's eyes went wide. The blade in Titania's hand disappeared with a silent *pop* that pressed uncomfortably on my eardrums. Titania stepped smoothly out of the way, and I nearly fell on my face at the sudden release of pressure. I barely avoided looking like an utter fool by catching myself on one outstretched hand.

Titania prowled around Estaria, her fingers flexing and curling into claws. "What?! How long has it been since you were named Winter Lady? A month?"

"At least two," Oberon rumbled from across the room. He lobbed a grape high into the air and caught it easily in his mouth. Dark red juice spurted, staining his lips and teeth a dull crimson. He caught me staring and grinned manically at me. The Goblin King was going to take up a special place in my nightmares. I just knew it.

"Two months?" Titania's voice crept dangerously close to a screech. She modulated her tone but spiced it with an undercurrent of threat. "What have you been doing in all that time? Diddling your handsome captain, no doubt?"

Estaria's eyes flicked back to Frost and back again so quickly that I nearly missed it. Other than that slight sign of the romance I also suspected between the two, Estaria held her composure remarkably well. "No, my Queen. I am still upset by my brother's death. I don't believe it was an accident. He—"

Titania raised her hand, cutting her off. "This old, worn-out drivel? I've heard enough. I grow bored. Husband, ready yourself to take the Winter mantle." Oberon set down the grape he held in his hand and grabbed the armrests, bracing slightly in his chair.

The silvery blade crackled back into existence, and Titania pointed it directly at Estaria. "I told you then and I'll tell you now, there is no conspiracy to take Winter away from your family, although you seem to have managed the very thing you feared all on your own. How tragic for you. The bards will use your name as a warning for other foolish leaders who dare to contradict their Queen. If they remember you at all." Titania drew her arm back to strike, her face a perfect mask of serene benevolence.

Something the Fairy Queen said jarred my memory. "Family," I murmured under my breath without realizing I'd spoken out loud.

Titania's blade froze in mid-air. My words had stopped its descent more swiftly than my shadow blade had mere moments before.

"What was that?" Titania's eyes glittered dangerously.

"Who gave the mortal leave to speak? Or is she just dense?" Oberon bellowed from across the room.

Sloane hissed at me. "Shut up, Cam!"

I ignored all of them and shook my head. Pieces of the puzzle I didn't know I possessed coalesced to make a terrifying picture in my mind. "What if we've been going about this all wrong?" I said, filling the gaping maw of silence. "I mean, it doesn't add up."

Titania looked over her shoulder at her husband. "Have manlings grown stupider since I last spoke to one?" She returned her attention to me and spoke slowly, enunciating clearly, as if she thought I was an imbecile. "An attack plus magical weapons equals attempted murder."

I snorted softly. "Your schools are *so* messed up if you think that is what a math problem is."

Silver lightning crackled menacingly at the Fairy Queen's fingertips, but I hurried on.

"What I meant was, this can't be just about Estaria's family and Winter. I think that someone has been going around, killing off members of the ruling families of the courts and making them look like accidents. Estaria's brother. Lord Treston's son, Niall. If I were a betting person,

I'd be willing to wager that, if you did some digging, you'd uncover other fatal accidents among the other courts' nobility as well."

Oberon sat forward in his chair and growled, "And are you a betting person?"

A sudden premonition gripped me, as if I were standing on the edge of a cliff with my toes hanging over and a strong gale blowing in behind me. I swallowed hard, choosing my words carefully. "I don't bet with people's lives."

Oberon grunted and leaned back in his chair, looking dissatisfied. That scared me more than Titania's callous rush to execution or Lord Treston's sorrow-induced rage. It was a stark reminder that I needed to watch where I stepped, or, more accurately, how I spoke. This was a proverbial minefield. Any word I used poorly could blow this whole situation to smithereens. Itty bitty, Cameron-speckled smithereens.

Titania interrupted my thoughts. "So, what if some of my nobles have died? Fae is a dangerous place. Only the strong survive." She shrugged casually, as if commenting on the weather.

"This isn't about survival," I snapped back. "This is about *murder*. Widespread, calculated, almost *surgical* murder." Something about the words hit home.

"Precisely," Lord Treston interjected. "Which is why we are here. The Winter Lady tried to murder my wife."

I shook my head. "No, I think that she's just a convenient scapegoat."

"A *convincing* scapegoat, you mean," Titania retorted.

"I didn't do it!" Estaria protested.

"And how can you say that with any certainty if you are experiencing regular blackouts?" Titania sneered.

Rather than engaging, I took a different path. "What if all our assumptions are wrong? What if these deaths haven't been fatal accidents at all but premeditated murders designed to weaken the courts? Think about it. Niall dies and there is no obvious heir left in Spring. Etienne dies and his death thrust his younger sister into a role that she is unprepared to handle. By attacking Lady Aubrette and setting up Lady Estaria to take the fall, the killer strikes two courts at the same time. He or she further weakens the Spring Court and, if everything works out, gets Lord Treston to kill the Winter Lady, which would fragment the heart of Winter's power."

"A convoluted theory," Oberon said.

"Agreed, husband. Either make your point, manling, or I will make one of my own," Titania said, flicking her sword at me.

"I think it was Hemlock, the Winter emissary," I blurted out. "He's the only one who makes sense. He could create the ice weapon and I think he might have harbored sympathies for those who oppose the Court system. He and his accomplice worked together to frame Lady Estaria for the attack on the Spring Lady, hoping to spur Lord Treston into hasty retaliation that would've ended cataclysmically when the Winter mantle had no heir to inherit it."

Titania ran her tongue over her teeth, considering her words. "Very well, manling. Entertain me. Who is this accomplice?"

Okay, new problem. I had no fucking idea. But I had one shot, and I needed to make it count. I spoke slowly, my mind spinning in the background as I tried to put together all the pieces into a convincing narrative.

I cleared my throat and spoke slowly, choosing my words with the utmost care. "Assume for a moment that all the rumors are true. There is a treasonous plot brewing in Fae to return it to the wilder ways. All those nobles dying in 'accidents', weren't victims of foul play at all but assassinated in ways that only looked like accidents. However, the victims were too important, too well-guarded. It couldn't have just been one person doing it all, could it?" I answered my own question before I could be interrupted. "No. It would've been nearly impossible for one person to do so unless they were a ninja assassin on steroids. No, the much more likely scenario is that there is an organized group working in concert to topple the Court system."

"No, the more likely conclusion is that the Winter Lady went mad and killed my wife. Because that is the truth!" Lord Treston exploded. "Governmental overthrow only happens in the manling realm. Not in Fae."

"That's because you've never had an organized government for any length of time before this," I retorted. "Think about it. This attack was perfectly timed and designed to frame Lady Estaria. The ice dagger. The knowledge of her blackouts. The ability to strike boldly in the middle of the Spring Court. At Lady Aubrette herself! It all speaks of knowledge, ability, and proximity."

"If we believe your wild theory," Lord Treston scoffed.

"Treston? Interrupt her again and I will have you removed from this room. In pieces." Titania's voice was void of emotion, but Treston's teeth snapped shut. She waved a hand at me. "Get to the point, and quickly, manling, before I tire of your verbal flailing."

The frostbite on my knee ached, and I rubbed at it. Suddenly, more of the puzzle pieces snapped into place in my mind and I spoke with ever-growing confidence. "We know that there are four people who were in Spring at the time of the attack who could've created this ice weapon." I held up a finger for each name. "Lady Estaria, Captain Frost, Krampus, and Hemlock. But Captain Frost and Krampus disappeared roughly around the same time, well before the attack. Meaning they couldn't have created the ice weapon and handed it off to an accomplice. It would've melted before the attack." I folded two fingers down, leaving two pointed upwards. "It would be the height of stupidity to save the person who you'd just attempted to murder instead of making a clean getaway, and Estaria is not a stupid person." I folded down another finger. "Which only leaves Hemlock."

"But we know he was in the banqueting hall. He couldn't have done it," Commander Maeweather interjected.

I pointed my upraised finger at him and waggled it. "Which brings us back to the accomplice theory. Hemlock might not have struck the blow, but that doesn't absolve him of creating the weapon. In fact, I spotted him in the hallway moments before the attack. He could've easily created the ice weapon and handed it off."

Oberon drummed his nails against his armrest and then clicked his tongue. "A pretty theory, but it has one gaping flaw. There is no actual proof. Not of a conspiracy. Not of an accomplice. Nothing."

"Not true. We have frostbite," I said, a hint of triumph leaking into my tone.

"Frostbite?" Oberon sounded confused.

I conjured a small shadow blade. It sprang to life in my palm with surprising ease. Before anyone could move, I turned it on myself. I cut away a square of cloth in my leggings, exposing my knee. A fresh wound with ugly blackened edges oozed clear pus at the sudden removal of the cloth. The ointment I'd spread on it had helped a little, but after my recent mistreatment of the wound, it felt as painful as it looked. I looked up triumphantly.

Titania furrowed her brow at my knee and spoke dryly. "Dare I ask what that is? Or will the answer lead us down another rabbit hole of conspiracies? Perhaps with an overzealous tailor and a giant this time?" Titania waved her hand at me dismissively, but Oberon leaned forward in his chair to get a closer look, despite his wife's disbelieving tone.

I ignored him and pointed at my knee as I directed my words at Titania. "This is what happens when someone touches conjured ice who isn't from Winter."

"Let me see if I understand your theory," said Titania. "You propose that Hemlock created an ice weapon moments before the attack on Lady Aubrette. He handed the dagger off to an associate who then carried out this heinous crime. Then Hemlock hurried back to the banquet hall to create an elaborate ruse of an alibi. Have I followed your absurd line of thought, mortal?"

"Yes," I said.

"We are to believe that this is a more logical conclusion than catching a murderess red-handed, standing over her victim with the weapon in her hand?" Titania put a heavy sneer into her voice.

I fought to keep my tone even. "But it wasn't in her hand. It was shattered and melting on the floor. Why would she have let it shatter when she could've just reabsorbed the ice? Which is my point. Whoever made the blade didn't do the deed. When the knife shattered, it could have fallen on some exposed skin, causing frostbite to Hemlock's accomplice."

Oberon stroked his beard thoughtfully. "As much as I enjoy a good conspiracy theory," he said, "I'm not sure that this one can be substantiated. You're asking us to believe in an, as yet undefined, accomplice on your word alone."

"Not on my word alone," I protested. "There's evidence out there!"

"Ah yes, the supposed frostbite." Oberon settled back in his chair and steepled his fingers, tapping them lightly against his chin.

"Yes! The frostbite."

Lord Treston snorted. "You want us to search every person in this castle for a trace of hypothetical frostbite? Impossible! Even if we started now, word would get out and your supposed accomplice would either escape or create a glamour to obscure the wound."

Titania slapped the palms of her hands on the chair. "I agree. The mortal has a certain flair for the dramatic. I'll grant you, it is an entertaining story, but that is all. A story. Again, *human*, you have no proof. Now, if we are finished with this charade, let us continue with the unfortunate business to hand. I would prefer not to draw this out any longer."

"Wait!" I said desperately, looking around the room. My eyes landed on something at the back of the room and suddenly, I knew I was right, and I had all the evidence to prove it.

"A wild ogre chase will not net you an accomplice, even if there is one lurking in the castle somewhere," Oberon rumbled. Annoyance laced his words.

"No more waiting," Titania said. Her blade crackled with silvery magic as she stood.

"Not lurking *somewhere*," I said. "Lurking *here*." Eyes widened and small gasps sounded. I raised my finger in the air and let it fall to point across the room at the pair of musicians. "Why, in the warmth of the Spring Court, does someone wear gloves? Especially when doing so means that he cannot perform for the most important people in all of Fae."

All eyes turned to Brio, who was rubbing his wrist distractedly. He jumped to his feet, backing away slowly. He held up his gloved hands, then glanced at them and tucked them swiftly behind his back. "I am allowing my journeyman the honor of performing for such a prestigious audience. It is my role as her tutor and master to provide her with opportunities to show her skill. It is a sacred duty. One I take most seriously."

"Which is why you always allow her to play when everyone is mingling after expecting silence for your performance, of course," Sloane said sweetly from across the room.

I directed my next words at his journeyman, Jazria. "And does he do this often? Allow you the honor of playing in front of the most powerful people in Fae instead of him?"

The musician's face paled. She slowly shook her head.

Brio continued backing away as all eyes turned to him. "I don't know what the manling is talking about," he said, looking a little panicked. His breath came in short bursts. "She is delusional! She's gone mad from being exposed to our magic. She's grasping at anything to serve her Winter mistress!"

"There is a simple way to prove whether she is mad and a simple way to prove your innocence. Luckily, they are the same," Titania said, raising her sword and stalking towards the bard. "Take off your gloves."

Brio's eyes rolled wildly in his head. With more speed than I would've given him credit for, he yanked a dagger from a hidden sheath at the small of his back.

Instinctively, I threw myself forward towards the Winter Lady while simultaneously calling a shadow blade into existence. There was no way I was letting him kill Estaria. Not now.

But I'd misjudged his target. Brio turned away from the Winter Lady and flung himself at the prone body of Lady Aubrette.

"No!" Blythe shrieked, throwing herself across her godmother's body in a brave, desperate attempt to save her surrogate mother from the fatal strike. Everyone else looked on in shock as Brio charged the Spring Lady, murder in his eyes. And no one else was close enough to intercept the bard as he attacked a helpless woman and a girl.

I watched in horror as he raised the blade high. Treston moved to save his wife, but he was too far away and wasn't fast enough. Brio launched himself through the air, intent on landing the fatal strike with the entire force of his body behind the blow.

But the strike never landed.

With a roar, Oberon propelled himself out of his chair. The speed of his sudden movement sent the chair tumbling backwards and grapes cascading to the floor to squelch underneath his massive feet as he charged at Brio.

Oberon lowered his head, driving through Brio's hapless body just as the bard launched himself into an irreversible strike. Oberon cut Brio's attack short while the bard was in midair. The wickedly pointed tips of Oberon's horns pierced into the bard's body like a harpoon through silk. The Goblin King threw his head back with a roar of triumph. Brio struggled weakly. Oberon shook his head violently from side to side, working the horns ever deeper into the doomed bard's body. Rivulets of blood dripped down Oberon's face and into his beard from the gory crown he wore atop his head. All I could think of was how the bard's blood was almost the exact same color as the grape juice that had spattered Oberon's beard mere moments before.

Brio twitched spasmodically on the tips of the Goblin King's antlers. The bard was dead already. His body sprawled limply as his life blood flowed down Oberon's antlers. The Goblin King lowered his head and shook the bard loose.

The musician slipped off the pointed tips of the Goblin King's horns with a squelch and slid limply to the floor. A pool of blood quickly formed underneath the bard's still body from the multiple puncture wounds. The viscous liquid seeped into the hardwood floor, staining the dark wood a disturbing dusky crimson.

An annoyed huff broke through my stupefied horror at the bard's violent end. Titania stood with a hand on her hip, shaking her sword at her husband as though admonishing a schoolyard bully. "Now we'll have to get that suit cleaned and you know blood doesn't come out of that fabric easily. Do try to be more careful in the future."

Oberon looked unrepentant. He ran a hand over his face, wiping the dripping blood back into his hair like the most disturbing leave-in conditioner imaginable, then licked his fingers clean. "Yes, my love," he said, utterly unabashed.

Titania snorted. With a wave of her hand, she shifted the sword into a slim, silver knife crackling with magical sparks. She glided over to Brio's body and knelt at his side. "Let us see if your theory holds merit, mortal."

"What?" I exclaimed. "Didn't you just see him try to attack Lady Aubrette?"

"His actions, while disturbing, do not prove her innocence," Titania said, pointing her dagger at Estaria. "And since my husband was a touch too enthusiastic in his reprimand, it's not as if we can question the bard now, can we?"

Titania returned her attention to the dead musician. She deftly sliced through the delicately tooled leather glove on his right hand and peeled it back. She slowly revealed long fingers and tanned skin. She flipped the dead man's hand over. It was unblemished by any telltale dark marks.

My nerves ratcheted a notch higher. What if I was wrong? But Brio had attacked Aubrette right in front of our eyes. He *had* to be behind all this. I couldn't be wrong. Could I?

Titania stood, lifted her skirts daintily to avoid the pooling blood, and stepped over the body. My pulse thundered loudly in my ears, punctuated sporadically by the gasping sobs coming from Blythe, where she still crouched over her godmother protectively.

Titania swept her pristine skirts to the side as she carefully sliced through the second glove. All eyes in the room were glued on her progress. Finally, she worked the tight leather off the dead bard's fingers and tossed the mangled glove into the pool of spreading blood.

My breath caught in my throat. There. On the inside of his left wrist, just below the cuff of his elaborately embroidered shirt, was a series of small slices, blackened at the edges by magical frostbite.

Chapter 41

Titania lifted her knife as she rose from her crouch. "Husband, I must confer with you."

Oberon's face was grim as he offered her his bloodstained hand. Titania accepted it and daintily glided away from Brio's body.

She spun to point her dagger at each of us. "No one leaves this room until I give my leave."

Faint murmurs of agreement met her words. The royal couple moved off to the side of the room. Titania waved her hand. A shimmer of silver sparks danced to life like hungry, carnivorous fireflies around their heads. Not a sound escaped the swarm as the Queen whispered urgently to her King. Almost absentmindedly, Titania flicked her wrist at the journeyman musician who stood gaping at her dead master. Silver cords sprang out and trussed up the girl in an instant. She fell to the floor with a crash, looking like a terrified mummy as she ended up splashing into the pool of spreading blood.

Estaria fell into Captain Frost's arms, sobbing softly. He stroked her hair and murmured comfort designed for her ears alone. I looked away quickly to give them privacy.

Lord Treston hurried over to the bed where his wife lay. He placed an awkward hand on Blythe's shoulder. The girl turned to face him, tears streaming from her dazzling green eyes to cascade down her beautiful face. It might have been a trick of the light, but the pink crystal in the ring around her neck looked duller than before. I reminded myself that I needed to retrieve the ring from Blythe before we left. I couldn't leave it here with all the unanswered questions surrounding it. The girl threw herself into her godfather's arms as if he were her last bastion of hope. I suppose, in some ways, he was.

Letitia drifted over towards her family. Blythe snaked an arm out and yanked her cousin into a fierce group hug. Something tugged at my heart to see the remnants of the family band together. Even Aubrette seemed to breathe easier in her unconscious state. Her color had improved since I entered the room. A bloom of color tinged her cheeks to a peony pink. I smiled faintly. Maybe she'd make a full recovery after all.

A hand touched my elbow. I turned to see Sloane. She eyed my hand skeptically. "I'd hug you, but I also feel the overwhelming urge to tell you that you're an idiot. And brilliant. A brilliant idiot. However, I made I promise to my mother never to hug someone with a knife."

I glanced down, surprised to see I still held my shadow knife. I released my hold. It dissolved back into shadows. I wiggled my empty hand at her. "There. Better?"

Sloane flung herself at me, crushing the air out of my lungs with the force of her hug. "You're an idiot," she muttered into my shirt.

"A brilliant idiot," I reminded her, returning the hug.

"How did you figure that all out?" Sloane asked, pushing away from me.

"I'll tell you, but not right now," I whispered, as the shimmering sparks faded from around Titania and Oberon.

The Fairy Queen strode to the center of the room, commanding silence. "There is always a price to pay for power, and this is the moment of reckoning," she said coldly, looking at each of the fae nobles. "For far too long, my husband and I have been battling the forces that threaten our realm alone, protecting you and all the inhabitants of Fae from descending back into the madness and chaos that once consumed this realm. As our enemies grow and multiply, so must our allies. We can no longer hold back the tide of rebellion on our own."

A sword crackled to life in her hands once more. I noticed that Oberon now held an ebony-colored bow nocked with a green-and-black fletched arrow pointed at the floor. "My Queen is saying that it is time to choose a side. Will you stand with us against the forces that threaten to tear down the beautiful order we have created together, or are you our enemy?" He lifted the bow slightly, not pointing it specifically at any one person, but the threat clear in the tension of his bowstring.

Lord Treston was the first to move. He fell to his knees, bowing his head and raising a fist to his heart. "You have my fealty, my sword, and my life. I will stand with you," he said, sincerity ringing clearly in his words. Letitia and Blythe knelt a moment later, echoing the Spring Lord's words under Titania and Oberon's fearsome gaze. The guards followed suit, pledging unwavering loyalty.

The Fairy Queen slowly turned to face Estaria. The Winter Lady had composed herself and looked every inch the ice queen once more. Titania raised an eyebrow. "Are you choosing death over service, Lady Winter?" Her tone brooked no compromise.

Estaria, to her credit, didn't flinch under Titania's gaze. "Will you help me find my brother's killer?" Estaria asked. "I swore an oath to see blood repaid with blood and I do not break my oaths."

A wicked smile twisted Titania's lips. "It is good to know you hold as true to your oaths as I do to my own. I swear to you I will help you find your brother's killer, if he is still in Fae, and will turn him over to you to face whatever justice you mete out."

"Then I am yours," Estaria said, falling to her knees and raising her fist to her heart. Captain Frost followed his Lady a moment later. A loud crack resonated throughout the room like a gunshot. I crouched, looking around to see where this unexpected threat was coming from. Purple and icy blue spirals of frost danced across the floor in a mesmerizing pattern of whorls and swirls. The intricate design pulsed with magic for a split second before fading into nothing, leaving the wood underneath bone dry as if the frost had never been there.

A silvery laugh caught me off guard. Titania pressed a delicate hand to her chest and inclined her head to Estaria. "It is nice to see you fully accept the Winter mantle, Lady Estaria. I look forward to seeing how you wield your newly uncovered powers under my banners in the future." Estaria dipped her head, a faint blush of pride at the Fairy Queen's words creeping up her cheeks.

Titania finally turned to face Sloane and me. I snuck a peek at Sloane, who shrugged infinitesimally. Titania raised a single eyebrow in silent query.

I swallowed hard and spoke carefully. "Umm, no offense, but all I want is to find our friends and return to New Orleans as soon as possible," I said, adding a hasty "your Majesty," at the end.

Titania considered us for a moment more before letting her sword flicker out of existence. "Very well. I suppose our battles are not yours, after all. However, I would… request… you do not speak of what you witnessed this day with anyone not in this room. Surprise is a weapon that I wield with the same efficiency as my blade. In return for your silence about the events that have transpired here today, you may leave our realm without fear of repercussion for your unorthodox visit."

I looked at Sloane, raising a questioning eyebrow. She shrugged, apparently unable to see a downside to the Queen's offer. "Sounds like a fair exchange," I said. "You have my silence about what has happened in this room today." A *whoomph* shuddered through my chest as the deal was sealed.

"And mine," added Sloane quickly.

Oberon nodded once in our direction before turning his attention to the trussed-up musician wriggling impotently on the floor. He pulled the arrow back to his ear and the woman's eyes widened in horror. "Shall I dispatch this one for you, my love?" Blood dripped down his antlers and made his matted curls glisten. Oberon offered to dispatch the journeyman musician so casually that he might have been asking if he could get Titania a cup of tea. Jazria's eyes went wide and wild. She increased her frantic, futile efforts to free herself from the magical bonds.

Titania turned her cat eyes towards the terrified journeyman. "No, I don't think so. Brio is… was… an unexpected traitor and one we can no longer question. His journeyman might provide us with answers he cannot. Bring her with us but guard her well. She might be our only lead to find this missing Hemlock and the other rebels."

Oberon nodded and slung his bow over his shoulder, where it promptly disappeared. He crouched next to the musician and, with a grunt, hefted her over his massive shoulder.

"Oh, and husband?" Oberon turned at Titania's words. "Make sure she remains gagged the entire way home." He nodded and placed his hand on the handle of the door.

Before he could open it, a weak voice sounded from the bed. "What..." Aubrette let out a hacking cough, pressing her hand to her bandaged wound as she winced at the pain. Lord Treston flew to his wife's side and helped her to sit. Once she had regained control of herself, Aubrette looked around the room weakly. "What have I missed?"

Chapter 42

Blythe threw herself at Aubrette in the fiercest gentle embrace I'd ever seen. The Spring Lady looked startled as the girl convulsed in silent sobs.

"Daughter? Is that you, Blythe?" Aubrette dropped a hand to the girl's head and stroked her fine blonde hair as if she hadn't seen Blythe just that morning.

"Godmother! I thought you'd...you'd..." Blythe looked up at Aubrette through watery eyes and then dissolved into a new deluge of wracking sobs.

Aubrette's hand hitched in midair just for a moment before clutching Blythe to her gently. "Oh, Blythe, I'd never leave you! You are my precious... goddaughter," Aubrette said, pausing ever so slightly on the last word as if it felt strange in her mouth. Tears filled her eyes, making them glisten a brilliant azure blue.

A tingle started at the base of my skull, as if a distant memory was dancing just on the edges of my conscious brain. Instinct told me that the sooner I figured out what my subconscious wanted me to remember, the better off I'd be. Unfortunately, I didn't currently have the time to delve into memories to figure out what was ringing warning bells in my mind.

Oberon opened the door and a flood of people rushed into the room. Guards took possession of the bound and gagged musician. Healers rushed to Aubrette's side. Servants covered Brio's body with a clean cloth that did nothing to obscure the coagulating puddle of blood.

Estaria and Captain Frost threaded their way through the chaos that had descended upon the room towards us. The Winter Lady dipped a low curtsy, and her Captain matched her gesture with a respectful bow.

Estaria rose gracefully from her curtsey and spoke. "You have helped me to uncover the mystery behind my brother's death, even if I have not yet found the culprit. For that, you have my unending gratitude."

"Not for saving your life?" Sloane asked skeptically.

Captain Frost dipped his head in a sincere bow. "For that, you have *my* unending gratitude," he said. He raised his lady's hand and gently kissed the back of it. Estaria smiled warmly up at the stoic captain before returning her attention to us.

"I assume you wish to return to your home as soon as possible, but know that you are welcome in Winter should you ever return to Fae. It would be my honor to host you in my court on your next visit," she said earnestly.

I squinted at her overdramatically. "No ice spears this time?" I asked, taking a step back and raising my hands in mock self-defense.

Estaria chuckled. "No promises, but I will try to give warning before attempting to impale you or your friends."

I pretended to consider her offer seriously and then shrugged. "I'll take it." Grinning, I stuck out my hand. After a moment of hesitation, Estaria took it. She squeezed my hand warmly as we shook. Well, as warmly as a member of the Winter Court could.

Lord Treston cleared his throat from behind me. Estaria let go of my hand and turned to face the Spring Lord. "Lady Estaria, if I may interrupt, I believe we have some matters to discuss, beginning with a heartfelt apology on my part." He clicked his heels together and performed a tight little bow.

Estaria dipped her head in return. "Of course, Lord Treston." She turned to me. "Excuse me, please," she said.

"No ice spears," I reminded her under my breath.

A mischievous smile tugged at the corners of her mouth. "No promises," she repeated before moving off to have a discreet conversation with the Spring Lord. Captain Frost nodded briskly at us before following his lady.

Letitia approached, a brilliant smile lighting her too thin face. "The healer thinks it's likely that my aunt will make a full recovery! Of course, there will be a scar, but no one predicted she would wake up this soon. It's a miracle!"

"That's amazing!" Sloane exclaimed.

"Unbelievable," I echoed. Something clicked in my head as a memory came sharply into focus. "Umm, did the healer say what was going on with her eyes?" I asked.

"You mean, why are they blue instead of green?" Letitia shrugged. "The hypothesis is that it was a rare reaction to the ice magic."

"Hypothesis?" I asked.

Letitia waggled a hand in midair. "It's the best they could do. There aren't many known survivors of a deadly attack from an enchanted ice weapon, so who knows?"

"Right. Who knows?" I mumbled. But the explanation didn't convince me.

Letitia grasped each of our hands in hers, changing the topic. "I assume you would like to return as quickly as possible to New Orleans, and I will probably be busy here for a while, but I needed to pass on my thanks before you left. Let's catch up as soon as I'm back, okay?" She smiled and turned to go.

I held onto her hand, stopping her. I had my own hypothesis to test. "Umm, Letitia?" I said awkwardly. "So sorry to do this right now, but I think that your little cousin has something of mine. I need it back before we can go."

Letitia narrowed her eyes at Blythe. "She's gotten into some bad habits lately. Sticky fingers and the like. What did she take this time?"

I gestured at my neck. "The small silver ring on her necklace. I don't really care how she got it. I just need it back."

Letitia looked over and narrowed her eyes at her cousin. She nodded. "I remember. It was on your chain that broke at the feast. Not to worry. I'll get it for you." She hurried off with a determined look on her face.

Sloane raised an eyebrow at me while Letitia whispered heatedly into Blythe's ear. "Is that the same ring...?" Sloane asked. She waggled her eyebrows significantly as she tailed off.

"That I think houses the last soul that escaped on Halloween? Yeah." I tried to watch Letitia chastise Blythe without looking like I was staring.

"How'd she get it, anyway?" Sloane asked curiously.

"She must've lifted it. I didn't even feel it when she picked my pocket. The girl's got skills."

"You sound like you're impressed," Sloane observed.

I tipped my hand back and forth slightly. "I am a little. But I also feel bad for the kid. Fate dealt her a rough hand."

Sloane nodded thoughtfully as Letitia returned. The fae woman pressed the ring into my hand. "Please accept my apologies on Blythe's behalf."

I accepted the ring and tucked it deep into my pocket. "I've got it back now, so there's no problem. Thanks for talking with her." I checked the tattoo on my wrist and let out a little sigh of relief. The blue dot was still hovering near the center of the compass.

Letitia held up a finger and smiled mischievously. "Well, there is one problem."

My stomach dropped. "What's that?" I asked.

"You owe me a shopping trip. A *full* shopping trip," Letitia said, her smile blooming into a full, unrepentant grin.

Sloane burst out. "What? How? Cam *hates* shopping!"

I groaned, but Letitia looked proud of herself. "We made a deal that Cam wouldn't get pulled into any maniacal schemes, and I think this is the very definition of a maniacal scheme," she said, gesturing at the room.

"Really? You're going to hold me to that after I just uncovered the mystery behind your aunt's attack?" I asked. The look on Letitia's face told me it was hopeless to protest.

"Absolutely. Deals are sacrosanct in Fae," Letitia said.

Sloane nodded seriously. "Agreed."

I groaned. "Fine. When we are all back in New Orleans, we'll go shopping."

"I'd love to see this," Sloane said with altogether too much enjoyment for my taste.

"You should come!" Letitia exclaimed. "The more the merrier!"

"Says who?" I grumbled.

Chapter 43

Sloane and I faded back to the corner of the room as more people in Spring livery crowded into the room. I wasn't sure if we were free to go and was just about to make an executive decision on the matter when Lord Treston approached.

He bowed curtly to each of us. "Without your assistance today, things might have been much worse."

"I'm just glad we could help," I said sincerely. I didn't even want to imagine what ripple effects might've spread to Earth if the plot had succeeded. Although, now that I had the time and an adrenaline crash, I could picture all sorts of horrible scenarios.

"Indeed. I find myself once again in your—"

I held up my hand, forestalling any further words of gratitude or debts. "I think we can all agree that we narrowly dodged catastrophe today. However, if you don't mind, my friends and I would really like to get back to New Orleans as quickly as possible. I know you have a lot on your plate, but when you have a moment, could I cash in that boon from before? If you can send us home, then we'll be square, okay?"

Treston blinked in surprise and then a warm, genuine smile broke over his face. He extended a hand, and I accepted the grip with a smile of my own. "I've never met anyone quite like you, Cameron Blaze."

"Consider yourself lucky then," Sloane said from behind me. When I turned to glare over my shoulder, she was studying the ceiling intently and even whistled softly under her breath.

Treston chuckled and pressed my hand firmly once before letting go. "I have a few things to attend to here first, but I will arrange for your transport back to your home as quickly as possible."

"Great. Th—" I said. "Umm, I mean, all the best for Aubrette and her, you know, recovery."

Treston looked over his shoulder to where Blythe was beaming at her godmother, and Aubrette seemed to improve almost by the second. "I will inform her of your well wishes. Now, if you will excuse me?" He bowed again, deeper this time, and hurried back to his wife's side.

It took Sloane and me about two minutes more to realize that we were just getting in the way of the flurry of activity in the relatively small space. Quietly, we slipped out of the hubbub and spent the next fifteen minutes trying to find our rooms.

Luckily, Magnus and Andrei had already returned by the time we arrived. Magnus crushed me in a massive hug as soon as he saw me. I hugged him back just as hard. I was thankful that he and Andrei had returned tired, but unscathed. Apparently, they'd found Krampus asleep in a cave. After waking him and hearing his story, all three had rushed back to the castle, where they were promptly put under the strict guard of Captain Maeweather's most trusted men. They'd been locked in their rooms and unable to convince anyone to tell them where we were or what was happening. It took me one look at Magnus to realize he'd been a hair's breadth away from shifting and tearing down the castle stone by stone until he found me.

When it came time for Sloane and me to share our adventures, we had to rely on innuendo and vague statements because of our promise of secrecy. Despite the initial frustration, Magnus and Andrei eventually understood why we were being so cagey. They pieced together enough of what we left unsaid to comprehend the gist of what had happened, even if the details were lacking. After swapping stories, we all agreed that it was time for us to head back to New Orleans. A small whirlwind of packing consumed the next few minutes.

Soon, we all gathered back in my room with our packs in hand. I checked for the third time to make sure that Goliath was tucked up safely in his special pocket in my bag. He'd still been quietly asleep on my pillow, and I'd almost forgotten about him. I also brushed my hand against the pocket that held the ring and my mother's charm that I'd retrieved from its hiding place in the drawer, rechecking their presence for the umpteenth time. I wasn't about to leave either in Fae on a mere oversight.

Then, it was a lot of sitting around and waiting until Commander Maeweather appeared and escorted us to the most elite magicians in the Spring Court. Apparently, the magic was complex and draining, but by working together, the seven of them could send us wherever we wished to go in the mortal realm. After a brief discussion, we settled on my apartment, mostly because it was empty. Magically appearing in the middle of the city where a Norm might see us, or worse, record us, seemed like a bad idea. After our escapades in Fae, I'd just put myself in the Collective's good graces. At least, I hoped so. But there was no way I was going on their shit list if I could help it.

Magnus intertwined his fingers in mine as the magicians chanted and drew strange sigils in the air. "This is so cool!" Andrei exclaimed, trying to wriggle around to see everything at once.

"Calm down, pup," Magnus said, but he didn't look like he really meant it. Andrei must've thought so too, because the kid ignored him.

I smiled up at the large werewolf holding my hand. "There's no place like home," I said.

"Agreed. But I never thought I'd get the chance to say, 'Beam me up, Scotty!' in Fae of all places. However, now seems like an à propos time," he whispered.

Sloane leaned around me. "You're a Trekkie? Okay. You can stay. I guess." She extended a fist.

Magnus chuckled as he tapped his knuckles against hers. "Glad to hear it."

A warm fuzzy feeling crept up from my stomach and landed somewhere in the region of my heart as I watched the two of them. Or maybe it was the prospect of going home. Either way, I was smiling like an idiot when the world flashed white.

Chapter 44

When I opened my eyes, the four of us were standing in the middle of my apartment. My cozy, little one-bedroom apartment. A breath of relief whooshed out of me. I didn't know how transport from Fae was supposed to go, but that was relatively anticlimactic. A flash of light and we were back.

As soon as I blinked the stars from my eyes, I headed towards the bedroom. I wanted to get my phone to check the date. A small tinkling noise of metal on metal tugged at my ear. I fished around in my pocket and pulled out the pink quartz ring. I was glad I'd gotten it back before leaving Fae. As I looked at the ring, something seemed off about it. The azure light that had been on the inside of the pink quartz had vanished. I checked my cinnamon-colored tattoo on my inner wrist immediately. The blue dot had also vanished from the tracking tattoo. That was weird. I'd checked it when Letitia got the ring back from Blythe. The tracking dot had been there. It couldn't just vanish, could it? Maybe the journey from Fae was messing with the sigil's magic and it needed some time to catch up with the sudden transfer of surroundings. I flicked the ring thoughtfully as Magnus, Sloane, and Andrei erupted into excited chatter in the room behind me.

I set the ring on my nightstand and snagged my phone from its charging cable. I paused with my thumb hovering over the home button. My mouth was suddenly dry. Time flowed differently between Earth and Fae. Even though we'd been gone for just over two weeks in Fae time, that could've been anything from an hour to a century here on Earth. The positive thing was that all my stuff was still in the apartment, so it couldn't have been that long. I pressed the button and blinked in surprise at the date on my screen. I double-checked it before running back into the living room.

"It's been a month! We've been gone a month!" I said as I waved the phone.

A frown broke over Magnus's face. "Are you sure? We were only in Fae for a couple of weeks."

"Time flows differently in Fae. It could've been a lot worse," Sloane reminded him, heading towards my kettle to make a cup of tea.

"Check for yourself," I said, holding the phone up so Magnus could see it. He glanced at and nodded thoughtfully.

"I can't wait to tell all my friends I went to fucking Fae!" Andrei crowed.

"Hey!" Magnus said. The older wolf caught the kid in a playful head-lock. "Don't let your dad hear you talking like that, or he'll have your hide. And then he'll have mine." He rubbed his knuckles on the top of Andrei's head with a chuckle.

Andrei wriggled loose and glared at Magnus while he tried to smooth his hair back into the teenager-approved state of dishevelment.

"Speaking of Damon, I'd better get the kid back home," Magnus said over Andrei's grumbling.

"Sure. Do you want to call ahead and let him know you're on the way?" I asked, holding out my phone.

Magnus shook his head. "No, I don't think so. The Pack headquarters isn't too far away. Besides, Damon would probably handle this news better face to face." He hitched his pack a little higher and spoke to Andrei. "C'mon kid, let's go."

"Fine, but if you touch my hair again, it's on," Andrei said. He tried to sound tough, but his irrepressible good humor snuck through, robbing his words of any threat.

"Sure, kid," Magnus said, placing a hand on Andrei's shoulder and steering him towards the door. Something about watching Magnus walk out my front door snagged at my heart.

"Hey! Magnus?" I said, taking a couple of quick steps forward.

"Yeah?" He turned with a quizzical brow lifted.

"Umm." My brain stuttered to a stop. I didn't know what to say. I didn't enjoy seeing him walk out my front door, but I couldn't form the right words to communicate that to him.

Magnus read everything I didn't say in that moment of hesitation. A small smile curved his lips, and he strode over. He caught me up with an arm around my waist and another tangling in the back of my hair. The kiss was hard, electrifying, and over much too quickly for my liking. When he lifted his head, his gray eyes were twinkling with more than just merriment.

"I'm ready to take you on that date, Cam, whenever you are. You just say the word," he breathed, for my ears only. Slowly, like he was forcing himself to let me go, he released his hold and stepped back.

Andrei's voice drifted from down the hall. "Hurry up or I'm leaving you!"

Magnus rolled his eyes but shot me a roguish wink before disappearing down the hall.

I chuckled under my breath and shut the door behind them. I was already on the brink of daydreaming about my next encounter with the handsome werewolf.

Sloane cleared her throat loudly from where she was standing in the kitchen. "Something you want to tell me?" she asked as she settled down at the kitchen table with two mugs of steaming tea. She slid one over to me. I shoved my phone in my pocket as I sat across from her.

"Maybe? I don't know. Magnus and I are, well, kind of a thing, I guess."

"When a man kisses you like that, it's way more than 'kind of a thing'," Sloane declared confidently.

"Yeah, but we haven't really had much of a chance to talk and..."

"Girl, he's the type of man who you should do all sorts of things with and to and on. Talking is near the bottom of that list." She winked suggestively.

"Hey!"

"Hey, what? Get your priorities straight!"

I shook my head and toyed with the tag on the tea bag. "Maybe you and I have different priorities. Besides, there's been a lot going on."

"There's *always* a lot going on. When are you going to make time for you? To do normal, girly, living-your-life things?" Sloane raised her mug and looked at me pointedly through the fragrant steam.

"I know, I know. It's just, well, something happened in Fae and I'm not sure what to make of it."

"With Magnus?" Sloane said eagerly.

"No, with Blythe and that ring," I said.

"I'm suddenly less interested," Sloane said, sitting back in her chair.

"The same ring that I thought housed the last escaped soul. Remember? The problem is that I don't think it's there anymore," I said, waving my arm at her. The cinnamon-colored tattoo was still clear on my inner wrist, but the final blue tracking dot was noticeably absent.

"And you have my interest again," Sloane said, leaning forward to examine the sigil tattoo. "So, what do you think happened to the soul?"

"Is it too much to think the spirit just ran out of ghost juice and couldn't continue to exist on this side of the Abyss?" I asked with little hope.

"Probably."

"Well, this next part is going to sound convoluted, but it's my best guess for the moment." I rubbed at the back of my neck, trying to work out the uneasy kinks in my muscles while I put my thoughts in order. "I think the ring came into contact with the Spring Lady. Remember when Brio attacked, and Blythe threw herself across Aubrette to protect her?"

"Sure. And then he got impaled by far too many pointy things to be healthy," Sloane said, shivering at the memory.

"Well, a couple of things happened right after that. Weird things. Aubrette, who'd been knocking on Death's door, sits up and starts talking. Strange, right? And not only that, but she calls Blythe '*daughter*'. Not *goddaughter*."

Sloane shrugged. "So, the diagnosis sucked, and she misspoke. What's the issue?"

"And the thing with her eyes changing color?" I asked.

"You heard Letitia. A weird side-effect," Sloane said.

"But what if it's not?" I asked.

"What are you saying?" Sloane frowned at me.

I sucked in a deep breath. "What if Aubrette isn't Aubrette?"

"I'm not following."

My voice dropped to barely above a whisper. "I think the soul in the ring's crystal may have jumped into the Spring Lady's body during that brief contact. I don't know enough about the rules of souls or whatever. Maybe there are two souls battling for dominance inside Aubrette or this rogue soul pushed Aubrette's soul out in the ghostly version of murder..."

"Or she got better and misspoke," Sloane interrupted.

I pointed at the blank tattoo. "Then where's the soul? When it was in the ring, the tracker picked it up. Now? Nada. Nothing. Zip. So, where is it?"

"Fine. For the sake of argument, I'll play along. Why didn't this rogue soul try jumping into you? I mean, you wore the ring around your neck for weeks. It had to come into contact with your skin. Or Blythe's for that matter."

I cracked my knuckles and thought. Finally, I said, "Maybe it had something to do with Aubrette's injury? Blythe wasn't hurt, and I'm too stubborn to surrender to a trespassing soul without a fight."

"Ain't that the truth," Sloane murmured into her teacup.

I glared at her. "Maybe Aubrette was so close to death that the other soul could gain a foothold." I threw my hands up in the air. "For all we know, she actually died and maybe this soul just capitalized on an opportunity."

Sloane didn't look convinced. "If this soul body-snatched the Spring Lady, who do you think is riding along inside her now?" she asked.

I bit my lower lip. "You know, something about my last encounter with Aldrich Kingsley has been bugging me lately."

"A lot about my last encounter with Aldrich Kingsley bugs me," Sloane muttered darkly.

"Put aside the fact that he tried to kill us for a second and listen. Right before he died, he asked me if I saw her. That she looked so beautiful."

Sloane shook her head. "Who?"

I continued as if she hadn't spoken. "Add in the fact that Aubrette, or Faux-Aubrette, called Blythe '*daughter*.'" I raised my eyebrows significantly at Sloane.

She sucked in a breath. "You don't think..."

I pointed a finger at her. "That's precisely what I think. I think the third soul that escaped on Halloween was Carina Kingsley. And she is now doing a ghostly ride along in Lady Aubrette's body."

"Then thank goodness the Lords and Ladies of the Courts almost never cross over into the mortal realm. It would be hard for Carina, if that even is her, to hunt you down," Sloane said, looking relieved.

"Why is that?" I asked.

"Because it would leave the Fae realm too unstable, especially with the time slippage. I mean, imagine Estaria popping over to have a cup of tea and a chat. Then, when she went back, found out decades had passed in Fae and all the while, no one had held the Winter mantle of power."

"No, I mean, why would Carina Kingsley want to hunt me down? If I am right and that's her soul using Aubrette's body, shouldn't she be happy to be back in Fae with her daughter?"

Sloane held up a finger. "You are forgetting one important thing."

"Which is?"

"Assuming you are correct in your hypotheses, the night Carina's soul escaped was the same night you killed her husband. Which means she was there, and she knows who is responsible for Aldrich's death." Sloane tipped her finger to point directly at me.

"So, you think she's coming after me?" I asked.

Sloane shrugged. "What I think is this is all a little far-fetched. However, if I was an escaped soul that no one knew about with a second shot at life, I wouldn't be above revenge. Which is why it's a good thing that Aubrette-slash-Carina is, for all intents and purposes, trapped in Fae. But then again, this could all be a crazy conspiracy theory that your sleep-deprived brain has created." She nodded at the mug sitting in front of me. "Drink your tea and get a good night's sleep. I bet that this will all seem like a bad dream in the morning."

I nodded pensively as I wrapped my hands around the mug. Despite her assurances, I was not at all comforted, but perhaps she was right and all I needed was a good night's sleep.

Epilogue

Two days later, Sloane stood next to me at the back gate of Mama's house. Goliath tugged lightly on the hair behind my ear as I fidgeted uncomfortably in front of the cheerful yellow house. Somehow, Mama had pulled together an impromptu memorial service for Ben. Even though the funeral and burial had taken place while we'd been stuck in Fae, Mama said that she'd like to hold a memorial service now that we'd returned. She said it didn't feel right to celebrate Ben's life without Sloane and me, which only added to my feeling of overwhelming guilt. It felt like I was going to drown under the weight of it.

Sloane tugged my hand and gently pulled me through the gate. The courtyard behind Mama's house was crowded with local Supes. I knew some of them and waved as Sloane pulled me towards the house. Slow jazz music spilled over us and out onto the sidewalk. Soft lights hung from tree branches. They glowed over the somber scene as a jazz quartet played quietly from a small stage in the corner.

Sloane and I got separated as we were drawn into conversation with various guests. Everyone seemed to have a story to tell about Ben. The wellspring of guilt in my gut grew deeper with every memory I overheard being shared. After all, it was my fault we were all here mourning his passing. I grabbed a mason jar full of sweet tea off a table to disguise my rising discomfort. When that didn't work, I was about to bolt.

Abruptly, the music cut off. I looked around to find out why. Mama accepted the hand the trumpet player extended down to her. The man graciously assisted her up on the stage and adjusted the microphone for her more diminutive stature. Mama murmured a thanks to him before stepping closer to address the expectant crowd.

There was a tremor of sadness in Mama's firm voice, but she spoke clearly and with confidence. "I know that many of you said your final farewells to Ben last month, but I'd like to thank y'all for coming together as a community this evening to honor and remember a fine man."

A series of murmured 'Amens' and 'May he rest in peace' rose from the gathered crowd.

Mama nodded her head in acceptance of the comforting sentiments before continuing. "If anyone knew a thing or two about death, it was Ben." Chuckles greeted those words and a small smile ghosted over Mama's wrinkled face. "He used to tell me that, regardless of the labels we put on ourselves throughout our time on this planet, at the end of the day, it's pretty simple: We're born, and we die. We all have that in common, which makes us, at our core, the same. Just folks all traveling the road of life the best we know how."

The crowd murmured their agreement at Mama's words. She smiled around the full courtyard, her eyes a little misty. "Ben's journey down that road wasn't always the easiest, but he had a knack for finding joy in even the darkest of situations and sharing that joy with anyone lucky enough to come into his life. He loved spending time with y'all." Mama spread her arms wide, tears spilling down her cheeks, but her voice stayed strong. "And I know he would've loved to see y'all here tonight."

"Although he would've hated to be the center of attention!" someone called out from the crowd. Chuckles rolled around the crowd at the truth of the words. I smiled past the lump in my throat.

A broad smile split Mama's face. "Ain't that the truth! But you know what else Ben liked to say? He liked to tell me that grief is a burden that can be shared. In the sharing, you could find a little more joy in celebrating the transition from this life to the next. So, tonight, I'd like y'all to lay down your burdens of grief and share the joy that Ben brought into our lives as we honor his homecoming tonight." She turned and accepted a glass of sweet tea from the lead musician. Mama raised it to the crowd. "To Ben!"

As one, everyone in the courtyard lifted their glasses and echoed her. "To Ben."

The band started up a slow rendition of 'Gonna lay my burden down', with the trumpet player leading the way through a somber introduction. It didn't stay that way for long. In traditional New Orleans style, the song shifted, the tempo increased, and soon everyone's toes were tapping as the band paved the way for a true Louisiana send-off.

For Ben.

Tears welled up in my eyes and I faded towards the edge of the crowd, not yet willing to engage fully, despite the comforting burble of conversation that drifted up over the strains of jazz music from the courtyard. I pulled my shadows around me as I stood next to a flower bed that I'd seen Ben spend hours cultivating. I wished for nothing more than a semblance of privacy in which to pay my final respects.

It was there, standing alone next to one of Ben's gardens, that I finally released the last of the guilt into the living earth that Ben so lovingly cared for. I silently cried and cried, watering the garden with my sorrow for my friend, until I had no more tears left. And I felt lighter for it. Who knows? Perhaps there'd be vibrant new flowers blooming on this very spot in the spring. I imagined that Ben might have planted them just for me. That made me feel happy. I'd have to come back and see.

I don't know how long I stood there, but when I let my shadows fall back, I felt better than I had in weeks. As I rejoined the party, I even smiled a little.

The first person I saw was lounging against a nearby tree with a familiar, sexy lean. My smile grew, and I walked over. Magnus looked at me as I joined him.

"Hey," I said.

"Hey yourself. How are you doing?" he asked, his tone careful. I read the deeper meaning in his words.

I considered my answer, then nodded. "I'm good. Not great, but good."

Magnus smiled down at me. "At least it's better than fine."

I chuckled. "It is that." I raised my jar of sweet tea, and he tapped his beer bottle against it. We stood there in companionable silence, watching dancers sway to the familiar strains of jazz in the air.

Finally, Magnus spoke. "If you ever want to talk, I'd love to hear more about Ben. I can only imagine the stories you have." He left the offer hanging like an olive branch between us.

I kept my gaze focused on the crowd as I took in his words. I finally sucked in a deep breath. "Someday. But not today. Today, I just want to soak all this in. To listen to others tell their stories about him. There'll be time enough later to tell my own."

"As you wish," Magnus said easily.

I don't know how long we stood there, enjoying the silent comfort of each other's company as the musicians skillfully shifted the music into more of a party vibe.

A low whistle rang out. I turned to see a group of tough-looking men and women waving Magnus over. I recognized Julius, Parker, and Will among the group. Magnus tried to shrug them off with an easy salute of his beer bottle, but the low whistles started turning to wolf whistles as the shifters noticed me at his side.

"It looks like they aren't taking no for an answer. Why don't you go on? Don't feel like you have to stay here all night on my account," I said, even though that is exactly what I wanted him to do.

"Well, I have some good news. Since more than enough time has passed and you have been under almost constant surveillance by two members of the Pack, Damn has declared that you are free of any possibility of werewolf contamination from that incident with Andrei and the demon. Thought you'd like to know." He lifted the bottle to his lips and took a sip.

"I figured that out ages ago, but...wait!" I smacked him lightly on the arm. "You're a full member of the Pack! You didn't tell me that! Congratulations!"

He grinned widely. "Thanks. It's nice to have a place to call home again."

I waved at the wolves in the corner. "You should go celebrate with them then!"

He smiled down at me. "Honestly, there's nowhere else I'd rather be than right here with you. Besides, they just want to catch up on the gossip. The shifters have gotten noticeably warmer towards me since Damon moved me off maverick status."

"We can always do something later. This is a big deal! Go! Be with your Pack!" I exclaimed, making small shooing motions with my hand.

Magnus looked torn. "I don't want to leave you alone," he said.

I snorted softly, "I know way more people here than you do, newbie." I smiled to soften my words. "Trust me. I'll be fine. Now go! Celebrate! Drink many beers!" I said, gesturing grandly towards the waiting wolves.

Another round of boisterous shouts rang out from the werewolves. Magnus waved an arm to quiet them down, which had the opposite effect.

He sighed. "I'd better get over there before they do something truly embarrassing. Are you sure you're okay?"

"Go on. I'll be fine," I said. Magnus nodded at me and turned towards his new Pack mates. A little part of me wrenched as he walked away.

"Wait!" I called, reaching out towards him. Magnus turned with a questioning look on his face.

I closed the distance between us. "Look, I know this isn't really the time or place all the storybooks say I should do this, but whatever. I doubt anyone would ever confuse me with a princess. And I don't think Ben would mind me taking advantage of the moment to find a little joy."

Magnus looked confused. "Cam. You're rambling."

"Right." I cleared my throat. "What's the word I'm supposed to say?"

"What?" His brow furrowed further.

"You told me to say the word, but never told me what the word it is. Which makes it damned confusing to say the word. So, I'm asking what the word is so I can say the word."

Confusion clouded Magnus's expression for a moment more before understanding broke across his face. He chuckled as he took my hand. "Cam, don't take this the wrong way, but while you are an exceptional fighter, you suck at the language thing sometimes."

"Well, if I'd known you wanted me to come at you with a knife, that would've been so much easier!" I protested, feeling a rush of heat flood my cheeks.

"Nope, I like this way better." Humor lit in the depths of his eyes and made them sparkle as he looked down at me. "Are you sure this is what you want?"

I looked up at him and felt like my feet had finally found solid ground. My voice was soft, but the single word was firm. "Yes," I said.

"Then that's all I need to know," Magnus said, raising our entwined fingers and lightly kissing the back of my hand. Another, louder round of whistles and shouts rose from the rowdy Pack behind him.

Magnus rolled his eyes. I laughed. "Go," I chuckled. "Before they really make a scene."

"Nah, they can wait. I've got much more to celebrate right here." His gaze burned the chill of the Louisiana winter right out of me. A low howl from the group of shifters warbled through the night before dissolving into laughter.

I smiled and squeezed his hand. "You've got a lot to celebrate tonight, but I have a feeling if you don't get over there soon, they are going to cause a ruckus."

Magnus let his head fall forward. "I think you're right. But you should know that I'm leaving you under protest."

"Noted. Now go before they shift, and we have wolves all over the courtyard. Mama wouldn't be happy. She might withhold treats and, trust me, you don't want that."

Magnus squeezed my fingers once more before turning towards the Pack. They welcomed him with shouts and pats to the back as he walked over. I smiled as friendly banter drifted towards me on the wind.

"Now that's a sight," a voice said from behind me. "It's rare that one bears witness to a new beginning." I turned to see Mama walking up behind me.

I tipped my head towards the werewolves. "I know. Magnus was just made an official member of the Pack."

"Not what I meant," Mama said with a knowing twinkle in her eyes. She opened her arms. I bent down to give her a hug and a kiss on the cheek. She whispered into my ear. "He's a fine boy, your wolf. Ben would be happy you found each other, and he'd be tickled that it happened at his party. He'd take all the credit and never let me hear the end of it."

I pulled back, tears forming. "Mama, we haven't had the chance... I mean, I'm so sorry that I..."

She patted my hand. "Hush now, child. For all his powers, Ben was an old man. He knew his time was short, and he'd be the first to warn you against lingering over any feelings of self-recrimination or the like. He was as stubborn as the day was long and, as he liked to remind me, was quite capable of making his own choices, thank you very much." She put her hand on her hip and waggled a finger under my nose in a passable imitation of the old necromancer.

I gave her a watery smile. A small tug on my hair just below my ear reminded me of something. I raised my hand to my shoulder and Goliath scampered onto my palm. Carefully, I extended the small mouse towards Mama.

"Oh, my stars! I'd wondered what became of Goliath, but no one could find him at the Embassy." She held up her hand and the tiny familiar darted across to her. Mama held him up to her cheek for a furry little cuddle before carefully depositing him in the front pocket of her colorful skirt. "Thank you for bringing him back, child."

"I think his home has always been here." I shrugged. "Besides, I don't think Goliath found me to be as relaxing a companion as Ben was."

Mama guffawed and patted her pocket. "Probably not, but I have a feeling we'll find a way of working things out between us. After all, we both loved Ben. Sometimes, Goliath seemed to be such a part of him. It was like they both shared the same soul across two bodies, but that would be ridiculous, of course!" She chuckled through what looked suspiciously like a gathering of tears as she stroked the tiny creature's head.

Something about the way she phrased that made me think of my hypothesis about Carina Kingsley. "Of course," I agreed half-heartedly. "Umm, remind me. Why would that be ridiculous?"

Mama looked at me strangely. "Because it would violate the laws of nature. One soul for one body. You can't spread one soul over two bodies or have two souls in one body. It's too much. Even necromancers must abide by those immutable rules."

I frowned. "What do you know about souls coming back from the other side?" I asked, fidgeting absently with my necklace where I'd restrung the pink crystal ring next to my charm on a new chain.

Mama's mouth crinkled sympathetically. "Oh no, honey. Ben's gone. As much as I'd love for him not to be, his time has passed. Let him rest." She took my hand and patted it gently.

She'd obviously misunderstood me. I shook my head, debating whether to clarify. Finally, I decided not to and just smiled sadly. "I'd love nothing more than to have one more conversation with him over a cup of tea and some of your home-baked goodies."

"He wouldn't want you pining after him, child."

I wiped a finger under my eye, dabbing away the gathering moisture that had suddenly pooled at the corner. "I am, and I'm not, if that makes sense. I'll miss him. I *do* miss him. The strangest things remind me of him. The smell of fresh beignets. Daffodils. Goliath," I said, pointing at the little mouse as he stuck his head out of Mama's pocket.

"Ben would've been the first to tell you that's what makes life so sweet. That it's finite. You never know when your end is right around the corner. He'd have told you to grab the happiness you find in this world and hold on to that as tightly as you can. He'd say to let everything just pass you by while you bask in the sunshine of your own bliss."

Mama peeked around me and then gave me a conspiratorial wink. "And I can see a hunk of a werewolf who looks like he'd bring you a lot of joy. Might I suggest you grab on to him and not let go 'til at least the middle of next month? I mean, if it was me, I'd hold on clear 'til spring, but then again, I do so hate being cold."

"Mama!" I protested through a grin.

She chuckled and held up her hands. "Just think about what I said, child."

I snuck a glance over my shoulder to see Magnus chatting easily with his new Pack mates. He caught me looking and shot me a warm smile before returning to his conversation. That one private look warmed me better than the Louisiana summer sun in the middle of a heatwave.

A red-haired woman detached herself from a nearby group and sauntered over to us. For a moment, I thought it might be Meridiana, my friend, who also was a demoness. However, when a rooster popped its knobby head up from her arms, I quickly realized my mistake. I should've expected to see Brigitte at a wake. After all, she was the local goddess in charge of helping souls cross over. By local traditions, Brigitte was a loa of death and not a goddess in the strictest of terms, but I wasn't about to split hairs over her title. Besides, if I asked, she'd probably tell me to fuck off, anyway. All things considered; I was actually on fairly friendly terms with the deity. Her pet rooster, though? Not so much.

"Hello, Brigitte," I said. The rooster shifted his beady black eyes to me, bobbing his wickedly sharp beak in my direction. "Hello Cluck Norris," I added hurriedly.

"So lovely to see you again, Cameron," Brigitte said. The rooster's head bobbed aggressively towards me. Brigitte stroked the rooster's black plumage, which shone with an almost purple iridescence. Cluck Norris settled back into her arms, but kept a wary eye on me.

"Thank you for coming, Brigitte," Mama said. "Ben would've appreciated the kindness."

Brigitte smiled warmly at Mama. "I wouldn't have missed it, Atli. I wanted to tell you he's in safe hands, resting comfortably."

Mama's eyes welled with tears. "That's mighty kind of you, Brigitte. Mighty kind, indeed. Thank you." She wiped the corner of her eyes with the corner of her skirt. She jostled Goliath out of his comfortable resting place and the little mouse scampered up her arm. Mama cupped the tiny mouse in her hand. "Oh, would you look at that? We're running low on sweet tea. I'll just hurry on back inside and grab a fresh pitcher." She hurried off towards the kitchen, stroking the mouse.

I looked around and noticed a full pitcher on a nearby table. Brigitte followed my gaze and smiled gently. "All of us grieve in different ways. Atli, for all her legendary hospitality, is a private person when it comes to her own affairs."

I nodded, not really sure what to say. Brigitte ran a hand along the rooster's iridescent feathers. She looked at me speculatively.

"Hmm," she said, tapping a finger against her lips.

I froze. "What?"

Brigitte pointed her finger at me. "I've seen that before."

"Seen what?" I twisted to half look over my shoulder without turning, just in case there was something behind me I shouldn't be drawing attention to.

Brigitte leaned in and whispered, "The fuckening." She tapped the side of her nose somberly and gave me a slow nod.

"I don't know what you are talking about," I whispered back.

"Oh, I think you do." She pursed her lips and gave me a knowing wink.

"No. I really don't. And now I'm scared to ask."

Brigitte twitched her head in a manner eerily similar to that of her pet. "Surely, you must know the fuckening. *Everyone* knows about the fuckening," she scoffed.

I raised both palms heavenward. "Not a clue. And if it's some freaky sex thing, I don't want to know."

"The *fuckening*. You know, where there's a little niggle at the back of your mind all day, but you just can't put your finger on it. So, you live your day as normal, but it is anything except normal. In fact, things are going well. Almost too well. And then, just like that," she snapped her fingers in my face, and I jumped. "... the thing that was bugging you falls into place and there it is. The *fuckening*." Brigitte resumed stroking Cluck Norris with an air of self-satisfaction and sympathetic empathy.

"How did you... I mean, I just..." I stuttered to a stop.

Brigitte nodded sagely. "That's precisely how the fuckening works. Tell me about it."

"It's convoluted, and it's going to sound more than a little nuts," I said tentatively.

"Oh, my dear, that's the best kind!" Brigitte exclaimed.

I weighed my options, but it didn't take me long to decide that asking a death loa about souls and the afterlife was probably my best bet at answers. As quickly as I could, I laid out the situation and my guess that Carina Kingsley was now inhabiting Aubrette's body.

Brigitte nodded pensively as I concluded. She stroked the rooster's feathers and stared off into the middle distance. Finally, I cleared my throat. "So? What do you think?"

The loa's eyes tightened and her lips turned down in a thoughtful frown as she swung her gaze back to me. "If you are right, this Carina person would've forced the Spring Lady's soul out of her body. Essentially murdering her while keeping her body alive and functioning. But what better way for a bodiless soul to get a second lease on life? Unless, of course, she just got inordinately lucky and took possession at the moment of death." She stood there, absently petting the rooster's feathers as her gaze went unfocused and drifted towards the tree behind me.

I let her think, hoping she would offer answers. When the silence moved from awkward to disturbingly uncomfortable, I cleared my throat. "So, is it possible?"

Brigitte jumped like I'd slapped her awake and then dumped a bucket of water I pulled directly from the Winter Court all over her. "What? Oh. I mean, yes. Yes, of course it is. But such occurrences are rarely successful. Those that happen maybe once a millennium? I mean, there was that Lazarus thing, but we all know how that turned out." She waved her hand dismissively.

The churning in my gut increased from moderate storm to a category one hurricane. "So, it *is* possible? The body snatching thing."

Brigitte shrugged and waved her free hand through the air. "Of course. Anything is *possible.* Probable is a whole different story." She resumed petting Cluck Norris and mused aloud. "Carina Kingsley, who watched you kill her husband, is now inhabiting the body of one of the most powerful beings in Fae." Brigitte shook her head and chuckled throatily.

"Maybe. I don't know. If it is true, why are you laughing?" Anger rode on the coattails of my surprise.

"I've got to hand it to you, Cameron. If you're right, that is the most fucked-up fuckening I've ever heard of!" Brigitte chortled.

"Would you stop laughing long enough to tell me what I should do about it?" I hissed at her.

"Darling, just be glad that Carina chose someone like Aubrette, who is so essential to the Fae realm that it would likely implode without her physically there. It would be devilishly hard for her to get to you here," Brigitte said, laughter still tinging her voice.

"Sloane said something similar. Somehow, that notion isn't terribly comforting," I observed.

Brigitte patted my arm. "Perhaps not, but this is not a problem that can or should be solved tonight. This evening is for Ben. Spend the time to remember him, to share memories with friends, to heal a little. And then, perhaps consider indulging in some of the most ancient, restorative practices known to man with that werewolf of yours." Brigitte winked wickedly at me.

"Brigitte!" I exclaimed. A rush of heat flooded my cheeks at the insinuation.

"What?" She batted her eyelashes innocently at me. "All I'm saying is let tomorrow's problems be *tomorrow's* problems."

I considered her words as I looked out over the crowd. Magnus looked up at the same time. He caught my eye and smiled. Butterflies erupted in my stomach and spread to my everywhere.

Perhaps the goddess was right. I should focus on the here and now rather than borrowing tomorrow's trouble. I felt a silly smile stretch my lips and started walking towards Magnus.

"Go get him, darling!" Brigitte said from behind me.

I lifted my hand in a wave. After all, when a goddess gives you advice, it would be downright rude not to act on it.

Thank you!

Thank you for picking my book. If you enjoyed it, please consider adding a review. I would be grateful if you could spare a couple of minutes to leave a review by heading over to the book's page where you purchased it. It need only be a line or two and it makes a massive difference. It's easy to skip this step – I often did myself until I realized how much authors count on these reviews. I'd be so grateful if you would take a moment to post a rating and a few words. More reviews help other readers discover this series and, as I now realize, it helps your humble author enormously.
  Best wishes,

L.L. Gray

  Turn the page to read a sample of **Daggers and Deception** - Smoke and Shadows Series Book 5

Daggers and Deception

The story thus far. The universe was created. This was deemed to be an ill-conceived and eventually disastrous move. I'm sure there is still at least one hopeless optimist out there who still believes unicorns fart rainbows. However, on this Tuesday in February when I was face down in the stinking swamp slime in a remote part of Florida better left to the alligators, I was not among those delusional romantics.

A low growl rumbled off to my left, reminding me there was no time for jaded cosmic pondering or self-pity. I shoved to my feet with a loud squelch. The murky swamp tried to suck me with all its viscous, noxious power, but I resisted. I held my breath and waded forward until the toes of my boots found solid ground. Solid was probably an over exaggeration.

My prey-turned-predator let out another bone curdling roar. Before I could think better of it, I wiped my sleeve across my eyes. Swamp muck smeared slime across my face, almost completely obscuring my view of the charging creature.

I pawed at my eyes, trying to clear away the worst of the stinking ooze. I wished I hadn't. The monster charging towards me was enough to make me never want to visit the Sunshine State ever again. Hell, New Orleans might be too close if these creatures migrated!

The beast was over double my height and probably could've been Bigfoot's stunt double. Or smelly second cousin. The large, foul-smelling creature lumbered towards me, apparently unencumbered by the sucking drag of the swamp's murk. The bipedal ape-like creature looked like it probably considered the swamp a luxurious day spa, judging by the matted fur and muddy spatter covering it from head to toe. It bared its massive fangs at me and snarled.

"Logan?" I shouted as I scrambled backwards, trying to find better footing.

A tinny voice sounded in my ear. "Yes, Cameron?"

"Are you *sure* this thing needs to be captured alive?"

An annoyed sigh echoed through the earpiece I wore. "For the fourth time, yes. The client was very specific. The skunk apes of the region are in their mating season. As an ethical means of controlling the population, she is paying us to remove several of the females to a cordoned off area of the swamplands until the mating fervor has passed. In this way, the client can limit offspring without killing."

"If this client is so pro-skunk ape, tell her to come and catch them herself!" I grumbled.

"Two problems with that plan," Logan said.

"Which are?" I muttered. I touched the bandolier of small vials slung across my chest. I'd filled each with a sedative strong enough to put down a rhino. Or a rampaging ogre. I doubted anyone had ever conducted field tests on skunk apes. If I lived through this, I'd have to make my due contribution to science and let nerds in white coats know. I wondered what sort of academic journal might publish my findings. I even had a title in mind.

Never mess with skunk apes. Regardless of how strong your drugs are. A good life motto if I ever heard one.

Logan's voice interrupted my thoughts. "One, our client is bound to a wheelchair, which would make traversing the inner swamplands next to impossible."

"What's the second problem?" I asked.

The skunk ape was almost within striking distance. I pulled on my magic. I imagined a sword made of shadows. It sprang to life in my mind's eye. Regretfully, I dulled the sharp blade before it manifested. I wasn't used to working with an intentional handicap, but Logan's rules were clear. What the client wants, the client gets. Quickly, I ran the weapon through the forge of my will. A moment later, I felt the hilt slam comfortingly into my hand.

"She's anti-killing. No one in their right mind is pro-skunk ape," Logan said matter-of-factly. I grimaced. Cool logic had no place in the rotting swamps of Florida. Or likely, any rotting swamp.

I bit back a reply as the skunk ape threw a wild punch at me. I ducked and lunged to the side. My dulled shadow blade darted out, landing a satisfying *thunk* on the skunk ape's rib cage. The creature yowled in anger. It pounded heavy fists against its hairy chest as it stumbled backward. I narrowed my eyes in confusion. My lunge had put me within easy viewing of the creature's lower region. Nothing had been dangling between its hairy legs. But when it had pummeled its chest just now, there had been no evidence of bulges under the fur up there, either.

"Umm, Logan?" I said, readying myself for another attack. "I just found problem number three."

"Which is?"

"How do I tell if this is a male or female? I can't see any of the requisite bits!" The skunk ape snarled again and charged at me as Logan answered.

"Trial and error, I guess. If this one isn't female, get rid of him and let's move on to the next as quickly as possible. I have dinner plans I'd prefer not to reschedule."

I growled, and it wasn't at the smelly monster intent on taking my head off. I juked to the side as it charged me. It must not have been too smart because it fully committed to my feint. The skunk ape charged to the left, lumbering forward with a snarl directly through the space where I no longer stood.

I dug my fingers into its matted fur as it rushed by me. With a little extra help from my enchanted boots, I leapt up onto its back. The creature threw its head back and roared its anger to the overcast skies. I used the opportunity to snake my arm around its massive throat. That secured my position enough that I could reach the sedative and end this quickly.

Or so I thought.

I let the shadow blade dissolve and reached for the bandolier of vials at my chest. As quickly as I could, I wiggled one free. I yanked the protective cover free of the needle with my teeth. Which is when the skunk ape did its best impression of a rodeo bull. I lost my grip on the vial, which went sailing off into the swamp. I groaned but used my now free hand to help keep my seat on the bucking, twirling ape.

Look, I have nothing but respect for those people crazy enough to get up on the back of an angry horned bovine. But do you know the difference between a bucking bull and a bucking ape? And no, it's not the thumbs. It's the arms. The skunk ape was remarkably flexible, and its fingers were strong and dexterous. I felt it scrabble at my back, trying to gain purchase. Luckily, my leather fighting gear didn't allow for much of a grip. However, it was only a matter of time until the ape found enough of a hold to pull me off.

I looked around desperately, searching for anything to use to my advantage. Unfortunately, the swamp was the ape's playground, not mine.

Logan's voice sounded in my ear. "Status report. Did you neutralize the target?"

"No, I haven't neutralized the huge, angry ape! I decided to take it to tea instead. Turns out it prefers crumpets to scones. Shut up and let me think!"

"You don't need to be testy about it," Logan grumbled.

"What I need is some peace and quiet to think of a distraction be-fore...wait! Logan! Do a fly over," I shouted.

"Now? You said it wasn't down." Logan sounded unsure.

I felt the ape's fingers wrap around my calf. It gave a bellow of triumph. "Right frickin' now! Do it!"

"Do you even know the rules you are breaking right now?" Logan muttered through the earpiece.

I dug my fingers into the stinking fur and held on with all my might as the creature started tugging on my leg. "Don't know. Don't care. Get here fast or it's going to go all Hulk-smash on my ass like the big green guy did to Loki in that superhero movie."

"I don't know why you watch that drivel. Not even close to an accurate description of the Norse or, well, anything," Logan grumbled. "Coming around now."

The ape twisted under me, clawing at my leg with its other arm. If it latched on with that one as well, I was done for. I screamed and wriggled with all my might. I'd just reached the conclusion that I might have to resort to biting the foul creature when I heard the whir of an approaching helicopter.

The ape must've heard it too. It looked up in confusion as Logan's helicopter whizzed overhead. Its fingers loosened on my leg as it gaped skyward. I took advantage of the brief reprieve. Holding on to the creature's back with just my knees, I pulled two vials from the bandolier. As quickly as I could, I yanked the caps off the needles and shoved them through the ape's thick fur. Once I felt the needles pop through the skin, I jammed the buttons on the vials down, forcing the sedative into the skunk ape. The creature threw its head back and roared. If I thought it was angry before, it was nothing compared to the rage resonating through the swamp at being wounded.

"Status?" Logan's voice crackled through my earpiece.

"Sedative deployed. Now, let's just wait and see how long..." The creature between my knees started to sway. Its head bobbed back and forth. It grunted and fell to one knee. Sensing the impeding crash, I pushed off its back and scrambled to safety, trying to land on the firmest ground I could find. Just in time, too. The skunk ape crashed face first into the slimy muck underfoot. It let out a massive belch and then lay still.

"Well. That escalated quickly. Or should I say, deescalated quickly," I said as I nudged the skunk ape with a boot. It batted weakly at me. Then it rolled over onto its side and stuck its thumb in its mouth. The sounds of snuffling snores drifted up from under the hair paw a moment later.

"I take it that means you were successful?" Logan's voice crackled in my ear.

"Yep. Bring that chopper back around and load this one up," I replied.

"Two more to go, if this one is a female," Logan said as I picked up the sound of the helicopter approaching once more.

"Good Lord, I hope this one is female. The faster we capture all three, the faster I can get home," I said.

"Why the rush? You've been practically begging for any job regardless of how far away it is from New Orleans. Do you have dinner plans as well?" Logan sounded curious.

"Oh, no reason in particular," I said, going for breezy. That was an utter lie. I wanted to get home for one very specific were-wolf-shaped reason. Magnus. Almost as soon as we'd returned from our misadventures in Fae, Magnus had left again on some super-secret wolf-y mission. He hadn't been able to tell me much except Damon, the Alpha of the New Orleans Pack, had requested his presence on the mission. I knew enough to read between the lines. You didn't turn down a request from an Alpha unless you really hated your throat and wanted it forcibly removed. Anyway, whether it was the mission or the crappy cell connection, communication with my handsome something-more-than-a-friend-but-not-quite-a-boyfriend werewolf had been next to impossible. But he'd texted me two days ago to say he was coming back to town tomorrow.

I was excited. Sue me.

"I know that tone. Who's the guy?" Logan's voice was getting hard to hear as the chopper came closer.

"A werewolf." I shouted to be heard.

"Ah," Logan's voice was calm and thoughtful. "Piece of advice? Multiple showers. You don't want Eau de Skunk Ape disrupting his sensitive nose."

It couldn't be that bad, could it? I took a tentative sniff of my clothes and nearly reeled back at the stench.

Multiple showers. Got it.

And then a date with a werewolf. I couldn't hide my smile.

I was muddy, slimy, stinking, and cold by the time we finally caught the third female. Once I'd discovered that the females tended towards a brownish color with mossy green highlights, whereas the males seemed to stay in the gray spectrum, it had been easy to differentiate the creatures. Logan whizzed off in the helicopter with the last skunk ape in tow. I waved goodbye and then started the trudge back to where I'd left the car.

It was unseasonably cold in Florida for the soaked, swamp-hiker. I alternated between shivering and sweating by the time I reached the spot I'd left the car. Despite that, I stripped down to my bra and panties and tugged on some oversized sweatpants and a t-shirt before I even considered getting in the vehicle. Thank all the gods it was a rental. I could expense the cleaning charges I'd no doubt incur to Logan. I shoved my fighting gear into a plastic bag and tied the top of tightly. My dry cleaner was a good guy who was used to strange requests from me, but even he'd raise an eyebrow at this mess. I sighed and made a mental note to add the dry cleaning to my expense charges when I sent my bill to Logan.

I slid into the car once I was marginally cleaner and much less slimy. I reached for my phone. Maybe Magnus had texted again. To my surprise, the phone started vibrating as soon as I flicked on the screen. The incoming call was an unknown number. Not unheard of in my line of work, but enough to set my nerves jangling. I slid the green icon over and answered the call.

"Cameron! It's been much too long!" The male voice was cheery and vaguely familiar.

"Umm, hi?" I cleared my throat. It didn't sound like Magnus. Could it be one of his Pack mates calling? "New number. Who's this?"

"I'm hurt." The man's pout was obvious in his tone. "I thought we had something special. We do work rather marvelously together. That is, until you betrayed me to a nest of vampires." He *tsked*. "Naughty, naughty."

I punched the dashboard. Lightly, because it was a rental. Otto. The thief I'd screwed over on our last job. Sounds like he'd figured out my little trick. A sudden thought struck me. Otto wasn't above spying. Although I doubted he would've tracked me here, I didn't want to give him the satisfaction of knowing that he'd gotten under my skin. On the off chance he was watching, I sat up straight and pasted on a smile.

"Otto," I said breezily. "Last time I saw you, you were running away like a scared little puppy."

"Vampires, Cameron. You sent a nest of ancient, angry *vampires* after me." Was that a hint of anger I heard in the thief's charming tone?

"Yet you survived. So, what's the problem?" I asked.

"I have a job in the New Orleans area—"

"And a death wish?" I interrupted. "If Alessandro catches you in New Orleans, I doubt you'll be pulling *any* more jobs."

I heard the smile in Otto's voice as he continued, ignoring my interruption. "And you're going to help me."

I snorted out a laugh. "In what universe?"

"In the universe where I have a phone book and know your secret. What do you think Alessandro Nicoletti would do if he found out?"

My blood ran cold. On that last job, I may have insinuated to Alessandro, the head of the vamps in New Orleans, that Otto had stolen a priceless artifact while squirreling it away for me.

May have. Did. Who am I to quibble over nuances?

Regardless, there was no way Otto knew about my trick! He couldn't! Could he? I retreated into snark while I desperately tried to find Otto's angle. "News flash, bub, phone books haven't been around for years."

"News flash, princess. I remember when they were invented," Otto retorted.

Right. He was old. Like ancient Greece, old. Although he went by Otto now, his given name was Autolycus. Son of Hermes, master thief, and pain in my ass. Given how much he annoyed me, I'm sure he rubbed several people the wrong way. I wasn't sure how he'd survived this long. However, as someone who'd willingly just tackled multiple skunk-apes, perhaps I shouldn't cast aspersions on making sensible life choices.

Rather than buckle under vague threats, I went on the offensive. "Look, I'm busy. I just wrapped up a job in Florida and have another commitment tomorrow night."

"Perfect," Otto interjected smoothly. "Meet me for lunch at the Golden Nugget in Biloxi. I'll give you all the details then. By my best guess, we should have this thing wrapped up by the end of the week."

I recognized the place. It was a casino right across the Louisiana border in Mississippi. Which was conveniently outside of the Collective's jurisdiction. The Supes on the Collective were a scary bunch who kept the peace in New Orleans by any means possible. When they encountered an issue, their problem-solving mantra seemed to be *'the bloodier, the better.'* It didn't surprise me Otto would opt for meeting in an entirely different state from where the Collective did business.

"I know it," I allowed. Then, because it was Otto and I wasn't above riling him up, I asked sweetly, "Why not the Big Easy?"

I heard him shudder over the phone. "Vampires, Cameron. It's the vampires. It's always the bloody vampires."

I chuckled to myself, adding a mental point to my side of an invisible tally list. "Out of curiosity, what makes you think that I'll actually show up?"

This time, it was Otto who chuckled. "Same reason. Vampires. No one wants to be on their bad side. Even you."

"That's assuming that your vague insinuations about a secret are enough to get me there," I said with an over-inflated sense of bravado to see what I could get out of him.

"Oh, they will," Otto said and disconnected the call.

Son of a...

I looked at the darkened screen on my phone before hammering my fist against the steering wheel.

It looked like I was headed to Mississippi.

Don't forget, your FREE book is waiting!

A killer pair of shoes, a party of a lifetime, and a demon. What could possibly go wrong?

Cameron Blaze owes a demon a favor and what better way to pay off a debt than to have a girl's night out? The plan was simple. Find a killer pair of heels, go to a great bar, and party into the early hours of the morning. Cameron thinks that she has everything planned. The shoes on are, the drinks are poured, and the party is in full swing. She just forgot to account for one small thing. Magic going haywire.

Sign up here to get your free book!

https://www.subscribepage.com/llgray

Also By

Smoke and Shadows Series

Shadows and Relics

Pixie Pranks (exclusive novella)

Felons and Fangs

Bones and Blades
Tempest and Treason
Daggers and Deception

About the Author

L.L. Gray was born in Wisconsin and split her time being a musical theatre nerd, a book worm, and a burgeoning coffee addict. She began writing her debut novel after obsessing over fantasy books for most of her life. When she's not writing, she can be found playing soccer (or football for you non-American folks), singing loudly to any and all showtunes, or traveling the world in hopes of trying out new coffee shops. L.L. Gray currently lives in Abu Dhabi with her husband and two daughters.

**Psst, it's me. L.L. Gray. Nice to meet you! Connecting with fellow lovers of the written word and crazy adventure stories is important to me. If that sounds like your cup of tea (or coffee, or other beverage) please hop over to my website (www.llgray.com) and join my newsletter where you can grab a FREE, exclusive goodies or hang out with us on my Facebook readers group.

However, if email is more your speed, then please feel free to drop me a line at info@llgray.com should the mood strike.

I hope you stay in touch!

Acknowledgments

First, I need to thank my fabulous team. They have become like a second family to me. I couldn't do it without die-hard supporters like them. Special thanks to Ellen, Anna, Roland, Mariaan, Caroline, Michael, and, my wonderful mother and the best cheerleader I could ever hope for.

I'd also like to thank you, the reader. I hope you enjoyed reading Cam's wild adventures as much as I've enjoyed writing them. If you'd like to stay in touch or be kept up to date with upcoming releases, please head over to my website. If you'd like to hang out with some like-minded readers on Facebook , come and join our wonderful community.

And last, but definitely not least, I'd like to thank my wonderful husband, Nick. Without your support, none of this would have been possible.

www.ingramcontent.com/pod-product-compliance
Lightning Source LLC
Chambersburg PA
CBHW072055190726
48294CB00005B/1520